COLA BOY

Ryan Battles

Published by ZANI

For information contact:
info@zani.co.uk

Editors
Mike Boorman
Rob Buckley

Book Cover Design
Pete Collins

Dedication

This book is dedicated to the memories of
Alex, Gregg and Mike.

Good people and good times.

Special Thanks

Thanks to everyone who has bought this book. I wrote it to purely entertain, so I hope you enjoy the read and the ride. Special thanks to Zani publisher, Matteo Sedazzari and Dean Cavanagh for believing in me and the story. Also to DJ Dribbler (Harry's Kebabs) who provided inspiring guidance along the way. And this book wouldn't have been possible without the support of these good people: Samantha (Mrs) Battles, Nick (DJ Parsons) Ward, Scott (Horsey) Walker, Graeme (DJ Fisher) Powrie, Pete (DJ Nice) Collins, Iain Hagger, Craig Mathers, Craig Douglas, Martin Forbes, Jimmy Webster, Tom Legge, Grant (Going Viral) Weinberg and everyone I kicked around with in Aberdeen, Dubai and London in the 90s. I can't complete the thanks without a special mention to my sons Jack and Maxwell Battles who question everything I do today and did yesterday. Thanks for the awkward questions boys.

DISCLAIMER FOR LAWYERS AND FAMILY

This story has been written as a work of fiction to entertain. There are some seeds of truth running through it since yes I was born in Aberdeen and I did live and work in Dubai as a journalist in the 90s, bringing my records with me. I took these seeds as inspiration to develop fictitious characters and plotlines for Cola Boy. Business names integral to the story are fictitious. Any resemblance in the characters to an actual living person is coincidental. References to real world brands are done so in passing, without malice and for several, in celebration of what they are. Opinions expressed are those of the characters and shouldn't be confused with the author's. Some historical events and chronological references may not be entirely accurate. I stand free against bigotry, racism, homophobia, corruption, injustice and misogyny. I have no desire to ever travel to Dubai again.

Table of Contents

Chapter 1

I looked over beyond the headstones and saw them approaching. Baggy white shirts hanging over their loose-fitting black jeans, a purposeful stride in their walk, pushing and shoving each other as they trudged over the sodden grass and fresh burial mounds of earth.

As they got closer, I could see their faces were bruised, shirts ripped by the chest buttons and knuckles red raw. But they weren't sombre. They were smiling.

'Battered 'em,' I could hear Gaz muttering into Kev's ear, who was standing just a few feet behind me at the side of the congregation. 'Fuckin' cut us up on the road giving us the finger. We got 'em, though. Got ahead of them, slammed on the brakes, got 'em out of the car and fuckin' battered 'em. Job done, eh?' he said, turning round to slap a slightly bloodied Archie on the back.

I couldn't believe what I was overhearing or seeing today, today of all days. Their unceremonious arrival made me lose my concentration as my footing started to slip on the boggy grass as we gradually lowered the casket straps. Jesus, Andy was a slim and fit guy – he was an ex-Royal Marine after all – but this felt like we were burying an ex-submarine. How could he be so heavy? Must be the coffin. What the hell is it made of? Lead? Mustn't fall in. Must... hold... it. Hold... it... Fuckin' hold it, Jimmy. Why the hell am I wearing slip-on shoes in a bloody bog?

My right foot slid forward an inch, then stopped. Then a few seconds later, slipped a couple more inches, then three, then four, then thud! Thank God. He was down, laid to rest, not in the most graceful of ways but the three other pallbearers had done their job far better than me and held him steady… well, almost steady.

22. Gone too soon. Motorbike accident but Jesus, he was only going at 30mph on the roundabout. Torrential rain, though, that night and his back tyre gave way. He slid across the road snapping his neck on impact with a dyke. I was just about to DJ at the Cotton Club and took a call from my newspaper's night reporter 10 minutes before my set.

'Hey, Jimmy, it's Rob from the paper. You got a minute? Have you got a friend called Andrew Buchan?'

Yes.

'I thought so. How old is he?'

22.

'…Look, I'm really sorry, Jimmy, but I've just done my check-in calls with the police and ambulance and there's been an RTA. And they named him: Andrew Buchan. He was pronounced dead at the scene.'

I couldn't quite believe what I was hearing and stepped outside the club away from the banging House, sheltering from the wind and rain in a shop doorway. I asked Rob to double-check the details. Spelling of the name. His age. His address…

It was our Andy.

I returned to the DJ booth in disbelief to tell the rest of the guys and word soon spread throughout the 100 or so crowd that Andy was gone. Tears were shed as pills kicked in and we continued to play – it's what Andy would have wanted, we all agreed. Back at the flat later, tears kicked in again, pills were shed, spliffs were lit and Alfredo's Café del Mar cassette tape played till dawn as we reminisced about the good times with our fallen soldier.

Since then, Aberdeen was starting to get me down. The football was on the decline – back-to-back losses against Dundee United and Hibs and knocked out of the League Cup by the not-so-mighty Dundee. The Fergie years of regular silverware were long gone and here we were now being managed by Roy *fucking* Aitken. He may have played a few games for the Dons near the end of his career, but he was still Celtic to me. Not a Red. And not worthy to be manager of the famous Aberdeen FC**.

At 24, my commitment to playing amateur football was starting to wane. No fags on the Friday before a match had become six or seven Marlboro Lights. No fags on the morning of the match had become two or three before noon. No fags in the car on the way to the match had become one or two while cranking up the tunes in the red Vauxhall Nova. And no fags during the game had become a quick one at halftime.

If Socrates can smoke 30-40 a day and play for Brazil, why can't I have five or six and play for Glendee Rovers? 'Cause yer nae Socrates, Jimmy,' the manager would spit back.

My relationship with Natalie had also turned toxic. It had been on and off for a year now, with a few pub scraps thrown in – not between the two of us – but with other blokes she was rumoured to be shagging behind my back. A fair few bars stopped letting me in, especially if they knew some of those cunts were already inside. But with Aberdeen being a small city with a limited number of good clubs, we always, *always* ended up clashing in some place later in the night.

The only plus was my job at the local newspaper, which was going pretty well: Chief News Reporter, landing front-page splashes three or four times a week and I'd recently convinced the Editor to feature a new music column on Fridays about 'clubbing'.

Some of the world's best House DJs were flying in and out of the city every weekend playing in front of hundreds of pilled-up clubbers and until now, the paper had failed to recognise this was a scene and was growing.

Me and my pals had flown a number of these DJs up from England to play at our monthly nights: the likes of Junior Boys Own, Judge Jules, Seb Fontaine and of course local boy done good, Graeme Park of The Hacienda – what a buzz as these nights went right off. Final track was followed by lock-ins and after-parties till sunrise; though watching the winter sun come up over the North Sea, shivering and quivering on the beach at 6 in the morning, was more endurance than euphoria.

Every couple of months was spent on the train heading down to London. This is where I knew I really wanted to be. Aberdeen had reached its limit for me, was on repeat mode and I craved more. I wanted to explore the new, the unknown and the un-imagined. To discover the non-conformists, the subcultures and the counter cultures. Seek out the underground and find the edges. And if I was lucky, hopefully, get a decent girlfriend along the way for a change. London seemed to have it all.

We'd leave Club UK around 5am and wander around Wandsworth searching for a 'cab' or any car that would take us back to our B&B near Victoria station. 'B&B' – Ha! Now there's a loose definition. Neither a 'bed' nor 'breakfast' was needed for these trips to London. More like 'D&G' – 'Dump and Go'. These itchy and scratchy rooms around Victoria were just a place for me and Andy to turn up, dump our bags, get changed and head out – only seeing the receptionist again at 6am the following day, when we'd sheepishly walk back in through the front doors hiding behind our cheap sunnies, Andy swiping some 'London Tours' leaflets off her counter for roaches as we sketched past to our room. The nine-and-a-half-hour train journey back north to the Granite City was twitchingly painful at first but usually sorted itself out by Doncaster being a couple of Stellas in.

But surprisingly, the call didn't come from the Big Smoke. In the end, it came from somewhere else. Somewhere I'd only vaguely heard of.

Mondays were always a struggle after these London weekends. But this Monday turned out to be harder than the rest. Just a couple of hours into my early shift at the newspaper, the Editor called an all-staff floor meeting at 9.30am. 'Difficult times', 'print costs going up', 'circulation going down', more corporate blah blah and then those inevitable words: 'at risk of redundancy'.

Two weeks later after the expected, terminable dreary conversations with HR, the Editor called me into his office.

'Sorry, we've got to let you go, Jimmy lad. You're one of our best, but you're young. You've got a great career ahead of you, you'll do alright, and I think I've got something you'll be interested in. Now, Jimmy, have you heard of Dubai or Sharjah?'

'Somewhere in the Middle East, aren't they?' I replied.

'Aye, in the United Arab Emirates, the middle of the desert. And it's hot, bloody hot over there. Every day is blue sky and sunshine. Not like this shite weather we've got,' he said, as he looked out his window at the van drivers struggling to load up the evening papers while the rain battered them.

A new English-language newspaper had been recently launched over there by one of his old editor pals from The Sun and they were looking for senior reporters. If I was interested and up for the challenge, he said he could make the call and put in a good word.

Guaranteed sunshine, golden beaches, tax-free salary and a journey into the unknown? I didn't need a Stella to think this one through and was on the plane four weeks later.

Chapter 2

The first thing you learn when you fly into Dubai airport is that you're totally unprepared for the culture shock that greets you as soon as your feet touch the sand.

Standing in the passport queue, staring ahead at the line of dishdash-robed customs officers in their booths, unexpected beads of sweat trickled down my forehead and the small of my back. Part overwhelming heat, part nerves and part unjustified guilt seemed to consume me, which I couldn't shake as I fidgeted with my recently dyed blonde curtains hair.

This wasn't a friendly wall of warmth and welcoming – this felt like a wall of intense scrutiny and intimidation. There must have been at least a dozen customs and border control desks quizzing the arrivals. And positioned in front of each customs officer stood a well-armed soldier. Along the outer perimeter of our queue, more armed military slowly paced up and down with Alsatian guard dogs by their sides. I had nothing to worry about, but they were making me anxious.

The Daily UAE had arranged for a driver to pick me up. Despite stumbling over the simple question of 'Where are you from?' with the response of 'London. No, I mean Aberdeen. Well, Scotland, but I flew here from London,' and struggling to answer the other straightforward question of 'Where will you be living?' because at that point I didn't actually know except it was 'a hotel' and a driver would take me there, Passport Control eventually waved me through.

Asif, the driver, stood there holding a white board with 'Mr James' scrawled on it, scanning every white male passenger going past him until our eyes locked on each other – a knowing smile from him as the pale-faced 20-something from Scotland with 'Nae Idea' tattooed across his forehead approached.

He chatted and drove, worryingly looking back at me more times than the road ahead. The soft plastic back seats of this Nissan Bluebird were ripped through to the foam and the seatbelt fastener just didn't fasten. His radio station was tuned in to what I was guessing was some sort of Muslim prayers – long recitals broken up every now and then with something more melodic. Although it was only 10.30 in the morning, the desert heat must have been pushing 30°C and this Scottish loon was not used to anything above 20°C, as my pale blue Ralph Lauren shirt stuck to the back of the seat, and sweat patches gradually formed under my armpits. It was bloody hot. Too hot even for a cigarette.

We headed along the main Dubai-to-Sharjah road, cutting through the dusty, barren desert. The landscape was completely flat, stretching along the horizon in all directions like a plasterer had skimmed the entire terrain. Clumps of shrubs and lines of telegraph poles were the only visible signs of life trying their best to break the monotony of bleakness.

The six-storey red-bricked hotel stood alone in the desert on the outskirts of Sharjah. A small grocery store was affixed onto the side and an empty two-pump Emarat petrol station was opposite. No sign of a pub or nightlife or any kind of life – just a few stray goats lying lazily in the shade on the side of the hotel.

I had a meeting with the Editor in three hours. But before that, I needed to see the newspaper's general manager, a local called Hamza, who reported directly to the representatives of Sheikh Muhammed Al Zaheri, ruler of Sharjah and owner of the newspaper.

I heaved the £19.99 Debenhams 'Sale' suitcases onto the single bed and unpacked what I'd deemed back home were the essentials for a relocation to the desert: four pairs of Adidas trainers, one pair of suede Clarks Wallabees, one pair of black leather shoes, eight T-shirts, five short-sleeved cotton work shirts, two suits, three pairs of jeans, a pair of chinos, two Next beach shorts, one cagoule, two hoodies, the new editions of FHM, Mixmag and DJ Magazine, the latest Irvine Welsh book, Howard Marks' Mr Nice, a bag of records and a pile of socks and pants.

Then there were the 'essentials' my mum had insisted on packing: two dozen Aberdeen rowies, two packets of Tunnock's Tea Cakes, two boxes of Nairn's oatcakes, one tin of Dean's shortbread, six packets of Batchelors Pasta 'n' Sauce, four tins of tomato soup, two large bars of Galaxy chocolate, a family multi-pack of Golden Wonder crisps and extra smellies (four roll-on deodorants, four tubes of SR toothpaste and two Insignia shower gels).

Walking around the small, sparsely furnished room, there was nowhere to store the food, so I stuffed it all back into the case. The flimsy single wardrobe only had two plastic hangers, so I tripled up on T-shirts, hanging the best and folding the others to place on the shelf above.

Flinging open the maroon-coloured floor-to-ceiling curtains, the blinding sun illuminated the room as I unlocked the balcony doors. It was a balcony for one, barely wide enough for the single folding metal stool and coffee table. The stifling desert heat soon filled the room and after a few minutes, I closed the doors and curtains as there was no air conditioning to be found. The only respite was from the tired-looking brass ceiling fan slowly rotating with minimum effect.

After an unexpected snooze on the softly sprung bed, it was time to hail a cab and head to the Daily UAE offices.

'As-Salam alaykum. Welcome to Sharjah,' Hamza said, as he remained seated behind his excessively large mahogany desk, tapping his cigar into the glass ashtray.

'I trust you had a good flight. Now, can I have your passport, please?'

I handed it over.

'Thank you. Now sign this, please.'

He passed over a piece of paper typed in Arabic and pointed to where I should add my signature.

'We will look after this now,' he said as he turned behind him, opening a safe and placing my passport onto a pile of what looked like a rainbow of passports from around the world.

Okaaay, that was unexpected and didn't feel right, I said to myself, questioning this casual submission of British freedom and protection.

'You have five nights already paid for at the hotel. After that, you must find your own accommodation. Plenty of accommodation in Sharjah, it won't be difficult finding somewhere.'

'I wish you well here,' he said.

There was no offer of additional help and he abruptly motioned towards the door for me to leave. I headed down to the newsroom on the ground floor – a vast, brightly lit, open-plan area. Everything looked shiny and new – more desks than people. In fact, I could only see a handful of people, and they were gathered around a computer in the far corner of the room outside a glass-walled office.

I wandered over, introducing myself with a question to a short, bull-necked, 50-something who was standing with one hand placed on the back of the sub-editor's chair.

'Do you know where the Editor's office is?'

'There,' he pointed to the glass-enclosed room just behind while keeping his eyes fixed on the sub's computer screen.

'Do you know where the Editor is?' I asked.

'Fuckin' hell. What do you want?' he snapped back.

'I'm looking for the Editor. Got a meeting with him. I'm Jimmy Irvine. Start today as a senior reporter.'

'Go in there and wait. I'll be in in a minute.'

I sat down in the black leather chair and looked back through the glass at the group huddled around the computer. Mr 'Fuckin' Hell' was jabbing the screen with his pen over the shoulder of the sub-editor. His voice grew louder and louder until the pen flew across the empty newsroom, bouncing off a bench of computer screens. He turned around, red-faced, arms swaying, muttering and 'fucking cunting' to himself as he headed towards me and stepped into the office.

'Can't fucking publish anything. Spiking another fucking story. Another fucking royal connection. Another story fucking censored,' he angrily grumbled to himself.

'Welcome,' he paused, taking a deep breath and placing his hand on his desk to steady himself and inhale his cigarette.

'Sorry about that. Okay, let's get you started,' he said. 'The first thing I say to everyone new, Jimmy, is that you've got to understand that over here, the locals are always right, and you're always wrong. The locals are always protected and you're not. You fuck up here, son, and you either disappear or you end up in a rat-infested jail for a long time, chewing on your fingernails as it's the only thing you'll trust to eat.

'Tabloid stories don't survive here. And the writers who dare... well, they soon escape back to the UK or they... disappear. You don't see them again. You don't hear from them. You just don't know what's happened to them. There's a million square miles of Arabian desert out there. That's a lot of fucking sand to bury things in.

'Don't cross the line and you'll be fine. Forget about scoops. Forget about whistleblowing. Forget about investigations. Just report what you're allowed to report.

'We pulled four stories last night. Forced to pull. Four fucking stories came back down from Hamza, redacted with thick black marker pen scored across the pages. Four cunting stories. Two hours before print!

'Do you know what we did? Replaced them with travel features. Fucking travel features and big fucking travel pictures. Features about how fucking great Dubai is. How it's growing. How it's the biggest. How it's the best.

'Get used to it Jimmy. This is journalism in the UAE.'

Frustrated and seemingly permanently stressed, he was a typical cantankerous tabloid editor. And like a typical editor, you could tell he wouldn't hold back on unleashing a verbal bashing on anyone who fucked up.

After our brief 10-minute chat, which was more him telling me what his expectations were rather than me actually getting a chance to ask any questions, he handed me over to my direct boss, the news editor: an Algerian woman, probably mid-forties, studious black-rimmed glasses and thick curly dark hair, but with a friendly smile.

She quietly led me around the office, pointing out where the cuttings library was, the picture desk, the internet desk, the sport and feature teams areas, and where to find the IT guys.

On the surrounding walls hung grand canvas paintings of Sheikh Al Zaheri in his fine regal golden robes. There was no friendly smile about him, though. On each of the four paintings, he scowled down at you through his thick dark eyebrows and beard. Not so much an inspiring 'Your Country Needs You' but more of a 'My Country Orders You'.

The last few hours of this first day were spent learning the newspaper's editorial system and how and where to file stories. In between, there were long spells of listening to the eerie office silence and wondering 'where the fuck is everyone?', as only a handful of people were dotted around the floor and nobody was talking, just facing their screen and working.

■ ■ ■

At 50p for a pack of 20 Marlboro Lights, I was never going to be without a cigarette out here. Standing on the hotel balcony that night, I puffed through the lot, knowing that I still had a full sleeve left in the suitcase.

Staring out into the silent desert darkness, that unwelcome voice of self-doubt appeared as I realised just how alien and unfamiliar this land was. 'What the hell am I doing here? Why am I in the middle of nowhere? Where will I live? Where is everyone? Are there people like me? Where is the nightlife? Is there a nightlife? How do I get a beer? Is this really better than Scotland?'

Lots of questions flew around with few answers, but tomorrow was a day for flat-hunting. The clock was ticking and I'd be turfed out of this courtesy hotel by the end of the week.

My second shift at the Daily UAE didn't start until 2pm so I was up early to hit the estate agents by 9. I'd been told Sharjah was the poorer cousin of Dubai. Not just poorer but also a teetotal, god-fearing version of Dubai. Not as many international brands and fewer international people living there. There was absolutely no nightlife in Sharjah and from what I could gather, no life for anyone who wasn't Arabic.

I decided to explore the rental options over in Dubai first, heading to Deira, the poorer – or let's say the 'more affordable' – cousin of the Bur Dubai area (which was attracting the wealthier Western expats with luxury apartments, villas and five-star hotels). Deira was historically the commercial port of Dubai, a bustling, noisy, beehive of colourful souks, traders and dhows ferrying goods up and down the Creek. It was the old face of Dubai. The true Dubai. Dubai without the botox.

The first couple of apartments made my stomach churn. We walked through the Indian spice store out to the backyard and up a narrow flight of sandstone stairs. The humidity must have been beyond 80% as every step I took squeezed out more sweat from every pore. I was hot, thirsty and uncomfortable before the estate agent unlocked the door. I craved the coolness of walking into an air-conditioned apartment sheltered from the scorching desert sun. But this door did not lead to the relief and sanctuary I was hoping for.

We were greeted by a scurry of cockroaches darting across the hallway floor. Within seconds, they were out of sight but not out of mind.

Cockroaches. Jesus, why are there fuckin' cockroaches? I'd never seen so many cockroaches up close before. Beetles, yes. Slaters, yes. Earwigs, yes. But cockroaches? Nae thanks.

We turned sharply into a galley kitchen. It felt like we were interrupting. Interrupting a dinner for four. Not four people but four cats. Lying amongst their scrawny paws were fragments of bones and the festering remains of some kind of packaged meat.

Rice was scattered all over the floor and pools of cooking sauces were splattered from corner to corner. The stench of cat piss and sauces simmering from the sunlight burning through the window forced us out of the kitchen back into the hallway.

A short intake of breath was all we could withstand as the foulness travelled with us along the hall and into the living area. In the corner of the room was a double bed with a mattress. But this once-white mattress was now stained a dirty yellow, providing a second home for more vermin cats.

Without discussion, I left. 2,000 Dirhams (£400) a month they wanted for that hovel. The next apartment to see was 1,500 Dirhams a month and my expectations had been lowered as I headed down to the waterside of the Creek to gasp some fresh air and a couple of cigs before the next viewing.

The second apartment was a five-minute walk back through the souk behind the InterContinental Hotel. Right area, location good, I thought, until I arrived at the main building entrance. Directly opposite was the refuse zone for the hotel. Rows of glass bottle banks and dunes of rotting rubbish bags were stacked up and reeking along the adjacent wall leading from the steps of the apartment entrance down into the underground hotel deliveries area. There was no need to step into this flat for a guided tour – the decision had been made. Nae fuckin' chance.

The next day, after a recommendation from one of the English reporters, I upped my game and pushed the budget to 2,500 Dirhams a month. Would this get me the right apartment in the right area without the risk of being gnawed to death at night by devil rats or waterboarded by cat piss?

The four-storey apartment block had only just been completed. It was on the right side of Deira but the wrong side of Bur Dubai, making it affordable. The corridors smelt of fresh paint and sawdust. Some of the rooms were still being fitted by carpenters as I walked past them down to Apartment 12.

The agent unlocked, pushed open the door, flicked on the air conditioning, turned around and asked: 'Well, you like?'

I didn't need a tour. It was small and in a matter of seconds I could see it was perfect. A clean, more familiar, modern studio flat with an open-plan kitchen, twin beds and living space leading out to a curved balcony that stretched around the corner of the building, giving views of wasteland to the front and the Creek to the side.

The apartment felt instantly familiar and comfortable in a Western European way – a new TV, fitted kitchen with breakfast bar, white-tiled bathroom and shower room, and two chic low-backed black leather chairs. For me, this was bloody luxury. This was it, I thought. This is the beginning of life in Dubai. And it was the beginning. But it was the wrong beginning.

Chapter 3

The concierge reception area was still work in progress. Every morning for the first couple of weeks, I'd step around, over or under carpenters, painters and electricians as they laid cables, sawed wooden panels, fitted lights or just sat around waiting.

Their boss-man looked Arabic. Six foot, late 30s, thick black hair swept back in a Hugh Grant style. He never removed his Ray-Bans and always wore a black top – sometimes a polo shirt, sometimes a long-sleeved shirt, sometimes a tee, but always black.

Nothing seemed to happen until he arrived in the morning. Looking out from my balcony with a Marlboro Light drooped over the side and coffee in hand, I'd see him whizzing up in his Jeep Wrangler, sending a cloud of dust into the air as he abruptly braked, always at a sharp angle like he was tempted to do a doughnut.

He'd stay in the Jeep for a good five or ten minutes talking on his cell phone. I couldn't understand what he was saying as it was in Arabic, but you could tell his temperament from the decibels of his conversation. On a bad day, it grew louder without any pauses for breath. Whoever was on the other side was taking a verbal beating with no chance of reply. The call would end, the door would slam and he'd stride into the reception below, directing orders at the awaiting tradesmen. None of them was Arabic, of course. Arabs don't do manual labour. All of them were Asian or ASEAN, as I later learned.

Whenever I passed him in reception, he always smiled and made polite gestures like standing out of my way and clearing a path through the Jenga-like piles of toolboxes, planks, paint pots and cables loosely draped at garrotting height from wall to wall.

Every day, the small talk led to us both discovering something new about each other. He was called Ali. He was a Lebanese property developer and this was his third development in Dubai. He'd lived in London before this and loved telling anecdotes about his party nights at the Ministry of Sound. VIP treatment, 'English girls', private tables and exclusive parties back at the Metropolitan Hotel. It might have all been bullshit, but he talked a good game and bragging seemed to make him happy.

'You like parties? You like girls?' he'd ask, smiling. He'd finish our small talk with the same question almost every time.

There were four apartments on each of the floors. I was on the third in Apartment 12. This was positioned at the end of the corridor, furthest away from the lift and opposite the emergency exit staircase.

After three weeks, the workmen were no longer on-site and the reception area was immaculately operational, with crystal-white marble flooring, a couple of low-backed white leather sofas with cacti on the side and a teak wood-panelled concierge desk.

Ali said all the apartments had been completed except on the fourth floor where 'we have to make some special adjustments', he added, without sharing any more detail.

These 'special adjustments' seemed to be getting special treatment, as the sound of drilling and power saws was no longer contained to just daytime but continued into the evenings as well. Vans were being unloaded at night and I could see Ali down below from the balcony, directing the workmen with boxed goods in and out of the apartment block followed minutes later by several thuds from the floor above and sometimes a loud muffled voice – Ali's, I guessed.

I'd only spotted one other resident in the block in the six weeks since moving in. A white Western-looking man, clean-shaven, curly, mousy brown hair, maybe in his mid-forties. Always in a smart, loose-fitting work shirt and beige trousers or chinos. He'd leave at 7am every morning, except on a Friday, holding his briefcase and walking over to the main road to flag down a Dubai Taxi.

With no other visible signs of tenants, it surprised then intrigued me when 'visitors' began arriving in the evenings.

From about 10pm on Thursdays, a stream of Mercedes, Porsche, Jeep, the odd Lamborghini and taxis would pull up at the front of the building. Out would stumble groups of young Arabic men with white Western girls in tow. Their delicate gazelle-like legs and high heels appearing first from the low-rise car doors, followed by a swaying shoulder-strapped designer handbag and then the full show of sprayed-on miniskirt and micro boob tube. Jostling, joking and sometimes stacking it in the gravel, I'd then see Ali dart out from under the entrance canopy to greet them with a joyous 'As-salam alaykum' and usher them inside.

You could hear the bassline pounding the floor above into the early hours. He was a good-looking, popular man, Ali, and must be reliving his London party life in Dubai, I'd think, lying awake in bed. But despite the lack of sleep, the noise never bothered me; if anything, I was more gutted that I hadn't been invited to the fourth floor, yet.

Chapter 4

The club scene in the UK was reaching its peak in 1996. Every town and city had its own 'legendary' night of resident House DJs, headliner guests and live PAs.

Being east-coast boys, our clubbing artery flowed straight down the train lines of Aberdeen, Edinburgh, Leeds and London, never veering west to Liverpool or Manchester – there was no need to, in my mind.

Clubs had become theatres of not just music but art and entertainment. The more outrageous and controversial the entertainment, the more people wanted to be a part of it. Outside of London, Vague in Leeds had become my go-to party place – it was leading the way in terms of hedonism and hi-energy House with a friendly mix of heterosexual, homosexual and polysexual clubbers, all focused on battering the hell out of their weekends.

Nothing was taboo there, which was being referred to by Melody Maker and the mainstream press as 'the dance equivalent of Andy Warhol's The Factory'.

'Do you spit or swallow?'

That was part of the door vetting at Vague, as the glamorous hostess Madame JoJo sashayed up and down the line of clubbers outside, checking to see who was suitable to be let in. Those who refused to swallow JoJo's squirty cream sprayed into their mouths were given a curt, 'Not tonight, love. Try somewhere else,' while those who lapped it up and had made an effort in their attire or just looked 'so cute' were led down to the front and into the club.

At Vague, music was just part of the experience. Self-expression, performance art, friendships, a sense of liberation and unshackling from the monotony of daily routines were all there to be enjoyed for six hours in this colourful *club*Land of Oz.

Vague, Ibiza's Ku Club and Club USA in New York were the holy trinities of my clubbing experiences to date and I'd been taking bits from each into the club nights we created in Aberdeen, albeit in a scaled-down, low-budget, tight-arsed, Scottish kinda way.

Those clubs shaped this desire inside to push boundaries, be daring and be the first to try something new, though I didn't think Aberdeen's clubland was quite ready for the one-dollar wank booths of Club USA.

Flying Vague's Trannies With Attitude (TWA) up to Aberdeen for one of our nights was certainly risqué and daring enough, as they stepped off the plane in their red-and-white TWA netball outfits, high heels and towering wigs. At six foot-plus, TWA's Nick and Paul were turning heads in all directions, from oil riggers at the airport to customs, police and taxi drivers. By the time they DJ'd in the club, the city was abuzz with chat about '*the trannies in toon*' and the queue to get in snaked around a couple of blocks.

It was impossible to replicate that sexual energy of Vague outside of the Vague venue, but by the end of a night partying with the trannies anywhere, you felt like you'd been as close to having had sex as you could in public – hot, sweaty, loved-up, toking on a fag and a desire to go again 'one more time' or 'one more tune'.

But this freedom to express yourself, homosexuality, transvestism and what the press loved to call 'recreational' drugs were all strictly illegal in the UAE. Even dancing to music could land you in jail during Ramadan.

This was not the country to push the boundaries of clubbing.

Or was it?

■ ■ ■

I hadn't seen Ali in the mornings for a few weeks since the building work had completed. My only glimpses of him were looking down onto his baseball cap and silhouette as he greeted his late-night guests at the apartment block.

'As-salam alaykum,' he exclaimed as the lift doors opened and there he was, leaning casually against the wall, Ray-Bans firmly on, black polo shirt, lit cigarette in one hand and a bag of unmistakably 12" records in the other. But he was not alone. On the other side standing rigidly upright was 'Mr 7am', clutching his briefcase. He averted his eyes quickly to the floor, clearly not in the mood for a chat.

'Been buying records?' I said to Ali, nodding towards his bag of vinyl.

'Ha! Not buying, playing,' he said.

'Playing? Where do you play?'

'On the fourth floor,' he laughed. 'Not anywhere fancy, just the fourth floor. My friends love a party, so I spin these all the time. But I've only got 40 or so. There's no record shops in the UAE – well, none that sells House music,' he said.

I could feel a wee rush shooting up my back into my head. My chest tightened and I blurted out: 'Ha! Brilliant! I do a bit of that as well. Used to run some club nights back in the UK. And got a lot more than 40 records.'

'You got them with you?'

'Ha. Not all of them, no. I only brought about 50 or so over.'

I paused.

'So, there's folk out here who like House music and clubbing? I didn't think there was any kind of scene,' I queried.

'There isn't but these people like my parties. They've got a hunger for it. A hunger for everything I offer,' Ali smiled. The lift doors opened and the two of them stepped out first. They turned to each other in a knowing way, stopped and waited for me to carry on past them.

'Have a good day, Jimmy,' he said as I walked out towards the blazing sunlight.

Then, 'Do you want to play sometime?' he shouted, just within earshot as I was stepping out through the automatic main doors.

'Oh aye. Yes!' I said enthusiastically, giving him a thumbs up.

'Good. We'll talk later,' he said, nodding to 'Mr 7am', and then the two of them walked behind the concierge desk into his small office.

No matter where you travel, always take a bag of records with you – this is what I'd learned over the years. You just never know where the opportunity might pop up to jump on behind the decks.

The year before, on a jaunt down to London with some of Aberdeen's 'elite' hairdresser friends for the opening party of the Coco & Claire clothes shop in Covent Garden, I turned up with a fresh bag of tunes from TAG Records. A couple of hours later and several Budweisers in, their DJ asked if I wanted to slap them on. And that was it – we were off. Banging tunes till 10pm on the shop floor, a few snifters in the back office then more decks, records and nose bag at the after-party penthouse on Warwick Street.

Ali had obviously locked into the needs of his friends or guests, fulfilling their desires with his fourth-floor entertainment. Now here I was, in the right place at the right time with a bag of tunes, and it was time to get my own fix of this.

Chapter 5

I strolled into the editorial floor to start the morning shift. As usual at this time, it was empty except for one person sitting at the designated 'Internet Desk', surfing the world wide web on their allocated time slot, and a couple of other senior reporters from the UK: Geordie Joe and Cockney Dave. No sign of the Editor and my boss, the news editor, who didn't start her shift until later in the afternoon.

The three of us sat around Joe's desk chain-smoking our way through packs of Marlboros – always in disbelief that fags were cheaper than water out here.

'What you covering today then, lads?' I asked.

'Seiko product launch down at the Creek in an hour,' said Dave with a knowing grin.

'Hold on a minute. Don't tell me. You better not be getting a freebie watch out of this one, are you Dave?'

'Only five journos have been invited and I'm banging the PR. She's promised a goodie bag at the end of the launch, which "you'll love", she said. And come on, if you're going to write about a product launch, you need to use the product, don't you? Makes it an authentic and honest review,' he said, fully aware of the hypocrisy of what he just said.

For the journos out here, it was all about the goodie bags. An unsaid agreement between Arab business owners and the

Arab-owned press. 'We look after you. You write something good.'

Scanning Dave's belongings and clobber, he was a walking goodie bag himself. Alfred Dunhill tie – freebie; Hermès leather briefcase – freebie; Montblanc pen – freebie; Ralph Lauren socks – freebie; Versace cufflinks – freebie. And that's not including the free lunches and dinners at some of the finest restaurants in Dubai. His slightly chubby face and tightly stretched shirt were visible signs of those growing excesses.

'I'm fookin' double-booked over two events,' said Joe. 'Hard Rock Cafe got a pre-opening brunch down at Jumeirah Beach. And then the Arabian Leopard Protection Foundation has invited the paper to an announcement on funding and some environmental research project.'

'Hard Rock Cafe with champers and burgers, or eco lovers with pie charts and projectors? Hmm… I just can't decide,' he laughed.

'Jimmy lad, if you can take this one for me, I'll pay you back. Next juicy freebie is yours, I promise,' he said.

The Arabian Leopard Protection Foundation was located five miles out from Sharjah. The presentation was due to start in an hour, so with no other plans in my diary, I agreed to take this gig so Joe could go off and enjoy himself. No doubt I'd see him later at Champions Bar, fucking wasted after his 11am start on champers.

I flagged over a dusty Sharjah taxi from outside the office and we headed out into the desert. With no AC in these rickety old Nissans, it was windows down, but it made no difference as hot air and then sand swirled around the inside of the car, forcing me to bend down and cover my eyes while the driver adjusted his red-and-white-checked ghutra headscarf to give him some protection.

We bumped and bashed our way across the makeshift desert road, failing to avoid potholes as I rolled around in the backseat thinking what a mug I was and what a cunt Joe was for passing this onto me. 'Bet that fucker has bloody been out here before,' I cursed to myself.

The foundation's HQ was nothing more than three portable cabins with a couple of Land Rovers parked in front. To the sides of the cabins were some fenced enclosures. They looked empty at first, barring a wooden shack of some sort with large boulders behind casting a protective shadow from the sun. But as I approached the fence, I could just make out the head of a leopard poking out, resting on its front paws, cooling in the shade of its makeshift home.

Dr Janssen had created this volunteer organisation a couple of years ago and was slowly managing to draw attention to the dwindling numbers of indigenous leopards surviving in the region and the gradual destruction of their natural habitat. Sheikh Al Zaheri, owner of our newspaper (sorry, that's Sheikh Dr Sultan Bin Muhammed Al Zaheri, Supreme Council Member and Ruler of Sharjah, to you and me), had recently granted it a legal status and was expected to make a generous donation soon.

It quickly became clear that there was no other press here today as Dr Janssen opened the cabin door and showed me to a single chair positioned in front of a white screen and projector. No coffee, croissants or champagne on offer here, just water. Joe – you wanker.

Only approximately 120 leopards are thought to be alive now across the Arabian peninsula, Dr Janssen went on to explain. Their numbers are in decline and they are at risk of extinction as the UAE cities encroach further into the desert, destroying natural environments, and nomadic tribes continue to hunt them to protect their livestock. Not just killing them but capturing and selling them onto the black market for thousands of dollars.

'We are two minutes away from the final hour,' he warned. 'Without protection, these beautiful animals will become extinct before we know it.'

Dr Janssen's message (which he wanted the story to focus on) was to take action now and protect the leopards by investing in sanctuaries for captive breeding and to clamp down on the growing black-market trading.

'It's not just leopards, of course,' he told me. 'You can buy anything on the black-market. Orangutans, golden eagles, lions – they're all for sale if you want them and you've got the money.'

I wasn't aware of a black market in exotic animals out here, but this sounded like a possible story where Dr Janssen was only scratching the surface. His focus was leopards but what the hell was going on with all these other animals? Where were they being sold? Who was buying them?

'Where would you go to buy them then?' I asked.

'I'm not sure,' he said. 'But the UAE's secrets are kept in the souks.'

Back at the office, I filed the story with the suggested headline of

LEOPARDS FACE EXTINCTION AS SHARJAH EXPANSION THREATENS HABITAT

knowing fine that would never get approved but it was always amusing to spook the sub-editors now and then with an uncomfortable headline. It was 6pm and the editorial floor was getting busier as the night shift of subs and editors took to their desks ready to publish another edition of the Daily UAE.

For me, it was the end of my shift. The end of a hard day I

joked to myself: one interview and one story. This was nothing like the daily paper back in Scotland, where I could be bashing out three or four news stories and a 700-word feature in one shift.

Time to get home, freshen up and hit the '100 Dirhams Night' with Joe at 8pm down at Champions Bar. This was the drunkest night in town for the world's expats. For an entrance fee of 100 Dirhams, you could drink and eat as much as you want all night.

Everyone came there to party. Some got laid and some got laid out, as four hours of downing beers, tequila shots and Long Island Ice Teas inevitably ended up with Brits scrapping other Brits, quickly followed by the blue lights of Dubai police and ambulances.

Set in the basement of the Marriott Hotel, Champions Bar was just the warm-up for your Thursday night out.

'Areet, Jimmy,' bellowed Joe as he stood proudly in front of the two tequila slammers and two Heineken pints he'd lined up at the bar for my arrival. 'How were your big cats?'

'Fuck off,' I replied jokingly as I reached out, clasping his hand for a matey shoulder bump. 'You stitched me up royally with that one. Middle of nowhere in a roasting tin cabin? Thanks, pal! Trust *you* had a good time?'

Joe laughed and we downed our tequila shots – well on our way now to another night of unknown inebriated adventures.

The neon-lit, American-styled sports bar got busier by the minute as Dubai's expat community swung in through the saloon doors – teachers, oil workers, media and marketing types, airline cabin crew, pilots and, every now and then, a few Arabs, usually Lebanese, never locals. The air hostesses always looked amazing. Permanently tanned, slim and toned – you felt like you'd gate-crashed a beauty pageant with the best-looking girls from every country here to unwind and party before their next flight.

But while the girls looked great, the music sucked at Champions Bar. Guns N' Roses, Dexys Midnight Runners, Madonna, Spice Girls, Chumba-fuckin'-wamba, Vinda-fuckin'-loo, Jive-fuckin'-Bunny... this was a wedding disco on crack, with sex-crazed, adrenalin-junky, 20-somethings replacing your sweet grandmas and cute children on the dancefloor.

As we downed our fifth Long Island Iced Tea, the two of us glided towards the small dancefloor squeezed in at the end of the bar, heading for a group of six girls who were sharing two-pint pitchers of cocktails and dancing to Chumbawamba.

Soon, we 'got knocked down', then we 'got up again' and we mouthed 'a whisky drink', then 'a vodka drink', then a 'lager drink' to the girls before we 'got knocked down' then 'got up again', jumping around in circles with them. We hadn't even spoken – it was pure drunken energy we were somehow connecting through, as cheesy karaoke hit after cheesy karaoke hit was played, drowning out every attempt at a conversation.

'Alison', 'Kent', 'air hostess' were the only three words I could make out from trying to talk to her as we swayed around the dancefloor in our group.

'They're fookin' Arabian World cabin crew,' shouted Joe into my ear, who'd been leaning into one of the girls.

'Just got off a Jo'burg flight. The little blonde one with those loovely puppies that need soom strokin' says they're going to the Highland Lodge next.'

The Highland Lodge nightclub was the climax of the night in Dubai – all the expats ended up there at some point. At 4am, you could even stumble from the dancefloor to its outside breakfast bar and tuck into a Full English before heading off home.

We piled into a cab with two of the air hostesses – Alison and Michelle. Joe's eyes were transfixed on Michelle's 'puppies' tightly packed into her black vest top, as he struggled to maintain eye level every time she spoke.

'Dubai Taxis' were in a different league to Sharjah's. Most of them were a Mercedes C Class, spotlessly clean and the drivers wore a smart uniform of cream shirt, golden tie and brown trousers. They were always respectful, polite and friendly. But us pissed-up Brits were their worst nightmare: abusive, rude and always taking the mick.

Geordie Joe had told me a few of his lively stories down the Bigg Market and Quayside on a Saturday night back home in Newcastle. It was not uncommon for him to strip off and run stark-bollock naked into the bars, before seconds later being turfed out and rolled onto the street by the unamused bouncers.

And he wasn't one to shy away from an argument, as his slightly crooked nose and faded scar above his right eyebrow signalled. He could quickly turn from stupid clown to psycho cunt depending on his mood and boredom threshold on a night out. A wrong glance or comment from any bloke could trigger the inner nutter from Joe.

'DFS' was one of his nicknames back home, he'd once boasted. 'Drinking. Fighting. Shagging. That's what I do.'

'What are you doing?' shrieked Michelle as Joe clambered over her in the backseat to get near the window.

Sitting in the front seat I could hear the commotion and laughter from the girls but couldn't see Joe properly as he was sitting right behind me. But their laughter soon turned to screaming as a huge gust of air blew into the taxi: 'Don't do it. What are you doing? Oh my God. He's fucking mad.'

I didn't need to wait much longer to find out what was going on as a hand suddenly appeared outside from the top of the windscreen followed by Joe's upside-down face grinning at me and the driver. He was on the fuckin' roof!

The driver went into panic, yelling at me, yelling at Joe, yelling at the girls and unable to stop with other cars so close behind on the dual carriageway. Joe inched himself further down the windscreen, stretching his arms out to grab the wipers while the speedometer flashed 60kmph. His face now at the bottom of the windscreen, he laughed uncontrollably as his belly was on full show, squashed against the glass, letting us read in all its fine glory 'Toon Army NUFC' tattooed across his gut.

But he wasn't completely daft, Joe. He'd timed this all to perfection. The driver pulled off the dual carriageway onto the slip road and gradually slowed down to a stop. We could see the bright lights of the Highland Lodge were just a few hundred yards ahead of us as the driver confronted Joe, threatening to phone the police and repeatedly calling him a maniac.

Alison and Michelle were hysterical with laughter, falling over each other, wiping the tears from their eyes. Joe handed the driver an extra 100 Dirhams on top of the fare, apologised, patted him on the back and walked over to Michelle. He scooped her up in one swoop and onto his shoulders, marching towards the club. He clearly thought he was back in Newcastle's Bigg Market.

The other taxi with the rest of the AWA air hostesses had witnessed the whole thing. They ran up to us outside the club, laughing and shouting up at Michelle sitting on top of Joe pretending to whip him like a jockey.

The bouncers, who had no doubt seen it all before, shook their heads, smiled and waved us in.

'Oi Oi!' came the voice from behind, followed by a swift whack on my back as I approached the bar. It was Dave or 'Davey

Tags' as I was now starting to refer to him, as he had so many designer labels hanging off him.

Good-looking guy from Islington, north London, always wearing the best clobber, mixing it up with Paul Smith, Tommy Hilfiger, Prada, Armani and sometimes his Gucci loafers, though he usually regretted it after a night out with Joe. He now only had one matching pair left after Joe's night-time games of desert frisbee where he'd launch Davey's shoes out of a taxi window into the darkness on the way home.

'How was Seiko?' I asked, as he stood grinning at Alison standing at my side.

'And who's this lovely?' he replied, blanking me and introducing himself to Alison while trying not to lose his balance and hold onto his wobbling pint.

He may look good, but Davey Tags was not sounding good tonight. His 12-noon product launch with Seiko was accompanied with champagne flutes, followed by lunchtime beers and cocktails at the Hyatt Regency. Now, 11 hours later, his liquid feast was swirling around inside him like a rollercoaster of inebriety.

Sometimes he'd talk coherently for a minute, but then he'd drift off into a slur of mumbles punctuated by extreme Cockney 'fahks', 'fahking', 'fahk it' and then a cross-eyed 'fahking come on, let's get some fahhhkin' shots.'

He pulled me and Alison towards the bar, his outstretched arm revealing what I assumed was the freebie Seiko watch from earlier in the day. Green dial with brown leather strap, very stylish. Jammy cunt.

The barman lined up three tequila shots. Alison and Davey sprinkled the salt on their hands and grabbed the slices of lemon. I always preferred it neat, followed quickly by a few swigs of beer. In the 10 seconds it took me to down the shot and Heineken chaser, Davey had stacked it and was lying flat on his back on the floor. Davey had succeeded with the '1, 2, 3, Down!' part, but with the flinging back of his head, he'd failed to stop the rest of his body from tumbling backwards.

'Taxi for Davey,' I said to myself and then to Alison.

Unable to stand without draping his arms over me for support, I knew it was the end of the night for both of us as he'd need an escort back to his apartment.

Alison smiled and didn't seem too fussed when I said I had to go. But then she unexpectedly gave me a goodbye peck on the cheek before wandering over to join her cabin crew and Joe, who by now had his shirt off dancing to ABBA. 'Fuck knows what's going to happen to him tonight,' I wondered as I dragged Davey outside, rolling him into a Dubai Taxi, luckily grabbing one of his loafers lying by the wheel just before we closed the door and headed off.

Davey remained passed out until we pulled up to his apartment block. I asked the driver to wait while I helped him get into the lift and then up to his flat. Davey blindly chucked a few more 'fahks' in my direction then KO'd on his couch, face-planting into the cushion. I tucked one of his loafers into his arms and decided to take the other one away with me, hoping he'd phone later that day in a panic about his precious missing Guccis.

The taxi meter was at 240 Dirhams and the clock showed 01:55 as we turned off the main road, bumping along the stretch of gravel leading up towards my apartment.

We were not alone. I could see the headlights of several cars parked outside and a throng of people milling around the reception.

'As-salam alaykum,' he said as I opened the taxi door. Standing in front of me in a black T-shirt and jeans was Ali. And an Ali without Ray-Bans.

'Ah, Mr Jimmy,' he laughed, surprised.

'Ali, how you doing? What's going on here?' I replied, looking around at the cars and people.

'Ah, just one of my little parties, Jimmy. You know: some girls, some boys, some music. Good times.' He smiled, patting me on the shoulders.

Ali turned to greet another car full of what I'm sure were Russian girls. You could always tell the Russians as their faces were as harsh as stone, chiselled cheekbones, tall and skinny, fake boobs and dripping in designer – or more likely knock-off designer – gear.

'You want to play, Jimmy?

'Tonight? Now?' Ali shouted over, as I walked towards the building.

Chapter 6

Four Arabic men were fooling around on the sofas in the reception area. Young guys in their 20s, muscle ripping T-shirts, gold neck chains, stonewashed jeans and black trainers. Ali brought them chilled bottles of Heineken from his office as they pushed, shoved, whispered then laughed with one another at what looked like excitable anticipation of what was to come.

'I'll knock on your door in about 20 minutes,' Ali said to me as we waited by the lift.

The lift doors opened and out stumbled two Arabic men, similarly dressed to the guys in reception but in an even more euphoric state. They were hanging onto each other, jokingly slapping each other's backsides, fist-bumping, talking and laughing loudly in Arabic. Their eyes passed over us as if we didn't exist, then they bounded their way through reception and out the front doors.

'My friends, come with me,' Ali beckoned over the four men on the sofas, holding the lift doors open as we all squeezed in.

Ali and the men chatted away excitedly until we reached the third floor.

'20 minutes, my friend,' he shouted after me as the doors were closing and I walked down the corridor to my apartment.

I reached under the bed and pulled out the bag of records, flicking through them trying to figure out a good solid start of a

House set then selecting a few 'big guns' and anthems to take it up a level.

I swapped my sweaty Lacoste polo shirt for a fresh one – pastel green this time – and sprayed the Lynx Africa all over. I stretched out on the bed, counting down the minutes.

Knock, knock. Knock, knock. Knock, knock.

Knock, knock. Knock, knock. Knock, knock. Knock, knock.

KNOCK, KNOCK. KNOCK, KNOCK, KNOCK!!

I jolted up. I'd passed out and was all fuzzy as I stumbled over the record bag falling into the side of the other twin bed. I opened the door and there... was... not Ali... but one of his guests. At 6ft with spiky black heels on, her eyes levelled with mine, just a few inches from my face, I stood back to see this slender figure in a silver minidress, her cleavage something she was no doubt proud of and happy to boast.

'Mr Jimmy,' she said in a Russian accent. 'Mr Ali has sent me to get you. But... before we go, we do this.'

She delicately put her hand on my chest and brushed past into the room. Motioning me over to the chair and coffee table, she reached into her petite 'Chanel' purse and pulled out a little bag of white powder. Within seconds, she had expertly chopped out two generous lines of coke. She looked up, smiled, then bent down, hoovering up her line in a nanosecond before handing over the 100 Dirhams note.

This was A-class fucking rocket fuel, I said to myself, seconds after dusting off the remains on the table. Couple more deep snorts and it shot straight to the brain, instantly supercharging the much-needed rocket boosters.

She stood up, kissed me full on the lips and said: 'Now, we go.'

Buzzing, we marched up the fire exit staircase opposite. As we approached the fourth floor, I could hear more voices and the music getting louder. She pulled open the fire door and smiled at the beast of a bouncer standing there in a black suit.

I looked down the corridor and it was a sea of bodies. Girls were dancing and writhing against men, some sliding their hands up and down their bodies and the backs of their shirts. All the apartment doors along the corridor were open except one at the end by the lift. Beams of disco-coloured lights streamed from the doorways into the hall as groups snaked their way in and out of the apartments.

She led me into the first apartment, which was bathed in red lights with a muted white glow from a table lamp in the corner where the Technics 1210s were, and behind them, Ali was focused on mixing in the next track. I turned around and looked further into the apartment, but unbelievably, what I could see was not just one apartment but all the apartments on the fourth floor.

They had knocked through or probably never even built solid walls between the apartments. Sliding partitions had been pulled back to open this vast space that easily stretched further than the length of a tennis court. In the adjacent apartment, the kitchen had been converted into a bar area where girls and guys were perched on metal stools, knocking back champagne flutes.

Plush crimson couches were neatly spaced out along both sides, enough of a gap between each for couples to retain some kind of 'privacy'. Some I could see were blatantly tucking into the marching powder on the tables, while others were stretched out getting more intimate.

My escort smiled and walked off into a throng of dancing bodies as Ali reached out to shake my hand and planted a cold beer in the other.

'Mr Jimmy, my friend. You like?' he said.

'Anything you want tonight, you just ask me. Anything you see here and you want is yours. But first, you must play,' he grinned and we walked back over to the decks.

'Looking good, Ali. What a party – nice fuckin' scene,' I gushed as the charlie kicked in again.

'Just like the VIP parties back in London. Everyone gets what they want and everyone is happy,' he boasted.

Standing behind the decks usually gives you the best vantage point of the room and this was no different, as I could pretty well see all the way down to the solid wall of the end apartment. It also makes you the centre of attention, usually attracting wasted eejits asking for requests or pestering you about the names of tracks. Strangely though, nobody here seemed to care who was DJing. I didn't even get a second glance from anyone. Everyone was just focused on, well, everyone.

'A little something to keep you going tonight,' Ali said as he placed what looked like a full G of bagged powder under the right turntable before turning his back and walking back into the crowd.

In a good way, everyone danced to what I played, but it felt like they'd dance to Black Lace if I dropped it. Bringing out the big guns of Ken Doh's 'Nakasaki' and Gat Decor's 'Passion' made no difference – there was just no reaction.

Then it became clear.

Paying more attention to the room than the mixing for 10 minutes, I could see how this whole operation was working. And it was an 'operation' and some people here were 'working'.

The girls were demanding champagne from the punters at the bar, who were gladly buying, then moving to the couches and cosying up to each other. This was then followed by the guys reaching into their wallets to count out a number of notes.

The girl would then motion to the suited gorilla who would come over and take the money before briefly speaking into his walkie-talkie and stepping to the side. A few minutes later, I'd see her take the young Arab by the hand and lead him down towards the 'closed' Apartment 13 opposite the lift.

I hadn't seen Ali since he'd left that little present an hour or so ago and paranoia was starting to kick in a bit as I'd nose-bagged into it on repeat after every few mixes.

Who the fuck are these people?

I don't know anyone.

Nobody's talking to me.

Where are my pals?

What's the point of fuckin' DJing here?

Do I need a beer?

No, a shot. No, a line. No, a water.

Fuckin' need water.

I was now existing only in my own head, the room feeling more fuzzy and alien by the minute and getting seedier as the crowd thinned out but the cycle of money, coke and hookers continued to spin around to the backdrop of the House tunes.

Then, through into the next apartment… I could see…

…him.

But it couldn't be, could it?

I was fucked, really fucked, and couldn't be 100% sure at first, but…

…Joe, fuckin' Joe, was sitting on one of the couches laughing with Ali and what I assumed were two hookers.

Jesus, what the fuck is he doing here? Last time I saw him was at the Highland Lodge, where he locked into a sure thing with that air hostess.

I was fidgeting and puffing on my cig, scenarios flying around in my head, none of them making sense. I wasn't prepared to deal with a raucous Geordie Joe and knew I had to make a sharp exit. I stopped staring and ducked down behind the decks to tidy up the record bag, trying not to step on the vinyl I'd wildly discarded after failing to re-sleeve them.

I pulled out a nine-minute mix of Helicopter's 'On Ya Way'.

Can't kill the music, that would attract attention, but I need to get the fuck out of here, I was saying to myself as I dropped the needle on the record.

Fuck it, I'll get it back later, I decided, leaving it to play out for the next eight minutes while I gathered up the record bag and headphones, ready to make a sharp exit.

I could see Joe leaning over the table, hoovering up a line, closely followed by one of the girls. Right, time to make a move.

The bouncer was no longer on the door by the fire escape – he'd since moved his attention to further down the corridor, marshalling the flow of girls and punters in and out of Apartment 13.

As I gingerly stepped down the fire escape, I could feel the sun rising across the desert, the light piercing the windows and boring into my skull, inflicting its perennial form of torture upon those who dare to face daylight after no sleep.

My heart was beating ferociously and I was sweating from all pores as I stumbled into the apartment. I drew the floor-to-ceiling curtains shut, trying to block out the blinding white light, then peeled off my polo shirt, curled up in a ball on the bed and looked at my watch… 5.25am. The press conference was at 9.30am.

Chapter 7

Most press conferences in Dubai over the summer months were held indoors as temperatures outside regularly tipped 50°C. Not that the government would officially admit to that temperature, though, because once it hits 50°C, the government decree is that all outside labour has to stop.

But Dubai was going toe to toe with Abu Dhabi to see who could build the biggest, the tallest, the most ostentatious and blingiest buildings in the world. Nothing was going to stop the race between the egomaniac sheikhs, so Dubai's state-owned TV and radio stations would only ever report temperatures up to 47/48/49°C, and those poor sods on the building sites were bussed out of their squalid labour camps at the crack of dawn and forced to work through a 50°C+ midday sun until sunset.

Today, though, of course, this conference was an exception to the rule and was out-fuckin'-side, located down at the Creek. Not only was it out-fuckin'-side, but the event theme itself was the last thing I wanted to get involved with after four hours of pretend sleeping, lying in sheet-drenched sweat and a failed chipolata wank to FHM's photo spread of Gemma Atkinson. Nope, sleep had not been my friend last night.

Now I had to set off and report on the unveiling of the world's longest fuckin' cake! I couldn't believe it but, of course, I'm the one who'd agreed to cover this story yesterday, thinking with a clear rational head at the time that it would be an enjoyable morning of 'free food' and 'free drinks' for a few hours and an 'easy story' to file.

Food couldn't be further from my mind as I stepped out of the taxi at the Creek and walked into a cacophony of performing folk bands with banging drums and tambourines and throngs of spectators lining up behind the steel barriers protecting the cake.

2.5km it stretched for, as it twisted and looped its way on top of adjoined tables around the Creek. Once the record was confirmed, they were going to remove the barriers and let everyone grab a slice. If this was in Scotland, today would have also marked the world's biggest food fight, but the mainly Asian crowd were too well behaved for that and probably didn't fancy being arrested.

My sunnies were barely big enough to cover my eyes, as I wished somehow they could wrap around and protect my pounding head, which felt like it had mushroomed overnight. Never had I wanted one of those Arabian ghutras to cover my bonce more than now.

It might have still been the morning, but this unforgiving sun had focused a magnifying glass on me, doubling up on efforts to burn through to my soul. I wanted to cry, I wanted to sleep, I wanted to shower. I did not want fuckin' cake.

Weighing in at 74,000kg, this was also now the world's heaviest cake and the Dubai officials and chefs looked as happy as pigs in marzipan shit, as the Guinness World Records adjudicator declared both records official.

I was not at my inquisitive journalistic best as I asked the chefs some feeble questions, partly hoping they wouldn't answer and would tell me to go away or take pity and offer a complimentary bed in their five-star hotel for an afternoon's kip:

'Do you like cake?'

'Have you ever made a cake this big before?'

'If you had to do it again, could you make it bigger?'

'Did you have your cake and eat it?'

And to the government officials:

'How important is it to put Dubai on the world's cake-making map?'

'Will this cake boost tourism?'

'What does the future for cake-making in Dubai look like now?'

With their responses captured in the Dictaphone, I sweated towards the taxi rank, jostling back through the feeding hyenas (who were in their thousands) helping themselves to as much cake as they could fit into their mouths, bags, pots and prams. Yes, some people were actually loading up prams, shovelling in wedges of this heavyweight champion of cakes at the expense of their crying toddlers standing by their sides.

The editorial floor was quiet as always in the middle of the afternoon. I could see Davey Tags over in the far corner, logged onto the 'Internet Desk' with his back to me.

I quietly walked up to him. 'Looking for porn?' I joked, as I lent over his shoulder.

He jumped. 'Fahk. Ha, ha!'

'Looking for Gucci loafers more like. Lost one last night. Can't fahkin' believe it,' he grumbled.

'Was it Joe, Jimmy? Did he do it again? Did he frisbee my loafers?'

'I've nae idea. I was wasted myself and barely remember us getting into the taxi,' I said.

'Maybe it fell off while I was dragging you up to your apartment. Did you check the lift or ask the concierge if he'd seen it?'

'No mate, there was nobody around this morning when I left. Can't believe you had to carry me out of the Lodge. In front of those Arabian World girls as well. Fahk sake,' he said, resting his head in his right hand.

He looked deflated about the whole night, but it was too early to kill the shoe gag. Had to let him suffer a bit longer as there was still some mileage in what I had planned with his loafer.

'Sure it'll turn up,' I said, with a pat on the shoulder as I walked off towards my desk.

DUBAI'S SLICE OF HISTORY AS HUNGRY MOB MAKES A MEAL OF IT was the headline I filed, along with the 400-word story. Another one to test the subs and keep them on their toes.

I then dug into my bank of pre-written stories that all of us ex-pat journos had hidden away in our notebooks for hangover days like this. Last week, I'd phone-interviewed the Spicey Girls, a cover band from the UK who were flying over next month to perform at the Hard Rock Cafe. This will one will do. I'll file it in an hour or so and that'll be my quota for the day to keep the news editor happy.

HOT AND SPICEY GIRLS TO GO HARD IN DUBAI I typed into the headline space.

'Whaey aye man! There's the loover boy,' came the Geordie bullhorn as Joe strolled into the office, eyes fixed on me with a big grin. 'You're a looky boy, Jimmy lad,' he said.

'What you talking about?' I said. 'Didn't pull anyone last night. Ended up taking this pissed-up fucker back home in a cab.'

'It's not about last night. It's about what's to come, Jimmy boy. That Alison lass wants some Aberdeen Angus, you looky fooker. Kept talking about yous all night. Thought it was 'sweet' how you looked after Dave.' Davey briefly turned around then back again, burying his embarrassment in his keyboard.

'They want to meet us on Thursday, once they're back from their London flight. They said they'd see us down at Champions Bar.

'Last night was just the warm-up,' he joked as he rubbed his hands over his belly. 'This Thursday night, Michelle will be getting some of this Toon loovin'.'

'Where did you end up then last night?' I asked knowingly, but curious as to how he would respond.

'Ach, man. Michelle and the lasses fooked off in a taxi together. No room for me and no invite back for afters this time. I stopped off at the Lebanese Bakery, noised up some lasses there, but no luck, so headed home on me fookin' tod.'

Hmm. No mention of coke and hookers then, Joe, I said to myself.

None of us wanted to stay long in the office that day with everyone – except Joe, who clearly still had some 'enhanced' energy inside him – really wishing they were dead but comfortably dead, like lying on a king-sized bed in an air-conditioned room with a large bottle of cool water by your side, just in case you wanted to come back to life.

I filed the 'Spicey Girls' and left Joe and Davey around 6pm to struggle on with their stories, Davey still lamenting his missing Gucci loafer while Joe continued to tease.

As I unlocked and stepped into the apartment, my right foot slipped as I skated on the 12" of that Helicopter track that had been pushed under the door.

Quality tune. Didn't want to lose that one, so was relieved to see it back in one piece and now safely tucked into my record bag.

I had no energy even for a cigarette. I dragged myself into the shower then collapsed onto the bed. The curtains were still shut and I longed for the imminent deep sleep.

Chapter 8

The only animals I'd ever bought were fish. Goldfish. And not even bought them really. Just won them at the funfair for lobbing a ping-pong ball into a glass bowl.

To think that you could go down to a market here and buy a leopard or an orangutan or golden eagle just seemed unreal, absurd, wrong… but fuckin' intriguing.

'No scoops, no investigations,' the Editor had insisted on that first day at the Daily UAE. But I was a newshound, former chief reporter of '*Scotland's favourite family newspaper*', always on the hunt for a scoop, and once I had a sniff of a story, that was it, I was off to land it and bag another front-page byline. Everything was about the byline.

Dr Janssen had lit that investigative fire of curiosity inside – I had to find out more, and the Gold Souk in Deira was the place to start. It was the souk with the money after all.

This 100-year-old market was a bustling and glistening Aladdin's Cave of riches. A maze containing hundreds of shaded shops and stalls glowing in gold, some looking more high-end and professional than others. Tucked down the alleys off the main thoroughfare were the unlicensed traders selling out of suitcases propped up on wooden crates, and tiny stalls selling a mix of Arabic and Asian street food. I didn't know where to start – high-end or low- – but just had to start and see where that would lead me.

I'd smartened up as well: light grey suit jacket, white shirt and chinos. Had to look like I had money or at least was representing someone who had money.

'Yes, boss. You looking for watches, chains, necklaces, rings? What you want? I got everything. Everything in gold you need,' said the trader beckoning me over, competing for my attention against the other market sellers.

I blanked him and kept walking, jostling through the throng of shoppers, traders and hustlers all blending into each other. I wasn't sure what I was looking for yet, more trying to gauge how the whole Souk operated. What was the pecking order of good to shit? What was popular? What was genuine? What looked fake? Were there fakes here? I didn't know.

The traders had a traditional saying: 'If you can't find it in Deira, then you can't find it anywhere.' And here I was looking for a leopard or orangutan, which should be bloody obvious but at the moment, was like trying to find a needle in a golden haystack.

My cover-story pretence was that I was looking for a gold, diamond-encrusted watch for my father's 60th birthday. And once the conversation was flowing with the trader, I'd mention his love for and collection of rare animals and how I also wanted to surprise him with a new exotic pet.

It sounded ridiculous but I even ended up suggesting a matching gold collar for the pet as well, 'if only I could find someone who sells' such animals.

After telling this barely believable story to five or six traders, there was no sign at all that this was the place to find a matching leopard to go with a gold watch. Blank stares, smiles, shakes of the head and sometimes dismissive chuckles is all I received in return.

Time to move off into the alleyways.

Surprisingly, there were no uniformed police or security in this souk with millions of dollars' worth of jewellery. But you still felt relatively safe wherever you went, as the punishment for crime was so severe in Dubai. A minor theft or mugging could result in a three-year sentence in one of Dubai's overcrowded, rat-infested jails, followed by deportation for the non-locals.

Pungent smells of spices and spit-roasting meats soaked the air as I wandered further down the twisting, narrow lanes looking for a sign. You couldn't move anywhere fast, as these tight alleyways were a noisy congestion of people standing and bartering with traders or sitting tucking into their street food on the clay cornerstone kerbs that every so often jutted out, trying their best to trip you up.

Then I heard it. And then I saw it. Up ahead, stacked in two- and three-tiered rusting cages were squawking birds – actually, parrots and budgerigars. Cages filled with an array of bright-coloured plumage: blues and golds, greens and yellows, crimson reds, and greys. The first sight of animals in the souk. As I approached, I could see this was the front of a small, dimly lit shop that stretched further back off the street.

It was just after 6pm, just before sunset, and you could see the sunlight starting to recede from exposed corners on the lane. Unlike the main thoroughfare of the Gold Souk, which had artificial lighting ready to kick in around 6.30, the alleyways were only lit by oil lamps and the neon signs of brands like Coca-Cola, Sprite and the tobacco companies. I knew this would be the last shop to probe before the evening prayers started at 6.50 as nobody would be willing to talk once the mosques started broadcasting time for prayers across the rooftops.

'Beautiful birds,' I said to the young Asian man standing by the cages outside.

He smiled agreeingly.

'Where are they from?' I asked.

'Africa,' he replied without offering any more information.

Pointing at the large scarlet macaw, I asked: 'For sale?' He nodded.

'How much?'

'2,000 Dirhams,' he said, gesturing one finger at me.

'Hmm. I'm looking for something more exotic. Something more rare and beautiful,' I said.

We stood in silence as I watched the macaw hop along its metal pole and the seller, looking uninterested, gazed beyond me down the alleyway.

Unusually for a trader, he was not trying to force a sale. I peered deeper into the store and could see a back doorway partly covered by a heavy draped blanket and beyond that, what looked like the edges of more cages with the final glimpses of today's sunlight reflecting off the metal. My gut instinct was saying that I shouldn't leave – I needed to carry on the conversation here.

'My father will be 60 on Friday. He's a good man. I'm very proud of him and want to buy him something really special,' I said but received no response. 'He's a diamond trader, so what do you buy someone who already has diamonds and so much money he doesn't know what to do with it?'

He turned around with a little smile, gesturing towards the macaw's cage.

'No. I need the best, the most beautiful, most exotic bird there is,' I said.

He paused, muttered to himself, then slowly turned away and casually walked towards the back of the shop, pushing aside the dusty blanket over the doorway and stepping out into the courtyard where I'd spotted the other cages.

I lit another Marlboro Light, and admired the squawking parrots hopping and flapping around in their cages. Seemed like they had a nice life; looking as pristine as that all day, being admired by everyone, watered and fed and flying around... okay... maybe not the flying bit. Maybe they weren't that happy.

His walking away didn't feel like a signal to leave, so I stepped just inside the slightly cooler shade of the shop and waited. I was just about to put the second cig out when he reappeared by the back doorway.

'Come,' he motioned to me. 'Come,' he said again.

I flicked the cig out the shop front, just missing one of the macaw's bobbing heads and walked towards him.

'As-salam alaykum,' greeted an older Asian man standing on the other side of the doorway. Short and stocky with a salt-and-pepper beard and snow-white hair, he reached out his weathered hand as a greeting while the younger assistant retreated back into the shop.

'I have many birds,' he said, casting his gaze across what must have been a dozen cages lying side by side, each filled with not just parrots this time but falcons and toucans. 'You can buy any you like.'

'Beautiful, yes,' I said. 'But the falcon is very popular here. My father already has several falcons. And he has numerous parrots.'

One cage positioned in a more shaded corner had a partly draped sheet over it, lying just a couple of inches off the floor where the claws of a large bird were just barely visible.

He smiled as he caught me looking towards it.

'This, my friend, is very special. And, with this, is very expensive.'

I followed as he walked over to the cage and slowly removed the sheet.

'This is a Golden Eagle. You will not find a better Golden Eagle for sale in the UAE,' he said as I looked down on the sorry sight of this magnificent bird squashed up into a cage no bigger than a couple of beer crates. Four months he said he'd had it for. Four months chained inside this cage, its 2m wings closed tightly for all that time. Poor sod.

'I sell for 40,000 Dirhams but when she die, you get your money back,' he laughed. 'You sell the head, you sell the claws, the feathers and body. Many people want these and will pay thousands of Dirhams or dollars.'

'You buy?' he asked. 'You buy now?'

Of course, I couldn't buy now and explained I'd need to think about it and come back in a few days with the money if I'd decided this was the right gift for my father.

The spark was lit now. I had a lead and felt I was now on my way to a scoop with some good old investigative journalism.

Chapter 9

The Daily UAE pool cars were a lot better than what I was used to back in Aberdeen where we'd only have access to a few 1.1 Ford Fiestas or VW Polos. Ashtrays were always overspilling with fag butts and ash, and the remains of a reporter's lunch would be found stuffed in the side pockets, under the seats, in the glove compartment or in the boot. It was pot luck if you landed the one car where the radio and cassette deck actually worked. And pot luck if you didn't get the one with the mouse. Poor lass Jackie wouldn't set foot in the pool cars again after her '*mouse in the blouse*' incident.

Here in Sharjah, though, the Daily UAE provided the reporting team with nearly new white Audi A4s. Cassette deck and CD player, air conditioning, electric windows and leather seats were standard throughout.

You felt like Coulthard nipping around in these, and with nothing but sand on either side of the main roads between Dubai, Sharjah and Abu Dhabi, it was a blast opening them up to 120mph. You just needed to mind the speed bumps and random four-way junctions, which would spring out of nowhere in the middle of the desert. More than once, I'd unexpectedly flown through the crossroads at over a ton, only to catch a glimpse of the red traffic lights in the rear-view mirror as I General Lee'd onto the other side.

The Souk closed at 11pm, but from around 10.30pm, the traders would start loading up some of their stock into trucks to take back to warehouses for overnight storage.

I'd parked up about 20 yards away from a couple of Toyota saloons, which were set further back from the pickup trucks lined up at the rear of the souk stores.

It was dark, I wasn't wearing sunglasses but I had a full tank of gas, half a pack of cigarettes and Journeys by Coldcut playing quietly on the CD. A giant packet of tangy Doritos, a one-litre bottle of Coke and my Nikon SLR lay on the passenger seat.

'Beaky', as I referred to the old man, and his assistant started loading their birdcages just before 10.30. There was a lot, and it took them another 30 minutes before they strapped down the tarpaulin over the truck's cargo bed and climbed back into the cabin.

This was it. I turned on the ignition.

Lights... no, hold on, not yet.

I lowered my seat, leaning back out of view and waited until they pulled away, passing just 10 yards from the car as the beam of their headlights flashed across the dashboard.

I tried to keep back by about three or four cars as they weaved their way in and out of the Deira streets. At 11pm, Dubai was a busy place, as traders and shoppers from all over the city were on the road heading home, while hundreds of expats were filling taxis heading out for a night in the hotel bars.

Once on the main Sharjah road, it became easier yet harder at the same time to tail the lorry. The traffic thinned out, but that made me more conspicuous as their diesel-spewing truck could only chug along the inside lane at about 40mph.

I slipped in behind two lorries on the inside, occasionally drifting out to the right to keep an eye on Beaky. I could see in my rear-view mirror more pickups starting to sidle in behind what had now become a mini convoy, as we all slowly veered off the main highway onto a slip road – well, more of a slip 'track' than a 'road'.

The Audi was shuddering and jolting, as pothole after pothole battered the suspension. The bottle of Coke flew up off the seat, bouncing off the dashboard and onto the floor. The camera had also jumped off the seat and was now rolling around on the floor, with the Coke bottle butting against the metal undercarriage of the seat every few seconds.

Must get the camera. I'm fucked without that camera. Plus it cost me 300 quid, I was saying to myself.

Spread out like Stretch Armstrong, I struggled to keep my right hand on the steering wheel and one eye on the truck just a few metres in front as I leaned over and reached down to the passenger side floor with my left hand trying to scoop up the camera.

Bang! Fuck. Bang! Fuck. Bang! Bang! 'Fuuuuuuuucccck.'

My head was being bashed against the dashboard with every mother-fuckin' pothole, my view now falling below windscreen-level as I was almost horizontal, leaning over from the driver's seat.

Then...

RED LIGHTS! RED LIGHTS! Fuck! Brakes! Fuck! BOSH! Jesus, Fucking Fuck!!

The truck in front had suddenly stopped and I'd only just managed to stretch over a foot on the brake in time but almost flattened my nose in doing so. I face-planted into the glove compartment with so much force, I was momentarily stunned like when you get whacked in the head by a basketball. I pulled myself back up, gently dabbing my face, looking down at my hands for signs of blood.

No blood thankfully, but Jesus, my nose was throbbing like some sadistic bastard was pinching it hard every few seconds. I managed to lift up the camera and securely position it between my legs as the convoy started to roll forward again.

In the distance, I could see white lights dotted among the desert darkness. We were now heading towards them.

As we drew closer, the lights shone brighter, illuminating the area like something out of Close Encounters. I could see rows of warehouses and a hive of lorries, cars and pickup trucks. Beaky pulled away from the main line of trucks and headed towards the end of the compound. This area was quieter – fewer trucks and most of the warehouses were closed, standing silent in the darkness. I switched off the headlights and quietly rolled the car behind one of the buildings.

I planned to watch them from the car at first, observing their movements and trying to ascertain what was being kept in the warehouse. I pulled open the Tangy Doritos and unscrewed the bottle of Coke.

'SHIIIIITTTTT! FUCK! FUUUUUUCKKK! STOP!

'FUUUCK!! STOP!! FUUUUCKING HELL!'

The Coke exploded everywhere, fizzing and gushing its guts out uncontrollably all over the seats, the windows, the dashboard, my face, shirt, trousers and inside the packet of Doritos! My hands, face and arms were dripping with cola as I wrestled to get the screw cap back on, before flinging open the door and launching it into the sand.

I looked around at the aftermath of the Coke tsunami, which in a matter of seconds had spray-painted the inside of the Audi a new Pantone, 'Cocoa Loco'. A drip from the ceiling fell onto my head, followed by another and then another. I flipped down the vanity mirror, wiping the Coke from my face and pushed my fingers through my mop of hair, which was now congealing with hair wax and sugar. How was I going to tidy this shit up, I thought, looking around for a few seconds, but then checked myself; forget it – I've got to focus on the job at hand. Here. Now.

The Nikon had been partly protected between my legs during the cola carnage. Only one tiny splash on the lens cap and a few on the body of the camera. I checked the shutter and zoom, and all seemed okay. Time to go birdwatching.

I shuffled along the side of the warehouse, keeping as close to the corrugated metal wall as possible, staying in the darkness away from the fixed security lights at the entrance. Glancing down, I now regretted wearing the yellow-and-white Forest Hills – should've been in ninja-black. The all-black Adidas Sambas would have been better. Next time.

I stood still, at first just peering from the corner, observing the men lifting the birdcages off the back of the truck and carrying them into the storage unit. But I couldn't actually see inside the warehouse from where I was and knew I had to get closer. This lock-up was about the height of two double-decker buses and the length of about six. There's got to be more than just some pretty pollies in there, I thought.

Every front has got a back. I don't need to be here knocking at the front door, I thought, so I started shimmying my way around the perimeter to the back of the building.

'Sorted!' As I hoped, there was a single fire-exit door, and thankfully, health and safety had not been around to inspect as it hung lopsided off a couple of broken hinges, making it easy to force ajar just enough to squeeze my less-than-honed physique through.

The back of the warehouse was draped in darkness, as I crouched behind a stack of wooden crates from where I could spy the illuminated Beaky and his team arranging the bird cages into rows near the front of the entrance. Guess it makes it quicker for them in the morning to load up again when they return.

Shifting my view away from the front, on the left-hand side of the warehouse were dozens of pallets containing hundreds of cardboard boxes piled up high into the rafters of the building. Over to the right were larger containers, each separated from one another by about five feet, with tarpaulins draped over them.

CLICK!

Suddenly, it was total darkness.

Beaky was leaving as one of his lackeys switched off the main lights and started winching down the chains to lower the metal shutters at the front. First, the headlights of their truck disappeared out of sight, then their feet, then seconds later CRASH! CLANG! CLINK! I could hear them fastening the bolt and locks on the outside, followed by the spluttering sound of the diesel truck starting up before it drifted off into the desert silence.

Here I was now, alone in this hushed warehouse.

I blindly reached up, patting the wall by the fire door, grappling around in hope for a switch. I felt the outline of wire casing first and followed that along and up until… Yes, a switch. Flick and the lights came on; well, a single lightbulb, hanging down from an exposed copper wire, tied around the wooden rafters above. The dim lighting gave me visibility for maybe about five or six metres in front where a couple of the larger containers were stored.

Even though I was on my own, I still crept silently and slowly, looking around at all times as I got closer to the container. I was paranoid that they might suddenly return or maybe I was not alone. Maybe there was a sleeping guard dog somewhere? It certainly smelt like some kind of animal had been here.

I started to lift the corner of the tarpaulin draped over the container off the ground. Just enough, I thought, to poke my head underneath and get a good look at these boxes. As I gathered up one of the edges, I could see that this wasn't a wooden crate or storage container. Into view came a few inches of cold steel bars. As I raised it higher, the vertical bars stretched up and up beyond my height. A couple of feet into the cage, I could just make out two paws stretched on the ground, then another two paws by its side and then another set of paws a few feet away. The cage was too high and the blanket too large to completely pull off, so I had to prop myself forward, flat up against its side, flipping the tarpaulin back over my head behind me.

Leopard cubs. Shit. Look at them. There must be what? One, two, three, four of them? No, hold on, what's that in the corner? Another one, no, two. That's two and larger than the others, curled up side by side. Fuck, that's six. Poor fuckers.

The cage may have been eight-foot tall but it was only about ten-foot long and wide. I wasn't an animal welfare expert but I knew this wasn't exactly the Born Free Holiday Inn for them.

I quietly stepped back out, carefully drooping the tarpaulin back over the edge of the cage.

Now I need the picture.

I'd never photographed an animal before. And what do they say? 'Never work with animals or children.' There's probably a second part to that as well: 'especially wild animals asleep in cramped, dark cages and probably really cranky.'

I checked the camera settings. This would have to be a flash-and-run shot.

I flung up the tarpaulin, this time resting it partly on my shoulders like one of those Victorian cameramen with a cape drape.

Say cheeeese. FLASH. No reaction. They didn't stir, thank God.

FLASH. FLASH. Nothing. Good, they must be sound asleep.

FLASH. FLASH.

FUCK!! FUCK!!

The claws swiped through the bars, catching the side of the zoom lens as I flew back, tripping over my feet and landing on my arse. High-pitched growling and hissing exploded throughout the cage as the other leopards jumped up and pressed their heads against the metal grates.

I remained on the floor, examining the camera for any serious damage. Thankfully, no, just psycho-Simba's clawed signature on the side.

CAT CARTEL BUSTED AS ILLEGAL LEOPARD TRADERS CAGED

The story was already there, but was there more to this?

I stepped over towards the container opposite, similar in size with a couple of large sheets draped on top. Now a bit more apprehensive as to what lay behind these tarpaulins, I slowly edged it up. This time, there was no mistaking its inhabitant as it almost filled the entire cage. Standing on its stocky four legs, transfixed and barely moving, except the slow rise and fall of its chest as it breathed, was a rhino – a baby rhino.

Shit. It's bloody London Zoo here.

FLASH. FLASH. FLASH. This wee guy didn't move. Not interested in me or so bored he'd given up caring.

EXOTIC ANIMAL TRAFFICKERS BUSTED.

The story *was* bigger. It had definitely now moved on from BUDGIE SMUGGLERS BUSTED.

I didn't need any more and headed back out to the newly christened *Coke Mobile.*

Chapter 10

'Jimmy 5 Gins', 'Jimmy Riddle' or 'The Riddler', 'Smasher' and now *'Cola Boy'* were the nicknames I'd amassed over the years, along with the standard 'Fanny Heid' and 'Poof' thrown in from time to time, which just comes with the territory of growing up in Aberdeen.

Geordie Joe had ignored the significance of the scoop as I relayed it back to the guys in the office and instead, he focused solely on me 'shooting yer load' with the exploding Coke. Simba's right hook also had him rocking back with laughter, followed quickly by shouts of 'Pussy Boy' for the whole office to hear.

Thankfully, in the days that followed, he moved on from that particular moniker and stuck with 'Cola Boy', as Hamza and the newspaper's pen-pushers investigated the costs of the clean-up job in the pool car and word spread throughout the office. Even one of the chatty security guards at the gate was saying with a knowing smile, 'Morning, Mr Cola,' as I swiped in for my shift.

Cola Boy I could live with, but I didn't want Joe and certainly not Alison to know about those other nicknames.

Jimmy 5 Gins stuck from about the age of 18 where on nights out my pals noticed that after I'd knocked back the fifth gin, I became a moody, argumentative fucker. Friends, girlfriends, bar staff, bouncers, taxi drivers, kebab shop workers, James Whale phone-ins – yup, nobody escaped the '5 Gins' rant if they crossed my path. Waking up the following morning, I wouldn't remember a thing and be in total denial.

Jimmy Riddle or The Riddler was just embarrassing and that couldn't – just couldn't – get back to Alison or any girl in the UAE. It was one of those incidents that happened just the once, but as soon as it's leaked out to your pals, you are done for. And leaked it certainly did.

Heading back to Natalie's place after an all-dayer on the beers and cheeky Gianluca, I couldn't hold in the call of nature anymore in the taxi. I gave her a two-second warning before the seal was broken flooding the back seats with piss. There was no choice, as we were on the dual carriageway and the taxi driver couldn't pull over, though I'm sure he regretted not driving up onto the grass verge when I warned him five minutes earlier – 'I'm fuckin' bustin', min.' Natalie's white Levi's never recovered and neither did Natalie.

Smasher was more innocent than it sounds and stemmed from my childhood days when I was about 13. Playing football in a rainy back garden with some school chums, I perfectly left-foot volleyed through our kitchen window, not just smashing the glass but totally destroying the plates and cups on the draining board on the other side, scattering them all over the kitchen floor. My mum went fuckin' ballistic, cuffing me round the head in front of my friends. Pretty sure that goal was a Kenny Dalglish winner, though, in our wee game of 'World Cuppy'.

I pitched the animal trafficking story to the Editor, who at first was fuming I'd gone against his instructions not to carry out any investigative journalism.

But once I'd shown him the photos and assured him I had evidence, hard evidence, which was a lock-up in the desert, he said he would discuss with Hamza and if he agreed, they'd alert the Ministry of Interior for Sharjah. A police raid with exclusive access for us and the accompanying arrest pictures would be the best result for the paper, I suggested. I filed what I had and the Editor said he'd come back to me.

Davey Tags had bumped into Alison and Michelle earlier in the day, sunning themselves at the Dubai Marine Club. He'd spent enough time with them to make a good impression and finally laugh at making a tit of himself on that first night they met at The Highland Lodge.

'They're going to be at the Irish Village later, not Champions,' he said from his desk sitting opposite. 'They want to meet us there for a few drinks.' Joe and I looked at each other, winked, and said in unison: 'Game on!'

'Time to head home and spruce ourselves up, Cola Boy,' he said grinning. 'Tonight. Is. The. Night.'

■ ■ ■

Pastel lime or pink? I wasn't sure. Would the pink Ralph Lauren polo be a bit too bold and daring for tonight or does it show Alison I'm comfortable with my softer, more feminine side?

I stood in front of the bathroom mirror swapping the tops around before finally pulling another one off the hanger and settling on aqua blue with the red Ralphy motif – a safe bet, I thought. I slicked back my hair into a ponytail then slapped on a few splashes of Joop! aftershave. I crouched down on the side of the bed to tie my green-tabbed white Stans when suddenly there was a... Knock! Knock!

Ali was standing there, in his finest black clobber as always. He tilted his Ray-Bans down the bridge of his nose to make eye contact.

'Mr Jimmy. How are you?'

'Good, Ali, good.'

'Can I come in? I have good news for you. You have beer? Let's have a beer.'

I grabbed a couple of Heinekens out of the fridge, offered him a cig and we plumped ourselves into the neat armchairs around the glass coffee table.

'Have you met your new neighbours?' he said. 'Apartments nine and ten?'

'Neighbours? No, I haven't,' I replied.

'They are good people. Friends of mine. You must meet them later. Anyway, Jimmy, I ask, you had fun last week at the party, yes?'

'Sure,' I nodded.

'Good, good. I'm pleased you said that. I want you to play every week, Jimmy. All the guests spoke about you. The 'English DJ', they kept saying. 'Who is the English DJ?' 'We love the English DJ.' Especially the girls.'

'Scottish DJ, Ali,' I corrected him on the spot, half-smiling. I'm the fuckin' Scottish DJ.'

Ali was playing to my DJ ego, which I liked, though I was a bit suspicious as no fucker had even glanced over at the party, let alone spoken to me or properly raved to the tunes.

'Of course,' Ali laughed. 'The amazing Scottish DJ.' He pulled out his wallet, unzipped one of the small inner compartments and unfolded some silver foil to reveal a rock of gear. He casually filed a chunk off with a razor blade and smoothed out a couple of slugs.

Whoosh! No words were said as he threw his head back, leaning into the chair, finger snorting the loose bits of charlie up his schnozzle before passing over the 100 Dirhams note. Here I was now getting fucked with the wrong Ali. I should have left 20 minutes ago to meet Alison at the Irish Village and if any fuckness was going on tonight, I wanted it to be with Alison, not Ali.

'I need you to play tonight,' he said. 'At midnight. Be here for midnight. It's going to be busy. You'll enjoy it.'

Before I could answer, he slid the rock over in the foil. 'You keep and enjoy. I'll see you later. Midnight. The fourth floor.'

The gear kicked in as he reached the door to leave and as before, was fuckin' lush. Real clean. Real quality. Nothing too gnarly.

'Too right, Ali. See you tonight. I'll be here at 12 with all the tunes. Let's smash it!' I was starting to gibber as he glanced back with a nod and closed the door.

Needed to get my shit together but I didn't have long. I was wired and focused, super focused now and twitchy, darting around the apartment, tidying the place up at warp speed, neatening the bed sheets and pillows, kicking shoes under the bed and out of sight, shoving the pile of dirty dishes from the sink into the dishwasher.

'Sorted. I'll take her back here,' was the supercharged Class A masterplan. 'We'll go to Ali's party at 12, I'll play for a couple of hours, then we'll come back down here and let things take their natural course.'

I zipped into the bathroom, quickly checking up my hooter for any coke residue. Don't want to turn up late looking like Tony Montana while bullshitting some excuse like there were no taxis.

I flicked through the record bag, switching the tunes around from front to back, then left it at the side of the doorway with headphones on top. One final check scanning the apartment and all was good. Let's get this night started.

By the time I arrived at the Irish Village, I was almost an hour late. Thankfully, it didn't look like they were missing me as I walked up to the group, which was sitting around three tables pushed together covered with empty two-pint pitchers, beer glasses and smoking ashtrays. Davey Tags was holding court with the girls, who were shrieking with laughter, while Joe was slowly and ever so steadily carrying a tray of replenished cocktail pitchers over from the bar.

'Here he is,' he said, placing the wobbly tray down on the table.

'The Cola Boy has landed! Or maybe it should be Coke Boy,' he laughed. 'But that could mean something else, eh?' he joked, slapping me on the back while charlie-paranoia danced around in my head. Does he know?

Alison looked up smiling. 'Hi, Jimmy. We were wondering where you were?' she said, her face still beaming and showing off her cute dimples. She looked amazing in a white strapless top that accentuated her golden-brown tanned skin.

Her auburn hair flowed down, sitting just above her breasts, drawing my eyes in for a split second before she casually flicked one side back up behind her ear, revealing what looked like a tattoo of an exotic bird on her shoulder. Underneath the table, I could see her slender ankles sitting beautifully in a pair of... 'HOLD ON, FUCKING YES!' white Stans, green tab!

'That's it. She's the one,' I thought, judging sex, marriage, children and life happiness all on her choice of trainers.

'Couldn't get a taxi for ages,' I predictably lied, hoping there would be no further questions as I desperately needed another toot now. I craved that second rush to get back on top of my game before I started to clam up, but Joe quickly killed off that thought, returning again from the bar with a round of sambuca shots.

'Get this down ye man. You've got a lot of catching up to do. I've got two shots for you, one sambuca and one tequila, and, of course, your pint of Heineken on the side.'

Top bloke, Joe. Always up for a party. Never wants you to feel left out. Just don't go spoiling his party.

Knocking back the shots and Heineken did the job. The bugle call subdued a little and I started to loosen up in the chat with Alison, now snuggled nicely next to her, sitting elbow to elbow, butt cheek to butt cheek.

Davey was still the man of the moment, chatting away with three other air hostesses, while Joe sitting opposite me was locked into Michelle, arm stretched around the back of her chair playing with her hair, occasionally looking over at Alison and me with a mischievous glint in his eye.

Turns out Alison was the boss of these girls. They call her a 'purser', a senior cabin-crew steward who manages the rest of the hostesses on a flight. She'd been with AWA for three years and she flew with Virgin for five years before that. There wasn't a country she hadn't been to: Hong Kong, China, Australia, Bali, India, Kenya, South Africa, North America, South America – the lot.

'Impressive, but have you been to Scotland?' I cheekily asked.

She hadn't.

'Ach, well, y'see, ye need tae get 'at stamped on yer passport before ye can call yersel' a globetrotter,' I said, notching up the Scottish accent a level or two.

She was liking the banter, jabbing me in the ribs as I got cheekier, touching my arm as we joked, and I could sense that if I didn't fuck things up, tonight she'd be checking in at Castle Irvine.

Flying around the world, she was also a solid clubbing lass, rattling off stories about tripping at full moon parties in Thailand and Goa, and nights on poppers and ecstasy at the Sound Factory in New York. She'd also been a regular at Club UK and The Gardening Club in Covent Garden – both favourites of mine and Andy's when we were having our wee jaunts down to London for the weekend.

'You been around a bit then, Alison?' Joe butted in sharply with a smile that wasn't well-received by Alison. She grimaced back at him for a few seconds until I checked him with an 'Oiiiiiiii, come on pal, no need for that'.

Joe laughed it off, shrugging his shoulders: 'She knows I'm only kidding, eh lass?'

Alison looked coldly at Joe and squeezed my hand, while Joe smiled and turned his attention back to Michelle.

The proverbial ice had been broken now between the two of us. Alison, not me, had dropped in the drug references and it felt like we were cut from the same clubbing cloth.

Here I was, sitting with a rock stuffed into my jeans pocket, already one chunky sniff ahead of her. If she only knew. But how to broach it without freaking her out and attracting attention from the rest of the group.

You see, you didn't just go down for possession, here in Dubai – you'd end up in jail just for being associated with someone caught in possession or even just for being on the same premises as someone in possession.

You couldn't fuck up here at all. If you did, you'd be fucked over, languishing in one of those treacherous Dubai prisons at the mercy of the rapists, murderers and knife-packing Russian gang members. This was not the place to casually pass the gear round the table as a little digestif.

I stood up and offered to get a round in for everyone.

'I'll come and help,' she said.

'Okay,' I said. 'Just need to go to the loo first. I'll meet you at the bar.'

I took a presumptive gamble and smoothed out a couple of lines in the disabled toilets, leaving one for Alison on the cistern shelf, hidden inside the stacked loo rolls.

She didn't ask twice when I leaned in to whisper to her at the bar: 'There's a little livener for you in the disabled toilets.' And when she returned a few minutes later, she gave me a big smacker on the cheeks and an affectionate squeeze of my hand.

Within five minutes, the two of us had morphed into one of those chattering toy teeth you used to buy as a kid. We didn't stop for air as the banter flowed from the bar back to the table carrying the round of drinks. I told her about the party back at my apartment block and she was game. We'd have to leave in an hour.

The flirting notched up a level as she entwined her arm around mine sitting next to me, occasionally squeezing my hand, nuzzling into my neck in those wee moments of a coke rush.

Joe sitting opposite wasn't helping my paranoia, though, as he stared at the two of us once too often. But, of course, I knew he was a player – he just didn't know that I knew. That was all about to change, though.

'Joe, I'm DJing at a party tonight. You fancy coming?' I asked, looking at Michelle as well, who was now looking back at Alison for some kind of signal.

'What kind of party? Thought we were going to the Lodge?' he said.

'House party. Well, 'apartment' party but I'm playing 'House',' I laughed. 'It's in my block in Deira.'

I caught Alison giving a knowing smile and nod to Michelle who jumped in with: 'Let's go! Sounds like fun. Come on, Joe.'

Joe leaned over to Davey and the other girls. 'We got a party tonight. You coming?'

'When is it?' Davey asked.

'When is it?' Joe turned back round to me.

'Got to be there in an hour,' I said.

'An hour. Midnight. Fahk that mate,' said Davey, who was set on taking his little harem to the Lodge. Give me the address and I'll come later.'

We knew that was unlikely, based on Davey's previous of never making it past 2am before he was comatose in a taxi on the way home and being put to bed by either one of us or a very disappointed lass.

I ripped up the empty fag packet and wrote down the apartment address twice, giving one bit of the paper to Davey and the other to Alison, who handed it to one of Davey's air stewardesses who said they might be up for it.

As the taxi got closer to my apartment building, I was wondering how Joe was going to react. Was he going to keep quiet and pretend he'd never been here before or was he going to acknowledge he knew this place?

It was, of course, Geordie Joe, though. 'The talk of the Toon.' I should have known better.

'Fookin hell, man. I know this place,' he shouted out, grinning and slapping the back of the passenger seat I was sitting in. 'I've had soom fookin' cracking nights partying here Jimmy boy.' (I know you have Joe)

It was twenty to twelve and the usual melee of cars, punters and prozzies hadn't materialised yet. I opened the door to my apartment, leading everyone in, letting them admire this small but wonderfully tidy (the cleaning bit beforehand was bloody impressive) studio flat.

I grabbed four Heinekens from the fridge. The girls wanted vodka, so I free poured a couple of glasses with splashes of soda. No lime, sorry. I'm nae that organised! But at least the soda was cold from the fridge.

The bugle calling was loud again and without much thought... ACH, FUCK IT.

As the three of them stood on the balcony chatting away, I racked up four equal lines on the kitchen worktop, neatly positioning the rolled 100 Dirhams note across the top of them and stepped back for a few seconds, admiring the perfect symmetry.

'Hey, come in here, you lot. I've got a little something for you.'

I stood proudly behind the breakfast bar like one of those Gold Souk traders waving his hand across a tray of diamond earrings.

'Before we go up, there's a little present for everyone to get us in the mood,' I said, motioning my hand towards the neatly presented chopped lines.

'Jimmy boy, now what the fook is this?' asked Joe.

'You're a very bad man. Hold my beer.'

He winked, knowingly patted me on the shoulder and tucked in, swiftly followed by Alison. Both deftly seized the moment like seasoned pros. Michelle held back, insisting I go next, which I duly did, and then thankfully it was all for one, one for all, as Michelle completed the round.

'Whooh. Fookin' yes!' shouted Joe, turning round kissing Michelle fully on the lips.

'Fookin' nice one, Cola... no... hold on, you really are *Coke* Boy. It's the *Real* fookin' *Thing!*' he laughed.

We flew up the fire escape to the fourth floor, buzzing and gibbering. A knowing nod to the black-suited bear by the emergency door and we strolled into the main apartment. Nobody was on the decks, but the speakers were pumping out a Ministry of Sound CD compilation.

There were maybe about a dozen to 20 people chatting on the velvet couches and at the bar. Mostly guys from what I could see – only a few girls. All very civilised, for now.

Ali came into view, walking up from the apartment area beyond the bar. At first, he smiled, striding towards us, then he momentarily stopped and started to laugh as he came closer, pointing to Joe, who responded with a nodding grin.

'Mr Jimmy. And Mr Joe! You know each other?' he asked, patting us both on the shoulders as if he was reuniting two long-lost brothers. 'This is wonderful. Just wonderful.'

'Tonight is going to be a great night,' he said, turning his attention now to Alison and Michelle. 'Relax, enjoy yourselves, have fun. Jimmy is a great DJ! And friends of the DJ are my guests. Whatever you want tonight is on me. Let me get you some champagne first.'

Knowing how the face of this party was going to contort and twist throughout the night, I wanted to keep Alison close, so suggested the three of them base themselves at the snug area nearest the decks. A few minutes later, Ali was over with the champagne and glasses, pouring the flutes for the girls first in his ever-so-charming way.

Half an hour into my set and it was already getting lively. The convoy of Mercs, 911s, Jeeps and taxis must have been docking outside as the numbers started to swell inside and by now there were a lot more girls – 'working girls'.

There was a steady stream between the decks and the sofa as one by one, Alison, Joe and Michelle came over to hoover the lines I'd served up for them on the 12" sleeve – Raze 'Break 4 Love'.

Alison started dancing in front of the decks, showing her support, hoping to entice more people from the bar area to join in and get the House vibe going. This wasn't that kind of party though, as I knew. These girls weren't shy, didn't need encouragement from her and would eventually start dancing with the guys… all part of their business-like seduction.

As the number of punters and pros grew and the couches filled, they started gravitating towards the decks. As before, they only had eyes for each other, the bleached blonde Russky girls gyrating against their girlfriends and then against the Arab guys, putting on a teaser show of what was to follow if you paid them.

Nobody (except Alison) reacted to any particular song, no matter how much of a banger it was – it was just a continuation of writhing seduction to the music, which eventually led to them wandering off hand in hand in groups of two, three and even four down towards Apartment 13.

I looked over to our table, and Joe and Michelle had gone. Instead, seated there were two girls with their legs draped round a very happy bloke in the middle and, of course, a fresh champagne bucket at the side of the table.

Ahead, I could see them. Where I'd spotted Joe the last time, Michelle was sitting on the couch in a little alcove over to the left. On either side of her were Joe and Ali. In the middle, more champagne and when I looked over a few minutes later, one then two heads bent down and flicked up as Michelle and Joe tucked into gear off the table.

Ali knew I was only going to play a two-hour set, so 2am was our witching hour, the cut-off point to get the hell out of here and move onto some serious business with Alison downstairs.

With 10 minutes to go, Alison checked in on Michelle, asking if she wanted to leave.

She was fucking wasted, though, comfortably lodged in between Joe and Ali on the snug sofa, and had no intentions of heading off soon.

'I'll be at Jimmy's downstairs. Come down later if you want,' Alison said leaning over.

Michelle looked back at her with those manic eyes: 'Love you, babes,' she said.

Ali walked back over to the decks with Alison, thanked me and loaded up his Cream CD. Time for Alison and me to disappear and leave them to it.

My ears were still ringing from the tunes as I unlocked the door. I'd forgotten to leave on the AC and had left the balcony doors open, so the apartment instantly felt hot and muggy. Alison headed straight to the fridge, pulling out a couple of beers while I sat down and scraped out just enough to make one last line.

Within seconds of her finishing her little toot, I leaned over and kissed her. She responded passionately.

As we rolled up onto the bed, I whipped off her little white top, revealing her perfectly pert tits with white bikini tan lines around her dark brown nipples. At the same time, she was unbuckling my belt and pulling down my jeans.

She reached into my boxer shorts to pull my cock out, but he hadn't got the memo. Instead of bursting with excitement to what was undoubtedly the hottest naked body he'd ever been in front of, the little fucker had shrivelled up into a coke-infused walnut.

Alison was fucking horny, though, and – give her her due – she kept going, trying her best to suck life into this flatlined cock, but he was not having it. I pushed her back onto the bed and went down on her wet pussy. Thankfully, focusing my best efforts on this led to her coming a couple of times and she seemed happy.

'Fucking charlie,' I said grimacing, half-embarrassed, looking down at my pathetic pea-nis and not sure how she'd respond.

'Fucking charlie,' she softly chuckled back at me, taking my hand and placing it between her legs and back into her soaking pussy. There was not going to be much enjoyment for me tonight, I thought, but Alison's certainly going to make the most of it.

After an hour or so of us playing around and a few more failed attempts at resuscitating my comatose pecker, she nestled her rosy flushed face onto my chest and drifted off to sleep.

I lay there, admiring the beauty of Alison's slender body wrapped around me, gently caressing her back. That tattoo of hers on the shoulder looked a bit fucked up though. I'm sure it was a kingfisher – you know, those little birds with the long thin beaks and blue plumage. But this beak was short, stumpy and squared off… I kept tracing the outline gently with my finger, questioning my limited knowledge of ornithology. Sure, it wasn't right but then… I too felt myself gradually give in to sleep… … …

At first, I thought I was in a deep dream. I could just hear these faint muffled voices, but they steadily grew louder and angrier, followed by a woman yelling: 'Fuck you! Fuck you! Fuck you!'

I realised they were coming from outside the apartment door. I gently moved Alison's arm from my chest, not wanting to disturb her, and quietly crept up to the front door to see what was going on. The voices were louder and clearer now. I peered through the spyhole, holding my breath, and through the fire door opposite, I could see Ali pinning one of the Russian prostitutes by her neck against the wall on the staircase.

'You thieving bitch!' he shouted. 'You fucking thieving whore. Where is my money? Where is my fucking money?'

'Fuck you. Fuck you. You cunt. Fucking cunt. Fucking cunt,' the girl spat back in her Russian accent.

Then 'WHACK'. Ali stood back and swiped her across the face with the back of his clenched fist. She screamed as she lost her footing and tumbled headfirst down the stairs.

Open-mouthed, I stopped breathing and couldn't believe what I'd seen. Suddenly, Ali turned around and seemed to be staring back through the glass door right at me. Even though he couldn't see or hear me, I froze and slowly inched to the side away from the spyhole.

There was silence for a minute and then I heard a second voice. A man's voice. Not loud or angry this time.

I leaned into the spyhole again. 'Shit. What the...?'

It was Joe.

'What is he doing?'

The two of them briefly spoke then headed down the staircase and out of sight.

My heart was racing now, as I crept past the sleeping Alison and slowly slid open the balcony doors as quietly as I could. I did not dare stand up to look over the ledge in case Ali and Joe were already outside, so I crawled along round the side of the balcony, which looked over the ground floor exit of the fire escape.

I remained crouched down, momentarily taking in the ridiculousness of a naked me crawling around on all fours at 4am, off my chops and now with a hangover kicking like a mule through the charlie.

At this time of the morning, Deira was deathly silent and still; it was too early even for the fishing dhows and souk traders. The only sound I could hear was the voice in my head – the voice that was asking so many questions and warning not to get spotted.

I heard the CLUNK! of the metal bar being released as the

emergency-exit door was pushed open below. I tentatively peered over the edge but saw nobody at first. Then, Ali, faintly lit by the fire-exit sign, appeared and briskly walked round to the front of the building. A brief burst of an engine starting and a minute later, he was silently rolling his Jeep back round to the fire exit, headlights off.

He ducked back inside the building, leaving the Jeep's back-seat doors open.

What's going on?

I didn't have to wait long to find out.

At first, it was Ali who appeared, slowly edging into view and cautiously walking backwards step by step. A few more seconds and I could see he had his hands tucked up under the armpits of the girl's limp body. Joe then gradually came into sight, holding her outstretched legs as they struggled towards the car, awkwardly slumping her frame onto the backseats.

Shit. Is she... dead? Fuckin' dead?

No. No, can't be. Maybe she's okay. Just out cold.

Concussed. They're taking her to hospital. That must be it.

I could see but not clearly hear the two of them speaking before they climbed into the front of the 4x4 and quietly drove off into the darkness.

I sparked up a Marlboro Light on the balcony, trying to process what I'd just witnessed, before accepting that I was still wasted and sleep was a much better option than trying to deal with comedown paranoia and the head-splitting early stages of a hangover.

After a few hours' of sleep (which was really just twitching with my eyes closed), Alison and I both stirred around 7am with other things on our minds. Thankfully, my pathetic pecker was no more: now fully recovered, at your service madam, and ready for action. The boy did well for the rest of that morning as we lay there flushed in salty sweat, beaming with satisfaction, wondering if we should actually bother getting out of bed at all today or just carry on with the good times.

Chapter 11

Life as an Arabian World Airlines air hostess was glamorous and privileged. Tax-free salary, free accommodation with no bills to pay, free airline tickets to fly home for holidays, flight discounts for family and friends, and, of course, jetting off to exotic places while staying in luxury hotels, with all expenses paid for.

Not anyone could become an Arabian World hostess though. The two-day recruitment and sifting process was gruelling, and AWA was known to favour girls under the age of 30, slim and attractive – unlike some of those sour-faced flying grannies on British Airways or the American airlines.

There was an air of mystique about the Arabian World cabin crew whenever I saw them. The regimented bright red lipstick, dark eyeliner and mascara were as much part of the uniform as their pale blue, cropped jackets, knee-length skirts and the navy pillbox hats. A professional and stylish look, nothing overtly sexy but still mesmerising and strangely seductive.

While you were seduced by their spell, some of the stewardesses, I learned, had also been seduced by the riches of what the UAE could offer.

The 'paid-for' lifestyle of the AWA crews meant they had a lot of disposable income, leading to a materialistic obsession and a keeping up with the expat Joneses of Dubai. Many drove their own 4x4s while the more established stewardesses had upgraded themselves to convertible Mercs or BMWs. Luxury designer bags and shoes were as common among them as a GAP hoodie back home.

But for some, their own wealth was never enough and like a magpie, they were attracted to the shinier, more sparkling, more expensive trappings of the UAE. Trappings that were provided by members of the royal families or their extended web of super-rich and powerful Emiratis.

It was known among the crews and the expat community that some of the hottest stewardesses were handpicked to fly on private charters by the younger princes, disappearing for days to an exotic location and embracing the 'fun'. For a short while, their willingness to succumb to the playboy princes' sexual demands and bank accounts would be rewarded with gifts of jewellery, clothes and cars, but soon they'd be discarded like a used golden johnny and replaced by the next girl, with their initial gifts of jewellery and cars forcibly returned.

To date, Alison said she'd managed to avoid being press-ganged into these private royal flights and, over the past three years, had worked her way up to purser level, stashing away her tax-free savings while living comfortably in one of the AWA staff accommodation blocks on the Sheikh Zayed Road. She said she was also renting out her old flat in Kent, so more cash was flowing into her bank account every month. Proper smart lass this one.

Michelle, however, was not a nester. This Scouser spent money as soon as it touched her bank account, always pleading poverty to Alison by the end of the month.

The two of them had shared the apartment for just over a year, with Alison becoming more of a sisterly guardian towards her, being five years her senior and having flown with Virgin

Atlantic beforehand. For Michelle, this was her first airline job, having only ever been abroad once before – to Tenerife on a hen weekend.

Visiting their apartment always felt like luxury to me. Spacious, open-plan living room with a 12 person, L-shaped sofa and wrap-around balcony, which stretched either side of the living room to both of their en suite bedrooms. The hallway was furnished with exotic collections from their worldly travels; tall wooden carvings of leopards greeted you at the door, an Aboriginal didgeridoo was fixed up on the wall; oversized plant tubs decorated with brightly coloured ornate drawings were dotted around the floor, next to a set of bongo drums and what looked like ceremonial Arabian swords hung just above the white-tiled arch as you stepped into the lounge area.

The second-floor flat Andy and I shared back in Aberdeen was the polar opposite of this. Nae fancy hallway, just a front door that opened onto our toilet-shower room. Then two box-sized bedrooms either side of the toilet with single beds in each, one fitted out as a makeshift kitchen, the other we used as a living room. There was no 'best room'; either you went to sleep in a room reeking of weed or a room humming of that night's curry. The decks were kept in my room, so it tended to be the party place whenever folk came round – the hardest bit was trying to get the wasted cunts out when I needed some kip.

My room also bore the scars of fucked-up parties, the most obvious being the satanic black circle scorched into the centre of the carpet where an overly fucked Archie had lit lighter fluid 'for a laugh', only to set fire to his trousers as he tried to stamp it out. The Great Fire of Aberdeen 1995 was only just avoided by Gaz and the rest of the lads throwing pans of water over him, quickly followed of course by a shower of beer.

No, the girls' apartment was in a different class to all that.

Their drinks selection for a start could have rivalled The Savoy. Fully stocked cabinets (there were three) boasted an array of the finest and most unusual spirits and liqueurs from around the world, amassed as I later found out through the black-market trading among the Arabian World crew.

Safari? Batavia Arrack? Amarula? Peddlers? Mama Juana? Nae idea. And then there was 'Donkey Piss Tequila'... I'll give it a miss, thanks.

Not being a connoisseur of liqueurs and spirits beyond absinthe and a vodka and Coke, I always stuck to a straight bat of Heineken, Rolling Rock or Red Stripe when offered. Tennent's Lager was still nowhere to be found, proving now to be one of the rarest lagers in the Middle East.

I'd only seen Alison a couple of times in the past month since we first got together. Her rotas had been brutal, taking her to Sydney twice, Thailand twice and Sri Lanka.

Such was the uncertainty of her rotas and being placed on standby for a flight at a moment's notice that I'd sometimes only discover she was on the other side of the world through bumping into Michelle or another one of her pals at one of the bars.

She was back now for three days R&R before her next flight, a quick there and back to Heathrow – a 'bungee' flight, in cabin-crew lingo.

'Haven't seen you at the fourth floor for a few weeks, Jimmy. What you been up to?' Michelle mischievously asked as I sat down with Alison. 'Had better plans after midnight?'

Since witnessing that night of Joe and Ali's 'body snatch', I'd tried to avoid Ali, claiming to have been unwell on one of the Thursdays and then purposely 'overdoing it' on another after an all-dayer champagne press trip.

I couldn't even mention the incident to Alison, fearing that if I passed on what I'd seen, it would make her somewhat implicit or put her at risk of whatever ramifications might come. Forget any talk of assault or murder – the two of us could be arrested for just being together in the same apartment after midnight, let alone having sex outside of marriage. Those were the harsh sharia laws of Dubai.

'Ha ha, Shell! Been partying a bit too hard beforehand and peaking too soon,' I replied, joking it off.

'That's what happens when Alison's not here to keep me right. I turn into a lightweight,' I said, gently nudging Alison on the side.

I knew Shell and Joe had been seeing a lot of each other, as Joe had not been shy on dishing the sordid details of their 'fuck-fests' in our office chats. In the Lodge toilets, in the car park, in a phonebox and in a fucking taxi (that one cost him a few hundred Dirhams to stop the driver calling the Dubai rozzers) – they were at it all the time.

Michelle was good fun but mouthy, and once she was on it, a fucking sweary, argumentative, mouthy Scouser. Alison was a lot calmer – also a good laugh, but more considered and never one to really lose her shit.

'The parties been good?' I asked her.

'Banging, Jimmy, but not as good as when you play. Ali's spun a few times, but his tracks are old now. He always looks bored and busy on his phone, then he ditches the records and pings on the CDs. We need some live mixing action, Jimmy,' she said, pleading for me to play soon. 'I won't be here for a couple of weeks, though. Got a busy rota. Heading back to Heathrow tonight, then Jo'burg, then Hong Kong. So, make sure you play when I'm here.'

The door-buzzer pierced the chat and Michelle jumped up to check the intercom.

'That'll be Joe,' Alison said. 'We won't see them now.' She knowingly smiled and right enough, I heard Joe's 'Areet pet' greeting as Shell opened the front door and the two of them disappeared into her bedroom.

'Caught any big cats since I've been away?' Alison asked cheekily while pouring a beer for me.

'Ha! Nothing yet,' I replied.

It had been three weeks since I filed the story to the Editor who said to 'leave it with him'. Whenever I asked him for an update, he just said: 'It's under control. It'll happen when it'll happen and you'll be the first to know.'

Christ, he was sounding more like a local, only forgetting to add the clichéd 'Inshallah' at the end of the sentence, which was the default Arabic cop-out meaning 'God willing' or, in Scottish talk, 'in yer dreams, pal'.

'How long have you known Joe?' Alison asked out of the blue.

'Just since I arrived – about four months. Didn't know what to make of him at first. Still don't!'

'He's lived out here a few years, hasn't he? Bet there's a few stories about him – the big, loud Geordie – you can't miss him,' she said. 'Hope he's good to Shell. She needs a good guy for a change. She had a real nasty bastard of a boyfriend back in Liverpool. Used to steal her money and hit her. Even turned up in Tenerife on that hen weekend.

'She was walking down the street with her pals, heading to Bobby's and Busby's for some drinks, and the psycho pulled up in a taxi, jumped out, punched her bang in the face and dragged her into the car.

'He accused her of shagging someone over there, calling her

a slag. She'd only just arrived that morning. It was her first night out!

'Poor girl never saw her pals again, as he flew her back from Tenerife the next day.'

'He's never spoken to me about any of his ex-girlfriends,' I said. 'He does bang on about banging Michelle, though, so I think they're pretty happy for now!'

Alison nodded, adding: 'I've certainly heard them!'

■ ■ ■

Shell reached over to her glass of water on the bedside cabinet, washing down the remains of Joe's cum as he lay there naked, out of breath from their vigorous session. She thought a good fucking would have taken her mind off it, but with just a couple of hours to go before her flight pickup, she was feeling more anxious.

She tapped out a cigarette and sat up against the bed headboard.

'Are you sure this is going to work?' she turned to Joe. 'What if I get caught? What's going to happen?'

'Don't be daft, lass. This is a well-oiled machine,' he said. 'Works every time. Don't stress. The worst thing you can do is panic. It's just a routine flight there and back.'

His reassurances weren't getting through, as Shell played out scenarios in her head. The 'come with me, please' shoulder tap, the strip search, the fucking jails, the fucking rapes, her family, her life, her little...

'By this time tomorrow you'll be back here with me and an extra £500 in yer pocket,' said Joe gently stroking her neck. 'And trust me – once you've done it once, it's a doddle the rest of the time.'

Shell stood up and walked over to the bathroom, trying to erase the fearful thoughts in her head and remind herself how useful the £500 would be.

'Nobody's been caught,' she mulled. 'And I've never heard of any crew being arrested. Just that marketing bloke from that record label that Alison knew. Caught with 10g but the idiot hadn't even hidden it properly, just stuffing it into the back of a camera.'

It was time to start preparing for her pickup and applying the Arabian World warpaint and uniform – a routine she liked to do in private, so it was a cue for Joe to go.

'Remember to text me your room number,' he said. 'He'll be there at 2. And just keep cool, keep fookin' cool lass.'

Joe kissed her on the lips before turning and walking out towards the elevator. Shell closed the door, paused leaning against it and wondered 'was this the last time I'd see him?'

The AWA minibus arrived on time as always, collecting Shell and four others from outside the 'Red Building', then it was off to the AWA's 'Green Building' to pick up the rest of the cabin crew.

You rarely ended up on a rota with one of your friends, as the vast number of flights and the hundreds of air stewardesses greatly put the odds against you. But the few times it did happen always led to a more adventurous or more mischievous stopover, followed by a hellish hangover and a miserable flight of endurance on the journey back.

Shell scanned the crew on the minibus. Thankfully, there was nobody she recognised. This time, she didn't want to be with a friend. She knew she was not herself and wouldn't be going out for drinks with anyone in London. She had other things on her mind.

Chapter 12

Ali had led a charmed life. The son of two Lebanese doctors, he was born in Fulham, privately educated, but flunked his exams and failed to get into university. He took three years out to 'discover himself' at 20, travelling around India and Thailand before running out of cash and returning to the UK.

What he 'discovered' on his travels was no more than the fact he loved to party and he liked drugs – so much so that he decided it would be a great career choice.

At first, they were just small beach parties with a little bit of hashish-dealing on the side. Then he got friendly with one of the main promoters in the Goa rave scene who suggested stopping his little parties to come and work for him, putting on these 'Psytrance' events for a couple of thousand tie-dyed backpackers.

He enjoyed the good times at first, becoming a bit of a face in Goa and reaping the typical rewards of a promoter – the money and the girls – but then it all started to go wrong after the third raver OD'd at their beach parties.

Two girls were from England and the UK press was all over it as the deaths happened separately in the space of just four weeks. The 21-year-old was also the daughter of a TV soap actor, which had catapulted the media coverage from newspapers to TV news and TV talk shows, and then questions raised in Parliament.

BRITS DIE IN GOA DEATH RAVES screamed The Sun.

Ali's rave empire started collapsing around him, as the local police clamped down hard on the back of the media and political pressure. The parties were stopped during the investigations and the money started drying up shortly after. The relentless police questioning and forensic examination of how the raves were being managed eventually forced Ali to disappear from Goa, returning to the UK via Pakistan and Russia before eventually arriving home at the bank of mum and dad for help.

Propped up by their funds and the healthy commissions he was landing in his new job as an estate agent in London's W10 and W11 postcodes, he once again built up his reputation as a party organiser and promoter. This time, though, notching it up a few levels from the dreadlocked hippies to the cash-rich yuppies.

His 'private parties' at the likes of Annabel's and Chinawhite soon morphed into 'exclusive VIP' events when he realised the rich and glamorous kids of Kensington and Knightsbridge were willing to pay anything to fulfil their sexual fantasies.

'The Mad Hatter's She Party' was discreetly hosted in palatial West London houses operating under the radar on a strictly invite-only basis. Acceptance was based purely on the size of your bank account or if you were a girl, the size of your tits, your looks and your willingness to embrace the 'free love' Bacchanalian spirit of the parties. Theatrical performers would be hired adding to the fantasy wonderment while drugs flowed freely served on tea trollies by naked bellboys.

Now, while Ali was slowly building up a similar scene in

Dubai, his business partner Omar kept the London operation running smoothly and so far without incident.

■ ■ ■

Shell had surprisingly slept well in her Heathrow hotel room that night, the seven-hour flight and fuckfest with Joe beforehand taking its toll on her and knocking her out as soon as her head hit the pillow.

As 2pm approached, though, she grew more anxious again, not knowing what to expect from this Omar. She chain-smoked through her Silk Cuts, wishing she could have downed a couple of vodkas as well, but knew that would be asking for trouble. If any of the crew smelt alcohol on her breath, she would be immediately reported and arrested.

She switched on the TV, flicking between Home and Away and Murder She Wrote, not being able to really focus on either.

'Got to pull it together. Keep calm. Just a routine flight. Just a routine flight,' she kept saying over and over in her head.

She opened the door to Omar, who was standing there, grinning like the Cheshire Cat, clearly looking forward to meeting his new drugs mule.

'Hi, Shell darling. How you doing?' he said loudly and brashly, as he pushed passed her and perched on the end of her bed.

Shell stood.

'I'm good, Omar… Good.'

'Ali talks very highly of you,' he smiled. 'And you're even prettier than I imagined, darling.'

A little alarm bell immediately went off in Shell's head as this six-foot and what looked like 20-stone-plus, dark-bearded and perspiring Arabic man sat there on her bed, looking all fucking smug with himself.

'He says you'll be a master at this.'

'What? What the fuck is he talking about? Has Ali told him I'm a fucking Howard Marks or something?' she thought.

'You'll be one of our best,' he added.

Shell faintly nodded, playing along, but moved quickly onto business matters.

'You got it then?'

He smiled.

'First, let's have a drink.' He reached over and opened the minibar.

'Oh. Of course, you can't, can you? Shame,' he said as he popped open the beer bottle and sunk back down onto her bed. Shell could hear the springs straining underneath.

'Fuck. This fat prick wants to fucking hang out,' Shell believed, feeling more agitated. 'Fuck that. Gotta get him out of here quick.'

'They've changed my pickup, Omar. Got to be there an hour earlier for a new safety briefing. We better crack on with it, as that's not long,' she said.

He looked at her for a few seconds with a little smirk then gulped down half the bottle and stood up next to the console table.

He laid out three clear bags filled with white powder.

'10g in each. Just the three bags, Shell. Won't get lost in there, will it?' he said motioning his head towards her waist with 'that fat fucking grin', she was thinking.

'Now go and do your bit,' he said condescendingly, pointing Shell towards the bathroom door.

She didn't answer him. She picked up the bags and walked

into the bathroom, locking the door behind her, fearing he might try something on.

She pulled down her jeans and pants, closed her eyes and thought of Joe and their foreplay when he's playing around and fisting her. Within seconds of fingering herself, she was wet enough and ready to start sliding the stringed pouches up her one by one.

'Pervert's probably listening against the door,' she suspected as the third one went in, leading to an unexpected groan. She washed her hands, pausing for a few seconds looking at herself in the mirror, then zipped up her jeans and unlocked the door.

'All done. Gotta get ready now, Omar,' she said, stepping out of the bathroom with a fake smile.

Omar stood staring at Shell then squeezed his overhanging gut past her and into the bathroom. He lifted up the toilet cistern, flipped open the sanitary bin and pulled down all the towels from the shelf, checking to see if she'd 'mislaid' any of the goods.

It wouldn't be the first time that one of the girls had bottled it and deliberately left the drugs behind.

'Open your pockets,' he said. 'Open. Your. Pockets,' this time more forceful.

Shell turned out her jeans pockets, showing they were empty.

'Now your trainers. Your. Trainers.' He picked them up, running his hands inside and lifting out the soles. 'Good girl. Good. Girl.'

'Enjoy your flight,' he said slowly, turning his head away from her and casually flinging the trainers on the bed.

He didn't turn round as he lifted the security latch off the door and walked out into the corridor.

She closed the door. 'Prick,' Shell said out loud as she sat on the edge of her bed lighting a cigarette and looking at her watch. Less than two hours until pickup.

■ ■ ■

They landed 15 minutes early at 8.45am Dubai time. Surprisingly, this had been a good flight for Shell. Six players from the England Rugby team were onboard, escaping rainy London for some sunshine and relaxation. She had no idea who they were, even when they shared their names and was clueless about the sport, but their banter and chat-up lines had her in stitches during the service and she hadn't once thought about what she was packing inside her.

Hyatt Regency was the hotel they were staying at. Not mentioned once or twice in their chat, but about a hundred times to both Shell and her Italian purser, who despite wearing her wedding ring was clearly still fair game in the eyes of these sports stars.

'Here for a week. Don't forget to come and say hello,' the one with the lesser squashed nose warmly said as he stooped to step out of the aeroplane's exit door and onto the airbridge.

Wouldn't be the first or last time so-called celebrities had flirted with Shell and the crew, but to date, nobody had taken her fancy enough for her to casually 'drop by' their hotel pool one day and say 'hello'.

She filed off the plane with the rest of the hostesses, dragging her trolley behind. She always loved this moment of procession, striding through the airports with her crew like peacocks, always looking ahead but acutely aware of the turning heads gazing in awe around them.

As they approached the main Dubai Customs & Immigration

area, there was still a number of passengers waiting in line, some by the looks of it facing lengthy questioning at the booths. Black or Asian travellers always seemed to be the people they particularly made uncomfortable at Passport Control, while white Westerns usually breezed through. Never understood why, Shell wondered, trying not to think about being stopped.

Cabin crew had their own customs line, of course, allowing them to get in and out of the airports quickly. It was a spot-check-only policy, so only now and then would a customs official decide to pull aside a crew member for a trolley check and more detailed questioning.

'Keep cool, keep cool,' Shell was saying over and over in her head as she deliberately struck up a conversation with the purser, just as they approached the dishdashed customs officer standing to the side.

The two of them started giggling about the rugby players as they handed over their passports.

'Keep laughing, keep chatting,' she kept telling herself, not daring to look up into the eyes of the officer.

And then, yes, yes, Yes, YES!

A cursory glance down at their documents and he waved them through.

Shell smugly chuckled to herself even more as she briskly walked towards the terminal exit and the awaiting AWA minibus.

'A well-oiled machine. I bloody did it. I bloody did it,' she sat proudly on the bus, excited about seeing Joe again and celebrating the safe delivery of their little shipment.

At £200 a gram, the street price of coke in Dubai was more than double what you'd pay back in the UK. The risks were higher and the penalties more severe, so the bumper price reflected this. You'd have been told to 'get tae fuck' for that price back in Aberdeen but with a growing expat population from not just the UK but Australia, South Africa, Italy and Holland as well, there were enough cash-rich and party-hungry customers to fulfil demand.

Shell may have brought in only 30 grams, but over the past few years, Ali had finessed a seamless operation, with 10 air mules now on his payroll and sometimes three or four UK flights a week returning with a special delivery from London.

What Shell didn't know, though, was that these 10 air stewardesses had chopped and changed over the years, the 'chopped' disappearing suddenly, never to be seen again.

Chapter 13

'Jimmy. It's on.'

'What's on?'

'Come in here,' the Editor beckoned me into his office standing behind his desk.

'I've just got off the phone with the Ministry of Interior Sharjah and they're going to raid your warehouse tomorrow morning. We've to meet them by the camel racetrack at 4.30 before sunset, then they want you to direct them to the warehouse. They've got to catch them at the warehouse with the animals before they head into the souk,' he said.

'You better get a bloody early night because we need to be on the ball with this Jimmy.

'You remember how to get there and which warehouse?' he held his gaze like a cobra, ready to strike if I didn't answer positively.

'Of, of course,' I stuttered slightly, trying to retrace the route in my head.

'Good, I'll book the photographer now and I want you to be there at 4.15. Fifteen minutes before they arrive, so we can recap on our briefing. This is going to be some scoop, Jimmy lad. An exclusive for the Daily UAE,' he said excitedly. 'A scoop that could go global. Put the Daily UAE on the map!

'You can't tell anyone else, though. No friends, no staff. We've got to keep this quiet. Just you, me and the photographer. Don't want it leaking out and blowing the whole fucking operation.'

I sat back down at my desk, as Davey, who had been watching, leaned over.

'You getting a bollocking?'

'Aye a little bit,' I shrugged my shoulders, pretending to brush it off as something insignificant. 'Little fuck-up on my facts. Got the date wrong for the Dubai World Trade Show, didn't I? Only a day out, though, nothing major.' I smiled then turned round to my screen and finished off writing:

DUBAI GETS OFF ITS TROLLEY WITH WORLD RECORD SHOPPING BASKET

This place had truly lost its head up its superlative arse, as it had indeed created a new Guinness World Record for the largest shopping basket. A two-tonne mesh of steel rods and wheels standing at 9m tall had been built to promote Dubai as the world's leading shopping destination.

As a journo, it was all about your bylines on stories and adding to your portfolio of cuttings, but on this occasion, I was begging the sub-editor to just type 'Staff Reporter' on the byline. Just like that time in Aberdeen when I had to report on the beach cafe trying to become the Scottish version of McDonald's by marinating everything in Irn Bru –

MADE IN SCOTLAND FROM BURGERS by Staff Reporter

There were some stories you just didn't want to be associated with.

Despite the good intentions of an early night, I was still lying in bed awake at 1am, my brain over-analysing what was to come in the next few hours, sidetracked at times by thoughts about Alison and when I'd next see her.

We weren't *serious* serious, but things were going well and it felt like we were becoming 'a couple', although neither of us had actually said it. She shared her rota now, so I knew when she was in and out of Dubai, and an extra billy bonus was the wee gifts she'd started bringing back on her trips, like the fake Ralph Lauren polo shirts from Bangkok and the Calvin Klein boxers. No need to buy cigs again either, as she had an endless stash of Marlboro sleeves – more spoils of the cabin crew black-market.

I knew it had to work both ways, though, and I couldn't just be freeloading off her without giving something back in return. I couldn't compete with money – a reporter's salary out here was at least £1,000 less a month than an air hostess's – but the free ching, parties and the fact she was with Dubai's soon-to-be-top journo surely had to be a fair deal? Didn't it?

She never mentioned any ex-boyfriends out here and so far, neither had any of her friends to Joe or Davey, so I didn't have that raging paranoia burning inside like it was with Natalie back in Aberdeen.

What I always had to watch out for, though, were the pilots.

Like nurses gushing over doctors, for many stewardesses, it was their dream to marry a pilot. And I could see why.

These guys were on six-figure salaries, living rent-free in plush villas, not apartments, usually owned a couple of flash cars, maybe a jet ski and a motorbike as well, were intelligent, sometimes multilingual, and somehow nearly all of them were good-looking. Tall, well-groomed and could charm the pants off any girl.

If one of these Clark Kents locked onto your missus, you were done for.

I didn't see 2am on the digital clock as the alarm beeps shot through my head at 3.45am. Surprisingly fresh, I jumped into the shower, the adrenaline pumping through me, then I pulled on my black T-shirt and jeans, remembering the black Sambas. This time I was ninja-ready! Dressed like a ninja, but actually driving a white Audi maybe wasn't exactly incognito.

The darkness felt heavy as I turned into the racecourse car park. Two security lights in the far corners cast an amber glow over the immediate spaces around the perimeter, leaving a black hole of emptiness in the middle where hundreds of cars would usually be parked on race day. I could see another white Audi sitting under one of the lights with its headlights on. 'That'll be the photographer then,' I gathered, as I silently rolled towards it.

Sure enough, sitting in the driver's seat was the photographer, Dan and next to him, the Editor.

'Nice of you to turn up,' the Editor said, pointing to his watch as he rolled down his window. I looked down at mine: 4.25. Ah, fuck.

'Still here before them,' I cheekily replied, chancing my luck.

The two of them stepped out of the car and we stood in between the two Audis.

Dan was briefed with his shot list, the Editor outlining the must-have snaps: the police going into the warehouse, the arrests, the cuffing, the cages, the animals. On no account were me or the Editor to be captured in any of the images. The Ministry had been clear this was an official government operation and they wanted all the credit in the news report.

'Jimmy, you need to capture all the colour of this bust. Every fucking detail must be written down. How many cops? What were they wearing? Guns or no guns? The time of the raid? How many cages? All the fucking animals listed. If they've got names, get the fucking names – Pluto, Dumbo, Bambi, Baloo, I don't care. How many arrests? Where are they from? Then get quotes from the Deputy Director General. Got it?'

We headed towards the warehouses in a convoy. I was leading from the front, followed by three Dubai Police 4x4s and then Dan and the Editor in the pool car. This time there was no pack of Doritos or exploding Coke at my side, just some cigs, a notepad, two pens, my Nikon camera and a walkie-talkie the police had handed over for the operation communications.

With sunrise still 20 minutes away, we managed to roll the convoy under the twilight of darkness round the back of a warehouse positioned opposite our target.

The agreed plan was to wait until Beaky and his team arrived. I would then confirm the suspects on the police radio and only after they had unlocked the warehouse shutter and opened up would the police swoop in. We were to follow behind, once the commanding officer radioed approval.

We didn't have long to wait before we saw the headlights of the first trucks entering the compound. Two, three, four, five drove in together, but stopped at two of the warehouses nearer the entrance. In a flurry of action, dozens of men were loading up cargo from their lock-ups, preparing for another day of trading down at the souks.

Within 10 minutes, the site had changed from a ghostly emptiness to a noisy bustling throng of diesel engines and chatter as each of the warehouses started to open up, one by one.

Is this them?

The rattling truck passed the first six warehouses, then seven, eight, then nine, ten and kept getting closer.

'It is them,' I said to myself as the truck pulled up in a dusty cloud outside the corrugated-framed shutter and out stepped Beaky, his assistant and a couple of other skinny looking labourers.

I checked the channel on the walkie-talkie then clicked the

speaker button to confirm their identity. Seconds later, the police vehicles swung out from behind the building, just as the young assistant had ducked under the warehouse shutter to hoist it fully up with the metal chains.

The police 4x4s blocked in the trucks as the dishdash-robed officers jumped out and marched over to confront them. After a brief conversation, two of the officers started inspecting the trucks while the others walked inside with Beaky.

I watched from the car as they disappeared for what became an uncomfortably long time. Then the radio crackled. 'You come. Come now.'

The Editor and Dan gave me a questionable stare, as we strode over towards the police. There was something strangely unnerving now about the stillness of the operation in front of us.

'Come with me,' the Deputy Director General said, motioning further into the warehouse.

FLASH. FLASH.

'No. No cameras,' he barked and waved his hand, as Dan started snapping away.

We stood in the middle of the warehouse, at first everyone slowly turning a full 360° to take in all corners of the space. Then I started to sense everyone's eyes lower and fix on me. The Editor's, in particular, were rather fiery and burning like a laser onto my cheeks.

'Nothing,' the Deputy Director General said, throwing his hands up in the air and gesturing all around the hollow building. 'There is nothing here. Where are animals? No animals. Where are cages? No cages.'

'HE says there are no animals here,' he pointed towards Beaky, who was standing quietly with his head bowed next to one of the officers.

Fuck. All I could see were just stacks of empty wooden pallets lying around and a dusty old pick-up truck near the back.

How could this be? I didn't respond to the Deputy Director General nor to the Editor who was shooting questions at me, which were now all blurring into one continuous drone of white noise.

I stepped away from the group, wiping the sweat from my neck, and shuffled up towards the far end of the building to take a look at the abandoned truck.

As I squeezed around the back of it, I looked across the corrugated wall in both directions.

'Hold on a minute.' I checked again, looking left, right, several times.

'Where's the door? There's no emergency exit. There's no fuckin' door.

'This, is the wrong warehouse!'

'It's the wrong fuckin' warehouse!'

I marched past the Editor and police – again, ignoring their questions but snapping back at them, 'Hold on!' – and headed outside to the front.

The sun was up now, and we were causing quite a scene as groups of traders had gradually migrated towards the warehouse to watch what so far was an Arabian farce.

I shouted over to the police, 'Stay there. Don't let them go!' as I ran up the side of the adjacent warehouse and around the back.

'Yaa beauty!' There it was. The broken door, still slightly ajar hanging off its hinges.

I stepped inside, this time not quietly but briskly and confidently walked up to the first container flipping up a corner of the tarpaulin.

And there they were.

'Yes, my boys. We've got you,' I shouted out to the leopard cubs pacing around the cage.

As the police escorted Beaky over to the front of the warehouse, his head and shoulders dropped lower. He meekly handed over his keys to the officer, which I knew were going to unlock the shutters and Bingo! They did.

My shoulders were now pushed back and chest puffed out with a smug grin on my face, as the shutter was winched up and the officers swarmed through the warehouse, pulling off the tarpaulins, revealing a Noah's Ark of leopards, cheetahs, baby rhinos and, of course, the golden eagle.

If that wasn't enough of a result, the police started ripping open the pallets of cardboard boxes piled high on the opposite side of the warehouse. As each one was torn open, out tumbled dozens of boxed Pioneer TVs, car stereos and hi-fi speakers.

Counterfeit. This must be all fuckin' counterfeit and there's hundreds of them, I was saying to myself, as I witnessed the collapse of a mini empire.

Not only had I smashed animal trafficking, but I'd blown apart a counterfeit operation as well.

ABERDEEN LOON DOES GOOD IN MIDDLE EAST BUST

I could see the headline now back in the local paper. Mum would be proud.

Chapter 14

Hamza was not the most visible of people. He remained up in his office on the third floor, either locked into meetings with representatives of Sheikh Al Zaheri or reviewing first drafts of the next day's Daily UAE, with a thick black marker pen and a ruler by his side, ready to redact anything that didn't meet his approval.

Unlike the UK press where the Editor was the ultimate decision-maker, Hamza wielded the power here, being the sheikh's official representative. His direct line to the Editor's office burned red hot in the evenings between 7pm and 9pm, as he demanded certain stories be spiked. The whole newsroom would be on edge until the call finished, wondering which of their stories had just 'been Hamza'd'.

Aside from that, you only ever saw him when you needed to collect your passport for an overseas business trip or a holiday back home. Despite being 'property of the Crown at all times', Hamza kept my British passport along with all the other employees' in his safe and you had to make an appointment if you wanted it back.

So, it sent seismic tremors across the newsroom when we saw his apparition suddenly appear at the entrance, briefly pausing to scan across the editorial floor before snaking his way around the first few banks of desks heading towards the Editor's office, just opposite my desk.

'As-salam alaykum,' he greeted everyone as he passed.

Most people stuttered and hesitated in response, failing to believe in those first few seconds it was actually him. Then like meerkats, all heads popped up and followed him around the floor, wondering just who he was here to see.

'He's heading to the Editor's office,' I was thinking as he got closer. 'Must be serious. Must be a real fuck-up for him to come down. This could really kick off.'

I sparked up a Marlboro Light, ready to enjoy the show, and locked eyes with Davey sitting opposite me.

'Fuuuck,' he mouthed back, raising his eyebrows.

I was just about to reply with another 'fuuuck', but paused and lost a heartbeat as Hamza stopped and stooped at the edge of the desk, staring down at me.

'Mr Jimmy,' he said. 'As-salam alaykum.' He outstretched his arm to shake my hand.

I clumsily shuffled up from the seat, dropping my cigarette, almost lighting a stack of newspapers on the desk in the process.

'Wa alaikum as-salam,' I replied, shaking his hand and now standing steady.

'Our Royal Highness Sheikh Sultan bin Muhammed Al Zaheri, ruler of Sharjah, wishes to express his gratitude for your work in exposing the illegal trading of the Arabian Leopard and other endangered animals. He has requested your presence at the palace on Friday for a private meeting.'

This time, I could see Davey mouthing a different kind of 'fuuuck' over to Joe.

Hamza shook my hand again.

'A driver will meet you here at 10am. Wait for him at the front gates.'

He turned around to the Editor, who by now had left his glass fishbowl to see what all the fuss was about.

'Good. This is a proud moment for us all,' he said. Hamza gave a courteous nod to the Editor then turned around and headed back towards the newsroom exit.

'Fuckin' hell,' I said to the Editor, once Hamza was out of sight.

'The sheikh. The fuckin' palace. That's some invite!' I was grinning excitedly now, imagining what delights might await me once I was in the company of the sheikh.

'This could be the mother of all freebies, Davey boy,' I joked, still envious of the Seiko strapped around his wrist.

But whatever the experience or reward, this was going to be a day never to forget.

Chapter 15

We agreed that we wouldn't go out partying the night before, so Alison had offered to cook a celebratory dinner at her place on the Thursday ahead of my royal date in the morning.

When I arrived, the champagne was already open with two half-drunk glasses on the dining table, as Alison and Shell darted back and forth from the kitchen, tinkering with the music in the lounge, not being able to settle on 'the right tunes for cooking'.

Surprisingly, for a change, there was no sign of Joe. I was relieved, though, as he never did things by halves and any talk of a 'quiet night' would just encourage him to make it the most fucked-up night this side of Newcastle's Bigg Market.

'Seeing him later down the Lodge,' Shell said. 'Leaving you two lovelies alone,' she added with a wink, sinking the rest of her champers.

Growing up in Scotland in the 70s and 80s didn't exactly expose you to the world's finest and most culturally diverse cuisines. The closest I got to a taste of Italy was whenever my mum sent me down the chipper to buy four macaroni pies or when she came back from the local SPAR with a Chicago Town margherita pizza.

As for anything Indian or Chinese, just don't mention it. You're talking another century, before my folks were willing to trust 'really foreign' food.

The food of choice in the Irvine household was Scotch Broth, Findus Crispy Pancakes, homemade Shepherd's Pie, fish fingers, chips and smoked kippers. For dessert, I'd usually treat myself to a Double Decker, Galaxy bar or chocolate mousse. It would take a family trip down to Edinburgh at 16 before I dared go off-piste and order an exotic lasagne and tiramisu.

'Just an Italian version of your Shepherd's Pie mum,' I described lasagne, at the risk of being disowned, tarred and catapulted out of Scotland into England.

Alison and Shell were creating an 'authentic' Thai dish, inspired they said by their nights out in Bangkok. Alison was busy grinding the herbs while shaking her cute butt in denim shorts to the tunes, while Shell was slicing up the chicken thighs, also swaying her slightly chubbier but very squeezable backside in time to the bassline.

'This is proper Thai. Street-food Thai. You'll love it, Jimmy,' Alison said, who since hearing about my royal recognition had been treating me like a prince or – dare I say it? – a pilot.

Dinner for three was served.

'What you going to wear, Jimmy?' Shell asked as she sunk her chopsticks into the Thai bowl.

'Got a kilt?' Alison chuckled, topping up her flute with some more Veuve Clicquot.

'Aye, funny one. Bit fuckin' hot for a kilt out here. Gonna go with the linen suit. Nice and cool,' I said.

'What do you think he's going to give you? A watch? A sword? A car?... A wife?' We cracked up at the thought of being gifted an Arabian bride and coming back to their apartment with a new flatmate.

Everyone knew that official guests to the palace never left empty-handed and stories had been told of some even being rewarded for 'outstanding duties of citizenship' with a new car – though, to date, nobody actually knew the names, let alone had met any of these fortunate people.

'If there are any handbags being offered, Jimmy, don't say no,' half-joked Shell.

'You just bought a new Chanel bag last week. And a Prada one the week before,' Alison jumped in to cut her off her wish list.

'Got to keep adding to my collection, sweety. Louis Vuitton would be nice, Jimmy,' she said, blowing a kiss at me from the other side of the table.

Shell stood up to take her empty bowl over to the kitchen, as I rolled my eyes at Alison in a reassuring 'if there's any gifts, it won't be for her, it'll be for you' way.

Shell notched the volume up on the stereo, then headed out into the hall and into her bedroom.

'She's happy,' I said. 'And since when did she become all Flash Sally with her designer handbags?'

In her room, Shell pulled over the desk chair to the side of her wardrobe and stepped up. On her tiptoes, she reached above, sliding the false ceiling panel to the side and felt around the inside edges.

'One, two, three, four, five, six, seven, eight, nine, ten, 11,' she tapped them as she counted each of the pouches. Each one was filled with 10g of cocaine.

'All there, all good,' she said, relieved as she felt the final smaller bag, which was for her own private use.

Since her first successful courier service back from London, Joe had asked her to store some extra shipments while he controlled the price and supply around Dubai with Ali.

'High demand and low supply equal higher prices and more money for you Shell,' Joe said, as he convinced her to hold stock.

Shell hadn't said anything to Alison about her little side-hustle, but everyone was in such a good mood tonight, she thought it was 'time to take the celebrations to the next level'.

She smoothed out three lines from her private stash on the dressing table.

'And just a little livener for myself before,' she said to herself as she tapped a small amount onto the back of her hand and sharply snorted.

She danced back into the living room, pulling out another chilled bottle of bubbly from the fridge.

'Come with me. Bring your glasses,' she sang in time to the beat. Alison and I looked quizzingly at each other, then shrugged and like the Pied Piper, duly followed her back to her room.

'We need to celebrate properly,' she said, reaching out and hugging us both. 'Not just for Jimmy but me. It's a Shell-ebration!'

'Come on.' She beckoned us over to her dressing table. 'A little treat for you – tuck in.'

'What you Shell-ebrating, Shell?' I asked, clocking the white lines.

'I'll tell you after this,' she replied, pointing to the gear over and over in time with the bassline beat. 'Come on, come on,' she kept saying, dancing by the table.

Here I was again, faced with the devil on one shoulder and the angel on another, just like John Belushi's Animal House. To sniff or not to sniff? That is the question.

'A quiet night. It can still be a quiet night, can't it?' I asked myself.

'Can't turn up fucked at the palace.'

I looked at Alison.

'It's only 8.30,' she said. 'You'll be fi…'

I finished the line before she finished her sentence, and

turned around, planting a big fat kiss on her cheeks. She moved me out of the way and bent down on the table to complete our hat-trick.

'What's it all about then, Shell?' asked Alison as she continued to nod in time to the music.

'Well, let's say Joe's been verrrrry good to me,' Shell replied.

She slid back her mirrored wardrobe door revealing a stack of designer shoe boxes from Dior, Prada, D&G and other names I couldn't pronounce. Then, from under her bed, she pulled out four matching luxury handbags. Beaming and swooning over her collection of riches, she said: 'Isn't it amazing? I wouldn't have had this without Joe.'

'Fuck. He bought you all this?' I asked.

'Well, kind of. I'm doing him a favour. A biiiiig favour. You must keep this a secret, though. You must promise not to tell a soul.'

We nodded.

She stood up on the chair and popped the ceiling panel.

One, two, three...

'Hold these, Jimmy,' she said as she passed down the pouches.

Four, five, six, seven, eight, nine, ten, 11.

'Hold these, Alison.'

'Shit. Fuckin' hell, Shell. Is this all Joe's?' I asked.

'Well, Ali and Joe's. All I've got to do is look after it for a while. They pay me for this and for the other bit.'

'The other bit? What's the other bit?' I asked.

'There's a friend of Ali's I meet on my London trips. He's a bit of a knob but a good friend of Ali's and used to run the 'Mad Hatter's She Parties' with him. He drops off a few bags of powder with me at the hotel and then, well, you see... I take them back.

'It's easy... really easy. They've been doing it for a while. It's a well-oiled machine, as Joe says, and it's only a few of these little guys at a time. Nobody checks and even if they did, they'd have a hard time finding them.'

She laughed, then motioned her hand going up between her legs and puckered a 'pop!' sound.

'Up they go. And nobody sees. Then eight hours later: Pop!' She puckered again. 'Out they pop and hey presto, here they are for everyone to enjoy.'

I wasn't sure how Alison was going to respond, being her purser and boss, but already being nose deep in the bugle and now literally 'champagne charlied', she didn't seem too bothered and was going along with it.

It had been a while since I'd seen this amount of gear laid out in front of me – not since Andy had started a new vocation in dealing after quitting the Royal Marines. He'd switched overnight from being brainwashed by the military corps and anti-drugs into running a makeshift chemist of uppers and downers from his caravan on the outskirts of Aberdeen.

Forget about the nine-mile speed marches over Dartmoor or the sleep-starved 'Long Nighters', it was losing the privilege of weekend leave for a third time that finally tipped him over the edge, calling his officers a 'bunch of fukin' fannies' because they'd reprimanded him for not having his cabin bed in order.

Quitting the Royal Marines and returning to Aberdeen penniless, homeless and fuckin' angry, we treated him to a few 'smiley' nights out while he kipped on the floor at our flat.

Loved up on pills and now a believer, within a few weeks he'd set himself up with God knows who, but was shipping out speed, pills, hash, jellies and gear from his rickety Sprite Alpine 4 berth he'd bought for 200 quid and pitched on the edge of Kirkhill

Forest just outside the city. He'd also bought himself a motor-bike. But then...

'Anybody else know?' Alison asked.

'Just Joe and Ali and now you two.'

'You've got to be careful, Shell. This is serious. How much is he paying you?'

'In the past four weeks... about £2,000. Nearly double my wages,' she said as she topped up our glasses with the Moët this time.

It was risky, but it did all sound simple and for a woman, yes, an impenetrable hiding place. Why would customs suspect you? Sniffer dogs wouldn't catch a scent and even if you did get pulled over, they'd just do a spot check on your luggage.

I could see how Shell had been tempted. And the more we drank, the more appealing it became to earn some extra readies. But there was a line not to cross – I wisnae sticking anything up my backside.

Chapter 16

The bright light of the morning sun pierced through the gap in the blinds and slowly forced my eyelids open. I tilted my head to see Alison lying next to me, curled up on top of the sheets still asleep, her crooked kingfisher giving me the evil eye.

The AWA ashtray on her bedside table was full and the bottle of Moët empty. I rolled my head back over to look at my side; ashtray also full and six empty bottles of Rolling Rock, one with a bunch of fags floating among the dregs of beer at the bottom.

I lay motionless, just staring up at the ceiling fan, which was still on high-speed rotation. Not usually audible, but in this stillness of the morning, the whirring of the blades was pounding through my head like a plane engine. The switch for the AC and the fan were on the wall by the bedroom door, which felt so far away I'd need to call a cab to reach it.

Can't reach. Try… No… Try… No… Try… Fuck it. I gave up on the thought of moving.

I tried to piece together the blurry visuals of the night before, but it was still too early and the memory fog still too thick.

We didn't cane it did we? Or did we?

I don't think we did. Did we?

I didn't feel that post-charlie fuzziness and paranoia that would be kicking in now if it had been a big night on the gak.

And hold on... yup, there were nae flakey coke bogies up my hooter.

Hungover, yes. But not fucked, thank fuck.

I slowly gazed around the room, our clothes wildly discarded and spread out across the floor from the door to the bedside. That bit I remembered.

Still squinting and fighting the sunlight, I caught a blurry outline of the digital clock on the VCR opposite the bed.

...08:11... I... think.

...08:... 11...?

08:... ... ...

Is that definitely... an 8?

Or is it a 9? Is it an 8?

Is that a 9? It's not a 9, is it? Can't be a fuckin' 9. Better not be a fuckin' 9.

I rubbed my eyes again and focused on the clock.

'Fuck. 09:11. It's fuckin' 09:11! Fuck! Fuck!! Fuck!!!'

Here I was in bed on the Sheikh Zayed Road in Dubai, when I needed to be shipshape and spritely back in Sharjah for a royal pickup at 10.

I bolted out of bed, scooping up my clothes as Alison started to stir.

'What you doing, babe?' she groaned with her eyes still closed.

'It's fuckin' 12 minutes past fuckin 9,' I shouted back, yanking up my boxers.

T-shirt, jeans and trainers on, I shot out of her apartment to the lifts.

'34th floor. Why couldn't she live on the first floor?' I was saying as I pressed buttons for all six of the lifts, trying to hurry them along.

I bundled into the back of the Dubai Taxi, instructing the driver to take the quickest route to Sharjah. His clock on the dashboard now showed 09:24.

'Important meeting, boss?' he asked, glancing at me in his rear-view mirror.

'You could say that. Just need to get there pronto,' I replied, not in the mood to start sharing details of the royal breakfast.

A fag-reeking T-shirt and jeans was not the intended attire for the palace, so we had to detour via the apartment first.

No time for a shower. I threw off my T-shirt and practically gassed myself all over with Lynx spray. Choking and cursing, with now-stinging eyes, I grabbed a clean white T-shirt from the wardrobe then slipped on the sandy-coloured linen suit.

09:49. The taxi was waiting for me outside.

A quick splash of water in the face. Mirror check. Done. Let's go.

'Hey, Cola Boy,' came the familiar voice as I darted through reception.

I glanced back and there was Joe, grinning at the door of the concierge office with Ali and 'Mr 7am', who was holding his briefcase as always.

'Gotta go,' I shouted back as I flung open the taxi door and barked 'yella' for the driver to floor it.

Compared to the UK, the police in Sharjah were pretty lax about speed limits. There was no such thing as a speed camera and, in any case, you were given a grace of 20mph above any limit before the minimal risk of a fine, if you were actually pulled over.

This driver thankfully was a pro and eagerly seized the gauntlet of professional rally driver, weaving expertly in and out of the traffic across the Sharjah city centre.

10.08. The cab screeched to a halt as he broke sharply outside the security gates of the Daily UAE. I thanked him with a

100 Dirhams tip and walked over to the staff entrance. Through the metal security bars, I could see on the other side a glistening white Rolls-Royce with a UAE flag flapping next to the prestigious Silver Lady figurine on the front of the bonnet. The well groomed driver was standing next to the vehicle in his pristine white Arabic robes, talking to the Editor.

Shit.

'Nice of you to turn up, Jimmy,' he said. 'We were wondering where you'd got to. Had something more important to do this morning, did you?'

'Sorry, chief. We were stuck in traffic. It was just murder getting here.'

He wasn't impressed and rolled his eyes.

'You better get going. Don't want to keep a sheikh waiting.'

The driver opened the backseat door of the Phantom, welcoming me in.

'Don't fuck up,' the Editor mouthed through the window, as the chauffeur closed the door gently behind me.

I couldn't believe how soft the toffee-brown leather seat was, as it cocooned itself around me, oozing in comfort. The floor was carpeted as well – a cream shagpile without a speck of dirt. I removed my shoes and let my feet enjoy the plush luxurious feel. The backseat was slightly elevated from the front, creating a sense of superiority and a 'I'm considerably wealthier than you' feeling. Except, of course, I wasn't.

Then I looked up.

And wow. I mean, fuckin' wow.

'Is this gold?' I asked, pointing to the ceiling, not daring to touch it.

'Yes, sir. All that shines in here is gold. All that sparkles is diamonds.'

The ceiling was skillfully painted as a night sky and solar system. Hundreds of tiny stars sparkled all above me, punctuated by golden planets running from one side of the car to the other. Looking closer, I could see intricate Arabic script also glistening in gold around the four edges.

The middle armrest compartment was open, providing cold water, two glasses and a small bowl of dates.

'Please. Have some water, sir,' the chauffeur offered as he pulled away from our security gates.

Unlike those tin-box Sharjah taxis, I couldn't feel any vibration from the road. In fact, if I couldn't have seen outside the windows, I would have sworn we weren't even moving. It just felt like we were gliding above the road, wrapped in a bubble of bliss, and it wasn't long until this soothing swathe of luxury lulled me into a deep sleep…

…We were still 1-0 down and the tackles were flying in. Souness was up in my face, but Miller was at my shoulder.

The ref blew for full-time and we walked off the pitch, straight into the office of the Daily UAE.

I sat at my desk reaching down to adjust my shin guards. When I looked up, I could see Natalie marching towards me, dragging a rattling old suitcase behind her. I carefully moved the newspaper over to hide the lines of coke, as Alison took her hand off my lap and swung her chair back round to the other side of the desk.

Just behind Natalie's shoulder, my mum came into view with a face like thunder wearing that pale blue winter coat she's had since I was a wee boy. She must have just been to the shops, as she was carrying a SPAR bag filled to the top with groceries.

I stood up to greet Natalie, but was more focused on my mum, thinking: 'Any second now, that bag is going to burst.'

*Roy Aitken, sitting opposite in his Aberdeen FC** strip with boots on, stopped typing to look up from his screen. 'You're fuuucked,' he mouthed.*

'How can I be fucked, Roy?' I said. 'You're the one fucked. You're the one that lost us the game.'

Natalie towered in front of me, much taller than what I remembered, as my mum kept walking yet didn't seem to be getting any closer.

'Why are you here?' I asked her.

'Jimmy, my love, I'm pregnant. But it's Roy's baby. It's Roy's baby. It's Roy's baby. Roy's baby.'

Sir. Sir. Sir. Sir. Sir. Sir. Sir.

I shot open my eyes to see the chauffeur leaning into the back-seat from the door with his hand delicately tapping my shoulder.

'Sir, we are here. The palace.'

For a few seconds, I'd completely lost my bearings. The dream had been so vivid, I had that fleeting moment of questioning what was reality and what was the dream. Was Natalie pregnant? Worse still, was Roy Aitken the fuckin' father? And was he really here, writing for the Daily UAE?

I shook some sense into my head, finished off the bottle of water and stepped out of the Roller.

We were now inside the boundary walls of the royal palace, parked outside the grand entrance – a towering archway of gold, white and blue patterned marble, reflecting the grandest of Islamic architecture and symbolism.

Two white-robed royal aides greeted and escorted me into this magnificent open space the size of Hampden. Dozens of colourful, multi-foiled arches and marble columns grandly stood in all directions across the vast silvery white floor – a surface so shiny you could have skated across it.

Lined up along the far edges of the walls for as far as I could see were dots of white-robed Arab men, sitting patiently and quietly on marble benches, each seat interspersed with spectacular displays of floral arrangements. I'd read before how all Emirati men are permitted an audience with their sheikh, a tradition going back to the founding sheikhs of the UAE and here they were waiting and waiting for what could take all day for just a few minutes with their glorious leader.

Here I was, though, skipping the queue and being whisked through the corridors to meet their esteemed leader.

The aides invited me to wait on a velvet upholstered bench in front of the floor-to-ceiling door by the sheikh's reception room. Six other men sat opposite. Some looked over, curious to see this non-national dressed in his linen suit, while others kept their heads down, flicking their worry beads, praying quietly to themselves.

The initial adrenaline and excitement started to wane as the time ticked on. Looking at my watch, it had been 40 minutes since they'd seated me here to wait.

And while the architecture may have been impressive wherever you looked, there were nae magazines to read and pass the time. This was no doctor's surgery.

An hour had come and gone, and I was becoming impatient and irritable as the pains of a hangover started to take effect.

How can a sheikh be running late? With all these helpers around him, surely someone's keeping an eye on the time?

I reached inside my jacket and tapped out a Marlboro Light. Hunched over with my elbows resting on my thighs, I lit the cigarette while staring down at the spotless floor.

A minute later, to my right at the end of the corridor, I could hear raised voices and looked round to see a group of men shouting in Arabic. They were briskly marching this way, their arms flailing in the air and eyes fixed on where we were sitting. I took a long inhale on the cigarette and gently blew out the smoke, admiring the rings slowly wafting up into the air.

I casually looked over to the men opposite. They were staring intently right back at me.

I couldn't understand a word of what was being said, but as they quickly approached, they were definitely angry. Like, really angry. Fergie hairdryer angry. And their eyes were fixed on me.

Two of them suddenly grabbed me by the collar on either side while the other twisted my wrist snatching the cigarette out of my hand. Still shouting in Arabic, they started to drag me away from the seat.

'OI. FUCK OFF! FUCK OFF, YE CUNTS! What the fuck you doin'?' I shouted and wrestled, trying to free my arms from their grip. By now, all of the sheikh's waiting guests were looking up, watching this spectacle. Like a domino effect, the heads in the queues turned one by one, as I was dragged 100 yards across the floor to a small wood-panelled door. They barged it open revealing a narrow stone staircase, not so grand this time, but still looking pristine.

Trying not to lose my balance and remain upright, they hurriedly bustled me down the stairs; only at the bottom did I miss the step and stumble over my ankle. They forcefully stood me up and stepped back still shouting uncontrollably in Arabic. Then, from behind, one of the (what I'd gathered by now were) plain-clothed palace guards grabbed my shoulder, spun me around and shoved me through a fire-exit door and out into a sandy courtyard.

Confused and startled about what the fuck had just happened, I turned around and one of them flicked the cigarette at me before slamming the door shut.

Two uniformed security guards sprinted up from their sentry box at the end of the courtyard. Again, without any pleasantries or explanations, they frogmarched me out beyond their security checkpoint and gave me a final shove onto the barren road outside the palace walls, before walking back to their gatehouse.

Being asleep in the Roller when I arrived, I had no sense of bearings, as the palace boundaries seemed to stretch infinitely in both directions from this small gatehouse, which I guessed was not the main entrance.

The guards didn't look like they were in the mood to assist with directions, so after a few minutes just standing there, trying to regain my composure, I flung my jacket over my shoulder and decided to walk left, following the partially sand-covered road running alongside the palace perimeter.

The dial on my watch showed 12.30, as a camel appeared about 100 feet away, nonchalantly stepping up from the desert dunes onto the tarmac, pausing briefly in the middle, before continuing to the other side without a care in the world.

In the midday sun, there were no mad dogs or Englishmen here. Only a confused Scotsman and a camel.

'What the fuck did I do wrong?' I kept asking myself. 'Who did I upset?

'Did I say something wrong?

'Or... the cigarette... Was it the cigarette? There weren't any 'No Smoking' signs in the palace so it couldn't have been that, could it?'

Like a flipbook, my brain retraced the images from graceful arrival to catapulted exit.

Everyone I'd seen from the palace entrance to the sheikh's waiting room. All those men… waiting patiently…for hours…

But did I see any of them light a cigarette…?

No…

Not one…

…Shit.

Not one of them had a cigarette. Shit, I should have spotted it, especially in this country, where a lit cigarette was like an eleventh finger. That was it. No smoking in the palace!

Fuck, I've gone and fucked it. 'Don't fuck it up,' he said. I could picture the Editor's face mouthing those words to me over and over.

Alison will be gutted. Returning empty-handed was not part of the plan. She'll be lying on the beach right now, dreaming about what gift I'm bringing back to her. Even worse, she'll be telling her friends, knowing that I'd successfully managed to leave her flat and just about get here on time.

The whole newsroom had wished me luck the day before as well. Joe and Davey in particular were looking forward to grilling me on all the lavish details when they next saw me.

'Ask him about his harem, mate. How many birds has he got?' Davey had joked.

Thirty minutes walking in the unforgiving, blistering heat and the perimeter wall still stretched as far as I could see, like the bloody Great Wall of China. No cars had passed either and there had been no other signs of life since the camel crossing. All around me was the static hissing of silence as the sun beat down, intensifying its glare with every step I took.

Thank fuck I was wearing this light suit and not the thicker one I'd brought over from the UK. It didn't stop me sweating buckets, though, as my T-shirt was now starting to soak through in patches and I could feel perspiration trickling out of every pore in my body. It must have been pushing 40°C.

Rescuing myself from the desert was one thing – but I was more concerned about rescuing this shit-show of a morning that I'd royally fucked up.

What the fuck do I tell Alison? What do I tell the fuckin' Editor?

But… will anyone actually know the truth?

Does the sheikh really care? He's a busy man, isn't he?

I was just one of hundreds there today. Must be more important meetings than me and the leopards.

Only I, the sheikh and the security guards know what happened. Maybe I could blag my way out of this… no, not maybe. I must blag it. There's no other choice, is there?

Over and over in my head, I played out the scenarios of truth or blag as I trekked along the side of the road. Truth always ended up more painful – lose the girl, lose the job, lose credibility – while blagging had a 50/50 chance of a good outcome: keep the girl, keep the job, get married, have kids, get promoted and live a good life.

Ahead, on the hazy, flickering horizon, I could see the dot of a car heading towards me.

Yes. Thank God. I'll wave him over.

As the car came closer, I could see the distinctive green and white markings of a Sharjah taxi.

Yes, even better – a taxi!

I started swinging the jacket over my head with one arm, motioning him to pull over with the other.

He got closer and closer and closer and then…

WHOOSH! The driver glanced at me with a smile as he sped past, blowing up sand from the road into my face.

What a cunt.

'YOU FUCKIN' CUNT,' I yelled after him, throwing the jacket onto the road.

What the fuck is wrong with this place? It's full of cunts. The United Emirates of Cunts!

I perched on the side of the road pulling my jacket over my head and shoulders for some shade. I lit a Marlboro. No chance of upsetting anyone out here with a fag.

A cockroach scurried out of nowhere, then lay still, taking shelter in the shade between my shoes. I didn't have the energy to move and just stared down at the little guy, wondering how the hell he survives in this furnace. Then, after a few minutes of absolute stillness, he suddenly burrowed back into the sand and was gone. It was now 1.20pm. Like the cockroach, I also knew I had to keep going. Rest, then walk. Rest, then walk.

I stood up and cast the jacket over my head, propping it up slightly at the front so I could see a few metres in front. And continued. Slowly.

1.35pm. I'd been walking for nearly an hour and my lips were sandpaper dry. The palace wall was still unforgiving, providing no shade as it pointed endlessly further into the desert.

Could have been back in the Roller with a cool bottle of water by this time. What I wouldn't give now for AC, shade and water.

AC… shade… and… water.

AC…

…shade…

…water… need water.

Water…. ……………………..shade………………..wat…

….. …..

……

…

At first, I wasn't sure where the little 'toot!' came from. I slowly lifted up the jacket more at the front, but the road ahead was still barren and blindingly bright.

Toot! Toot!

I stopped and slowly turned round, trying to keep under the shade of the jacket.

Tyres. I could see two wheels of a car on the road just beyond my feet. I poked my head out further... it was the taxi. The cunting Sharjah taxi! The saviour! The United Fuckin' Taxis of Arabia!

'As-salam alaykum,' he called over from behind his steering wheel, beckoning me into the back of the cab.

I smiled, so dehydrated I'd drink my tears of joy.

I opened the door and looked in. Three other Asian men were in the backseat and a dishdashed Arab in the front.

A shared cab. Shite.

But I was in no state to be picky as I squeezed into the backseats, squashing one arse cheek against the door and the other against this old bloke's backside, while contorting my neck at 90° against the ceiling.

The 30-minute ride back to the centre of Sharjah felt like an eternity, as every inch of my body ached with every bump and turn of the taxi.

But I'd made it. I was back.

Alive.

Though inside I was still dying, dying of embarrassment.

Chapter 17

I smeared the aftersun all over my beetroot face.

No need to worry about turning red in the cheeks when I fibbed this story to Alison – I was a flashing beacon of redness after the desert hike. Could have guided in passenger jets with this Rudolph face.

I'd arranged to hook up with Alison at the Dubai Marine Club after the palace. No time was set so there was no rush and it allowed me to think through my story.

There was no specific expectation from Alison, just that I'd hopefully return with some kind of reward or gift from the sheikh – and hopefully something suitable for her. There was no expectation either from the Editor. He just wanted to be proud and hear how his journalist and the newspaper had been recognised by the sheikh for their brilliant investigative work.

The sunburn I could pass off in a clichéd pale-skinned Scottish way – explaining that I'd stupidly not put on any sun cream and the palace was so busy with visitors, I had to wait outside in the grounds first for an hour.

At least part of that was true.

I did have to wait an hour… before…

…erm… I was thrown out.

The Marine Club was the go-to beach for the air hostesses and pilots on their days off.

Spotless soft, white sands stretched into the clear turquoise waters and being a members' club, it was never close to being crowded. Most of the time, it felt like your own private beach, with the nearest sunbather hundreds of yards away.

As journos, we were given free membership. The club was regularly hosting cultural and sporting events, which Joe, Davey and I were more than happy to attend and write about. Sometimes, we even felt compelled to go for a swim in the sea after a press conference. It was hard work.

I was really hoping that Alison would be on her own at the club, as I didn't want questioning eyes from her friends boring into my skull as I started to unravel my version of events at the palace.

'Hi, Jimmy,' said Maria, as I walked up to the reception desk, ready to swipe my member's card. Maria, the receptionist, was one of those super-sporty, super-fit Aussie types. The guys all had a crush on her, but knew she only ever dated other Adonis-like athletes, so there was nae chance for any of us.

'Hey, Maria. You good?'

'Yes, thanks,' she replied, looking up from her computer screen.

'Is Alison here?' I asked.

'Yes, yes she is. She's over on the jet-ski side with one of her friends.'

'Thanks.'

Okay, bugger. She's not on her own. Wonder who she's with? At least it's only one pal, I suppose.

I pushed open the glass doors leading out onto the decking area. The mid-afternoon sun was torching the white sands – I'd had enough sun for today, thank you and pulled the baseball cap down further.

The beach was quiet as usual, the silence only broken by the faint booming of a jet ski skimming across the water. Scanning the shore from the deck, I could see Alison in the distance, sitting amongst four empty sunloungers, talking to someone – not one of her stewardess pals, but a guy.

I slowly plodded through the hot sand towards them, squinting, trying to make out who she was with. Thankfully, as I got closer, I could see it wasn't a pilot or worse, Joe – it was just Davey.

I say just, but Davey of course could smooth-talk the knickers off yer granny.

Always clean-shaven with perfectly coiffed dark hair, he had that Cockney swagger and cheeky smile. He may have put on some timber since he came to Dubai, but his hairless and shiny bronzed torso seemed to compensate for that. I'd also put on the pounds over the past few months, but the raspberry-ripple complexion of my body today was not something to show off.

While talking the knickers off yer granny, Davey was also the type who'd sell yer granny for a story. He was a tabloid dog through and through. Unlike me and Joe, who had both come from local newspapers, Davey had freelanced for the red tops of The Sun and The World News back in London.

He was desperate to secure a permanent job at either, but luck never seemed to be on his side and at The World News he'd become a bit of a joke character since his infamous trip to Berlin with Playboy TV.

Hoping to secure the full-time position of Features Writer, he volunteered himself with every press invite or story lead that came through, no matter how gritty or sleazy.

Now, a weekend away with Playboy TV in Berlin may have sounded like a wet dream come true for any journo, but for Davey it turned into a horror show. A horror-sex show.

Playboy TV was filming a series, 'Europe's Hottest Cities', exploring some of the most sordid sex clubs and internet porn channels on the continent, and The World News had agreed to give them some coverage by flying out a journalist.

Keeping costs to a minimum, their team consisted of a local 'fixer', cameraman, a sound-boom jock and then the journalist.

Arriving at one of Berlin's S&M dungeons for filming, it dawned on the crew that shooting before the club opened up to the punters meant there was no subject (victim) to film.

With the cameraman on camera duty and the sound guy on sound-boom duty, all eyes turned to Davey, who was nervously standing there with what now looked like a very immaterial and easily dispensable notebook and pen.

Fast forward ten minutes and Davey was fully gimped up head to toe and strapped to a crucifix. As if that wasn't enough indignation, unbeknown to everyone, the dominatrix re-entered the room for part two of the humiliation and unzipped the flies on his black rubber gimp suit. Expertly holding a burning candle, she slowly tipped it over, dropping hot wax over his petrified pecker.

With the zip on Davey's gimp mask firmly shut, no words were audible – just ascending scales of muffled screams as his body twitched.

Cameraman and boom jock were true professionals. They filmed everything.

Before Davey even arrived back in the office for his next freelancer shift at the News, all the journos, secretaries and the Editor had watched the footage, several times over, in hysterics.

In the weeks that followed, the gags never ended, as his desk mail would be stacked with S&M catalogues, rubber knickers stuffed in his drawer, handcuffs locked onto the back of his chair and then the final nail in his rubber coffin, a visit from The World News's 'Lady Lust'.

Booked by the Features Editor, Lady Lust goose-stepped over to his desk in her revealing police officer's uniform with whip in hand and cuffs. Stomping one of her high-heeled leather boots onto his chair between his legs, she swiftly ripped open his shirt and straddled him. Davey though was not in the mood for a public strip-search and eventually managed to untangle himself, before bolting to the toilets.

He didn't get the full-time job and never bothered asking for more freelance shifts after that.

'Hey, Cola Boy,' Davey shouted over as I approached.

Alison spun round from her sunlounger, then stood up and flung her arms around me, grabbing my face with both hands for a kiss.

'Well…? Well? How was it? asked Alison. How did it go? How was the sheikh? What did he say? Aaaaand… was he generous?'

'Yes, Jimmy mate. I don't want to miss this. What happened?' asked Davey.

I joked off the running late from Alison's that morning, describing the Rolls-Royce and the grandeur of arriving at the palace in this chauffeur-driven luxury.

As planned, I then explained how the sheikh's advisers were very apologetic as I had to wait outside in the grand courtyard for nearly an hour while he personally met with each of 'his subjects'.

'It's his duty as ruler, they said. They had to be prioritised ahead of me. Which was fine. But there was nae offer of sun cream!'

'You Sweaty Socks never learn!' Davey laughed, ribbing me about the ruby face.

Alison winced, looking at my burnt nose sympathetically.

'His room was bloody huge. Like ten times the size of your apartment, Alison. Circular shape with what I assume were his royal advisers seated around the sides. He sat at the top in his plush regal throne with two less fancy chairs placed about 10 feet in front of him.

'One of his guards escorted me to the seat and then stepped back a couple of yards behind.

'I didn't know what to say to him.

'And he didn't say anything at first for what felt like ages.

'Then he said, "As-salam alaykum", and thanked me for saving the animals of the UAE. He said he has a collection of exotic animals himself and breeds tigers at the palace but they are well looked after. He calls them his "children".

'Even takes them for walks and swimming in the sea. Can you believe that?

'He mentioned God a few times. No, a lot of times and how it was God's will that the caged animals were saved by me and the illegal traders will now be punished.'

I paused, sensing now that both Alison and Davey were less interested in the details of what was said and eager to get to the headline of what he offered.

'That was it really... Then just when I thought I was going to be asked to leave he said that I must be rewarded and it was his duty as sheikh to reward 'such honourable actions'. He blessed me in Arabic then turned round and nodded to one of the advisers.

'This dishdashed bloke then walked over and asked me to follow him. I thanked the sheikh. Kinda bowed or nodded really. Not sure if that was the right thing to do, then followed him.

'Turns out this adviser is the Cultural Affairs Minister.

'Rather than giving me an actual gift there and then, he

asked what reward in my eyes would best represent the culture and traditions of the UAE. He said I didn't need to answer now and I can take my time. Then all I have to do is tell Hamza and he'll make the required arrangements with the minister.

'So, we need to think about it.' I smiled at Alison. But Alison was not smiling yet.

'Oh.' She paused, thinking for a few seconds, then: 'But... what does that mean? Culture and traditions of the UAE?'

'A fahkin' camel Jimmy,' Davey butted in, slapping my back. 'Ask for a fahkin' pet camel. Or an oil well, mate.' He laughed.

'Well, we can think about it,' I said. 'Maybe take a trip down to the Gold Souk? Gold, after all, is part of Dubai's culture, isn't it?'

Her eyes lit up and now she smiled.

Knowing just how slowly everything moved in Dubai, I knew I had time on my side with this. Inshallah, like mañana in Spain, was deep-rooted in the culture.

'Will I see you next Tuesday?'

Inshallah.

'Will I get paid at the end of the month?'

Inshallah.

'Will you shower me in riches to impress my girlfriend?'

Inshallah.

And now through naming Hamza as the middleman, I'd created another excuse to further delay any presentation of an actual gift.

'Gold. Nice idea, Jimmy,' Davey said. 'Get yourselves down to the Gold Souk and find something mint for Alison and you're sorted. Maybe a matching collection of watches: one for you, one for Alison and... if you've still got spare change, one for me, mate!'

Alison seemed happy now at the suggestion. Living comfortably in Dubai for three years, there wasn't much she didn't have but she didn't seem to wear much jewellery so maybe this was the best idea.

I'd never been the jewellery-buying type – always too skint for that. The only time I'd bought something that sparkled was for Natalie's 25th when I was desperately trying to impress her. She was layering her expectations on thick, months before her birthday, talking about the new VW Golf her folks were buying her, how her friends were grouping together to whisk her away for a weekend at a beauty spa near Edinburgh and even how she'd invited her ex-fiancé's parents to her birthday 'family do' because they were always 'generous'.

On a reporter's salary, which barely paid my rent and weekends out with the boys, I needed a cash-boost and turned to Andy.

I didn't want a club night full of speed freaks with jittering jaws or moody coke heads so we agreed he would only sell pills, limited to 200 a night and only good shit we'd both tested beforehand. At £20 a go, he could make £4,000 on a busy night. 20% would come to me but out of that £800, I had to look after our head of security to make sure he didn't bust Andy or let any other dealers muscle in on the club.

Two months into our little agreement and I'd more than pocketed the cash needed for Natalie's Tiffany earrings. I had a club full of happy smiley people, a happy Andy, happy head of security and soon to be happy Natalie. Good times.

Two months of this little earner then extended to three, then four, then five… there was no need to stop the happy vibe as the money rolled in.

Outside the club, the coppers just couldn't work it out at first. Most of Aberdeen's 'Sunset Strip' at kicking-out time would be swarming with packs of girls falling over each other, shouting abuse at the police and pissing in the street. Littered among them would be wankered blokes trying to knock ten bells out of each other.

Outside our club night, though, there was no aggro and the coppers would be greeted with hugs, not thugs, at closing time. The loved-up crowd would want to chat and wish them well, rather than wish them 'fuckin' deid, ya cunt'.

My little arrangement with Andy was bloody booming until he bought himself that motorbike...

Davey seemed genuinely pleased that the palace trip had turned out well for me, almost like a friend would. Part of me, though, thought he was secretly wishing me to fail. While friends to an extent, there was always a sense of journalistic rivalry between Joe, Davey and I. While I'd accepted the explanation at the time as a mistake by one of the sub editors, I'd later heard whispers that Joe had stooped to switching my byline for his on the Sheikh Maktoum Humanitarian Award story. It was desperation and jealousy in my eyes, as he was trying to land a 'royal' byline for his own portfolio. That was the week both Davey and Joe's stories were floundering around the middle-to-back pages of the newspaper, while I'd nailed the front page with

ILLEGAL ANIMAL TRADERS ARRESTED IN DRAMATIC POLICE SWOOP by Jimmy Irvine

And then bosh, followed up three days later with another front-pager

SMUGGLERS JAILED IN 5M DHM COUNTERFEIT BUST by Jimmy Irvine

My double whammy of that raid at the warehouse had been bigger than I could have imagined. The Ministry of Interior's counterfeit investigations department had uncovered nearly

2,000 fake Pioneer electrical goods hidden in not just that warehouse but two other warehouses in the industrial park housing counterfeit goods shipped in from China.

Being on first-name terms now with the Deputy General, I was the first and only person in the media he called to give the scoop.

The Editor was loving me and Hamza was even liking me, sending emails of 'excellent work'. Meanwhile, Joe and Davey scurried around like rats, desperate to find their own 'exclusive'.

Davey stood up from the sunlounger. 'Time to go and get my beauty sleep,' he said.

Turned out that Shell and a couple of the other girls had been on the beach with Alison earlier in the afternoon. Davey had joined them just to 'say hello' (in Alison's words – more like 'flirt' in my words), but as soon as Alison told him I was coming here straight after the palace, he'd plonked himself down to get comfortable with the girls and wait.

Thank fuck Davey had never been to the fourth floor, I thought – he'd be like an excitable puppy round those Russians, but would probably leave a bankrupt and broken man. Like that night a couple of months back when he snapped his banjo wire while being ridden by a Nigerian hooker.

Typical Davey – we don't think he knew much about that night. We saw him crawl into a taxi outside the Lodge. Then, according to him, one of the African prostitutes who always targeted the taxi ranks opened the other door and climbed into the backseat with him.

He vaguely remembers her trying to jerk him off in the back of the cab, and then there's a long memory void until he wakes up in screaming pain in his bed, looking down at his blood-soaked cock and a skinny naked ho swiftly dismounting and tut-tutting back at him.

He staggered to the bathroom, squealing with cock in hand, trying to stem the blood with a sock. He didn't come out for half an hour, desperately applying his own first aid, but when he did, the hooker was gone… along with his wallet, his cigarettes and a pair of his Gucci loafers.

No sex or wanking for eight weeks, the doctor told him. He could just about stomach no sex or wanking but losing a pair of his loafers? He'd hit a new low.

Chapter 18

The pressure was off from Alison for at least another week, as she jetted off on a long-haul flight to Sydney. Even on her return, she was unlikely to be in the mood for shopping, as these flights tended to make her tired and miserable.

After a couple of days sleeping and not wanting to see me or anyone else, she'd usually be back to her spritely gorgeous self, inviting me over to make up for lost – or rather lust – time.

Then, before you knew it, she'd be off again, on a bungee to Jo'burg or London. It was an unforgiving and relentless job, but selfishly I didn't really have much sympathy. Every time I lay in her bed, looking around at her stunning apartment, hearing her stories of staying in four-star luxury hotels in exotic locations and the alien concept to a journalist of receiving a 'company bonus', I thought: 'This is a fuckin' good life.'

Then I'd turn over, running my fingers over the small of her back, gradually working down to her sweet, rosy-white butt cheeks, and slowly slip inside her as she started to groan.

'Aye, Jimmy, this is nae a bad life.'

■ ■ ■

Since the night Shell had revealed her little covert operation with Joe and Ali, Shell had certainly been a happy girl, especially for those few days after her London flights when they paid her.

Shell was building an obsession with shoes and bags and Joe. Not sure where he stood in that top three, but he was certainly her ticket to happiness, something Alison said she was desperate for after that Scouser-cunt boyfriend had bashed her about back home.

On the nights that I was at their apartment, when Shell triumphantly returned from her Heathrow flights, we were all treated to a little reward, as she was more than generous in dishing out the powder for a 'wee celebration, Jimmy', she'd say in her mock Scottish-Scouse accent.

The machine for Shell did indeed seem to be well-oiled.

Now it was time for me to have a chat with Ali.

I'd never asked him where he got his gear from. It was always unspoken gratitude on my part as he left a wrap under the decks on the nights I DJ'd on the fourth floor. He knew my vice was gak not girls… unlike Joe, who was feasting on both.

It was not for me to mention it to Alison or Shell, but on the nights they were away flying with AWA, Joe was entertaining and being entertained at his usual table on the fourth floor.

Like the first time I spotted him there, he'd be cosied up to a girl on the couch, hands wandering around their thighs, stopping every five minutes to hoover a line off the table.

Unlike the other punters, though, he never ventured down to Apartment 13 with them hand in hand. They'd stay at the table downing champagne for a couple of hours, fool around with some heavy petting, then they'd get up, he'd shake hands with Ali and leave.

These girls weren't like the sour-faced, stick-thin Russkies, though. They looked more friendly, more natural, more bubbly, more… Arabian World… And they were AWA air hostesses.

It was a ticking time bomb to when Shell would find out – one that I didn't want to witness, as I knew both of them were fiery and wouldn't hold back on launching into a full-scale verbal or physical attack. I decided the best plan would be to play dumb and deny all knowledge if either Shell or Alison came probing.

The best time to talk to Ali about his operation was not when I was on the ching and topped up on Budweisers behind the decks, so I knew I had to find him fresh in the morning before heading off to work.

Like clockwork, 'Mr 7am' seemed my best bet to catch him, so I set my alarm for 6:15am allowing plenty of time to freshen up, gee myself up for making a bold proposal and then 'coincidentally' bump into the two of them downstairs in reception.

As usual, the lift was empty as I headed down to the ground floor at 6:56. The doors opened, and I stepped out into the reception as the glare of the sun pierced through the glass front doors and radiated off the lustrous marble floor.

I lit a Marlboro and leaned against the concierge desk, waiting. The office door behind was slightly ajar and at first there was nothing to see in there, but then I spotted hands moving in and out of the two-inch view. Hands grasping piles of banknotes on the table and neatly packing them into a briefcase.

6:58. Fuck. Better stand back. Don't want them to think I've been watching.

I retreated back into the lift, holding down the button to keep the doors open, ready to make my entrance again at 07:00.

Then bingo. At 07:00 on the dot, I heard their voices approach the office door and I stepped out of the lift.

'As-salam alaykum.'

'Wa alaikum as-salam,' we greeted each other.

'Jimmy, good morning. You are well?' Ali asked as he nodded to 'Mr 7am' who, without acknowledging me, started walking out of the reception towards the front doors.

'I'm good, Ali. Good.'

'And your girl, Alison, is she good?'

'Yes, Ali, she is good. Off on a flight now for a few days, though, so won't see her for a bit.'

This was my moment, so without any further small talk, I bluntly segued into: 'Actually, I wanted to talk to you about her. A favour. Perhaps we could have a chat about it, if yer free?'

'Of course, my friend, of course. Come, come,' he waved me into the office. I followed him behind the counter and he beckoned me over to take a seat as he closed the office door.

This wasn't a typical working office. There were no filing cabinets, no pictures on the walls, no stationery or mini-calendars on his desk, and no window. There was just a plain, wooden-topped desk with metal legs and a grubby cream coloured telephone placed on the side. Behind that, there was a well-aged and slightly bashed steel safe with a small mini-fridge placed on top. Two chairs were positioned either side of the table, one swivelled with an extended back like the crew have in Star Trek, which was obviously his, and the other just one of those cheap plastic conference-type chairs that get stacked up in their hundreds after events.

We sat down and Ali flicked open his cigarette pack, offering a Marlboro Red. We both sparked up and inhaled for a few seconds.

I'd decided that I didn't want to probe too deep into his operation, preferring to be ignorant about his dealings should anything go wrong. I didn't need to know all the details of how he and Joe worked with the AWA crew and how much gear was coming back into the UAE from London and how often.

This was going to be a one-off request. A quick hit, just to get some extra cash so I could buy Alison the 'sheikh's gift'.

'She is a special girl, Ali, my Alison. And she has a special birthday coming up – her 30th," I lied. "I gotta get her something amazing, something that sparkles, something that she'll never forget, something that'll make her and her friends go 'wow'. But, the problem is Ali I get paid a shit salary and this special 'wow' lives down at the Gold Souk.'

Ali kept his eyes fixed on me, listening and not giving anything away in his facial expression.

It dawned on me, just as the words started flowing out in the next sentence, that while Alison, Shell and I had all become used to Shell's Class A jaunts back and forth to Heathrow, maybe Ali didn't know she'd openly confided in us. He certainly wouldn't know we all enjoyed sampling his goods on her return as well.

But it was too late. I was off and couldn't find the verbal handbrake. I started talking about Shell.

'... this well-oiled machine, she says... So, I thought I could meet your man Omar when I head back to London and help give a little boost to next month's operation. I only need to do it once, just so I can get this extra cash. What do you think?'

Ali remained stony-faced, with no sign of his usual charismatic smile and upbeat friendly chat. He sat in silence behind his desk, stubbing out his cigarette and lighting another.

Then.

'Jimmy...' He paused.

'...Jimmy.' He paused again, tapping the ash off his cigarette.

'...The Scottish DJ.' He said slowly, mulling over his thoughts.

'You come, you play and I look after you. I always look after you. We both make people happy. You provide the music, I provide the girls and... yes, some other extras which you also enjoy.

'It works because we all know what we are here for and what we have to do. We know what we are good at and stick to that. And most importantly, we stay silent. Only a select number of people know what we do.

'It also works, Jimmy, because Shell is cabin crew and a woman. You are not a woman, Jimmy, and you are not cabin crew. How will you do this?'

While not quite having the Pablo Escobar qualifications of international drug smuggling on any scale, I did have a once-tried and once-succeeded method on a UK domestic flight back to Aberdeen after a post-club party in London.

Not wishing to miss out on a bargain, Andy and I had acquired a bag of pills one fucked-up twisty morning at half price in a bedsit just round the corner from our heavy night at Heaven in Charing Cross. Knowing we could sell at a decent profit back home, we brazenly walked to the TSB cash machine with our friendly dealer at 7am and made our exchange.

We spent the next few hours at the B&B before our flight back (yes, a flight this time as we'd had a particularly profitable month at our own club night), carefully unsealing the cellophane around the newly acquired 12" records, dropping the pills inside the covers and then resealing.

'Records,' I said. 'I need to buy some new ones in London for your night anyway. And the best place to hide the gear is in the records. They won't look. The last time, the customs guy actually held my bag of records in his hand. There were 30 pills inside the sleeves. Still holding onto the bag, he took them out one by one and he started chatting to me about how much he loves the Strictly Rhythm label while waving me through the scanner.

'Was more interested in where I'd played and what music was going down well.

'Coming back here, though, if I then seal them up in a metal record box, there's no way they'll be detected or sniffed out by the dogs.'

Finally, Ali cracked a smile, laughed and stood up.

'Music is the answer, eh, Jimmy? We have an Arabic saying here, Jimmy: "If you're afraid, don't do it. And if you're doing it, don't be afraid." Are you afraid, Jimmy?'

'No, not afraid, Ali. Wasn't before and won't be this time,' I replied, trying to sound confident while a little voice of doubt raised its ugly head in the back of my mind.

'More afraid of a pissed-off Alison,' I said, laughing, trying now to make it all sound as casual as sneaking in extra duty-free fags.

'OK, Jimmy. You leave it with me. I think. And I'll come back to you. Inshallah.'

He motioned towards the door, changing the subject to horse racing and next week's Dubai Gold Cup.

'My favourite sport, horse-racing. You should go, Jimmy. You might win. You might make some of that much-needed money.' He slapped my back jokingly.

He left me at the reception, turning back to wait for the lift while I headed out to the car replaying over and over in my head what I'd said, questioning whether I'd come across as a complete fanny or just a desperate and naive idiot.

Had I said too much about Shell? Too much about Omar? Too much about me?

I couldn't read him. One minute he's looking stern and silent, the next he's laughing and slapping me on the back.

Maybe he thinks I'm a joker or just a fuckin' joke?

Chapter 19

'We have a problem. No, actually *you* have a problem, Joe,' Ali said firmly.

Joe put down his cold beer and pushed his sunglasses up onto his head.

'Go on,' he said leaning forward over the sun-kissed bar table at the Hyatt Regency pool.

Ali also leaned in keeping his Ray-Bans on.

'Your girl, Shell – she's been talking. Talking a lot. Talking to Jimmy and his woman, Alison. Jimmy knows about Omar and Shell's little shopping trips back and forward to London. Knows so much about it, he wants to do it! Thinks it's easy.'

'What? Why would he want to do it?' Joe asked.

'Same as everyone. The money. He needs the money. Wants to buy jewellery for Alison. He is a weak man doing this. You buy jewellery only for the right woman. And Alison is not the right woman… Is she, Joe?'

Joe remembered when he first set eyes on Alison. It wasn't a boozy, cross-eyed and legless one down at the Lodge; it was at an AWA press event at the Hyatt Regency three years ago.

He was writing for the Khaleej Times back then and AWA were announcing a new addition to their fleet, the as-yet unnamed 'Airbus FFF' – a double-decked aircraft for 900 passengers with an inflight bar, games room and gym (for the luxury class only of course).

Alison was one of the air hostesses on parade, standing to attention in full Arabian World uniform at the side of the press-room podium and then serving drinks to guests after the big announcement.

With every drink she offered, Joe switched on the Geordie charm, but she didn't reciprocate much, remaining professional and polite before moving on to the other guests.

That didn't stop him tracking her down though. He spent the next few weeks patrolling the Dubai Marine Club beach like a friggin' lifeguard, scanning all the cabin crew as they sunbathed. Then, eventually, he 'coincidentally' bumped into her at the beach bar and unsurprisingly, she remembered the loud, obnoxious but funny Geordie.

They were chalk and cheese, but somehow, he managed to woo her with laughter into bed after a few nights out in Dubai.

She was classy, he thought. A 'posh lass', he'd say to Ali, and not one to be blindly coerced into their expanding operation with Omar back in London. He wanted to keep her away from all that. She was different from the other girls. Smarter. Less naive.

The definition of posh for Joe was 'not having a Geordie accent and your parents owning a detached house'. But Alison was not really that posh, just well-spoken, with a soft, southern accent. Her parents were distinctly middle class – both teachers and heads of departments at private schools in Kent. Life at home was certainly comfortable for her. She didn't have to want for anything, and being the only child, she was always spoiled and definitely a 'daddy's girl'.

But the more she got, the more she wanted, and like a magpie, was attracted to shiny new things.

One shiny new thing in particular out here was also her

downfall. A shiny new thing with a shiny bank balance. A balance so shiny the number of zeros in it could be worn as a necklace.

Fahad Zaheri, one of Sheikh Muhammed Al Zaheri's many cousins had also been enchanted by Alison's looks and English sophistication. And like many of the girls before and after her, what a royal family member wants, a royal family member gets.

After clocking her at another AWA corporate event, Fahad instructed his 'representatives' to approach her. No air hostess had ever turned down a royal come-on and Alison was no different.

She didn't dare tell Joe, flattered at the beginning, thinking it was part of her AWA duty to accept private dinner invitations at his palace. But after a couple of cordial evening dates, she was soon sucking the golden cock of royalty. Not wishing any of her colleagues to know, she refused to accept any of his flamboyant gifts and instead duly shared her bank details. She was on the game, but didn't want to admit it.

For two months, she lied to Joe, claiming to be back and forth on long-haul flights while she was actually relaxing on Fahad's private Sharjah beach by day and rocking the royal bed by night.

Inevitably, the fun times ended, though, once Fahad extended his bed invitations to a ménage à trois – not with another girl, but with one of his trusted representatives. While Alison tried to convince herself the prince genuinely adored her when it was just the two of them and the money was a generous gift rather than 'payment', being pounded by a 20-stone, sweating, hairy-backed, hairy-arsed Arab while Fahad jerked off over her face only meant one thing – she was meaningless, a commodity to be bought, used and discarded.

Joe had no sympathy when she broke down in tears confessing everything. He didn't want to be near her. In his eyes, she'd committed the cardinal sin for expat British girls: 'fucking an Arab for money'.

'Fuck you. And fuck off,' was his considered response.

So, like Fahad, Joe also sharply discarded her, knowing there were plenty more air hostesses in this town for him to play with.

That night at Champions Bar, followed by Joe's infamous taxi surfing, was the first time he'd actually spoken to her since he told her to 'fuck off'. But he didn't care; his eyes were set on Shell. He'd play the game and didn't give a fuck about Alison.

'Ah fook. Stupid cow. What the fook's she doing, blabbin' all that to Jimmy and Alison?' Joe said, responding to Ali.

Ali reclined back into his chair, pondering and looking out across the swimming pool, now busy with tourists and business folk on their days off. He turned back round to Joe.

'A single mistake ensures a double misfortune Joe. That's what I always say, isn't it? And the old Arab proverb is always right. Shell is on the mistake side and we sit on the misfortune end. I do not want to be on the side of misfortune Joe,' he said forcefully as his face reddened.

Joe knew that the two key success-factors in their little drugs racket were secrecy and monetary. They underpinned everything. The chosen AWA girls knew not to say anything to anyone – not to boyfriends, girlfriends or flatmates. And, in return, they'd get paid and make the money they wanted. And, again, they were warned not to attract suspicion by splashing their cash too often on anything too showy.

Two very simple principles. But now here was Shell breaking the most important one: secrecy, sworn secrecy.

Only one other stewardess had broken their trust since they started their operations: an Aussie, who on return from London with a mere 20g missed her scheduled drop-off with Joe.

For 48 hours, Joe tried to track her down, asking her flat-mates and other cabin crew in the bars, but she was nowhere to be found. Then he discovered that her boyfriend had also gone AWOL, not turning up for his cheffing shifts at the Radisson Blu Hotel.

Ali was incandescent with rage, as each hour went by with-out knowing where she was or where his gear had gone. Joe of all people had to keep him calm as they continued their casual questioning of cabin crew around the pools and beaches for days.

It took a week before word started filtering back to them that the couple had quit their jobs and fled Dubai overnight. A pilot later confirmed they'd been on standby for one of his flights and they'd flown to Hong Kong the day after she'd come back from London.

A couple of weeks after that, the rumours were flying around cabin crews that she'd discovered she was pregnant, which for an unmarried couple is illegal in the UAE. A combination of 20g and a foetus up her fanny, with the prospect of a double jail term-whammy if caught, had unsurprisingly forced her to panic and bolt.

Nobody knew what they'd done with Ali's cocaine. Had they sold it? Hidden it? Flushed it? Taken it with them?

Ali was not someone to leave any loose ends and made some enquiries of his own in Hong Kong. And let's just say, like a baby, the boyfriend was soon left being spoon-fed puréed food by hos-pital staff for a month after Ali's contacts had tracked them down.

Joe liked Shell. The sex was the best he'd ever had and she was the only girl to date that let him take her up the arse without resistance or him paying for it. She was also the only one who'd asked him for a golden shower. On both occasions, they were fucked out of their minds and fucking out of their minds. Lying naked in the bath at 7 in the morning without any sleep from the night before, she asked him in and pleaded with him to piss all over her.

Even for Joe this was a bit fucked up and didn't arouse him in any way, but Shell was in her own pleasure dome, writhing around with her eyes closed, smearing his piss all over her tits and face as he stood at the side of the bath, spraying his waterfall all over her.

The second time, they were on acid after one of Ali's contacts brought back some Double Dip Strawberries from Hong Kong. She went all fuckin' animalistic on him that night, getting down naked on all fours, snarling at him like a tiger. They hadn't even had any foreplay, let alone fucked, at this point and roleplay was not something that came naturally to Joe. He struggled to think of an appropriate animal to mimic as Shell's body warped and morphed into part-human, part-tiger.

Gorilla? Lion? Monkey? Was he a monkey? Could a monkey fuck a tiger? He was tripping his nut off. Thankfully, Shell didn't want any fucking at that point. But she did want monkey piss sprayed all over her, which he just about managed to do.

Took them about five days to come down from the acid and neither of them spoke about it again.

But despite the sex adventures with Shell, he knew this was a tightly run profitable business with Ali and, if some discipline was needed, then no amount of fucked-up sex would get in the way of doing what was needed to restore obedience.

'Leave it with me, Ali,' he said.

Ali sat in silence, mulling over a number of scenarios. Scenarios of misfortune.

Misfortune for him.

He no longer trusted Shell. And wasn't sure about Jimmy and Alison either.

'Lahore?' Ali said menacingly, deepening his tone.

'Lahore?' Joe replied worriedly, pausing before trying to reel Ali back in from doing anything rash. 'No, not Lahore, Ali. Let me deal with it here first. We don't need Lahore yet.'

Ali contemplated for a minute, rolling an unlit cigarette back and forth between his fingers, then gave a slight nod.

'You will fix this Joe, my friend. I know you will.'

Joe knew he had to fix it, but wasn't sure yet what to do.

Ali stood up and left, leaving Joe to finish his beer and think.

Chapter 20

'Hello, gorgeous,' I said, as I gave her a hug and a smacker on the lips.

Alison had returned from Sydney a couple of days before but, as always, was jet-lagged and exhausted, so I'd left her alone to recover, resisting the temptation to ring her. I knew by now anyway she always unplugged the phone by her bed, not wanting to be disturbed when she got back from the long hauls.

We now had a couple more days together before her next flight. Surprisingly, she didn't want to just chill out on the beach as she usually did – she wanted to head to the races, the Dubai World Cup. For the first time in years, she wasn't being asked to work there representing AWA and had a couple of complimentary tickets.

With comps that granted access to the sponsors' lounge and free champers, we spruced ourselves up for what is Dubai's biggest and most glamorous sporting event of the year. The great and good of the horsing world descend on Dubai for this annual meet, which, since launching three years earlier, had become the world's richest horse race, with £1.4m going into the pocket of the winner.

I looked out the trusted (okay, the only) linen suit, trying not to think about the last time I wore it. It was clean (ish) – well, the sweat patches had at least dried out since that desert trek from the palace. I ironed out a few of the big creases and sprayed some Joop! aftershave over the jacket. A more casual affair this time rather than a royal appointment, I decided to finish off the look with the white Stan Smith green tabs.

When I stepped out of the taxi at the AWA staff building, the suit was of course creased to fuck, making me look like I was wearing a crumpled paper bag. Art nouveau chic was not the intended look.

Alison was waiting inside the air-conditioned reception area. She really was a cracker. Stylish and sexy, she was wearing a light-salmon, wrap-belted dress. Sleeveless, it showed off her slender, tanned shoulders, while the front had a plunged V-neck that still retained her modesty. Her Louis Vuitton clutch bag matched the gold LV logo on the belt and her sparkly gold high heels completed the look. No doubt the heels were designer as well, but without a logo on them, I couldn't tell a Dior from a Debenhams.

With her hair tightly tied back like those girls in *that* Robert Palmer video, she really did look like a model and standing up on those pencil-thin heels, she was now above my height, of 6'.

ABERDEEN LOON OUT OF HIS DEPTH WITH SUPERMODEL GIRLFRIEND

... the local paper would mock.

At this point, I really wished I'd unpicked the Burton logo off my inside jacket pocket. I made a note to myself: don't take the jacket off today. Don't let her see the logo. The closest to designer luxury was my Stans and white Lacoste T-shirt but I suspected that both of those combined wouldn't come anywhere close to the cost of her tiny Louis Vuitton clutch bag.

The racing programme started early at 8.30am but the main event, the World Cup race, was in the evening at 7.15pm. We wanted to make sure we made the most of the freebies on offer, so had planned to be there at 2pm.

Alison had arranged to meet her other cabin-crew pals at the Rolex lounge. When we stepped out of the taxi just after 2pm, it felt like I'd walked into a Harrods theme park.

Rolex, Veuve Clicquot, Moët, Mercedes, Cartier, Omega and Patek Philippe all had branded feather flags fluttering in the wind, as throngs of perfectly groomed guests mingled and quaffed champagne in the corporate lounges underneath.

Sharp blazer and open-collared shirt was the uniformed look of the guys, accompanied by some eye-candy, of course, on their arms (paid-for or not, who knows?). I was doing well with one of those, but instantly felt conscious of probing eyes questioning the mismatch of the Lady And The Tramp as we walked among them.

Stans were certainly outnumbered by loafers and my T-shirt/crumpled linen jacket combo was certainly not sharp. I wasn't fooling anyone into thinking I was wealthy or belonged here, not even in that ironic scruffy kinda way that some millionaires like to do.

Back home, I loved a beige buffet, especially the ones my mum would make: mini-sausage rolls, sausages on a stick, mini-vol-au-vents, ham sandwiches cut up into little triangles, garlic bread and crisps. Loads of crisps; onion rings, salt & vinegar Chipsticks and cheesy Wotsits were de rigueur for any family celebration in the Irvine household.

Here, though, there wis nae sign of a Scottish buffet. Instead, I was faced with 'canapés' or 'cana-fuckin-naes' more like, as I passed on the oysters, then the sushi (cold fish? What the fuck?), then the scallops, then the prawns. No, thank you.

I was necking the champers as a substitute for food, watching the waitresses like a hawk as they came in with new platters, praying that there'd be some hot meat or potato stodge on one of these trays. But every time my hopes were raised, they'd come crashing down when I heard, 'Some sushi, sir?'

Alison of course was a different class and would daintily pick one piece of sushi and then a scallop or a prawn. Wisely, she gave the oysters a miss. I'd heard too many stories of folk being ruined for days after eating a dodgy oyster, so didn't blame her.

'You not hungry?' she asked.

'Not really. Not yet. Had something to eat just before I headed over to yours,' I lied.

Alison's AWA pals were lookers, of course – well, most of them bar one Welsh lass, who was a bit too peely-wally and ginger to be out in the afternoon sunshine. I couldn't help but notice the criss-crossed, painfully red tan lines on her exposed back from where she'd been switching bikini tops. She looked uncomfortable, probably wishing she was sitting outside a Caernarfon cafe in October rather than standing here in 30°C desert heat.

The five Arabian World lasses were joined by a couple of pilots, Rob and Neil, both English and both from the home counties – Surrey and Buckinghamshire. They gave me a slightly sniffy look up and down as Alison introduced us. That look of 'he's clearly not one of us', 'he could've ironed his suit first' and probably 'what the fuck is she doing with him?'

They'd also been diving headfirst into the free champers so the banter among the group was in full flow.

Alison leaned into the girls and started chatting, leaving me standing there wondering what the fuck I was going to say to these pilots. What would we have in common apart from just being here in Dubai?

I was really hoping she wouldn't but then she did. She

glanced over her shoulder to the three of us and said, 'He's been to the palace, you know. Getting a reward from the sheikh. Tell them, Jimmy, tell them,' before swinging back round into the chuckling craic of the girls, leaving me hanging on a story I really didn't want to tell.

'The palace? Now, that's pretty special. What did you do to deserve that?' asked Rob.

I wasn't going to go into all the fine details so kept it quite blasé and top line. Neil had checked out of the story anyway before it began, as I saw his eyes drifting over to one of the girls with Alison. Rob, in fairness, seemed more interested – well, at least kept the conversation going. Turned out he was a bit of a big-cat lover, having visited sanctuaries in India and Africa during his piloting travels.

I wasn't a big-cat lover, of course. 'I just wanted the scoop and would do anything to get that story.' Maybe I shouldn't have actually said that so bluntly, but I did. Kinda came out in a defensive way – feebly trying to show that my job had a harder edge to it than a pilot. A harder, more serious edge as a pilot flying 500 passengers at 40,000 feet in a metal tin over the Indian Ocean? Who was I kidding?

Rob nodded back, making no comment, before his unimpressed eyes started to wander as well.

All three of us reached for the champagne flutes as the waitress walked by, taking a couple of sips to break the awkward silence.

Then Neil piped up. He looked older than the rest of us, maybe late 30s, early 40s, sculpted cheekbones with a neatly groomed side-parting that was starting to reveal hints of greyness.

'I had an invitation to the palace once before as well, Jimmy. Sheikh Maktoum's palace in Dubai,' he said. 'Not Zaheri's.'

He turned to Rob, patting him on the shoulder.

'Now, Rob's heard this of course 100 times. But back in '94, we had an emergency landing at Dubai airport. We'd been battered around by a lightning storm then on descent, the landing wheels failed and we had to make a belly touchdown at 150mph.'

Here we fuckin' go. Superhero pilot stories to top everyone.

'I'm well drilled on these, of course, so the landing was no big deal for me, but the shuddering impact and tracer sparks flying all around the body of the plane sent all the passengers into a screaming panic. When we finally came to a halt and everyone realised everything was okay – i.e. they were alive – they all burst into applause.

'Then they were crying and hugging themselves and the cabin crew.

'Routine, as I said, but what was different this time was that the UAE football team was on board. Returning from a World Cup qualifier against Jordan.

'Some then knelt in the aisle. Praising God. Praising me.'

By this time, Alison and the girls had turned around, hanging on every word he spoke like the fuckin' Messiah.

'I got on the PA and thanked everyone 'for flying Arabian World Airlines today. Hope you enjoyed your fright.' A line which was met with laughter and more applause.'

Alison and the girls also laughed... in a hypnotic cult worshipper kinda way. 'Neil-fuckin-Manson' here could have the pick of any of these "wives" tonight,' I thought, glancing across their beaming faces.

'One needs a bit of dark humour in these situations,' he said smugly, smiling at the girls. 'Relaxes everyone. Then it turned out that the whole of the UAE football team and the manager recommended me for a commendation to Sheikh Maktoum.

Fast forward a couple of weeks and I'm sitting in his palace, sharing a cup of Arabic tea with him.'

Neil paused then unlatched his watch. A stainless-steel Rolex, green face and chunky. He turned it over and showed his wide-eyed disciples the inscription on the back.

April 08, 1994.

Forever grateful.

The Citizens of the United Arab Emirates.

'Wow,' said Alison, for the first time ever really pissing me off with just that one word.

I wanted to snap my fingers in her face and bring her back into the room but knew I had to play along with their holy saviour holding court for now.

'A small token of his thanks,' Neil proudly said, while letting everyone admire the watch in the palm of his hand.

Thankfully, he ended the story there, but of course in a way only a pilot could: 'Ladies, it's just all in a day's work of a pilot and cabin crew, isn't it?'

He then chinked everyone's glass and they gave a small cheer. Anticipating the impending awkwardness of being missed out on his toast, I sharply turned the other way and instinctively grabbed an hors d'oeuvre from the passing waitress's tray, washing it down with what was left of my champers.

Oh fuck. What the hell! Trying not to instantly gag all over them, I grabbed another flute of champagne and necked that.

But shit... I quickly stepped to the side and covered my mouth with my hand as an almighty champagne burp came shooting up my windpipe, trying to burst through my firmly clenched cheeks.

'You OK, mate?' Neil asked, as Alison also clocked me with a raised eyebrow.

'Oys... fuckin'... oyste...'

Uncontrollably, my body lurched forward, unleashing a tsunami of vomit over Neil's perfectly pressed blazer and shirt. Then, again, the second wave quickly followed. Trying my best to get the shell-shocked Neil out of my firing line, I bent down but unfortunately for him, jet hosed his designer loafers and up his trouser legs.

I swivelled away, hunched over and shuffled towards the back of the Rolex stand to find some shelter.

Breathe… Breathe… Breathe…

I could hear lots of screaming from the girls, followed by 'Fucking wanker! You fucking arsehole,' as Neil bellowed abuse in my direction.

I then felt a tender hand gently rub my back.

'What happened, babe?'

It was Alison.

I couldn't talk. Not yet anyway. I just wanted to stay hunched and motionless, fearful for another belly eruption at any second.

'FUCKING WANKER. HE'S A FUCKING WANKER. RUINED. FUCKING RUINED. RUINED. MY FUCKING LOAFERS. MY GUCCI LOAFERS. HE'S GOING TO FUCKING PAY. PAY FOR IT.'

I could still hear Neil incessantly unleashing F-bombs at me, as waitresses fussed around him with wet cloths, trying to make the best of what was an impossible task.

By this point, his flock of stewardesses had stepped back several feet from him, as the stench of champagne-oyster sick had become increasingly unbearable.

Alison wiped a cool damp cloth across my forehead and neck, telling me to 'breathe slowly… breathe slowly… breathe…'

The commotion behind started to die down, as Neil was led away by Rob and a couple of the waitresses. And just like Moses, he managed to part the sea of people in front of him, as the racing crowd stood back, gasping, covering their mouths and then swiftly their noses.

That was the last we saw of Neil at the races.

I, on the other hand, after a 40-minute sit down of back-rubbing from Alison, scoofing bottles of water and breathing exercises, got my second wind and was soon back on that horse, so to speak.

A cold lager (Budweiser, still no sign of Tennent's) followed, and that soon steadied the stomach and legs. Without any visible signs of vomit and no stench of sick breath thanks to Alison's spearmint gum (so that's what's in her tiny clutch bags), we were ready to mingle again as if nothing had happened.

The watching AWA crew had moved through the emotions of initial shock and horror to now sympathy and laughter. Sympathetic because 'we've all been there at one point, Jimmy, with oysters' and laughter because 'My loafers. My loafers. He's ruined my Gucci loafers.' Neil's outburst and mournful crying for his vomit-stained loafers was now being imitated and repeated with eye-watering howls, as our drinks flowed into the evening.

What is it with guys and their bloody loafers out here?

Chapter 21

Our day at the races certainly became a talking point amongst the AWA crews. Turned out that Neil was well known around Dubai, having flown for AWA for five years and before that British Airways for six.

He'd pretty much screwed his way through both airlines' roster of stewardesses, pausing briefly for two marriages, but both of those failed quickly as temptation was just too great to resist when he found himself in an exotic location, thousands of miles away from home, surrounded by glamorous 20-somethings.

Definitely a ladies' man and used to getting his own way, I had no sympathy for his embarrassing exit from the races and neither did anyone else by the sounds of it.

Ironically, Neil's boastful story of 'saving' those passengers and his gift from the sheikh had done me a favour. I now had an inkling of the value of a royal reward and how much cash I'd need.

His Rolex I was guessing was worth about £10k... It was given to him by the sheikh of a far wealthier emirate than Sharjah... and he'd fuckin' saved lives, human lives. I, on the other hand, had saved cats, birds and monkeys, and was being rewarded by the Steptoe of sheikhs.

So, £2k, maybe £3k at a push, would probably do it.

It was time to pay the Gold Souk a visit with Alison.

I hadn't been back since I'd tracked down Beaky, but I revelled in the opportunity to describe the operation to Alison as we walked through the bustling market.

I recounted the conversations with traders, explaining the ruse about my father to Alison before eventually leading her to the alley where Beaky's shop was. I didn't want to get too close, though, for fear of being identified, as I could see ahead there were still bird cages stacked outside the store, so someone was still trading.

Alison seemed interested in the blow-by-blow detail but maybe I was just kidding myself. She was probably wishing we'd just scoot along to the shopping bit. And eventually, we did.

With £3k in my head but only '£2k' coming out of my mouth to Alison, we started scanning the shop windows. This was a painfully slow process as Alison gazed into the glittering treasure troves on display, scrutinising every single ring, bracelet, necklace and pair of earrings she could see.

I wasn't expecting the Poirot-like deliberations and questions about each item of jewellery, and tried to encourage (hurry) her along by pointing out what I thought looked good.

She didn't really respond to my suggestions, just the odd 'hmm' or 'uh, huh' as she stood mesmerised peering through the glass of each window display.

Then, like a golden lightning bolt, it came from nowhere.

She fluttered her hazelnut brown eyes at me and said: 'Surprise me. You choose.'

And then....

'But a ring might be nice.'

She squeezed my hand and looked into my eyes, before planting a tender kiss on my lips.

'You, you want me... to choose?' I asked hesitantly.

'Yes, Jimmy. I love surprises. Aaaaaand I've given you some clues. Now come on, let's go. Back to mine.' She spun away from the window and pulled my hand.

Fuck. I was shaken, confused, silent, numb, the whole lot – like I'd been blindsided by a Tyson punch and the world had twisted into a muddled daze. What did this all mean?

I was hoping she'd just point out some earrings or a bracelet and then, bang, I'd be back here with the money in a few weeks and job done – 'Shukran, Mr Sheikh!'

But no, this was bigger… a ring? She'd raised the stakes in a way only women can – that way which fuses the wires in your brain, breaking the mainframe of man's binary emotional intelligence system. 'CODE REDS' were flashing all over the place in my head and I didn't have time to flick through the help manual as she excitedly continued talking in the taxi all the way back to her apartment.

She bounded in through the front door as I walked behind, slower and still flustered as my brain processor kept churning out conclusions that I didn't want to hear.

'Areeeeet, Cola Boy!' came the familiar voice.

From the hallway, I could see Joe's silhouette on the living room sofa lit up by the sunshine streaming in through the balcony glass doors.

Shell, in an oversized pink Benetton sweatshirt, was sitting next to him on the sofa. But not snuggled in like she usually was. This time there was a noticeable distance between the two. She was more snuggled into the sofa armrest than Joe, with her legs curled up onto the cushions, one hand tucked between her legs, the other holding a cigarette drooped over the ashtray on the side table.

'Grab a beer, man.' He pointed towards the fridge, as I

walked into the room. 'And sit doon, both of youz. We got a lot to talk aboot.'

Alison and I plumped ourselves on the opposite sofa facing Joe and Shell. I moved Alison's Cosmo magazine off the pile of other mags and used it as a coaster for the beer against what I'd been told was a very expensive glass coffee table – a gift, apparently, from Alison's uncle, she'd once told me.

Alison clearly was in a different world, a world of unicorns and fairy tales, and wasn't reading the room as she blurted out:

'Oh my God. You're going to make an announcement!' she said, eagerly clasping her hands together and leaning forward towards Joe and Shell.

Shell didn't respond, lowering her eyes towards the floor. Alison paused, glanced at me then looked back at Joe and Shell, winding back in her overly zealous assumption.

'Ha, ha! Good one, Alison. Nah, lass, you don't need to go buying a hat and I'm no Cilla Black.

'Look. We've all known each other now for a fair while – what seven, eight months, eh? We get on well, we've had some good nights oot in toon and parties up at the fourth floor. Fook, man, we're even friends, eh?

He paused, looking for a nod of agreement in return. Alison stared at Joe not sure how to respond; I gave a silent nod of the head, wondering where he was going with this.

'But sometimes, even among friends, there have to be secrets.' He held his gaze on Alison for a few seconds then turned to Shell, placing his hand on her lap. She flinched but let his hand rest there.

'Now, Shell, bless her, has told me she's regrettably shared one of our secrets with you two. A very precious secret between me and Shell. You know, the one about her special deliveries from London.'

Fuck. Fuck. Fuck. I've fuckin' royally dropped her in it, haven't I?

I didn't want to make eye contact with Shell, as the guilt started to consume me as I played over in my head the meeting with Ali and what I'd said.

Fuckin' idiot. Shouldn't have mentioned her. Should have kept her out of it.

'Ah,' I said.

'Ahhh fookin' ah indeed, Cola Boy. We have a well-oiled little operation here, you see, and we don't want anything to ruin that,' Joe said. 'It's a very tight circle. On a need-to-know basis and Ali doesn't tolerate fuck-ups.

'Now, you two didn't need to know. But now, thanks to Shell, you do. So, we now need to make sure nobody else knows. Do you understand?'

His eyes narrowed as he held his stare on both of us. 'No loose chat. You say nothing to anyone. No fuck-ups. Absolutely no fuck-ups. Ali doesn't fuck around if someone fucks up.'

'Joe, it's cool. We're not going to say anything. And we haven't said anything. We know the score,' I said, trying to reassure him.

'Ha! He likes you, Jimmy. Seems to like you a lot... Must be your choice of tunes.'

He finally broke into a smile, then swigged from his beer.

'Actually, he wants to chat to you tonight when you get back to your apartment so you better pop into the office to see him.

'Me and Shell had a little chat about all of this earlier and Shell won't be saying nowt to anyone anymore, so if you two keep a lid on it, we should all be good, shouldn't we?'

'All good, Joe. Nae worries,' I said, putting my arm round

Alison's shoulder, who also reassured Joe there was nothing to worry about on her side.

Shell stood up.

'Sorry... sorry, I'm really tired. Got a 4am pickup, so I need to get to bed now.'

She reached down for her glass of water, taking it off the coffee table. As she picked it up, I clocked what looked like a painfully raw burn mark wrapped around her wrist. Then, as her other hand picked up a magazine from the top of the pile, a similarly scarred wound was visible on that wrist, too.

There were no pleasant goodbyes exchanged between Shell and Joe as she walked off to her bedroom. Just a 'see you, lass – have a good flight' from Joe over his shoulder as she closed her bedroom door.

'Time for me to shoot as well,' Joe said, slowly rising from the sofa and finishing off his beer. 'Need to have my head switched on for tomorrow's interviews. Heading down to the powerboat qualifiers out by Jumeirah at 8. Helping out the sports desk with a bit of coverage. It's going to be bloody hot and bloody noisy.'

And just like that, he switched from drugs trafficker to sports journalist, and we were back talking about our day jobs.

'I've got an early one as well. But dull as fuck. Another Dubai Trade Show announcement down at the Ministry of Tourism,' I said.

I didn't hang around for too long after Joe left. Knowing that Ali wanted a chat tonight and I had an early start with Dubai's government bods, I explained to Alison it was best I headed off for an early night. Plus, I was still reeling from her Gold Souk bombshell and needed some space to get my head round what she'd been excitedly implying.

■ ■ ■

I pressed my ear up against the closed office door. I could hear nothing so gently knocked a couple of times. A drawer closed shut then seconds later, the door was pulled open and Ali stood there.

'Ah, Jimmy. Come, come. Come in.'

He offered me a cigarette as we pulled up our chairs around his desk.

'Joe has spoken to you?' he asked.

'Yes, Ali. And everything is cool. You have nothing to worry about with me and Alison, trust me.'

I decided for once to shut up and say no more, not wanting to put my foot or anyone else's foot in it again. I waited for Ali to talk as he toked on his Marlboro and took a sip from one of those small Arabic teacups.

'I trust you Jimmy,' he said. 'If I didn't trust you then I wouldn't have invited you into my world on the fourth floor. But this is now a different level of trust. Trust with money. Trust with your life. My life. Joe's life. Alison's life. Shell's life. And… Omar.

'This is a brotherhood trust. Trust that can never be broken or serious consequences happen.'

I understood and had no thoughts about breaking his trust. I just wanted to make a quick bit of cash and never have to talk about it again.

'So…' He paused for another puff.

'Me and Omar have been talking. You will go to London. You will meet Omar. But not on your own… Shell will come with you. Omar, you see, doesn't know you. *He* doesn't trust you. But he knows Shell. He likes Shell.

'You will go on Shell's Heathrow flight next Wednesday. She will get the ticket for you. You just need your passport.

'Once you meet Omar, he will explain more. What you need to do. You must listen and do exactly what he tells you.

'Then, my friend, I will see you back here on Friday night and we will both be happy, inshallah.'

I wasn't expecting to team up with Shell for this. Just thought I'd literally be flying solo without anyone else knowing. But as she was now a bit of a pro in this operation and me a rookie, I guess it made sense. And if this guy Omar had insisted on it then there was no other option.

'Okay, okay. Sounding good. I need to make about two grand on this, Ali. Will I make two grand?'

Ali smiled somewhat reassuringly and said: 'Do not worry, Jimmy. Omar will explain it all in London and you will be okay.'

He stood up and motioned towards the door, signalling the end of our little business chat.

'Now, what about your records, Jimmy? What are you going to buy in London? You're right we do need some new tunes for the fourth floor.'

Like most of my record-shop trips, I very rarely knew the name of a track I wanted to buy when I went in. Instead, you relied on a combination of chat with the shop assistant over the counter and if he liked you, he might suggest something decent, and the scribbled descriptions written on the record sleeves as you flicked through the 'House' and 'Techno' sections.

Then it was down to your personal choice and getting that buzzy feeling as you listened to 4/4 beats on one of the turntables, lifting the needle from start to first breakdown to the outro and then back again. Within 20 seconds, you usually knew if it was a banger or not.

For this trip, though, there was one banger I had to get hold of as it was setting clubs alight in the UK.

'Don't know yet, Ali, but everyone's talking about this Run-DMC remix – 'It's Like That'. Haven't heard it myself but the Arabian World girls have been raving about it. Will track that down and then see what else I can pick up around Soho.'

As we stepped back out into the reception, two other men were sitting on the couches, clearly waiting for Ali as they stood up on seeing us. Ali gestured with his finger for them to wait.

'Joe will speak to you more in the next couple of days, Jimmy. Joe and Shell. Have a good night.'

Chapter 22

With no bosses watching over our heads every minute of the day, Davey, Joe and I had mastered a way of weaving more leisure time into our working week.

Only having one official day off a week in a country of guaranteed sunshine, blue sky and white sandy beaches seemed unfair to the boys from perennially dreich Britain.

Apart from filing your quota of stories each day, you also had to swipe in and swipe out of the Daily UAE building – each swipe registering your attendance on that day.

With stories banked up in advance for those days of unbearable hangovers, we took work-avoidance one step further, creating a rota where one day a week, one of us would swipe in the cards of the other two while they went off to enjoy themselves down at the beach, water park or wherever took their fancy. Then an hour before the evening shifts started and the office filled up with sub-editors and editors, he'd file everyone's pre-written stories for the day and leave.

It worked like clockwork every time. Our Algerian boss was a lovely woman but probably far too trusting of 20-something journo lads from the UK. Occasionally, she'd text my pager in the evening, asking to call her desk phone to answer a query about one of the articles, but apart from that, I only saw her once a week for a 30-minute catch-up to talk about the stories I was going to cover next week.

Today, Davey Tags was on swiping duty for us. With Alison off on a Jo'burg flight, I'd decided to head off to the Radisson Blu hotel pool for the day where one of my chef pals there had blagged me an annual membership card.

Further out of Dubai by Jebel Ali, it was a lot quieter than the more central tourist hotels. It wasn't favoured by cabin crews, which was good because I really wanted some time to relax and think without bumping into any of Alison or Shell's friends.

Walking through the reception area out onto the poolside, I spotted only a handful of guests. The multi-sized pools flowed into each other, with wooden footbridges running across and dozens of palm trees standing tall around the edges.

Sunloungers snaked their way around the sides all the way down to the private beach area where, again, there were barely any people except a couple of families and one of the beach club assistants busy wiping down the loungers.

I placed Irvine Welsh's latest book Ecstasy: Three Tales of Chemical Romance on the lounger's side table, along with the sun cream, cigarettes and work pager. Saving the reading for later, I lit a Marlboro Light and looked out at the peaceful, turquoise Arabian Sea. Only the faint sound of a ripple could be heard as the water ever-so-gently ebbed and flowed across the shore.

Total tranquility. I couldn't imagine being anywhere more relaxed and idyllic.

Here I was, aged 25 now, in the middle of the Middle East, on my own, 5,000 miles from home, sunbathing on a honeymoon-style beach and getting paid for it. Nae bad.

The paradisal setting got me thinking about the situation with Alison. I'd never thought about marriage before. My older brother had already made a good job of fucking up his life by 25, having been married at 20, screwed his boss two weeks after the honeymoon, lost his job as a trainee teacher soon after, became a father at 21 and then divorced at 23. Add a couple of stalking charges on his ex- as well and he had become persona non grata. Witnessing the fallout and carnage of misery it inflicted on everyone involved made me want to keep a wide berth of marriage for a long time.

But Alison was the best thing that had happened to me in years.

No lies, no cheating, no bullshit and apart from her expensive taste in things, she seemed smitten with me and my humble offerings. To top it all, she was definitely a 10 out of 10 on looks. And, in Aberdeen, maybe nudging 11 out of 10.

I knew of other couples in Dubai who'd married just so they could live together without fear of being arrested. Legally, it was an arrestable offence just to share a bed overnight as an unmarried couple, let alone cohabit.

But I couldn't see us living together – well, not in Dubai. Alison was onto a good thing with her AWA-funded apartment and the airline wouldn't allow a non-employee to live there permanently.

An engagement could, of course, be a long engagement, I thought. There would be no need to rush into a marriage and all that kerfuffle of inviting family and friends. We could extend the engagement for maybe two or three years?

The ring itself was also a big enough symbol, surely – a symbol of commitment and intention – and if we were ever busted by the Dubai cops, surely that would be enough not to prosecute for unlawful shagging?

On the fifth Marlboro Light, I was becoming more comfortable with the thoughts of being engaged, although looking down the side of the lounger, I noticed I'd been subconsciously digging a deep hole in the sand with my right foot while mulling this all over.

Next on the 'will he, won't he?' agenda was the actual proposal. Was I going to propose? Did I really have to propose and concoct some grand romantic plan, or could I just give her the ring as a present and say: 'Hey, you're ace and one day we'll get married if everything works out okay, but how about this for now?'

I couldn't quite imagine myself bending down on one knee or anything overly slushie like releasing white doves from her rose covered balcony as I popped the question.

It needed further thought.

Then…

The pager suddenly vibrated on the table.

I was startled. The work pager had never gone off in the afternoon before. Davey wouldn't have even filed my story by this point so why would the newsroom be calling?

I hesitated, not wanting the realities of work to ruin my 'day off'. I sparked up another cig, knowing it might be my last peaceful moment before I'd have to read it and get ready to jump into action whatever that might be.

'CALL… HASINA… 866915… CALL… HASINA… 866915,' scrolled repeatedly across the pager screen.

Shit. My boss. But that wasn't her office number. That must be her home number. Why does she want me to call her home number?

I gathered my stuff and walked back into the hotel reception area to find a payphone.

I slowly punched in the numbers, mentally preparing myself for what awaited on the other end. Had she been tipped off where I was? Had she found out about me being catapulted out of the palace? Or was there a big scoop she wanted me to jump on right away?

'Ahlan,' she said in Arabic, answering the phone.

'Hello, Hasina? It's Jimmy. Jimmy Irvine. I got your page.'

'Ah, Jimmy. Yes, thank you for calling. Where are you, Jimmy?'

'Down at the Creek, at the Holiday Inn, about to interview their head chef for that feature,' I replied confidently, describing another story pre-written from earlier in the week.

'Okay, okay,' she said, with her voice slightly quivering. She then paused. 'Jimmy, I have some bad news. David has been in a car crash. A very bad car crash. He and several other people have been taken to Dubai Hospital in Deira.'

Shit. 'Is he okay?' I asked.

'We don't know yet. We'll get an update from the hospital soon.'

'What happened?'

'We're not sure. We just know that he and another car crashed into each other at speed. The other car had two children in it as well as the father.'

'Can I go and see him?'

'Not yet, Jimmy. It only happened an hour ago. He'll still be in the emergency treatment room. I'll update you when we know more.'

I put down the receiver and stood by the payphone, taking in what I'd just heard. Nobody wants to be involved in a car crash, let alone one in a foreign country.

Poor Davey. He'll be okay, though, I'm sure. Maybe a few broken ribs or leg. These Audis are damn sturdy and the airbag would have helped. But shit. Hope he was wearing his seatbelt.

There was no seatbelt law in Dubai and I for one was pretty lax on whether I strapped in or not. You never really felt like you were going to have a crash out here. The highways were six lanes wide and never that busy. Either side of them was barren desert so at worst, if you careered off the road, you'd just end up trench-deep in sand.

The biggest risk to crashing was driving through the busy streets of Deira where dhow traders casually dragged their carts onto the road in front of cars and people jaywalked in and out of the traffic.

I knew my day of lounging by the beach was over now and I'd have to get back to the office and 'file' my story. The office was probably the best place to get an update on Davey as well.

Joe was already there at his desk when I walked in about two hours later. He'd received the same page and update from Hasina. In the Editor's office, I could see Hamza and Hasina sitting opposite the Editor, deep in conversation.

'Fook, man. Doesn't sound good for Davey,' Joe said as I logged onto my computer opposite him.

'Not good? What's the latest? What have you heard?' I asked, fearing the worst.

'The Editor got a call from the police about 10 minutes ago. One of the kids in the crash, an eight-year-old girl, has died. And they're fookin' Dubai nationals, Jimmy. Emiratis. Police are saying it was Davey's fault,' he said.

Shit.

'Fuck. And what about Davey? How is he?'

'Hospital says he's stable. Sounds like he's going to be okay. But the other kid and father are still in intensive care.'

This was sounding messy for Davey. A dead child and the police quick to pin the blame on him. The accident had only happened about three or four hours ago. How could they be so sure he was at fault?

The Editor's door was closed shut but I could hear muffled raised voices as he stood behind his desk, appearing to direct some frustration at Hamza. Hasina glanced round from her chair, clocking me as I stared into their glass office trying to decipher what was being said. It was an impossible task, though – editors' offices are soundproofed for a reason. But as the minutes went on, it was clear there was a serious difference of opinions between the Editor and Hamza. I was damn sure it was about Davey and the fatality.

The three of them were locked in that room for over an hour. The heated discussions continued, only occasionally interrupted by the Editor taking calls on his desk phone.

Eventually, Hamza stood up and left, walking briskly past the two of us and out of the editorial floor.

Hasina stayed with the Editor for about 20 minutes longer, occasionally turning around and looking over towards me and Joe.

What is going on? I wanted to know what they were talking about. Who had been calling the Editor's phone? Was Davey okay? Why were they arguing?

Joe and I whispered these unanswered questions back and forth across our desks, ignorant about the reality of what was going on in that office and at the hospital.

Then Hasina stood up and opened the door. She briefly looked back at the Editor who raised his head in our direction before sitting back down behind his desk, pushing his hands up through the front of his hair before resting his forehead in his hands.

'Hi,' she said with a lump in her throat as she approached our desks, pulling over a seat.

'We have had some more updates from the police and hospital...

'David is going to be okay. He is stable with no life-threatening injuries, just some broken bones and bruising.

'The little girl, sadly as you know, died…

'Her brother, 12 years old… has… also…' She paused, taking a deep breath, looking down at the floor. '…sadly… died.'

She hesitated, trying to gather her composure.

'The father is stable and they expect him to pull through.

'The police have now arrested and could be charging David with manslaughter.'

Shit.

I leaned forward, clasping my hands and bowing my head. Two kids dead and now Davey up on manslaughter charges.

'How do they know it was his fault?' I asked Hasina, lifting my head.

'Well, we don't know. They are not saying much except that he has been arrested,' she said.

'Don't fuck with the locals,' I remember the Editor saying on my first day – you'll always lose. And I was finding it hard to believe that the police could be so quick to lay the blame on Davey without a thorough investigation.

I knew I had to get to Davey to find out the truth. I had to hear it from him first before I could believe any of this.

'Fookin' bullshit,' Joe blasted back at Hasina, as I quietly contemplated everything in my head. 'That's fookin' bullshit. How do the police know it was his fault yet? Where's the fookin' proof?'

From what Hasina had said, he was right. There was no evidence shared or witnesses being reported by the police. Without saying it, you could tell by her expressions and her unwillingness to immediately defend the police that she was probably questioning their impartiality at this point. Almost as if she had seen it or heard it all before.

Hasina took a professional stance and didn't want to question or speculate anymore. Moving back towards her desk, she asked us to file our stories from earlier in the day.

Now that she'd started her shift early, there'd be no sneaking off for me and Joe – we'd be here until 6pm probably, bashing out a couple or more stories between now and then.

Joe waited until 6.20, as I filed my last story with a sly smile about a world photography event.

TOP FLASHERS HEADING TO DUBAI PRESS PHOTO EXHIBITION

'Filed, Hasina,' I shouted over as I grabbed my cigarettes and sunnies, heading out of the newsroom.

Joe stood by the security gates. We'd both agreed earlier we should get down to the hospital to see Davey. Hear the story from him before it's too late and he's flung out of hospital into a cell.

A couple of Sharjah taxis were parked up opposite our building. The drivers sat with their windows rolled down, looking over at us. I whistled over to one as I walked up to Joe, but he quickly spun round and waved it away.

'Hold on, Jimmy. Let's take a walk first. We need to talk,' he said.

'OK, sure. What we talking about?'

He offered me one of his Marlboro Reds. I always preferred a Marlboro Light, not quite having the iron lungs to handle the Reds, but I took one anyway.

The sun wouldn't set for another hour, but it was still blasting out enough heat and humidity to make the walk uncomfortable.

'Let's grab a drink over here,' Joe said, pointing towards one of the windowless cafes which had a canopy casting a shadow over a table and a couple of metal chairs on the pavement.

'Two Cokes,' he said, holding up two fingers to the young Asian guy as we pulled up our seats.

'So, all is good, Jimmy. You are going to meet Omar next week,' he said in a lowered tone which was unusual for Joe.

'Shell, bless her – a loovly lass and a cracking fook, but a bit fookin' mouthy, isn't she? Anyway, Shell has sorted out your return tickets on AWA.

'You'll be on the same flight, the 11.30pm from Dubai, but you mustn't let on that you know her. Not on the flight or at the airport. You're booked into the same Holiday Inn hotel as the crew at the airport. But again, if you see her there, you must ignore her.

'The next day, you must be at her room by 2pm. That's when you'll meet Omar and he'll give you the goods.'

I was flicking through the timings in my head. It would leave a few hours to get from Heathrow into Soho to zip around the record shops and then back again to the hotel. No problem.

'Shell flies back on that day but you will fly back the day after. 24-hour turnaround for cabin crew is part of their job but for a passenger, it would be suspicious.

'Have you got your passport?'

Shit. 'No, not yet.'

'You need your fookin' passport, so you better get upstairs and see Hamza sharpish. And get your story straight. It's like the Spanish Inquisition trying to get your passport off him. He doesn't just hand it over, he likes to make you sweat...

'... Death. Make up a fookin' death in the family Jimmy. That usually works. But don't go straight for your mum and dad. Save them for later. Start out wider – aunties, uncles or cousins should do it.'

I'd been putting off the Hamza visit as I'd heard he was an

awkward bastard when trying to get your passport back and hadn't quite figured out my story yet. But Uncle Nick's death sounded like a good story to conjure up. Never liked my Uncle Nick anyway.

We finished off our drinks, arranging another chat with Shell over the next couple of days, and flagged down a taxi to drive us to the hospital.

The Dubai Hospital was a wonder of modern architecture with glistening shell-like glass-domed roofs, light sandstone buildings and an oasis of palm tree paths and perfectly manicured lawns connecting each of the departments. The A&E was positioned off a grassy roundabout with water fountains in the middle. Floor-to-ceiling glass panels surrounded the entrance, which was surprisingly quiet, without an ambulance to be seen.

Joe seemed to know his way around, confidently talking to the receptionists before urging me along to follow him now that he had the ward and room number for Davey.

We took the lift up to the third floor, Ward C, in search of Room 12. We followed the green line along the corridor floor directing us to Rooms 6–12. The corridors were long and winding, with only three patient-rooms on each stretch. Finally, after what felt like an army speed march, we turned the corner for Rooms 10, 11 and 12. As we approached Room 10, we started slowing down the pace, saying nothing to each other at first as we tried to make out what we could see at the end of the corridor.

Then, after a few more paces, we both stopped and turned to each other.

Fuck.

Standing outside Room 12 were two police officers. Dressed in their olive-green uniforms with matching berets, they were casually talking to each other as they guarded the door with semi-automatic pistols, handcuffs and truncheons strapped around their waists.

We pretended to appear lost and confused, standing between Rooms 10 and 11, as the two officers stopped their conversation to glare down the corridor at us. We turned on our heels and casually walked back round the corner and out of their view.

'Shit, he's fucked,' I said worryingly to Joe.

'Aye, we're not going to get near him now,' said Joe. 'If the cops are on his door then the next stop for Davey is a fookin' cell. Then it's the fookin' kangaroo courts of Dubai. He's at the mercy of the system now. Even if he's innocent, he's fooked.'

Heading back to our apartments from the hospital in the taxi, Joe and I didn't say much. I was certainly in my own little world of contemplation, staring out the car window at the Dubai landscape whizzing by. Davey was one of the good guys. Didn't do drugs, didn't fuck prostitutes (well, not intentionally), didn't fight, and there was a chance he was not at fault and didn't crash into that car killing two kids. Maybe it was the local who crashed into him?

He was your cheeky chappy from London, always happy and positive. Always flirting and joking with the girls and, a lot of the time, not having much luck as he couldn't hold his drink.

He was one of those guys you wanted to look after. Not someone who should get banged up abroad.

Joe was different. Joe lived on the edge, taking risks and not caring who he hurt along the way, so long as he had a good time or made money.

I couldn't give a fuck about Joe really, but Dave, David, Davey, Davey Tags – he didn't deserve this.

Chapter 23

It was the afternoon of my flight back to London.

My 'poor' Uncle Nick had been given 'less than two weeks to live' with terminal cancer – testicular cancer was the one I went with (he did talk a lot of bollocks, after all, so it seemed appropriate).

Hamza had predictably followed the Gestapo Interrogation Manual Vol 2 when I eventually got my shit together to ask for my passport back earlier in the week.

What should have been a short meeting with a couple of simple Q&As like...

'I need my passport. Can you hand it over?'

'Why do you need it?'

'To go and visit my dying uncle.'

'Okay, Mr Irvine, here you go.'

...lasted nearly 30 minutes, as he paused on every response, holding his inquisitive stare before firing another question about my family, where they lived, where I'd be travelling to, who I'd be staying with, how well I knew my uncle and whether I had any other uncles – all while arrogantly exhaling his cigar smoke in my direction and taking phone calls in between.

'Unprecedented,' he said when I explained I'd be flying to the UK and back within 48 hours.

'You are only going for 48 hours?' he asked again, puzzled. 'Your family will want you to stay longer, no?'

'It will be upsetting, Hamza, yes, but sometimes it's better to make a short goodbye rather than a long one. I also need to be back here working on the stories to help Hasina. And I don't want to miss a deadline for the Daily UAE,' I said, trying to sound like an exemplary employee.

Playing to his ego, articulating my professional dedication to the newspaper and probably making too many uncomfortable references to testicles won him over, as he eventually reached behind, unlocking his safe to sift through the staff passports and finding mine.

'I wish you a safe journey. Send my condolences to your family,' he said, standing up from behind his desk and handing over the burgundy red British passport. Never had it felt so good to be holding it again.

Uncle Nick's final countdown had to be shared with Alison as well. I didn't want her knowing the real purpose of my own bungee flight as that would unravel the whole palace palaver. And while she was a party girl, I didn't think 'small-time drugs trafficker' was on her wish list for a future husband's profession.

Thank fuck Alison was not rostered for the Heathrow flight as well. I hadn't thought that could have been a possibility, until she mentioned the day before that she was flying on the same night as me and Shell, but thankfully it was to Hong Kong for three days.

I avoided going around to Alison's apartment before we both set off on our night flights, not wanting to make contact with Shell and risk any awkward conversations. I didn't know how she felt before her courier flights back and forth to the UK, but certainly my rookie confidence was starting to wobble as flashes of Midnight Express ran through my head.

You know that airport scene where Billy's at Turkish Customs with his heart beating faster and faster as the officers search his holdall and pull out a frisbee. They ask him the simplest of questions: 'What is this? What's a frisbee?' and as Billy tries to answer, sweat drips down his face. Then, just when he thinks he's clear and on the boarding steps of the plane, he gets the dreaded tap on the shoulder from the police officer. Pulled aside and frisked on the tarmac, they find 2kg of hashish strapped to his chest. Game fuckin' over Billy.

My records were going to be Billy's frisbee and I'd need to be ice-cool if questioned.

I'd finished the shift at the paper as normal around 5.30pm. Thankfully it had been a quiet day – just a few press releases to rewrite and a catch-up with Hasina about the stories planned for next week. I think Hasina was deliberately going easy on me after hearing about my 'dying' uncle and the ongoing situation with Davey.

Davey was still in the hospital, recuperating along with the father of the deceased children, though unlike the UAE national, Davey had police officers guarding his room 24/7.

The Editor had taken the decision not to report the accident in our newspaper but the other titles in the region did.

DUBAI CHILDREN DIE IN HORROR CRASH. BRITISH JOURNALIST CHARGED.

There had been no word of anyone visiting Davey in hospital, either. Well, certainly none of the British expats had, including the Editor, though I suspected that Hamza or representatives of Hamza had, as the legal process was moving forward.

Hasina told me not to worry about Davey or my work, as she

also passed on her condolences about the impending 'death' of Uncle Nick.

She was right about one of those. I wasn't worrying about work, but I was concerned about Davey and starting to get twitchy about London, with less than two hours to go before the airport taxi arrived.

Thousands of people fly through Heathrow and Dubai airports every day. The chances of being stopped were slim, I kept trying to convince myself, as I started to pack a weekend bag. It's going to be okay. Keep calm. Don't do a Billy. Don't do a fuckin' Billy Hayes.

Two nights and two days travel equals three boxer shorts (always a spare, in case of emergency), two pairs of socks (never need a spare), four T-shirts (two for day, two for evening), one smart shirt (for the 'grieving family visit'), one hoodie (the navy Duffer), swimming shorts for the hotel pool and then the trickiest bit of all… footwear.

Being an obsessive trainer freak made travelling preparations a head-fuck of indecisions. To the uncultured, untrainered amateur eye, my collection does contain a lot of styles that you might think 'look the same'. Yes, they are all Adidas, but if you know your Superstars from your Indoor Supers, you'll appreciate the difference between the whites of Rod Laver, Forest Hill and Stan Smith and the colour blocks of ZX, Campus, SLs and Gazelle.

One pair to travel in but which ones?

Spotless white or colours?

In they went, out they came. On my feet, off my feet. Do they look best in these jeans or how about these jeans? No, the first jeans are better.

What about the T-shirts? This colour: black? Am I mourning yet? Not quite, but could help with the story. Now the pastels:

lime, yellow, pink? Or are pastels too much for rainy London? Maybe the white Ralphy or navy Lacoste will do.

And so it went on, the packing and unpacking, until I clocked my watch and realised the taxi would be here in ten minutes. Shit.

Passport? Check. Wallet? Check. Tickets? Check. A pair of balls?… Half-checked.

Time to go.

■ ■ ■

Up ahead, Shell was standing just inside the aircraft door, greeting passengers and checking their tickets before directing them to their seats.

She seemed relaxed, smiling and being all cutesy with a baby as a young couple struggled onboard with overhead bags and baby accessories swinging from their shoulders.

I'd never seen her in her uniform before and she looked unrecognisable with hair tied back under her pillbox hat and heavy red lipstick. The Scouse accent, though, was undeniably hers, something which could never be hidden.

Ever the professional and being attentive to the passengers standing in front of her, she didn't recognise me until it was my turn to show my ticket.

'Welcome to Arabian World Airlines. Ticket… please.' She hesitated ever so slightly as she looked straight at me. '24A, sir. Halfway down to the right. Enjoy your flight.'

She smiled but not in a knowingly kinda way. It was that always-on, professional smile of an air hostess. She was good at this.

I mumbled a thanks, and waited in the aisle behind the fumbling and flustered baby couple, as they tried to settle down into their seats.

I was the first passenger to sit in our row of three seats. Thankfully, it was a window seat (nice one, Shell), meaning I wouldn't have to move for any of the other two wanting to get to the loos. I could also rest my head against the window for a bit of shut-eye, not worrying about accidentally nuzzling onto the shoulders of someone sitting either side of me or getting bumped in the elbow by trollies being pushed up and down the aisle.

I started to flick through the in-flight mag, searching for movies to watch.

Nope, nope, nope, nope, nope. My Best Friend's Wedding? Nae chance. Picture Perfect? Oh, for fuck's sake. Then, ya beauty, Men in Black and The Fifth Element! Two blockbusters, which were being raved about and already released in the UK but were probably years away from being shown in a Dubai cinema.

Time to settle in. Shoes aff. Headphones on.

I was looking forward to a few beers now and some Hollywood entertainment allowing me to escape the realities of why I was here in the first place.

The Fifth Element needed more than a couple of beers just to keep hold of the plot, although passing out for about 20 minutes probably didn't help either. That Milla Jovovich, though, was something else – fit as fuck, but clearly one of those psycho birds that would cut yer balls off in yer sleep, just for shits and giggles.

And Gary Oldman. For me, he'll always be 'Bexy Boy' from The Firm. Top lad, never makes a shit film. True Romance – another one of his and a firm favourite, up there with the likes of Pulp Fiction and Carlito's Way.

As for Brucie, well, he's really John McClane, isn't he? Can't see him doing much after this, apart from knocking out a few more Die Hards.

Locking in on the back-to-back movies helped avoid any awkward conversations with the greasy-haired, 50-something, overweight English bloke sitting to my right. You could tell he was already getting on the nerves of the Arabic woman next to him, as I'd counted at least four times he'd excused himself to squeeze out of the seats and lumber himself down the aisle to the toilet.

He'd been trying to make small talk with her while knocking back the Heinekens and vodka chasers. You could tell the tee-totalling UAE national was squirming under her hijab, trying not to turn around and face his beer-soaked breath. Respect to her, though, as she remained calm and polite, refocusing on her book after courteous nods in response to his gibberings.

I knew if I gave him any sign of an in, like an accidental elbow bump or a casual side glance that caught his eye, he'd take it as an invitation to chat.

I remained stony-faced and sullen, staring straight ahead at the movie screen. I think he got the message. I only broke cover when food ('chicken or beef, sir?') or alcohol was being served.

Shell had been working our section all flight. To all onboard, we were complete strangers, as she carried out her duties to the highest standards with that painted-on, ever-jolly, professional demeanour. Even when I cracked a beery quip about tight-arsed Aberdonians, she responded with a polite smile like she would for anyone, before moving on to serving the next row.

I knew on the flight back I'd have to be as sober as an imam at Christmas and on top of my game, so now was the time to take full advantage of the free drinks, squeezing in one more beer before the seatbelts sign pinged for landing.

That structure to my left did the same. We even finished our beers at the same time then handed our empties over to Shell in sync. Still, though, the Eastern Bloc coldness I was giving him remained bitterly sharp and no words were exchanged.

Seated near the middle of the plane, we had to wait a good ten minutes until the rows in front of us cleared and we started to snake out. Standing up from my aisle seat, desperate for chatty boy to get a wiggle on, I cracked my bonce on the overhead locker as I tried too quickly to reach up and round to grab the holdall. The beer was definitely affecting my sense of balance and timing.

Wedged in between other carry-on cases and bags, I impatiently tugged and tugged at the bag with one hand until it suddenly flew out of the locker, the weight and momentum carrying it over my shoulder and smacking my co-passenger squarely on the back of his large head.

He stumbled forward, reaching out with both hands to prevent his fall, planting them both on the shoulders of the Arabic woman and knocking her onto the aisle floor. She screamed, hysterically, in Arabic. I think she'd finally lost her shit with him.

She carried on screaming, pointing at him, wildly waving her hands in front of his face, as Shell and the other stewardesses 'excused' and 'pardoned' their way past other passengers in the aisle to get near and calm her down.

She was beyond reasoning, though, not stopping for air to listen to what anyone was saying as she filled the cabin with what I assumed were fiery Arabic expletives.

I had to step in and offer an explanation. Over and around the machine gun of venom spitting from her mouth, I tried to explain to Shell and the other stewardesses that it was my fault – it was an accident.

I'd lost the Cold War and was now also apologising to Mr 24B, who in fairness accepted what had happened and the apology. Miss or Mrs 24C, however, was not willing to hear it from him, as every time he tried to explain, she screamed, with each screech notching up a pitch or two at a time.

Shell and her team moved the three of us over to the other side of the plane, which by now was clearing a lot quicker, as you could sense the frustration and anger building from the other 100 or so passengers waiting impatiently in line behind us to leave.

It took another 20 minutes before we were finally able to disembark. The wailing banshee of 24C only calmed down when we were forced by Shell's purser to write signed statements explaining what had happened. The woman had now filed an official complaint accusing this bloke of bloody assaulting her.

My plans of travelling without incident and incognito had been scuppered somewhat.

'Sorry, Shell,' I said to her and the purser as I walked off the plane onto the jet bridge.

Fuck.

Did that sound too familiar?

I daren't look back.

But her name badge did say 'Michelle', didn't it? Sure she could just brush it off as me being a bit of a boozy and flirty passenger.

Needed to get to the hotel now and sober up.

Tomorrow was going to be a big day.

Chapter 24

The Heathrow Holiday Inn was popular with many of the airlines. The foyer was a conveyor belt of crews from AWA, BA, KLM and Lufthansa, checking in for their overnight stays before flying onto their next destination.

I waited in line behind the cluster of Lufthansa air stewards. They looked exhausted, with very little chat going on among them. Guess there's no time to party for this lot – they probably just crave their bed and a good night's kip.

'Two nights, Mr Irvine?' the receptionist asked, double-checking the booking confirmation on her screen. 'Passport, please.'

She scanned it on the photocopier behind and handed it back to me.

'All good, sir. You're in Room 118. Dinner is served from 7pm and the bar closes at midnight. Breakfast is from 6.30 to 9.30. Here is your key.'

Very smooth. Good work so far from Joe and Shell.

I was glad to get inside the room and avoid Shell and the AWA stewards checking in. The onboard kerfuffle had certainly made me recognisable, and it might have thrown up questions with her colleagues as to why I was now staying in the same hotel as the cabin crew.

I neatly laid out my trainers (the Rod Laver green-white and

Campus red) underneath the console table, then hung up the hoodie and T-shirts. I left the boxers, swimming shorts and socks in the holdall – no need to bother with drawers for them. Next up was the bathroom to lay out the toiletries and discover what freebies were on offer.

I looked in the holdall, digging around the socks and boxers for the toiletry bag, pushing them around from side to side, before eventually tipping everything out. But there was no sign of it.

Idiot. I'd left it back in my apartment, hadn't I? Spending too much time on choosing trainers and then rushing out the door, I'd bloody forgotten it.

I scanned the complimentary bathroom smellies – nothing special, just Holiday Inn-branded shower gel, shampoo, conditioner and soap. I'd have to call reception for a toothbrush and toothpaste. The six-hour, beery, junk-food flight had left my mouth reeking like a Glaswegian sewer on New Year's Day.

Sorted. The maid service said they'd drop it off in my room shortly and within an impressive five minutes, there was a knock at the door and a middle-aged Filipina-looking maid was there with her housekeeping cart, handing over the toothbrush kit.

Easing off the post-flight hangover, I decided to head down to the pool for an evening swim. There was going to be no late-night bar distraction tonight. I needed to clear my head and wake up fresh for tomorrow's record-shopping and meeting with Omar and Shell.

The pool was a decent length – 20m according to the markings on the wall, with a small kids' paddling pool off to the side of the shallow end.

The dim lighting was moody and atmospheric. The darkness was punctuated by red spotlights dotted on the walls in between the rattan sunloungers, while strips of white lights lit up the bottom of the pool and along its tiled edges. Music played faintly from the speakers – nothing too upbeat, just background ambience adding to the relaxing atmosphere.

I placed the oversized white fluffy towel on the lounger, along with one of the pool reception's free magazines – Marie Claire. It was the best I could find in amongst Horse & Hound, Country Living and Red, plus Eva Herzigová was on the cover, next to a cover line saying: 'Sex Games – How far would you go to satisfy your partner in bed?'

I lowered myself into the tepid pool (no diving allowed) then pushed forward into front crawl, aiming for a target of 30 lengths.

This was the most relaxed I'd felt in days. With only one other swimmer, in the lane furthest away, it was bliss to have the place almost to myself and just glide in my own time up and down the pool. Even in Dubai, it never felt as good as this, as you usually ended up in outdoor pools with a 40°C sun beating down on you.

At 30 lengths, I hauled myself out of the pool and onto the lounger, feeling that, after a read and rest, I could jump back in and push another 20 before heading back up to the room for the night.

I dried myself off just enough so as not to soak the magazine, as I settled into the lounger for a read and perhaps a little doze.

'*No. 1: Play Captive. Have him tie your arms and legs to the bed, and slowly ravish you from top to bottom. You'll need ties, ribbons, handcuffs...*'

I was just about to move onto '*Sex Game No. 2*' when to my left, the 'Women's Changing Rooms' door pushed open and in strolled... shit! Shell and three of her fuckin' cabin crew!

With nobody else here, since that other swimmer had left, I was seconds away from being spotted.

I swiped the towel from the side and threw it over my head, slowly inching it down over my body. I lay motionless underneath, as I heard their chattering voices get closer as they looked to select a lounger.

Conscious that to them I now resembled some kind of murder-scene corpse, which would attract even more suspicion, I gradually started to snore and rolled over to one side pretending to sleep.

The Marie Claire 'Sex' pages were now soaking wet and stuck to the inside of my thighs. This was not a good look, should anyone dare to remove the towel.

Their chattering briefly stopped and then became a giggle as I heard them whisper:

'He's snoring. Look. Listen.'

They were now only a few yards away, making their way round to the deep end.

'Nice feet. Lovely tan,' I heard Shell whisper to the girls as she walked past, almost brushing my toes, which were sticking out from the bottom of the towel.

I was bloody stuck here now until they left. There was no escape, unless I pretended to sleepwalk with the towel over my head like a mummy rising from the dead.

It must have been an hour before they eventually left. I heard them splashing their lengths back and forward, maybe about ten, but then they spent the rest of the time sitting around the loungers chatting and gossiping.

Luckily, I had managed to conceal myself before they clocked me, because in the middle of their gossiping, I heard them talking about 'those nightmare passengers' on the flight over.

'Typical complaining Arabic bitch,' one of them said.

'He was so fat and annoying,' said the other.

And then: 'But the Scottish one. He was pretty cute. Think he had his eye on you, Shell.'

Shit. Had I been flirting with Shell during the flight? But hold on, who thought I was 'cute'? Whose body did that voice belong to? It was Irish, definitely Irish. Maybe she was cute as well?

Fuck. I'll never know.

Their voices drifted off as they walked off through the 'Women's Changing Rooms' door. I poked my head out from underneath the towel, just as the door slowly closed, only catching a glimpse of the backs of two of them: one petite, one taller, both brunette.

I unpeeled Marie Claire from my legs, the 'Sex' feature pages now embarrassingly part-ripped, part-smudged and part-lying in tiny, crumpled bits around the lounger.

Dried and dressed, I casually walked through the pool reception, briefly stopping to slide Eva Herzigová into the bottom of the magazines pile, hoping nobody would read it for a long time.

Safely back in the room, I dialled down for a pizza and settled in to watch Manchester United play Porto in the Champions League quarter-finals. United were my adopted English team through the Fergie connection and Scottish striker Brian McClair was still playing for them, though he hadn't scored many goals this season.

A comfortable 4-0 victory that night saw United progress into the semi-finals and I slept well.

■ ■ ■

As well as forgetting my toothbrush and toiletries, I realised as soon as I pulled open the curtains in the morning that I hadn't packed a jacket either. Luckily, it wasn't pishing down, but it was a typically grey, drizzly, London day that awaited me outside.

The Duffer hoodie would have to be my substitute jacket, and it was definitely not a day for the white Rod Lavers, so I laced up the Campus.

I wasn't shy on the full English breakfast, going back for seconds on sausages and bacon and topping up the coffee mug three times. I suspected this could be my last fill until after meeting Omar and Shell, and I needed a good lining of stodge and caffeine to suppress any nerves.

It takes roughly an hour on the Piccadilly Line to get from Heathrow into central London, so I knew I'd have to leave Soho around 12-12.30 to get back to the hotel for 2pm, taking into account the 50-50 chance of '*delays on the Underground*'.

I stepped out at Piccadilly Circus, admiring for a minute the giant ad boards towering above and sucking in the toxic fumes of the passing double-decker buses and black cabs.

Checking my watch, it was 10.05am. At this time of day, the West End was still quiet. The slow-moving, meandering tourists don't usually start flooding the streets until after 12.

Not raining, just drizzle, cool and not crowded, these were good conditions to zip around the Soho record shops and get the job done – x15 records (enough for a new set) and one small metal flight case (up to 50 records).

The hit list was Black Market Records – D'Arblay Street; Vinyl Junkies – Berwick Street; Flying Records – Dean Street; TAG Records – Shaftesbury Avenue; and Eukatech – Endell Street.

Best head to Black Market first as that place is fuckin' tight and gets uncomfortably packed. It was also probably the best option for the flight case, from what I could remember the last time I'd been in.

Berwick Street, Dean Street, Wardour Street: I always confused these three and unsurprisingly found myself on Meard Street at one point, trying to navigate between them all, as I was trying to snake around to D'Arblay Street, which was somewhere off one of them.

Eventually, after finding my way down to Black Market, I found myself in a different type of 'Meard'. Shop shut 'meard'.

'Opening times: 11am–7pm.'

Bollocks. It was only 10.30am. Change of plan.

TAG wasn't too far away and a firm favourite for tunes and so I decided to speed-march over there.

'Opening times: 11am–7pm.'

Fuck. I don't believe it.

It was now 10.42am.

I pushed on to the furthest away shop: Eukatech, just off Neal Street in Covent Garden. If it wasn't open, then I'd squirrel my way back into the Berwick Street area and focus efforts there.

'Opening times: 11am–7pm.'

Bollocks. It was 10.55am and while Eukatech might or might not open in five minutes, I wasn't convinced they stocked a range of flight cases, so about-turned and headed back into the centre of Soho.

An hour had gone since I popped out at Piccadilly Circus and I hadn't been inside one record shop yet.

While it was a comfortably fresh morning, the zigzagging hike around Soho and mounting pressure of the clock counting down were conspiring to build up a serious sweat underneath what now felt like an overly heavy hoodie.

Standing outside Black Market at 11.10, there was still no fucker to be seen. D'Arblay Street was empty except the builders' merchants on the corner, which had probably opened at daft o'clock.

I squatted down on the damp steps of a doorway opposite, unzipping the hoodie and sparking up a cig, now resigned to sitting and waiting. Shouldn't be long, I hoped.

11.15... nope

11.22...nope

Then at 11.28, a 30-something bloke with a ponytail under a black baseball cap stood in front of the Black Market door. He jostled around with keys for a few seconds then pushed the door open and beeped on the keypad, switching off the alarm.

I jumped up, headed straight over and in.

'Alrite, mite,' he said, looking a bit startled as I popped up just inches from his shoulder.

'Good, mate,' I replied, though, as always resenting the word 'mate' or 'mite' as the Cockneys pronounced it.

'Well, not that good,' I corrected myself. 'Need a flight case and some new tunes but don't have much time.'

Tom turned out to be a saviour. None of the grumpiness and sharpness you get from some record-shop assistants. He was generous with his recommendations, walking up and down the racks of records on the wall pulling out new releases, imports and a couple of white labels from cardboard boxes under the counter.

With a stack of around 20 in front of me, I got to work on the turntable while Tom pointed up to the small aluminium flight case on the shelf with a £50 flash-sign stuck to it.

I nodded. He lifted it down and flipped it open. 'Enough room for 50 records in there,' he said and there was some solid protective foam on the inside. The metal latches had padlock eyelets on them as well. Perfect. That'll remove the temptation for a nosey customs bod to poke around inside.

At 12.15, I needed to get a shifty on, so spurred on by adrenaline and vinyl indecision I opted to buy the lot. I didn't have time to go through and scrutinise the records again, but on the first round of listening, there was definitely something in all of them to work with.

The Tube chugged along with unbearable delays between stations on the Piccadilly Line. It wasn't until I reached Osterley that I could finally relax a bit. My watch said 1.25 and there were only five Tube stops to go before I was back at Heathrow, and just a few minutes' walk to the Holiday Inn. I was definitely going to be back by 2pm, but probably only just with little time to psych myself up for the drop-off and I definitely wanted to see Shell first before Omar arrived.

With 15 minutes to go and still carrying the flight case and the Black Market bag of records, I knocked on Room 307.

No response. I knocked again three times. Still no response. Then, just before the third attempt, the door opened.

'Jimmy,' Shell yelped with a big grin, welcoming me in.

With her hair wrapped up in a bath towel, she was just wearing jeans and a black bra.

'Sorry, you been waiting long? I was in the shower. Hold on, let me get a top on.'

She turned away and headed into her bathroom, holding her head towel up with one hand.

Jesus Christ. What the…?

I winced as her bare back revealed a bruising tangle of what could only be whip marks, mercilessly crisscrossed from shoulder to shoulder and down to the bottom of her spine. Her once smooth tanned skin now broken and resembling a child's scrawl of deep purple and painfully red lines.

How the fuck did she get those?

...Joe... could that have been fuckin' Joe?...

Then, within seconds, she darted back into the room, pulling down over her head a baggy Benetton sweatshirt.

I tried to mask my horror, forcing a smile and quickly starting up a conversation to remove the image of her scars from my mind.

I hurried into an awkward apology again for the flight debacle.

'Sorry, Shell. What a mess that was. It was all going so well until I started the domino effect with the bloke next to me.'

'You were a bit too pissed, Jimmy,' she said.

'Could have done without all the attention and the official form-filling. But everything should be okay. AWA will probably offer that cow a free flight voucher so she doesn't take it further. And for some of these Arabs, that's all they're really looking for.

'Just don't bloody drink on the flight back, Jimmy,' she warned as she sat down at the console table, brushing back her wet hair in front of the mirror.

'Of course not. I'm nae daft. Was just enjoying myself on the way out, wasn't I?'

'And whatever you do, don't mention what happened on-board to Omar.' She flipped round, putting her hairbrush down on the table with a sterner look.

'Sure. Sure.'

It was now five minutes to two and one thing was still playing on my mind. Should I mention the swimming pool last night? I mean, all is fine with Alison, obviously, but you know, it's always good to know who your other admirers are, just in case things change.

'Funny story. Last night, Shell, I was down at the swimming...'

KNOCK. KNOCK.

'That'll be Omar,' she said, cutting off the chat and making her way to the door.

Shell briefly peered through the spyhole then opened the door.

'Hey, Omar,' she said excitedly, greeting him with a hug.

'Hello, darling,' he replied, shuffling his large frame forward into the room. One of his associates I could see remained outside.

Omar was dressed head to toe in Nike, sporting a full black-and-red baggy tracksuit of splattered geometrical shapes and a pair of white high-top Air Jordans. In his right hand, he was clutching a black Nike sports bag. I didn't know if this sporty look was meant to convince people he was off to the gym, but at 20 stone, with as much agility as a sloth on ketamine, he wasn't fooling anyone.

'Jimmy?' he asked, looking over at me standing by the bathroom door.

'Yes, I'm Jimmy, Omar. How ye doing?'

He didn't reply, nor did he even attempt a handshake or any kind of friendly greeting. He just lowered himself down onto the side of the bed, nestling the sports bag between his feet.

Shell unlatched the minibar and popped open a bottle of Heineken for him.

'Good girl. Thanks, Shell.'

Shell moved over to sit by the console table, while I remained propped up against the door frame of the bathroom, unsure what the etiquette of a casual chat with our dealer was going to be.

'Did you see Home and Away earlier?' Omar asked, turning first to Shell and then to me.

'No, I missed it,' answered Shell, as Omar then looked over at me.

'Umm, no,' I mumbled, partly in disbelief at what he was asking.

'It was a good one. Really fucked up at the moment.

'You know Chloe, the teenager, who's stupidly doing drugs at high school? Well, her father, Max, has just taken a shotgun to the dealer. Turned up outside the school with a double-barrel like a psycho.

'Looked like he was about to pull the trigger and then... it cut... *"You know we belong together, You and I forever and ever..."*' He laughed as he launched into singing the theme tune. 'It's a good one. You've got to watch it tomorrow. Ah... but Shell, you'll miss it though, won't you, but Jimmy Boy, you gotta watch it.'

For the next 10 or so minutes, Shell and Omar forensically analysed Home and Away plots and characters. It was like being trapped in a soap geeks meet-up. I was more of a Neighbours man, anyway, and hadn't even seen that for about 10 months, so I had absolutely fuck-all to contribute. All I could do was pretend I was interested as a nodding spectator, while I puffed through three Marlboros and offered Omar more beer from Shell's minibar.

Omar stood up – well, eventually stood up after a couple of failed attempts to lift himself off the bed – and then cleared a space on the dressing table for his bag.

From the sports holdall, he carefully pulled out one, two, three... seven, eight, nine, ten sealed pouches of white powder, lining them up in rows of seven and three.

'10 grams in each, as always Shell. There's your three,' he said, sliding the bags towards Shell at the end of the table.

'The rest is yours, Jimmy.'

What the fuuuuuck?

'Seven? 70 grams?' I said in shock, questioning the vastness of this deposit.

I felt flushed, dragging my hand slowly down my face, looking over at Shell and then back at Omar. I cleared my throat, rubbing my eyebrow.

'70 fuckin' grams? 70?'

'Is there a problem, Jimmy?' Omar asked. 'You're not worried, are you? Ali said you had done this before. "Jimmy knows what he's doing," he said.'

I hesitated, trying to get a grip. I needed to reassure him I was the man for the job, but could I negotiate to take less?

'Of course, Omar. It's just when you pulled out the bags, I assumed there'd be an equal split there with Shell.'

'Ha, ha, ha, ha.' He laughed loudly and opened another beer.

'Jimmy, Jimmy. Firstly, you're not a woman. There is only so much a woman can conceal. Isn't that right, Shell? And secondly, Jimmy mite...' Fuck, there's that irritating 'mite' again. '...I hear you need to make some decent money on this. A lot more than Shell. And this...' He pointed to the seven bags of gear. '...is what it's going to take.'

I had not expected to be shifting 70 grams of coke out of London into Dubai. Three or four bags maybe but not nearly double.

There was no compromise, though. Shell and Omar clearly had formed a bond over the past few months, and she wasn't jumping in to help. I was also fully aware that one of his ogres was probably still patrolling the corridor outside, so I couldn't just innocently walk out of here saying, 'Naaah, not today.'

After Omar pointed to the bags, nobody spoke. All eyes were on me, waiting for a response. It was a do-or-cry moment, and I chose do. There was no other way. I did need the money.

'No problem, Omar. Lucky I bought enough records, eh?'

I joked, trying to thaw the ice that had momentarily set in the room since my initial reaction.

'All is good,' I said, trying to reinforce confidence in myself and him.

I lifted the flight case onto the bed and unlocked the latches. Flipping open the lid, I reached over to the table to start loading in the packages. I had some serious pre-flight preparation to do now.

'Hold on,' Omar said, placing his double-sized, slightly sweaty hand over mine, just as I was lifting up the first bag.

He looked me in the eye, his dark-stubbled, greasy-skinned, rotund face just inches away.

'No fuck-ups, Jimmy. Me and Ali don't do fuck-ups. 70 grams go in and 70 grams come out the other side. You better have this method of yours fuckin' nailed down.'

'As tight as a nun's fanny,' I replied cheekily. Omar, then Shell both laughed out loud. Confidence filled the room again, as Omar passed over a beer and I continued to load the record box.

Once full, I closed and locked the lid, explaining how this would then be padlocked by the time I fly and not reopened until I was sitting down with Ali in his office.

Omar was first to leave, but not before he polished off one more beer while this time talking about Blockbusters. This guy knew more about daytime TV than Lorraine fuckin' Kelly.

'He's not as good as old Bob that Michael Aspel, is he? Bit fucking stiff. And then the finalist got stuck on PL – 'What "PL" was the coveted title held by John Masefield, CD Lewis and Ted Hughes?' How could she not know that? It's Poet Laureate obviously. And that was to win a weekend away for two kayaking.'

'I've never been kayaking,' he said as he finally headed towards the door.

You wouldn't get far, I thought, as I watched him lumber past Shell.

Shell seemed really pleased with how our little meeting with Omar had gone. It was alright for her, I suppose – no change to her shipment and routine. I, on the other hand, was now going large on a maiden flight. No fuckin' around. A full run-up and dive-bomb into the deep end of small-time drugs trafficking.

'See you back in Dubai,' I said, giving Shell a peck on the cheek.

She excitedly waved me down the corridor to the lifts. A bit too jolly in my mind, but I suspected that becoming an accomplice in her world was now making her happy.

■ ■ ■

It was an early morning start on the day of my return flight and no time for breakfast as I dropped in and out of the hardware stores around Hounslow High Street. Check-out time from the room was 12 noon, so all the preparation had to be completed by then.

Shopping list done, I was back in the room by 9.30 with all the essentials: two padlocks, one small tube of glue, Stanley knife, tape, lighter fluid and kitchen foil. I'd also managed to grab the latest issues of FHM, Loaded and GQ on the way back – the choice of magazines in Dubai was even bleaker than in the Holiday Inn's pool reception.

Sitting on the floor with all the paraphernalia scattered around, I really wished Andy was here beside me. This was his area of expertise. While he'd ditched the Royal Marines, that military discipline and precision planning had really been drummed into him and his second vocation run out of his little caravan in the forest was a tight operation.

He didn't leave anything to chance and was meticulous with all the fine details. He even had camouflage netting draped over the caravan and tripwires with bells attached at 100m around the perimeter. And he never kept much cash in the caravan. No, no, no – only he knew where his little safety boxes were buried among the surrounding trees. Apart from that his training had also taught him to be ice-cool in stressful situations, something I knew I'd have to be very soon.

I tried not to think about the consequences of being caught but when you're sharing a room with just yourself and the voices in your head, it's hard not to let your thoughts wander off in all directions.

Not seeing Alison again. Not fucking Alison again. Actually, not fucking a girl again for a long time started at the top of my list. Then being raped or, worse, gang-fucked was a close second, but I really didn't want to dwell on that.

Then, from nowhere, my eyes welled up as my mind drifted to somewhere it hadn't been for a while.

The biggest worry was not Alison or the sexual violation. It was my mum.

It had been three years since my dad died. School sweethearts, they'd been together for 40 years. He'd literally swept her off her feet being one of those Rock 'n' Roll, jiving kids who danced brilliantly and was exciting to be around.

I can't remember a time when they were ever apart, except those last few months when my dad was in and out of hospital, which towards the end became more 'in' and less 'out'.

Being the only one of her three children left living in Aberdeen, I felt like I had to take on the role of surrogate husband. She's never stopped grieving, and it took at least a year before I managed to convince her to go out and spend an afternoon doing something enjoyable.

For those first 12 months, she barely left the house. The sentimental bond to menial tasks, such as grocery shopping, going to the bank or buying a newspaper, were deeply rooted in memories of her and dad doing these things together.

I managed all those chores for her until I realised that this is not what dad would have wanted. He loved her smile and seeing her happy. He wouldn't want her to sit inside all morose for eternity. I had to show her a way – a future that had some light in it, a way that allowed her to be happy again and celebrate the memories of times and places.

Ever so slowly, her smile did return, just in glimpses, like when we reminisced down at the beach that time when dad ran into the sea fully clothed to turn around my dinghy, which he thought was drifting out to Norway. The water was only about three feet deep and I was a competent 11-year-old swimmer, but he was one helluva worrier my dad.

Her biggest smile returned, surprisingly, when I told her about the opportunity in Dubai.

'Your father would be proud,' she said, glowing.

I didn't know how she would react and while, selfishly, I had no hesitation in accepting the job, I worried how she would cope alone. But she didn't want to stand in my way and at no point even hinted that she would struggle without me. In fact, she acted even more positive and independent in those final weeks before I left for Dubai.

'One year, two years tops,' I told her, promising I'd be back before she knew it.

Yet now, here I was, lying on a hotel floor with 70 grams of marching powder, lighter fluid and a knife like a scene out of Trainspotting, trying to smuggle it all into Dubai. If caught, I wouldn't be seeing her for a lot longer than two years.

I halved and quartered each of the 10g bags into small wraps so they could easily slip inside the record sleeves without showing any obvious outlines. First, they each needed to be wrapped in silver foil, then dipped in the lighter fluid to mask the scent of cocaine from any sniffer dogs.

Then, after carefully positioning the wraps inside the sleeves, with eye-watering precision, I dabbed minute blobs of glue onto the records' cellophane, smoothing my fingers along the top to reseal it.

I kept five 'clean' records out of the box. They would go in the carry-on Black Market polythene bag, along with the magazines – I was planning to make these a distracting talking point about music and DJing with customs or cabin crew, if questioned.

I slapped some record-label stickers on the box, deliberately ripping and roughly peeling some off again to make it look a bit more used and well-travelled. I did the same with the 'AWA' label that had been stuck to my holdall, picking it off and affixing part of it along the top so you only read '…WA', with half a logo showing. Then I unrolled a small strip of the 'FRAGILE' tape and wrapped that across the lid.

The final and most important part was the padlocks. Shutting the case, I looped the metal padlocks into the two latches. The box was now sealed and airtight – no scent was going to escape from this.

This was it. All I needed to do now was hold my nerve.

Chapter 25

The Heathrow terminal, as always, was heaving. Thousands of passengers were zipping around, either checking in or checking out from their worldly travels.

Thankfully, the Arabian World Airlines check-in zone was just a couple of letter blocks away from where I was standing. I'd only been in the terminal for a few minutes, but I was very conscious of the armed police patrolling and dreading the sight of any sniffer dogs.

Standing in the queue for the check-in desk became more tortuous with every passing minute. The wait is excruciating at the best of times, but I was constantly 360° scanning for the armed paw patrol, wishing the line to speed up and cursing the time-oblivious, disorganised families at the front.

Finally.

'Just the one item to check in, sir?' the AWA steward asked, as she weighed the flight case.

'Just the one, thanks,' I calmly replied.

And then, off it went. I watched for a few seconds as 15 fine records and 70 grams of London-chopped cocaine sailed its way along the conveyor belt, heading to the cargo hold of Arabian World Airlines Flight AW480.

Time for a beer.

By the time I settled into my seat on board, I was a lot more relaxed. I flicked through the in-flight movies again, but unsurprisingly, nothing had changed since the last flight and there was nothing to top The Fifth Element or Men In Black.

Pulling out Loaded magazine, Jo Guest greeted me on the front cover – her legs spread open straddling a black leather chair wearing sexy white stockings, push-up bra and without knickers, her hands carefully positioned between her thighs to protect her 'modesty'. The cover lines read JO GUEST: EVERYTHING YOU EVER WANTED TO KNOW ABOUT HER SEXUAL FANTASIES; PORN AWARDS WINNERS, plus a list of celebrity features and interviews: *Chris Waddle, The Charlatans, Faithless, Maradona, Prodigy* and *'Top Model Nosh'.*

Looked like there was enough in there to keep me entertained for a fair chunk of the flight.

After finishing the Sour Cream Pringles and can of Heineken, I remembered reading the Maradona and Charlatans features, but that was it. I must have conked out shortly after, as I was awoken by the adjacent passenger clambering back into her seat and elbowing me in the arm.

I looked up and the on-screen flight map showed we were now only an hour from touching down at Dubai.

24 hours ago, Shell had also landed at Dubai, eventually.

■ ■ ■

'Michelle, can you come with me, please?' the flight purser asked, with the airline's personnel manager standing by her side outside the Heathrow briefing room.

Michelle was just about to join her cabin crew for a pre-flight briefing and had never before been stopped.

'What? What's it about?

'Michelle, please come with me,' her purser replied, as they made their way along the corridor to a small windowless AWA office. 'Take a seat,' she said.

Michelle sat on one of the four armless, hard plastic chairs.

'Michelle, we have reason to believe...'

This was it. Michelle's heart beat faster and faster. She could feel the hot flush on her cheeks streaming down onto her neck and she was ready to burst into tears.

'...we have reason to believe you have been drinking alcohol before this flight,' the purser said.

Wait. Wait. What did she say? Alcohol? Alcohol? Not drugs?

Michelle started to breathe again.

'Alcohol? But I haven't drunk anything before this flight,' Michelle replied, regaining some composure and starting to drain the redness from her face.

'Your hotel room bill this afternoon showed you had six bottles of Heineken just four hours ago. We now need to breathalyse you and measure the alcohol in your blood,' the personnel manager stated strongly.

'I haven't drunk anything, honestly. Some London friends popped over to see me who I haven't seen for a while, that's all. They were the ones who drank the beer.'

As Michelle confidently predicted, the breathalyser test didn't reveal any alcohol in her bloodstream. But the purser and manager didn't apologise – it was all part of the airline's strict health and safety monitoring. Shell now knew, though, she'd have to be more careful and curb her in-room entertainment before future flights, to avoid becoming 'known' and popping up on any radar of suspicion.

■ ■ ■

Carefully, delicately and slowly this time, I lifted the holdall out of the overhead locker and calmly waited for our line of seats to start clearing into the aisle.

The four-hour sleep had thankfully removed the temptation for any more beer, and I was feeling match-fit and focused. There were now three more checkpoints to get through:

1 – Passport Control.
2 – Baggage Claim.

and then 3 – the 'Nothing To Declare' green zone. Get past the green zone, and I'd be home and dry.

The white-robed customs officer waved me towards his booth. I picked up the holdall from the floor and took a few steps forward, carrying my passport and the Black Market bag in my right hand.

With a face of misery that said 'don't dare fuck with me', he looked down at the passport and scanned it into his machine.

'You not stay in London for very long?' he questioned, holding onto the passport and staring dead-eyed at me.

'Family illness. My uncle. He doesn't have long to live, so I wanted to visit him before it's too late.'

'Hmm,' he muttered, glancing down to read his computer screen again.

Seconds ticked by, feeling like minutes...

'Why you hurry to come back? Back to Dubai?'

'My work. I'm a journalist at the Daily UAE and have some important interviews in the next few days.

'Hmm.' He held his stare, before looking down again at the screen.

He continued reading the monitor and flicking forwards and backwards through the passport. Then...

'OK, come.' He handed over my passport and ushered me through.

One down, two to go.

The baggage carousel had only just started spitting out luggage when I got there. There was the usual cluster of suitcases at first, then once all of those passengers had claimed what was theirs, there was a lull for ten minutes as the rest of us stared at the vacant carousel sluggishly going round and round and round. Everyone stood patiently, no doubt hoping none of their luggage had been mislaid or, in my case, seized and opened.

I was willing the sight of the record box with every luggage item that popped out from behind the black draft curtains.

It must have been another ten or so minutes, with dozens of suitcases, golf bags, prams, baby seats and overpacked rucksacks passing before me, when YES, there it was. As it came down the little ramp onto the carousel, the flight case ungraciously tipped forward onto its front with a thud.

I gently jostled the mum and dad in front to make room for an easy swoop off the carousel as it approached.

Lifting it past their kids, trying not to kneecap them in the process, I placed it on the floor about ten yards away for a quick examination. Result. Padlocks were completely sealed. No tampering or attempt to open them by the looks of it. Plus, there was some new 'FRAGILE' and AWA stickerage on the sides to give it an even more seasoned and authentic look.

Two down, one to go.

The 'Nothing To Declare' green zone was usually a small walkway of some 30 or 40 yards, and in the few airports I'd been to so far, I'd never seen it being nothing short of empty every time.

I picked up the pace to mingle in with a throng of passengers as we started walking through the green zone. As expected, there were no customs to be seen but the walkway was longer than what I remembered and, up ahead, I could see there was a left corner to turn.

The crowd swelled with trollies and pushchairs, as we came to the bend, and I was forced into the left-hand side…

…Shit.

As we came round the corner, 10 yards ahead on the left were two customs officers standing next to a long white table. I looked directly at them, perhaps for too long before shifting my eyes to the front and willing myself towards the exit doors sliding open just 20 yards away.

My heart was beating faster with every step and I was finding it harder to breathe as I was now within a few feet of the officers.

Then…

'Sir,' came the imposing authoritative voice as the officer stepped out in front of me, extending his open hand just inches away from my chest. 'Welcome to Dubai, sir. We'd like to examine your bag. Do you have anything to declare, sir?'

'No,' was all I said, as I could feel myself floundering inside and any more words risked sounding nervous as hell.

'OK. Step over here, please. And place your bags on the table.'

'Did you have a nice flight, sir?' the officer asked, standing by my side while the other pulled on white latex gloves and started unzipping the holdall.

'Good, thanks… Slept for most of it.' I forced a smile, trying to steady myself and keep calm, while my mouth became drier with every second.

Each item was carefully removed from the holdall and laid out on the table. The trainers, the T-shirts, the hoodie and CK boxers.

Then he picked up the Black Market bag. He pulled out each of the five records, examining them one by one, front, back and running his fingers around the edges.

'You DJ?' he smiled as he looked up.

'I try to,' I joked, trying to act casual. 'Just bought a load of records in London,' I said, confidently tapping the flight case.

'Expensive?' he asked.

'Very,' I said. Some are from the US and cost about 20 pounds or 100 Dirhams each. They're very delicate as well.'

He gently put down the record he was holding and delved further into the plastic bag. Then he briefly paused, as he started to pull out the GQ magazine at first. He hesitated again, peering into the bag, and signalled towards his colleague before standing up.

'Wait here,' he said and he walked off behind one of the security screens, clutching the carrier bag.

What the fuck is going on?

'Keep calm. Keep calm,' I kept telling myself, as the minutes passed and I lit the second Marlboro Light.

Mercifully, the remaining officer was not interested in making small talk and he turned towards the waves of passengers flowing past from the other flights.

I also faced the crowds of happy chattering tourists and UAE families passing by, trying my best to look relaxed and mask the nerves that constantly ebbed and flowed inside.

The image of Billy Hayes and the frisbee unexpectedly drifted into my head and I could feel a bead of sweat run down the side of my neck. I turned away from the officer, momentarily taking in some deep breaths as I could feel the uncontrollable tension building and the grip of fear starting to take control.

'Hold it together, Jimmy. Fuckin' hold it together, son,' I was telling myself. 'Good thoughts. Fuckin' good thoughts. Clear head. Football. Music. Alison. John Hewitt. Anything.'

I could feel the perspiration now seeping through the back of the T-shirt between my shoulder blades. Nothing yet was showing on the front, so I turned round, facing the table and the officer. But I knew it wouldn't be long before this nervous sweat would spread to other areas and become more visible.

Were they watching me on camera? Had a security scan penetrated the metal box and picked up the gear? Were they deliberately taking their time to put me under more pressure? Were they waiting for me to bolt towards the exit?

As the passenger flow dwindled, the remaining officer turned towards me. He held his gaze for about 10 long seconds before eventually saying:

'You like Dubai?'

'Yes... very much,' I instinctively replied.

'Why you like Dubai?'

'Erm... sunshine and beaches...'

'And the people,' I quickly added, trying to add some charm.

He grimaced and nodded, before stepping closer to the flight case, resting his hand on top and tapping it several times with his thumb.

Then, just before he was about to ask his next question, his colleague returned from behind the screen, placing the plastic bag of records and magazines back on the table.

'These. These magazines are not allowed in the UAE,' he said brusquely.

'No. No.

'Not like they were before. Not allowed. Not in Dubai.

'But now we fix.'

He placed FHM on the table. Cover girl Melinda Messenger now had a thick redacted black marker pen scored across her tits. He flicked through the rest of the magazine, stopping in places to show more redacted black marks over the tits of Melinda again, Carmen Electra's skimpy photoshoot and one of Melanie Sykes.

It was the same with GQ. There weren't as many scantily clad in there and none, of course, were topless, but poor Jennifer Aniston and Natalie Imbruglia had thick marker pen scored over their 'sexy' photoshoots as well.

There was no sign of the Loaded magazine, though.

'The other magazine? No. No. Very serious. Too much. Too, too much,' he said dismissively, waving his finger.

'OK. Now you go,' he said, stuffing the heavily censored FHM and GQ back into the bag and handing it over.

The other officer stepped aside from the table, and I flipped the holdall over my shoulder and lifted up the flight case, still trying to control the nerves racing around inside, fearing a 'just one more thing' Columbo question at any moment and a heavy hand being placed once again over the record box.

'Thank you,' I instinctively said, desperate to dart off quickly but resisting the urge.

I knew the back of my white T-shirt was so soaked through you could probably see patches of skin, but I had to calmly keep walking forward.

Ten yards to go... closer than a penalty kick...

Five yards... I can almost touch it...

Two yards...

The exit doors slid open... I crossed onto the other side. I was there. I was out. Fuckin' made it.

YE DANCER! I FUCKIN' MADE IT! My heart was still banging like a drum as I looked around in front for the taxi rank, not daring to look back into the green zone.

I was still paranoid about a shoulder tap, and it wasn't until I'd stepped out of the terminal into the humid afternoon air that a sense of relief started to descend, followed by a realisation of the absurdity of what had just happened. Sitting in the back of the airport taxi, a little smile of relief unlocked across my face, as I tapped the carrier bag of magazines by my side.

Distracted by tits. Who'd have thought it?

Thank you, Jo Guest. I bloody love you.

Ali, knowing the Heathrow flight times by heart, was expecting me. Standing behind the concierge desk in the reception area, he'd clearly planned not to leave that spot until I arrived, with a magazine opened up and a bottle of water and ashtray to the side.

I strolled in with a confident smile, as we clocked eyes on each other.

'Jimmy,' he said enthusiastically, opening his arms and stepping out from behind the desk. 'My friend. It is good to see you. You had a good trip?'

'Brilliant trip, Ali. Brought you back a present or two,' I replied with a bit of swagger, giving the record box a little sway on the side.

We made our way into his office and Ali locked the door behind.

'Ali, before we do the business. Can you tell me what the fuck is this all about?'

I placed the record box on the floor and laid out the magazines on his table. I flicked through them, showing him redacted photo after redacted photo.

He burst out laughing.

'They're not even naked for fuck's sake,' I said.

Ali held open the double-page spread of Melinda Messenger on all fours, purring on a leopard-skinned sofa, seductively staring back at you in her lacy black underwear.

'Ha, ha, ha. Did you have any more?' he asked.

'I did. Loaded magazine with Jo Guest. But they kept it.'

Ali laughed even louder, slapping the table in front of him.

'Pornography is illegal. And to them, my friend, this is porn. But they always keep the dirtiest for themselves,' he said, still mesmerised by Melinda's photo spread laid in front of him.

'Greedy bastards,' I said.

I lifted the flight case up onto the table and unlocked the padlocks, flicking up the metal latches. As I opened the lid, a pungent waft of the trapped lighter fluid filled the air, momentarily catching me by the throat.

I pulled out the records one by one, asking Ali for a knife. He turned the key on his desk drawer and ruffled in amongst the junk of scrap paper, pens, bull clips and rubber bands, before handing over a small stainless-steel dagger. Before he closed it, I glimpsed what was unmistakably a leather pistol case poking out from underneath a folder. No surprise, I guess, for a businessman of his ilk.

Intrigued by the methodology, Ali watched in silence as I slit open the cellophane around the record sleeves and started to neatly count out and line up the foil-covered wraps.

'Wasn't expecting it to be as much as 70 Gs, Ali. But here you go. It's all there.'

Ali unfolded a few of the foils then the wraps from within.

He smoothed out two small lines, inviting me to go first.

'Aaah. Good,' he said after testing the sample. 'No fuck-ups. And new tunes. You did good, Jimmy. You did good.'

Ali reached down to unlock the safe behind his desk and pulled out a brown Jiffy bag. Marked on the front was 'Scottish DJ'.

'See, Jimmy. I always had total trust in you.'

Again, desperate to be spending my time with Alison and not Ali, I made a polite goodbye, agreeing to catch up later.

'Say hello to Alison. She'll be a happy girl now,' Ali said, unlocking the door.

I zipped back upstairs to the apartment.

Two grand. Two fuckin' grand of bangers and mash (as Cockney Dave would say) was now lying on the bed, as I stared longingly at the neat pile of 500 Dirhams banknotes.

Job done. Now it's game on with Alison.

Chapter 26

For the previous two days, Alison had been wondering how I'd been getting on back in the UK, visiting Uncle Nick on his 'deathbed'. I explained it would be near impossible to call her with all the family I'd have to meet, plus jumping on and off flights from London to Aberdeen and back again in just 48 hours wasn't going to leave free time to chat. Apart from the ruse, I also didn't want any trails leading back to her should anything go wrong with the drugs run.

Lying on the plush, oversized sunlounger beds during the day, Alison's mind frequently drifted from reading Bridget Jones's Diary to thinking about the past six months we'd been together.

It was not the first time Alison had dated someone in the 'DJ scene'. Back in her hometown, she was known for being a bit of a DJ groupie, flitting and flirting between DJs from different club nights.

She thrived on being a 'face' by screwing a 'face', and got a buzz from finding herself in the DJ booths, VIP rooms and exclusive after-parties. In her parents' eyes, she was the perfect daughter, but she wanted to be the rebel daughter – well, a part-time rebel, one that could still rely on mum and dad to bail her out in emergencies.

The only time she'd been close to losing their support was

one Sunday morning after a particularly heavy weekend where she'd caned it on pills and ching for 36 hours.

It had seemed like the best idea at the time. At 4am, Alison was stood leaning against the kitchen worktop, relentlessly chewing on gum, gibbering to Georgia, who'd become one of her best clubbing pals over the past two years. The two of them were nodding to the music being blasted out from the decks in the after-party living room while watching the artist at work in front of them.

For 30 minutes, the girl in front had been face down on the kitchen table, her head pressed into her hands, trying to keep as still as you possibly could after necking three Es while Tommy Two Tics applied his steady hand on the tattoo needle, colouring in the white of the dove etched on her right shoulder.

Covered in tattoos from neck to toe, Tommy Two Tics was the favoured tattooist in town, known for perfecting some of the weirdest and most elaborate designs requested from his clientele. Always one for a party, Tommy wasn't shy on dipping into the nose bag either while tattooing, but knew to stop when the gear triggered his 'two tic' nervous twitch.

Still on a high, Alison followed on from the girl, eager to have the exotic blue feathered kingfisher inked on her shoulder. For over an hour, she sat topless at the kitchen table holding a hand towel across her chest, tucking it in under her armpits while Tommy applied his artistry.

Georgia, who by now was going a bit cross-eyed and chewing faster than a pneumatic drill, kept assuring Alison it 'looks beautiful', which was backed up every so often from another pilled-up kitchen gatecrasher, who'd stop on their way to the beer fridge and have a good look, saying 'Fucking Ace, Tommy. That's fucking ace.'

Tommy had been going for a solid three hours that night before the twitch hit. Luckily, he'd just stopped and moved the needle off Alison's shoulder to change the ink for the beak. But that was it, he knew he couldn't go on now, especially since that elongated dagger-like beak required such precision and a steady hand.

'Sorry, love, I gotta stop and draw a line here." Which he literally did. "Can't do anymore tonight. Too wasted. I'll finish it off the next time,' he said, as the second twitch shot through him.

Ever so quietly creeping into her parent's house and up the stairs to her bedroom at 10 in the morning, Alison had just peeled her top off, lifting it above her head when her mum knocked and walked in.

The red-raw, disfigured kingfisher stared right back at her, eliciting a scream, then a gasp as her mother covered her mouth in disbelief.

'What have you done? What the hell have you done?' The screaming quickly returned.

Alison, by now on a major comedown, with raging paranoia and anxiety setting in, had no energy or ability to argue, told her mum to do one, flipped her the bird and curled up under her duvet, hoping not to emerge until Monday morning.

Cocooned in the duvet with her dilated eyes wide open, she could hear her parents raging downstairs, as her mum explained to her dad what she'd just seen.

It was weeks before she and her parents could have a calm conversation about anything without the tattoo being mentioned and, by then, she couldn't wait to leave home and start her new life as a flight attendant with Virgin Atlantic.

Alison inserted the bookmark at the beginning of the

chapter: *Monday, 30 January* and closed the novel, resting it on the table next to her Sony Discman, the bowl of dates and a rainbow-coloured mocktail.

She slid on her Prada sunnies and stretched out, untying the strings on her bikini top. She pulled it down slightly, trying to minimise the tan lines as much as possible while not revealing too much, conscious of the prying eyes from the security guards positioned around the private beach.

Jimmy was definitely the best guy she'd dated in a long time, she was thinking as she closed her eyes. Out of all the DJs, he was, without doubt, the cleverest and not just a caner or dull records geek. His proper job as a journo was exciting and it was the first time she'd dated someone with qualifications, though his pay cheque at the end of the month wasn't exactly worth shouting about. He was cheeky and made her laugh all the time, plus she'd never been to the homeland of kilts and Ewan McGregor. He was definitely for keeping, she convinced herself.

'After tonight, that's it. No more. It's just me and Jimmy,' she swore adamantly.

In just a few hours, she knew she'd be back inside the luxury villa behind her, dining with Hasan, unsure if she'd later be sharing a bed just with him or with one of his other hand-picked air hostesses.

'My Jimmy is back tomorrow. And tomorrow is the start of a new me. From tomorrow, it's just Jimmy and me, nobody else.'

■ ■ ■

I was desperate to see Alison and really hoping she'd not been placed on standby for another flight – or, worse, was already in the air, on her way to another destination.

I had so much adrenaline rushing through me, still on a high from the London trip, and wanted to celebrate large with champers and an overdue fuck.

Buzz. Buzz. Buzz. Buzz. I kept pressing her apartment bell.

Shell answered.

'Hey, Shell. It's Jimmy.'

'Hey Jimmy. Up you come.' She buzzed me in.

I stepped out of the lift and saw another guy walking out of their apartment down the corridor towards me. He was mid-20s, crew cut hair, wearing a Hawaiian shirt with a skateboard tucked under his arm; probably British, definitely Western European.

'Arite?' I said as we passed each other.

He didn't respond, keeping his eyes straight ahead on the lift.

Oh well. Moody fucker.

Shell was waiting by the opened door.

'Hey, Jimmy.' She gave me a hug and closed the door behind.

'Who was that?' I asked.

'Oh, just one of the stewards. Was on a flight with him last week and we promised we'd catch up when back in Dubai.'

'Alison here?'

'No, she's not, Jimmy. She wasn't here when I got back from London, so I presume she's on a flight somewhere. Must be back soon though.'

'Fancy a beer?' she offered, walking through into the open-plan living room.

A little deflated that Alison wasn't there, I took a seat on the sofa. Shell would have to hear the story first, then, but not before she revealed her own close-call on her flight back.

'I should have known, Jimmy. One beer maybe won't get noticed but six just a few hours before a flight? Shit, that was stupid. The airline knows everything: when we check in, check out, when we eat, what we order, how much we spend. It's all recorded. Don't want to go through that again,' she said, pouring herself a large glass of Chardonnay.

'You'll have to cut back on the TV chat then. Get Omar out of your room sooner,' I half-joked.

A few more beers and Chardonnays in, we were clinking our glasses to a job well done.

'A well-fuckin-oiled machine.' We laughed loudly.

With the tunes playing from the stereo and our chat getting more bubbly and boisterous with each drink, we didn't hear Alison unlocking the front door.

'Hello, you two,' she said standing in the archway of the living room, looking a little perplexed at how cosy we appeared to be.

She whipped off her pillbox AWA hat and unfurled her hair from underneath. She flung the hat on the kitchen island and draped her uniform jacket over the bar stool.

I jumped up from the sofa and she came over, placing her tender hands on my face with a kiss before running her fingers through the back of my hair and neck. We didn't care that Shell was sitting just inches away, her eyeline now in full view of my erection, which couldn't be hidden as Alison kept hold of the kiss and teasingly pulled her nails down my neck.

Fuuuuck. I'd missed this.

'Alright, alright, you two,' Shell butted in.

We unlocked and I volunteered to get Alison a glass of wine from the kitchen, buying some time for the tent pole to subside.

'Where have you been?' Shell asked her.

'Was on a standby and got called out for a two-dayer in Delhi,' she replied, as I handed over her wine.

'Packed flights there and back. Bloody knackered,' she said, exasperated and flopping into the sofa.

'How was your uncle, Jimmy?' she asked, looking over at me in the kitchen, concerned.

'Aye, he's fine,' I instinctively replied, before quickly reminding myself he's meant to be knocking at death's door, ready to check out of this life. 'I… I mean as fine as can be with only a few days to live, you know.'

The three of us relaxed, dipping into more wine and briefly recounted what we'd been up to over the past three days: Shell's uneventful Heathrow flight, Alison's dull and tiring trip to Delhi, and my sombre visit to family back in Scotland.

Alison eagerly probed further into my wider family, keen to know who's who, how old and young they were, and where they all lived in Scotland. She was a talking cliché of a tourist, asking if the family had a clan tartan, did anyone in the family still wear a kilt, did my dad used to drink whisky every day (well, no – but, yes, every second day) and how many of my relatives were ginger?

I couldn't resist a wee bit of fun, though, as I explained there was a troublemaker in the family, someone who's always getting into scraps with the police or 'the polis', as grandpa calls them.

'Aye, he's my cousin Wullie or Oor Wullie, as my auntie affectionately calls him. Everyone's heard of him. He's in the papers a lot. He doesn't mean any harm, but trouble seems to find him.'

I left it there, looking forward to the day when she discovers the truth about who Scotland's Oor Wullie really is.

Shell was getting bored of our chat, as Alison continued to talk 'family', starting to sound a bit like a wedding planner.

'Is there anything else they eat apart from potatoes and soup?'

At that point, Shell smiled and stood up, walking over to the kitchen and scouring the cupboards for some food.

She filled a couple of ornate porcelain bowls with olives and dates. Knowing me well by now, she also tipped a generous portion of the supersized Lay's bag of salted crisps into a much bigger dish.

As she carried them over, the door buzzer went off.

Startled, Shell glanced at her watch.

'Shit. I'll get it,' she said, clunking down the bowls on the coffee table.

We heard her buzz the person up, before she nipped back into the living room.

'It's one of the crew from my London flight. He's got some extra fags for me. I'll be back in a bit.'

We heard Shell welcome the guy in and then the two disappeared into her room. A few minutes later, the apartment door closed shut again and Shell was back in the living room.

'Who was it?' asked Alison.

'Oh, you don't know him. He's new. Only joined a month ago and just figuring out how our little staff marketplace works,' she replied, reaching for her glass of wine.

Between my apartment and the girls, we were probably stocking more fags than Dot Cotton's lifetime subscription to Lambert & Butler. But they were so cheap there was little money to be made on them, it was purely for personal use or family gifts to take back home.

Alcohol was different.

Dubai couldn't become the 'Monaco of the Middle East' without allowing access to alcohol – something that Sharjah was painfully learning, as it remained a strictly dry state but was losing out severely on the tourist dollar. So, despite the strict sharia laws stating that alcohol is 'haram' or forbidden, the rules in Dubai had recently been flexed to grant hotels permission to sell alcohol in their restaurants, bars and on-site nightclubs.

Outside of this, the only legal way for expats to buy alcohol was through applying for a special permit to purchase at a few of the licensed stores in Deira, but this was a lengthy and frustrating process requiring you to submit your passport, payslips, employer's contract and your landlord's tenancy agreement to Dubai's police department. After a couple of months, you might be granted a liquor licence, which permits you to buy a 'limited' amount. But then, after 12 months, you've got to renew it again and go through the same process.

'Fuck that' was the view of most expats opting for the easy black-market route, though everyone still ran the risk of being fined or imprisoned, as you actually needed a licence to just drink in your house or even offer a drink to a guest.

There were two types of black markets across the UAE. The first was the 'hole in the wall'.

Dotted around the poorer Emirate states of Ajman and Ras Al Khaimah were a number of remote, abandoned warehouses, and fronting each of these was literally a 'hole in the wall', behind which a man would stand at your service. Then, behind him, filling the brick warehouse from floor to ceiling, were hundreds of crates of Heineken, Budweiser, Coors, Corona, Michelob, 'Smirnoff', 'Johnny Walker' and a whole lot more – but, sadly, still no Tennent's Lager.

You made your transaction, tried your best to conceal the cases in your car, then stealthily navigated your way back to Dubai, twisting and bumping along remote roads to avoid any of the police spot checks on the main dual carriageways.

The second black market was the airline crews. Removing the risk of police roadblocks and stomach-wrenching alcohol counterfeits, if you had an in with the stewardesses then the transactions could easily be done in any of the AWA accommodation blocks without anyone knowing.

This was more your refined black market of spirits and liqueurs, rather than beers, and came at refined prices. Hennessey, Veuve Clicquot, Moët, Jägermeister and Baileys would set you back double the price of the UK, while providing a healthy bump in the crews' monthly income.

Luckily, I was benefitting from the fruits of the cabin crews so didn't have to worry about desert treks to the 'hole in the wall' anymore.

As usual, I spent the night at Alison's. She only stayed at my place now if we'd been up to the fourth floor and were a bit worse for wear. I wasn't complaining – her gaff was a lot more comfortable.

Leaving her asleep in bed to recover from her Delhi trip and last night's hangover, I pecked her on the neck, winced at the kingfisher and snuck off just after 7.30, heading back to the apartment to get changed then into the office for a 9am (ish) start.

Looking over at Davey's desk opposite. I noticed that it had been cleared of all his personal stuff. His London-themed desk calendar, miniature cactus, Arabian World Airlines mug, the Lego Superman Blu-Tacked to his terminal and the sweaty bag of gym trainers kept under his desk had all gone.

What was he going through right now? Poor sod.

I'd heard he'd been released from the city hospital the previous week, but had been taken straight to the overcrowded Al Aweer Dubai Central Jail to await trial. And that could be a lengthy wait – in some cases, up to a year before actually appearing in court.

Davey was streetwise, but not street-tough, and I didn't fancy his chances if violence was to come his way. His Cockney guile might be his only self-defence. The charm and blag had helped him wriggle out of several awkward situations in the past, but that was on Civvy Street, not the slammer, and certainly not in a foreign country. His only other option might be if he had any way of accessing his money. Maybe he could pay for some protection and privileges? How the fuck that worked inside, though, I had no idea.

I'd never set foot in any prison at home or abroad and really wanted to keep it that way, but the question I kept chewing over was: should I go and see him or not?

The expat community here didn't have a good reputation for supporting 'friends' who fell foul of the law. One minute they're all your best buddies, but get arrested and they disappear in a flash. You soon realise that your only visitors are British Consulate representatives, your lawyer and, if they can afford it, someone from your family. But soon the family money for lawyers, the flights and hotels runs out, and the lonely stretch between visits from mum or dad gets longer each time.

You're on your own. Get used to it.

But Davey was a good guy, I kept reminding myself. I needed to know what caused the crash and I needed to hear it from him. I'd have to go and see him.

Twenty minutes into writing up one of my stories, there was a flurry of bodies streaming into the newsroom. I checked my watch. It's only 9.45. What the fuck is going on?

But there was the Editor, the features editor, the news editor, the chief sub-editor, the picture editor and one of the photographers feverishly talking and snaking their way around the desks to their seats by the Editor's office.

'Nice of you to make it, Jimmy,' the Editor curtly fired in my direction, as he marched into his office.

'Have you seen the news, Jimmy?" the news editor asked, her eyes expressing signs of shock and disbelief.

'Diana. Princess Diana. She's dead.'

The first task for the first reporter in the office on the first shift of the day was to switch on the TV and check the news channels. But, after two months, I stopped because there was never any exciting breaking news out here. I repeat, never.

But fuck. There it was. The news editor flicked on the TV and the SKY news ticker along the bottom of the screen read: PRINCESS DIANA KILLED IN PARIS CAR CRASH

What? Dead? How? Have they got this right?

I picked up the TV controller and flicked to the other News Channels. RAI, Al Jazeera, CNN, Bloomberg... everywhere I checked, the headline was the same: PRINCESS DIANA KILLED IN PARIS CAR CRASH

I stood motionless, frozen in disbelief, staring at the TV screen, almost waiting and wishing for the headline to be corrected to PRINCESS DIANA STABLE AFTER PARIS CAR CRASH

But no.

The Editor and senior team had been called in an hour before for an emergency meeting with Hamza upstairs. The pagination was going to be bumped up for tomorrow's edition. It was now all hands on deck to get reactions from across the UAE. Royals, foreign embassies, businesses, charities, celebrities – we would split the patches between us and hit the phones all day.

I was given royals and foreign embassies, while Joe – when he eventually turned up around 10.15 and also oblivious to the world's biggest news story – was tasked with charities and celebrities.

We pounded the phones all day, not breaking for lunch, just running on adrenaline, topped up with cigarettes and coffee.

By 10pm, we were wired, clocking up a 13-hour shift, filing four stories each and struggling to string any cohesive sentences together.

'What "L" is the capital of England?' Sorry, Bob. I'd have even failed on that one in this state.

The Editor and Hamza thankfully signed off the paper just after 10 and off it went to print for tomorrow's news stands.

Joe and I looked over at each other, exhausted. His hair was sticking up in all directions, like a wacky professor, constantly running his fingers through it as he chased countless UAE celebrity agents to try to get those two or three killer quotes. His top four shirt buttons were undone, each one unfastened throughout the day as the deadline pressures mounted.

I looked down at my yellow, nicotine-stained fingers. I was reeking. Both our ashtrays were overflowing and amazingly, for the first time ever, we had run out of fags.

Barely able to talk, we looked over at the news editor and, thankfully, she told us to go home.

'Good job, boys. See you tomorrow,' she said.

Dreaming of bed, I was praying for taxis to be waiting outside as we carried our wraithlike bodies out of the newsroom.

'Mr Cola. Sorry, Mr Jimmy. Mr Hamza would like to see you before you go,' came the voice from behind reception as we headed towards the main door.

'Sorry, what?' I replied, thinking I must have misheard.

The security guard on reception repeated the instruction as I turned to approach the desk.

'I'm fookin' off, Jimmy. Gotta get some shut-eye,' said Joe.

'Good luck,' he muttered as he walked out into the humid night-time air towards the taxi rank.

This was some sort of sadistic torture. Why would Hamza want to see me now? After a 13-hour shift on a day like this?

I took the lift up to the third floor, gasping for some water. I grabbed a small plastic cup and filled it from the cooler just outside his office, then knocked on the door.

'Aidkhul,' came his voice from behind the imposing mahogany door.

His room was also reeking, but not of fags – cigars. He'd also been putting in a shift today, I suppose.

Still puffing away, he sat within a halo of wispy smoke behind his desk.

'As-salam alaykum, Jimmy. Good to see you. Take a seat. Good work, today. A sad day, yes. A very sad day, but some excellent stories. His Highness will be very pleased. How is your family? How was your uncle?'

Exhausted, it was easier for me to answer it this time, as my natural demeanour at this point was definitely sullen, sombre and sapped.

Looking down at the floor then slowly up to Hamza, I said: 'Not good. They don't think he'll last next week.' I paused, too tired to say any more, and hoping he'd see this as some sort of grieving and not pursue further questioning.

'I am sorry to hear this,' he replied.

He tapped out the ash from his cigar, this time resting what was left of the body on the edge of his chunky, square, glass ashtray.

'Now, I have an important matter to discuss with you. While you were away, the Minister of Cultural Affairs contacted me. He informed me of an embarrassing episode during your visit to the palace.'

Fuck. Busted. This is all I need now.

I kept silent and looked into the plastic cup, momentarily thinking of chucking the water all over Hamza and going out with a bang.

'I can understand why you did not want to mention this. This was embarrassing for you, but Jimmy, more embarrassing for the palace. Embarrassing for His Royal Highness. The Minister has offered his sincerest apologies. This is not how they treat guests. You were not to know you cannot smoke inside the palace.'

He opened his desk drawer and placed a leather-bound 'Daily UAE' branded folder on the table. From within that, he pulled out two pieces of paper, one large and one small.

'Here. This is a certificate from His Royal Highness commending you for your commitment to protecting endangered animals. It is sealed with his royal signature.'

Okay. Thank fuck. Not busted.

'And this...' He held the small rectangular slip of paper in his hand. '...is a reward in recognition of your investigation, which you should have received at the palace.'

He slowly slid the paper over with his finger. It was a cheque. And what was that... 2,500?... No... hold on... 25,000... 25,000 Dirhams was printed on the bottom right corner with my name MR JAMES IRVINE in black bold type in the centre.

Fuuuuuck. Jesus fuck. Get in!

I couldn't believe what I was seeing through my tired eyes. That was the equivalent of around five grand in good old British pounds sterling.

ARABIAN ROYAL SHEIKHS MA HAND WITH £5,000 CHEQUE

How Aberdeen man became the animal king of the UAE. Read his exclusive story, pages 8-11.

A front-page splash back in Aberdeen, guaranteed.

'That's very kind of him,' I stuttered, still in disbelief and a bit fuzzy with exhaustion.

'It is an honour for you and for the Daily UAE,' Hamza added, reaching over for the cheque and neatly placing it back in the folder with the certificate.

'Here. Keep them safe in this.'

Then just as he was about to pass it over…

'There is one more thing, Jimmy. Your passport. Can I have your passport back please?'

He held out his right hand, keeping his left pressed on top of the folder on the table.

I patted my back pocket and could feel the outline. Yes, it was still there from when I'd set off from London.

I handed over the 'Property of the Crown' document, as Hamza slid the folder and the 25,000 Dirhams cheque back towards me.

Tiredness half-tempted me to say: 'Nice doing business with you, Hamza.' But, by now, at 10.55pm, it would have come out as an incomprehensible mumble and been a bloody foolish thing to say.

Apart from a few more 'thanks', I had nothing else to say, still wishing my way into a taxi and bed.

'Good night, Jimmy,' he said, motioning towards the door.

And then…

'Wait, let me get you a car.'

He picked up the desk phone, pushed the intercom button and briefly spoke in Arabic.

Placing the receiver down, he said: 'My driver will take you home. He will be at reception.'

Bloody hell. An unusually generous gesture from Hamza.

Stepping into the Mercedes S Class, I sunk into the cushioned leather seats, leaned my head against the window and closed my eyes, relaxed in the knowledge the chauffeur would drive straight to my front door.

What a day. Diana's death, the double shift and here I was, five grand richer than I was this morning and seven grand up on this time last week.

I had the money for Alison's ring and some serious wedge on the side for something else. But what would that be? I wasn't sure yet.

Chapter 27

Since Joe's 'little chat' with Shell, things had definitely cooled off between the two.

He still came round to the apartment, but less frequently and rarely stayed overnight.

I could only think of a couple of occasions in the past few months he had, and each time the four of us had been chang'd up to the eyeballs, jabbering away until the wee hours.

Their business arrangement was still in place and, despite the fuckfests drying up, Shell seemed more than content that she was making some decent dough on the side.

Shell enjoyed having Jimmy around the apartment and Alison had grown into a trusted friend, but recently, she'd started yearning for the days when Alison was off flying and she'd be left on her own.

Those had become her business days.

The days to make even more money.

Growing up in Liverpool's Toxteth in the 1980s and early 90s, Shell knew what the spectre of poverty felt like. She was surrounded by it every time she stepped out of the house – the burnt-out cars, the boarded-up shops, the husks of fire-ravaged buildings and the smackheads standing on the street corners. At home, it manifested through her dad – angry, violent and unemployed, like 50% of the other adult males in the area. Every day was a fight for survival and everyone in her family hustled, doing whatever it took to get food on the table and, when they could, a nice bit of clobber on the side.

Her older brother Stevie was propping up the family, more so than the dad, who had a little racket going on down at the docks selling off pilfered cigarettes from the African shipping containers.

At 22, Stevie was also unemployed with no qualifications. His car mechanic apprenticeship had ended abruptly, after the garage was torched one night, and nobody else could afford to take him on.

It was to be his football connections on the terraces that offered a new career for him. The top boys in the RRS firm had recently moved into the pharmaceutical trade, specialising in pills and speed, and as the city's club scene started exploding, so too did their dealings. Stevie became one of their foot soldiers, selling in the clubs and around the estates.

The hunger for uppers in a depressed, destitute city was relentless, and on some weeks, he was easily taking home between one and two grand. Always resourceful and canny, within a few months, he'd soon managed to double that to between three and four, and it was all thanks to Shell. Shell and her baby.

Halving the quality of gear to double the quantity, Stevie's lightbulb moment came when Shell was treating her toddler for constipation. Watching Shell scoop out the white-powdered, Macrogol laxative for little Ashleigh, he borrowed the bottle and got to work in his makeshift bedroom laboratory, using it as a cutting agent.

With Ashleigh tucked into bed, the two of them sampled a couple of lines that evening. Six wired hours later and a few bog rolls less, he had proved his theory right.

This need to make extra money was deep-rooted in Shell's Scouse blood. But it wasn't just money for her, it was money for her family – well, for her, her mum and her Ashleigh.

She omitted declaring that she was the mother of a four-year-old when she applied for the Arabian World Airlines job, fearing it would be used as an excuse to reject her. But when the job offer did come through, it was the happiest moment the family had shared in years, apart from Ashleigh's birth, of course – although that was a double-edged sword, as the father was that lass-beating cunt of an ex-boyfriend.

The money and lifestyle AWA provided was something to protect at all costs, and she'd kept motherhood a secret since she joined, even from Alison. Some nights she wanted to tell her and break down in tears, especially that day when she couldn't fly home for Ashleigh's birthday and the other time when she was poorly with chickenpox. But she couldn't. She couldn't take the risk. Nobody could know out here. She was alone.

But the ackers. Yes, the cash she sent back home would give her daughter a better life than she ever had. That was her focus and the temptation to double it, like her brother Stevie had done, was too great to ignore.

After the beating she took from Joe that night when he discovered she'd been talking to Jimmy and Alison, she sensed that in Joe's mind the matter was now closed and trust had been restored.

He'd made it clear that any future repercussions would be even more violent. This time he'd deliberately avoided bruising her face, gagging her face down, tightly fastening the wire cables around her wrists to the metal bed frame.

Kneeling naked between her straddled legs, he visibly took sadistic pleasure from fiercely whipping her bare back with his leather belt.

…four, five, six, seven, eight times he rained down with full force, each time verbally abusing her to 'keep your whoring mouth shut'.

'She's got the message,' Joe later arrogantly relayed back to Ali. 'No need for Lahore,' he said reassuringly.

But the only message Shell got was he was as big a bastard as her last boyfriend and now there was no loyalty. No fucking chance.

After a little shopping trip to the chemist opposite the AWA building, Shell now had her own mini-laboratory hidden away in the false ceiling of her bedroom. Carefully calculating and cutting out 40% of the cocaine, she forensically mixed in white-powdered laxatives and procaine anaesthetic, creating new wraps for her to sell independently.

She could hardly open a stall down the souk saying 'open for business', so she'd entrusted two other Scouse cabin crew she'd become friends with after a couple of messy Bangkok stopovers to act as her sales reps. Over the past couple of months, through some discreet conversations in the expat bars and on the beaches, they had identified a growing clientele of mainly British expats desperate for some nosebag in the desert.

What started as once a week was now twice-weekly visits to Shell's apartment to collect the gear, as demand was steadily rising.

Selling only to the Brits would keep Shell's little racket away from Ali and Joe's fourth-floor dealings as well, since that was still mainly an Arab and Russian crowd, plus Shell knew she could keep under the radar, so long as her sales team quietly operated out in the field while she remained anonymous behind the scenes.

Keep delivering for Joe and Ali.

Don't let them suspect anything.
Just smile, then fuck 'em over.
That was Shell's payback and pay cheque.

■ ■ ■

Since the London trip, I'd played at Ali's fourth-floor gatherings a couple of times, dropping in the new tracks and reshuffling sets around, desperate for some kind of reaction.

But despite the packed apartments, it was the same old response. Blokes' eyes on tits, hookers' eyes on money, no eyes on the DJ. The only one to get excited was actually Ali, when I spun Byron Stingily's 'Get Up Everybody' for the first time. He surprisingly lost his shit, jumping out of his private booth, knocking over the bucket of champers in the process, and started dancing in front of the decks. A couple of his regular sour-faced Russkies quickly tottered along after him, breaking into their soulless prances, but he was properly clubbing it like he was back in the Ministry.

Party for 60 but only one fucker actually appreciating the music. Not a good return on the 90-plus quid I'd splashed on records.

And so it was, on that second night of DJing to the damned since flying back from London, I decided it would be the last.

Still a little lively from the token gift Ali always left under the right-hand turntable, I sat on my balcony at 2am, feeling royally fucked off.

Feet resting up on the edge, I leaned back in the plastic chair, sparking a Marlboro Light, looking up at the hundreds of stars piercing the still, desert sky. I knew Ali was hooking me in every time, with the chance to play and the free bugle, but I hated how

I fell for it every time, like a fuckin' flapping seal waiting to be fed.

I knew I had to break the cycle. Had to break his grip. Had to cut off my ego from the honeytrap of DJing. Yes, Jimmy, you were DJing, but it's to a room full of unappreciative zombie whores and paralytic punters.

With a healthy £5,000 bonus now in the bank account and two grand of cash rolled up and hidden in my Sambas, the answer was there to be found surely.

Why the fuck was I relying on Ali?

I didn't need him or his sleazy desperados for a club night. No. I'm going to do it my way – a melting pot of Club USA, Vague and Amnesia in the desert with an injection of deep-fried Scottish club culture.

That's it. I can fuckin' do this. I've got the records. Just get the kit and the party will come. The magical magnetic pull of DJ and clubbers is always strong and there's a rave to be had in them thar dunes.

Tomorrow, I was going to take control. I'll head to the electronics stores in Deira to hunt down Technics and a sound system.

Go and make it happen, Jimmy. You can do this!

The gear had clearly wrapped me in the cloak of invincibility!

Then, just as I was lighting the third fag contemplating the creation of 'Desert Dance', 'Sandtazia', 'Desert Dome' or whatever the fuck I was going to call it, there was an uncomfortable rumbling from my backside, followed seconds later by another unexpected stirring and then another.

Swiftly darting from the balcony to the toilet, I unzipped my trousers just in time to guide the mini-explosion down the lavvie. For another 20 minutes, I remained perched on the loo, emptying my bowels every few minutes, confused as to what the hell was causing this torrent. Then, as I tore down on the last few sheets, I reached over into the sink cabinet, desperately scouting around for more rolls, but fuck, there weren't.

I dared to shuffle out of the bathroom towards the kitchen with my kecks around my ankles, praying I wouldn't be caught out by a sudden eruption.

Kitchen roll. Find the kitchen roll!

I shimmied along in tiny steps quicker than the chorus of Riverdance, clenching my naked butt cheeks hard, fighting the force of nature trying to burst through.

Kitchen roll. Kitchen roll. Where's the fuckin' kitchen roll?

I frantically pulled open all the cupboards. Nope, nope, nope, fuckin' nope, then fuckin' yes!

Hallelujah!

Stuffed behind the kettle was the arse-saving kitchen roll. But no, I don't believe it. Two sheets! Just two motherfuckin' sheets! I tore off the first with ease, then the last, the last bloody sheet, remained stuck to the cardboard roll. I frantically tore and picked away before it became a disintegrated, useless mess of tiny pieces.

One sheet. I've only got one fuckin' sheet!

Gotta find some more paper and quick.

'JI. Which JI is famous for shitting himself all over his apartment?'

Not now, Bob. Fuck off, Bob.

Then, in that moment of panic and desperation, it came to me. There is more paper in here!

Like tiptoeing through a minefield, I ever so slowly inched towards the bed, arse-cheek muscles still clenched like a vice, and reached under the pillow to pull out FHM and GQ.

As I held the mags in my hand, I could feel an uncontrollable rumbling rising again. This one's going to blow the doors wide open. With three giant rabbit hops, I leaped back into the toilet, just as the shit-tsunami hit.

The white-tiled bathroom floor was an innocent victim, sprayed in the sudden crossfire between door and toilet bowl, and I sat there again for another 30 minutes as the aftershocks continued to explode in varying degrees.

Melinda's seductive eyes looked up at me from the floor, but I just couldn't. I flicked the pages forward and there was Natalie Imbruglia, but she's way too cute and nice. Then bingo! The GQ eight-page Liam Gallagher interview. He's a fuckin' mouthy cunt. Have some of this ye shite bag.

I ripped out the eight pages and wiped that scowl right off Liam's face with my arse.

They'll never know, but Chris Waddle, Tom Cruise, David Beckham, Posh Spice, Mel Gibson, Mercedes-Benz, Audi, Burberry, Prada and Chanel all served their purpose throughout the night, as the unsightly plastic shopping bag of crumpled, shit-smeared magazine pages was filled to the brim.

Eventually, after 20 or so calm minutes of a nervous stillness, I cautiously removed myself from the toilet seat, hoping the worst was over, showered and then lay naked face down on the bed, clutching the last few torn pages of FHM just in case. It was now some time after 4am and shortly after I fell asleep.

Waking up at 9.30, I felt ten stone lighter while my arse felt like it had been at the mercy of a sand grinder. Forgetting to close the bathroom door, the stench of excrement was starting to take hold as the morning sun shone through the curtain gaps, warming up the apartment like a slow stew.

Despite being sapped of energy, I knew I couldn't lie in bed anymore while this acrid cloud was floating around the apartment.

The fleas had been up bright and early and were already tucking into their bathroom breakfast, as I pinched my nose with one hand and grabbed the bag with the other, trying to hold it as far away as possible. I quickly tied it shut with the handles then placed it outside the apartment door, checking first to make sure nobody was around. I'd take it to the garbage skip on my way out.

I slowly got myself together, showering again... for a lot longer than usual, spraying on the Lynx Africa from top to toe then giving it a good blast around the apartment as well and looking out a crisp, newly ironed Lacoste tee. Pulling on my boxer shorts was a painful affair and I had to abort the first time, retreating to the bathroom to apply Vaseline in some delicate areas.

Standing, definitely not sitting, on the balcony, I looked out across the Creek, which by this time was a bustling river channel of passing dhows with stacks of cargo precariously piled high on their decks. Sipping my second coffee, I enjoyed the morning sun on my face, pleased that I had booked the day off work, and was looking forward to making two significant purchases.

At 25, none of my friends were married or even close. The only person I knew who had ever proposed and got married was my older brother. Despite fucking up the marriage pretty quickly through his after-work shaganigans in the classroom, I heard the proposal had gone smoothly, albeit at a stinking Roquefort-cheese level of plus 11.

Influenced by his obsession with Richard Gere movies, he hired a stretched white limousine, which was chauffeur-driven to his bride-in-waiting's parents' house. Paranoid that his own Pretty Woman may have had plans to go out for the day, he rolled up outside at 8 in the morning.

Standing up through the limo's sunroof with a bouquet in one hand and a ghetto blaster in the other, he pumped out Phil

Collins 'A Groovy Kind of Love'. Nobody appeared after the first play of the song, but after a few toots on the horn from the driver and him calling out 'Lucy' several times, the front door was eventually opened by her mum.

At first gasping and shouting back over the music 'Fit are ye doin' Kevin?', it soon dawned on her that this was a marriage proposal. She rushed back inside, screaming 'Lucy! Lucy! Lucy! Get yersel' down here now.'

With Lucy standing in the doorway in her PJs, part-shocked but smitten by him and the occasion, she watched in gushing awe as he sang along with the words until the end. Dressed in an ill-fitting grey suit with blue pinstripes and a thin black-and-white leather piano tie, he walked up to her doorstep and bent down on one knee. 'Lucy McCall, will ye marry me?' he asked, opening up the ring box.

She said yes and the watching neighbours burst into applause. Hurrah!

Four weeks after their wedding, he was banging his boss. Fuckwit!

Crowd or no crowd? Music or no music? String quartets I've heard are popular, or someone on the classical guitar? Or maybe the bagpipes? But I didn't want to go too cheesy, certainly not to the level of my brother.

First things first – buy the ring. That was today's mission. Well, part of the mission. Technics are just as important, right?

I headed down to the Gold Souk and stood outside its ornate arched entrance, feeling as clueless as I was that time I was looking for leopards. Where the hell was that shop window that hypnotised Alison? The one where she dropped the biggest hint since Mrs Robinson told Benjamin Braddock: 'My husband will be back quite late.'

Wandering into the labyrinth of golden shimmering walkways, the traders tried to coax me into their shops as usual. And just like before, I ignored them. I didn't want to be harassed or pressured into buying the first ring on show. I needed time to explore and process the criteria of what makes a good engagement ring.

Sparkle? Yes. Gold? Yes. Or silver? Yes. Diamonds? Yes. Carats? Yes. I think two or three sounds fair enough. Settings? Um, nae idea what that means, but I've heard it's important. Budget? Maximum of £2,000. Hopefully, haggle it way down below that.

At the end of the day, it's all about the price and the sparkle. If I can get it for a good deal and it sparkles enough, we'll both be happy.

With my list of demands and best poker face on, I stepped into the first shop.

Two minutes later, I stepped out, flustered.

WHAT! THE! FUCK?

Modern? Vintage? Cut? Style? Colour? Clarity? Shape? Round? Square? Pear? Heart? Yellow gold? White gold? Platinum? And then there were the carats. One, two, three carats – who was I kidding? Half a carat was already maxing out the budget.

I was overloaded and bamboozled with questions and choices from the politely spoken smiling assistant. The pressure to choose. The pressure to buy. It was too much and I could feel the cool poker face dissolving into a perspiring crimson mess.

Embarrassed at such naivety, I walked a good couple of hundred yards and alleys away, paranoid that word would be spreading like fire from shop to shop that there's a diamond virgin about and he's fuckin' clueless, but has cash and is ready to buy.

Taking some time to compose myself with a cigarette and a bottle of water, I checked off the list of newly enlightened knowledge in my head, took a deep breath and entered 'Malik's Finest Gold Merchants'.

Malik's son, as it turned out, served me. Speaking in perfect English and sounding posher than a Nigel Havers tea party, Malik's son was a Cambridge law student. And unequivocally charming for someone a couple of years younger than me.

Feeling calmer, a lot calmer, and warming to his charisma and sense of 'fatherly' guidance, I narrowed the ring choice down to two after 20 minutes. One modern, one vintage. Both white gold. Both half-carats. Both round. One was 6,000 Dirhams (£1,200), the other 9,000 Dirhams (£1,800).

It was the shop lighting in the end that helped make the final decision. They both sparkled brilliantly under the bright lights and Malik's son, the expert after all, agreed. So, both were equal on sparkle, it was down to the price. After a little back and forth on the haggling and pretending to walk away, we settled on 5,200 Dirhams – 800 off the asking price. Job done. Next stop: Technics.

Like a nervous twitch, I kept feeling my jeans pocket every few seconds to check if the ring case was still there. I'd cleared the pocket, moving cash, cards and keys to the other side so there was no reason to dip into it other than to confirm the ring was still safely with me.

I tried to picture the proposal in my head as I walked through the crowded Deira streets towards the electronics stores. My mind was still racing with options of when to propose and where to propose. With no 'best man' or close friend out here, I had no one to turn to for words of advice either – not that I'm sure the boys back home would actually have been oracles of wisdom.

The last time Gaz gave me his 'sound advice' was when I bought that 'bargain' of an ex-company car, a Peugeot 406, from a dealership in Guildford. Gaz, being the self-appointed petrol-head in the group, agreed to drive us down in his motor from Aberdeen overnight to pick it up.

Arriving at opening time after the nine-and-a-half-hour journey, we stepped out of his Ford Escort resembling something between the Blues Brothers and Cheech and Chong: shades on, hair dishevelled, cigarettes in hands but honking of weed, we awkwardly clambered out, leaving behind the takeaway boxes, empty crisp packets, cans of Coke and chip-shop paper littered inside. Gaz's 'essential reading' of The Daily Sport was shamelessly displayed on the dashboard as we parked up just in front of the garage reception window.

Gaz applied his so-called mechanical knowledge to the questioning of the sales assistant, as he propped up the bonnet and prodded around, laid down on the floor to look under the chassis, and took it for a test drive with me around the block.

Despite 106,000 being on the clock, he said: 'It's a good car for £800. You should buy it.'

The journey back north proved him wrong.

The nine-and-a-half-hour trip down turned into a 16-hour drive from hell on the way back.

As I was tanking it along the motorway somewhere between York and Newcastle, smoke started billowing from the bonnet. That led to an embarrassing crawl along the hard shoulder at 20mph for 15 miles before coming off to find a garage, which after a lengthy wait, discovered the fan belt had gone.

And despite Gaz's unfounded confidence that everything from now on would be 'arite', everything was not 'arite' after that either.

Only a couple of hours later and still not in Scotland, the Peugeot started rattling and chugging like Chitty Chitty Bang fuckin' Bang. This time, the emergency garage from an unpronounceable village in the middle of nowhere discovered it was the catalytic converter that was fucked. Rusted and leaking. For three hours, I sat outside that garage by the side of the road before getting whacked with a bill of £120.

And Gaz? By this time, he was already on the final stretch, just a couple of hours away from Aberdeen. Apparently, he'd lost me in the traffic hours previously and thought I'd sped off ahead of him on the motorway so he just kept on going.

Nope, I definitely wasn't missing out on 'sound advice' from him.

Approaching one of the largest electronics shops in Deira, I felt no nerves for this kind of shopping. I knew exactly what I wanted. This was all about the haggle and getting the best price.

Seeing the large, red 'SALE' posters plastered across the store windows, I switched off the 'marriage proposal' deliberations and zoned in on creating the first House night in Dubai: *Paradise 49*, a nod to the Paradise Garage and original disco clubs of New York. It captured what the night would be about: free-spirited and hedonistic; on the edges of society; good people; positive vibes; high energy; and safe for all – black, white, gay, straight and everyone in between. Plus the 49 was our own touch on Dubai's temperatures never reaching 50°C!

Buying a bundle of Technics 1210s, mixer and sound system, I managed to negotiate an extra 200 quid off the sale price. And when I asked as I was leaving the overjoyed assistant, who must have been on commission, if he knew where I could buy a generator, he led me outside and over the street to another store where of course he knew the staff.

Promising to get me a 'good price', he spoke in Urdu to

someone who I assumed was the boss man, before coming back over smiling.

'2,500 Dirhams – 1,000 less than the store price,' he said, pointing to the price ticket on the generator box. 'This is a good price. Just for you.'

How they worked out their mark-ups and commissions between the two stores, I had no idea, but overall, it seemed like I was bagging a good deal, and I shook his hand and then the store manager's.

The set-up for the first ever *Paradise 49* would be delivered to the apartment on Friday. And thankfully, there was no mention of 'inshallah'.

Chapter 28

Traditionally, of course, you'd seek permission from the bride-to-be's father before proposing, but having never spoken to Geoff (let alone met him) and being 4,000 miles away from knocking on his front door… it wasn't going to happen.

I also didn't know if Alison had actually mentioned me to her parents over the past eight months. Knowing how strained their relationship had become in recent years, it wouldn't surprise me if she hadn't.

Her growing wealth in Dubai over the past few years had made her less dependent on bank transfers from mum and dad, and, with that, it sounded like their frequency of contact had also dwindled to two or three times a year.

On my side, the only family I needed to share the news with was my mum. Through the gateway of Janet, she'd tell my brother in Carlisle, my sister in Leeds, my Uncle Nick (alive of course) and, within 24 hours, half of Aberdeen.

Before those beacons were lit across the north-east coastline, I knew I'd have to get on the blower to the boys. They'd be mightily miffed if they heard second-hand. Not because they wanted to be the first to congratulate me, but the first to fire abuse and take the piss.

'Fuck off, Jimmy min!'

'Ye winding us up?'

'The Riddler's hitched!'

'Is she up the duff?'

'Does she carry a cane?'

'Is she 60?'

'Are you banging a granny? A blind granny?'

I could imagine what was to come. But I'd be the same, if it was one of them. That was the unwritten law of the pack – never praise, always ridicule.

The hotlines back to Scotland would have to wait, of course, until I'd convinced Alison that spending the rest of her life with me was actually a good idea.

Today was the day of the proposal. I wanted to keep it a secret until just before the grand gesture, so although we were spending the day together, I didn't suggest anything lavish or overly romantic, which would hint at something greater to come that evening.

Alison picked me up around 2pm in her yellow and black, Suzuki Vitrara. We'd decided to go 'wadi bashing' near Fujairah, about one hour's drive east out of Dubai.

I'd never tried it before, but Alison had 'several times' and, by now, she assured me, she was more than competent in steering off-road vehicles through the dry riverbeds and mountain passes.

The engagement ring had never left my side since I'd expertly haggled that price down at the Gold Souk. Tucked under my pillow at night and always in the front-right trouser pocket during the day, it came everywhere. But today was going to be the last day as its guardian. Tonight, it would pass to Alison. Safely and forever on her finger.

Out of her sight, I reassuringly patted my shorts pocket before jumping up into the passenger side of her 4x4.

'Ready?' she asked.

'As always,' I replied, thinking about both the trip and the proposal.

In the back, I could see Alison had stocked up on litres of water and had taken time to make a little picnic, packed inside a Harrods wicker basket. Beers and wine were chilling in the cool box as well, she said. Good girl. She was clearly up for making this a special day.

I slotted the Sasha & Digweed Renaissance CD into the player – the perfect tracks for our excursion into the desolate desert mountain ranges without a care in the world.

A converted Dubai speed-freak, Alison tore along the dual carriageway, topping 100mph as we left the city skyline behind us. Shades and baseball caps on, the tunes were pumped out, blasting the speakers while we both threw our hands in the air singing along to 'Perfect Motion'.

We hardly spoke as the music and wind swirled around us, drowning out anything we tried to say. But we didn't need to. Turning to each other every few seconds, our smiles were as wide as the horizon ahead. We were blissfully happy, lost in our own bubble of giddiness and joy.

Coming off the dual carriageway, we travelled along stony pothole-ridden tracks, passing through roadside villages and date-palm plantations.

The rugged Fujairah mountain ranges ahead pushed up from the dunes like crocodile teeth as the merciless sun beat down. 38°C was the temperature shining off the dashboard control panel. Dunked in factor-30 sun cream, I was prepared this time and had no worries about a lobster-grilling.

By the time 'Mismoplastico' started playing, we'd arrived at the gorge.

Alison turned down the volume.

'We're here. At the start of one of the wadis. Get ready to hold on tight – it's going to be bumpy,' she said.

The 4x4 jolted from side to side, as Alison slowly guided it across the boulders scattered along the arid riverbed. Our bodies thrashed around, as the SUV climbed rocks almost vertically before crashing back down with a thump on the other side.

'Shit. Are you going up...?' I asked, not believing what was in front of us.

Alison laughed: 'Don't worry. I've done this track before.'

The gigantic rock in front pointed upwards to the sky. You could not see beyond it. But now we were on it. The 4x4 gripped the base and we started to inch up its steep face. Alison moved up and down between the gears, the engine continually revving, and with her hands flitting quickly around the steering wheel, we zigzagged towards the top. By now, I was almost horizontal, like being laid out on a dentist's chair, head tilted back, seeing more of the sky above than what was in front. I gripped the top of the metal roll bar above with one hand and the underside of the seat with the other, wishing this to be over.

Alison didn't speak.

She was fighting the rock, navigating its contours to the top while mastering the mechanics of this three-litre engine.

As we reached the boulder ridge, the car tilted forward and levelled with a crash, which threw us up off our seats and down again with a back-and-arse-bashing thud.

'Wow! Woohoo!' I shouted, mightily relieved but buzzing off the adrenaline rush.

Ahead was a crystal-clear water pool with a stream trickling down into it from the overhanging rocks. Lush foliage was growing between the cracks of stone and two goats stood aimlessly above at the summit, blindingly lit against the deep-blue sky.

'Come on,' Alison said, as she switched off the engine and hopped out. 'I'll get the basket. You grab the cool box.'

The sun was fiercely beating down, forcing us to hot-foot it across the exposed burning rocks to find some shade by the side of the rock pool.

She unfolded the blanket, an intricate weave of gold, red and blue threads. Cashmere and suede goatskin, apparently. It certainly looked and felt expensive. And sitting on these scorching-hot, hard surfaces, I welcomed the protective layer of luxury under my tush.

Alison unpacked the picnic, taking out a couple of Scotch eggs, BBQ chicken drumsticks, a salad bowl and a couple of ciabatta rolls filled with prosciutto, salad and cheese.

'Damn. I forgot the oysters,' she joked.

'Aye, funny one,' I replied.

I uncorked the chilled Chardonnay and filled two of the plastic wine glasses. We leaned back against the shaded rock face, clinked our glasses, and took a moment to admire the glistening water and enjoy the cloak of silence wrapped around us.

'Beautiful, isn't it?' she said, staring ahead.

It certainly was. It was blissfully still and zen-like. If you were into meditating, this would be a prime spot, I thought, but maybe later in the day when it wasn't so bloody hot.

She reached over and held my hand, gently stroking it with her thumb while still gazing across water. At that moment, a crimson-coloured dragonfly flew into view, hovering within arm's reach of us. We sat motionless and held our breath while it hung in the air with its transparent wings feverishly flapping, creating a faint humming sound. Then, seconds later, another appeared just a few feet away.

'Never been so close to one, let alone two,' I whispered.

'Eek. Look at that,' she said, trying to muffle her excitement and not disturb the dragonflies as she pointed to the edge of the pool. 'Over there. Over there. On the right.'

A sandy-coloured lizard with black spots scampered across the stones. Then it suddenly stopped, paused for a few seconds and darted into one of the shady crevices in the rocks.

As suddenly as they appeared, the dragonflies flicked their wings and shot up vertically, before zipping off over the pool and out of sight.

'That was amazing,' she said, as she leaned over with a kiss.

She snuggled her head onto my shoulder. Up until this point, I'd been feeling as relaxed as a Tibetan monk, but then this unexpected voice of sappiness came rushing into my head with its hands flailing in the air like Cilla Black on speed.

Is this it? Is this your Surprise Surprise moment, Jimmy? This *is* it, Jimmy boy. This. Is. It!

Our little oasis suddenly felt like it had transformed into something wondrous from a Disney movie. All that was missing was Mr Bluebird flying onto my shoulder. I could feel the knots in my stomach tightening and my heart racing. I had to do it now. Everything *was* perfect. I patted the right-hand pocket of my shorts and gently moved Alison's head away to stand up.

'What you doing, Jimmy?' she asked.

I couldn't answer. I was running through what I was about to say in the next 10 seconds, desperately trying to grab the words floating around my head and rearrange them into an order that made sense.

Standing in front of her, I then crouched down on one knee.

'Aieeeeee!! Ya fuckkkkkkkker!!' I screamed.

The rock was blistering hot, scorching my kneecap.

'Jesus, fuck,' I shouted over and over, hobbling around, rubbing the knee trying to numb the pain.

'You okay, Jimmy?' Alison said concerned, getting up to come over and help.

'Fine, fine. Sit down, sit down. Get back,' I snapped, probably frightening off Mr Bluebird in the process if he was coming in to land. Alison was looking very confused now.

I bent down again, this time hovering the burnt knee a few inches off the ground.

Now at her eye level, I reached into the pocket and pulled out the little velvet pouch containing the ring.

Carefully taking it out, I held the 0.5 carat, white gold, £1,000 bargain-price ring between my thumb and forefinger.

'Alison. Will you…? Will you…? Would you…? Alison. Would you… like to get engaged?'

The words finally rolled up and over the large hump in my throat, spluttering awkwardly out of my mouth.

I'd said it.

'Engaged? Engaged? Engaged? En… gaged!' she said over and over.

'Yes, yes, engaged,' I said hurriedly, conscious of the seconds ticking away now without any sign of acceptance.

She squealed and threw her arms up in the air, then fell forward, wrapping them around my shoulders, yelling: 'Yes. Yes. Yes!'

Bloody hell, she said yes. I couldn't believe it; well, I could (or rather I'd hoped and prayed she'd say yes). I don't know what I'd have done if she'd said no. This was not the place to storm off in a strop.

Relief was followed by excitement, as I reached into the cooler for a beer, then topped up our wine glasses.

To say she was overjoyed was an understatement. We kissed and hugged over and over, both sharing how happy we were with each other and how we'd never felt like this before. She'd definitely been thinking about it as well, as every question she asked, she quickly answered herself.

'When shall we get married? In three months?'

'Where shall we get married? In England?'

'Small or big wedding? Let's keep it small.'

'What will your parents think?' I asked.

'Oh, they'll be fine,' she said dismissively.

'Do they know about us? About me?'

'Yeh, kind of. But they'll be cool.'

Her unconvincing response didn't exactly reassure me of gaining supportive in-laws, but they had a funny relationship, so best to let her lead on this one.

With the second opened wine bottle in her hand, Alison skipped over to the Vitara, switched on the engine and blasted out M People's 'How Can I Love You More?' from the Renaissance CD. The two of us danced by the side, replacing the tranquillity of Disney magic with the banging heady heights of a night at the Ministry.

We cranked up the party tunes for another half hour, before deciding we'd better pack up and start heading back to Dubai. There was one major problem, though. Alison was fucking wasted.

'I'm OK. I'm OK,' she insisted, with a little wobble as she clambered into the driver's seat.

In any other circumstances, I would have taken the keys off her and steered us home, even after a few beers myself, but being halfway up a mountain with a rickety riverbed of gargantuan prehistoric rocks to navigate over and having never driven a 4x4 before, I didn't fancy our chances with me behind the wheel.

She downed some water, more as a token gesture of 'Hey, look, everything's fine now' (the two scoofs wouldn't touch the sides of the one and a bit bottles of wine she'd necked), then she slipped into first gear and hit the accelerator.

We rattled and bumped our way along the wadi. There was 10 times more shaking and braking going down this time than up.

'You okay?' I kept asking, primed for a signal or a response where she'd say no and I'd yank up the handbrake.

'All okay, fiancé,' she replied with a chuckle, emphasising 'fiancé', while not taking her eyes off the rocks ahead.

If marriage is built on trust, then this was the first big test, as we tilted forward at a 90° angle, my chest pressed against the seatbelt, hands flat on the dashboard and sunnies slipping down the bridge of my nose. This was Alton Towers without the safety checks.

Alison's hands spun around the steering wheel as her sandals steadily controlled the brakes. Only once did her feet slip, as we suddenly lurched forward about 10 feet before a juddering halt.

'Whoa!' I exclaimed.

'Oops,' she cried out.

Perched halfway down the rock, she suddenly pulled up the handbrake and paused.

'Just need a minute,' she said, reaching for the bottle of water and taking some deep breaths.

Looking over, I could see her once rosy cheeks had faded and her complexion was a bit peaky. Actually, more than a bit – it was PEAK peaky!

I was really longing to see the landscape the right way up for a change, as I was also starting to feel nauseous.

'Don't think I can do anymore,' she mumbled softly.

'What?' I asked in total fuckin' disbelief, as my outstretched neck was pointing down the rock face and my hands were still tightly clinging to the metal roll bars. 'What? Now? Here? You can't go any further?'

'Don't... Think... So,' she softly replied, pausing for a deep breath between each word.

'OK, let's wait,' I said. There was no way we could swap drivers in this precarious position. To manoeuvre in and out of our seats without tumbling down the rock face at this angle would require acrobatic precision, which we did not possess.

Alison quietly placed her head in her hands and looked down at the floor.

Apart from question time with the customs officials, that became the longest 20 minutes in my life, as the two of us sat silently suspended on the rock, waiting for her queasiness to pass.

Eventually, after a couple more stops, we rolled out of the wadi onto the flat desert track that led back to the main Dubai road. We switched drivers, which took 10 minutes, as I waited for her to stop chundering at the side of the SUV.

As white as a sheet now, Alison closed her eyes and rested her head against the sidebar, taking the full front of the breeze as I drove us back to her apartment. Not wanting to attract the attention of any predatory traffic cops, I kept our speed to about 80mph and started wondering if she'd still be up for our 8pm dinner reservation at the Hyatt Regency.

That was the original plan for the proposal. But now that was out of the way, maybe I should cancel. Would save a couple of hundred quid if I did.

Nothing interrupted the barren landscape between us and the city skyline ahead. No camels, no leopards, no birds in the sky. Only the occasional cargo truck passed in the opposite direction, heading no doubt to a remote warehouse somewhere.

I looked over at Alison asleep. Never in my wildest Scottish dreams as a young loon could I have imagined getting hitched to such a beaut. Even in her drunken passed out state, there was no doubt she was a cracker.

In just over a year out here, I'd busted illegal animal traders, been commended by a sheikh, had numerous front-page splashes, earned amateur stripes as a small-time drug trafficker and was now driving home my own Arabian princess.

As we rattled onto the parking lot outside Alison's apartment block, she awoke, looking rather bewildered and befuddled. She must have been in a deep sleep.

Walking round the corner to the main entrance, the AWA staff bus was parked outside. Among the cabin crew handing over their trollies to the coach driver, we spotted Shell just as she was stepping on board.

'Hey, Shell,' I shouted as we walked over.

'Hey, Jimmy. Hey, Alison,' she shouted back.

'We've got some news for you,' I said smiling.

'Brilliant. Tell me when I get back,' she replied.

'Where are you off to?' I asked

'Heathrow.'

The doors of the bus closed and Shell kissed us goodbye from her window seat.

Chapter 29

The reaction to the news there was going to be a Mrs Irvine was met with two extremes from family and friends.

Calling my mum, she was shocked into silence.

'Are you still there? Helllllooooo?' I said, after rattling on for a few minutes about how happy the two of us were and how she'd love Alison when she eventually met her.

'Oh, I see,' were her emphatic words of endorsement, ten long seconds later, as she processed the news coming down the line from Dubai.

Followed gently by: 'Are ye sure?'

Eventually, she moved on to: 'Well, if yer happy, son, I'm happy for ye,' leaving me with the impression that maybe she wasn't going to be lighting those beacons across Aberdeen.

Standing at the phone box on the street corner opposite my apartment, I fed more coins into the slot and prepared myself for the next round of numbers to dial.

'A fuckin' trolley dolly? Ye got yersel' a trolley-dolly bride?' was Gaz's response as he shouted down the phone in laughter.

'Wait till the boys hear about this. Good on ye, pal. I need to get ma arse out there soon and meet this Alison. Ye know and introduce mysel' to her trolley-dolly friends. Let 'em see Aberdeen's finest stock!'

At 23, Gaz had all the chat and banter of a big-time player

when talking to the lads, but he'd only actually had one girlfriend since he was 16 and we'd only seen him pull once on a night out.

Being an offshore oil rigger probably didn't help with his three-weeks-on, three-weeks-off rotas. Every time he flew back from a three-week stint shacked up with 200 other bruisers on a North Sea rig, the first place he'd head to was the Nile Bar on Union Street.

Dropped off by the Aberdeen airport taxi at 2pm, he'd pull up a stool at the bar and would still be there at midnight. Any girl unfortunate enough to step into his arm's-length drunken snare over those 10 hours was unlikely to be enamoured by his increasingly lairy and mainly desperate come-ons. His Casanova chat disappeared after the fifth pint, making him as attractive as Rab C Nesbitt.

Now it seemed Aberdeen's finest Gaz bag wanted to take his ever-failing charm overseas and test it in a new country. And with his well-paid danger money from the oil rigs rolling in every month, I knew it wouldn't be long before he'd be on that flight to Dubai.

'Fuck off!' was the instant response from Archie. 'Fuck off, min. No fuckin' way. Yer engaged? Tae fanny? Fuckin' engaged tae fanny? Jimmy "the poof" Irvine hitched?'

This went on a bit as Archie questioned the news over and over.

'I cannae believe it. Fuckin' hell, min.

ABERDEEN'S BIGGEST FANNY HEID TO MARRY POSH FANNY.

'There's yer headline. I'll get onto the paper now,' he joked.

A postie since he was 17, Archie wasn't as flush with the cash as Gaz, but that didn't stop him moving quickly onto planning what would be the first stagger of all the lads, as I shared the newsl.

'We'll do one back here and one o'er in Dubai, right? Sure yer missus can sort out some deals on the flights, eh? Just let us know fit month and I'll start rounding up the troops.'

Since Andy had died, Archie had stepped into the organiser-and-logistics role for all of us. It was Archie who found the cheap Ibiza flights and apartments in San Antonio that following summer. And it was Archie who'd made the calls ahead of us arriving on the island to get us onto the guest lists for Amnesia and Pacha.

Now it would be Archie who'd meticulously plot my night of debauchery. Even though I couldn't give him a date, I knew he'd be off drawing up the sordid plans as soon as I hung up the phone.

■ ■ ■

Ali and Joe looked tense, as I approached them, walking back over into the apartment block. Standing behind the concierge desk with the office door open, they paused their whispered conversation as soon as they clocked me.

Ali turned his back and stepped into his office, as Joe said: 'Jimmy, can we have a chat?'

Ali stood behind his desk, Ray-Bans nestled in his thick hair and a lit cigarette in hand. The Martini Rosso-branded ashtray was filled to the brim with ash and fag butts.

Joe closed the door behind me.

'Jimmy. I'll be blunt with you,' Ali said sternly, without his usual charming smile. 'Is Shell selling coke? Selling my fucking coke?'

Shit. Where had this come from? I wasn't expecting this. Why would he think that?

'No, Ali. Of course not,' I said instinctively without much thought. 'Why do you think she is?'

'Are YOU fucking selling it then?' he snapped back, jabbing his finger at me.

I turned around, looking at Joe standing by the door then back at Ali.

'No way. No fucking way, Ali. I haven't been selling your gear. Why would I sell your gear?'

'What about that whore Alison? Is she selling? Is she selling with Shell? Are these whores in this together, Jimmy?'

Fuckin' cunt. He can't fuckin' call Alison a whore.

'Hold on, Ali. Don't you fuckin' call Alison a whore. Fuck you. She's my fuckin' wife-to-be,' I fired back.

Ali looked over at Joe with slightly raised eyebrows and a hint of a grin.

'Wife-to-be, Jimmy? You're getting married? To Alison?' He seemed surprised.

'Yes.' I nodded. He paused.

'Someone is fucking with my operation. Someone is fucking with *me*! And when I find out who they are, they'll pay the consequences, Jimmy. Pay the fuckin' consequences. You hear me?'

He tapped out another Marlboro, trying to calm down after his outburst. He yanked open his desk drawer and fumbled around to find a lighter, then slammed it shut.

'You better not be lying to me, Jimmy,' he said, holding his gaze with furrowed brows. 'Anyone found fucking with me will live to regret it. I don't care who the fuck they are, I will inflict an almighty pain upon their fucking souls.

'Go. Go.' He motioned for me to leave, as Joe unlocked and opened the door. 'And congratulations. I wish you good luck with your woman,' he said, with a wry smile.

'He doesn't know anything, Ali. You can tell,' Joe said, as the two of them remained standing in the office. 'And I don't think Alison does either. She's too clever a girl to try something on like this. She wouldn't be that desperate and wouldn't take the risk.'

'It's just that bitch, Shell. And she's being taken care of. Then you'll see everything will be okay.'

Chapter 30

It didn't take long for rumours of 'shit gear' to spread around Dubai's nosebaggers. Ali had been fiercely proud and protective of the high-quality reputation he'd built over the past few years. He and Omar had an agreement on the cutting agent applied in London – no more than 20% and only using an anaesthetised powder. He knew the expat crowd would pay good money for what they felt was top-notch charlie and he wouldn't drop his standards.

Now, though, word had worked its way back to him and Joe that people were spending more time wiping their arses than their noses after a night on his gak. Somewhere along his supply chain, it was being diluted and it didn't take Joe long to identify where.

Out of the 10 air mules on their books, only three were trusted with stashing extra in their apartments. Joe visited each of the stewardesses, removing a couple of bags from all three. 'Busy times. Good for business. Good for you,' he told the girls.

Back at his apartment, Joe laid out a neat line of six glass ampoules on the table, two from each of the stewardesses. In front of each, he'd scribbled their names down on a Post-it, making it clear which sample belonged to whom as he started to test for purity.

He measured out and added 20 milligrams of 'cocaine' to

each ampoule. The darker the brown, the higher the purity – anything between 70% and 90%. Anything light-coloured or clear from the chemical reaction meant very-low-to-fuck-all cocaine.

Ten seconds is all it took for the reaction to trigger colours across the glass tubes.

Kelly: dark brown.

Amelia: dark brown.

Shell: yellow piss.

Joe was raging. He double-checked to compare her colours against his test chart. At best, it was showing 50% pure, but it could be as low as 40%.

'Bitch! She's fucking us over,' he said to himself, spinning around and smashing his fist into his bathroom door.

'FUCKIN' BITCH!' he then shouted, as he threw another punch at the door, this time splitting the wooden panel into three cracks. He followed up with a right kick at the bottom of the frame, which broke through the wood, leaving splintered pieces scattered across the tiled floor.

He was shaking with anger, as his face flushed with fury.

She was making a fool of him.

He'd assured Ali he'd taken care of things since her loose chat with Jimmy and Alison, and she wouldn't step out of line again. He'd protected her and calmed Ali down when he'd threatened to make *the* call to Lahore.

Now, though.

NOW, THOUGH...

'I'M making the fuckin' call,' he said out loud, repeating it over and over, as he stomped around his room, his heartbeat pounding.

'FUCK YOU!' He kicked the sports bag, which skited across the floor onto the balcony.

'AARGH! FUCKIN' BITCH,' he yelled, as he shakingly unfolded the scrap of paper with a scrawled phone number, which he'd kept tucked into the back of his wallet.

He picked up the phone receiver and started dialling the code for Pakistan.

■ ■ ■

Shell had only visited Lahore once before. It was one of her first flights when she joined AWA. But since then, the rotas had scattered her around the rest of Asia, sometimes going back to the same place three or four times, but strangely never returning to Lahore.

This worked in her favour when she made a special request to the airline for a Lahore flight within the next month. Joe had insisted she go there to collect a package, which this time would be rewarded with double her usual payment.

It was too good an opportunity to turn down and with Ashleigh's birthday just five weeks away, she'd been saving to surprise her little girl with her dream present: a Shetland pony.

For the past six months, the violence in Lahore and across Pakistan had been escalating, as Shia and Sunni groups clashed. In the past four weeks, nearly 100 people had been murdered, as mosques, railway stations and courthouses were targeted with bombs and gunmen.

Kidnappings, street robberies and rapes had also surged across the city, and like the terrorist attacks, the police were failing to identify or arrest any suspects, with the majority of cases remaining 'unsolved'.

Anti-government protesters calling out corruption regularly clashed with the police on the streets, and in the past three months, nine lawyers and two high-court judges had been assassinated, as a heavy cloak of lawlessness slowly suffocated the city.

AWA was acutely aware of the risk to its airline crews. Its staff shuttle bus from the airport to the Ramada Hotel now had an armed guard on board, while the hotel itself had also beefed up security, with gun-clasping patrols outside the main entrance.

With such a melting pot of sectarian and political violence, it was no surprise that the airline had swiftly approved Shell's rota-request, as many cabin crew wanted to avoid the area and last-minute staff 'sickies' for Lahore flights were becoming more common.

Once inside their hotel however, flight staff were cocooned by the comforts, shut off from the troubles outside. There was no need for them to venture out of the hotel into the toxic streets. Unless, like Shell, you had business to take care of.

This time, there would be no meeting in Shell's room. Hotel security was too tight, and her local contact couldn't risk being stopped and questioned about his purpose. AWA head office guidance strongly advised crews not to leave the hotel during their Lahore stopover, but it was going to be a lot easier for Shell to walk out of there than her contact to walk in.

To avoid any suspicion from her colleagues, Shell had planned to enjoy the afternoon relaxing by the pool and would make her way to the Old City after dinner under the cover of darkness.

She wouldn't be on her own, though.

She felt more secure and relieved, knowing one of her trusted friends would accompany her.

They couldn't believe it at the time when Shell received the rota confirmation.

'Snap!' said Alison joyfully.

'Yes!' They both jumped around hugging each other in their apartment, as Alison revealed they would both be working on the same Lahore flight.

Shell had confided in Alison that it was also a 'business trip' and she had matters to take care of on that first night in Lahore. She didn't ask Alison to escort her, but Alison had insisted, aware of the current dangers and still having this moral sense of duty, like a protective older sister to the girl three years her junior.

They both dressed in traditional Pakistani clothing – Shell wore a long-sleeved tunic with loose trousers tapered at the bottom and sandals, while Alison had an ankle-length, all-in-one khaki dress with her black Puma pumps hidden underneath. Both wrapped plain silk scarves around their heads for added anonymity. At 10pm, they wandered out of the hotel into the dark and crowded streets, blending in with the throng of locals.

It was a 15-minute walk from the hotel to Lahore Zoo, where Shell had been instructed to meet the contact, Tariq, at the gates.

The streets were chaotic, noisy and dirty. Bell-ringing rickshaws and bicycles, beeping scooters, grass-chewing goats, tired-looking oxen and jostling crowds meandered and weaved their way along the narrow roads. Miles of telegraph cables hung loosely down from rooftop to rooftop. Exposed wires and broken electricity boxes clung precariously to the decrepit building walls as wild foliage sprouted in all directions from the brickwork and balconies above.

The main stores had long since closed their shutters. At this time of night, it was mealtime for the locals, as pungent steam hung in the humid air. Dozens of oversized steel woks and boiling vats continuously cooked fish, chicken, goat meat and other unknowns.

They didn't want to admit it to each other, but as they cagily walked around the streets towards their rendezvous, knots in their stomachs were tightening with every step. Tightening and pinching to a nauseous level.

With less than five minutes until the arranged meeting time, they'd both stopped the casual chat; only Shell would break the silence every so often, as she confirmed directions from the folded map discreetly tucked up her sleeve.

'Bottom of this road, then left… Straight ahead… Should be a right down here.'

'What am I doing?' Alison said over and over to herself, trying to stop her eyes from welling up as her chest tightened and her heart pounded.

'This is too much. I shouldn't be here. Where's Jimmy? Why am I not back in Dubai with my Jimmy?'

The iron gates of the zoo were draped in darkness; only a lone streetlight, engulfed by the branches of an overgrown tree, struggled to shine speckles of light through the leaves onto the street below.

Away from the commotion of main roads and bustling side streets, this area was quieter. The constant clicking of crickets in the undergrowth around the zoo walls was all that could be heard. Nobody else was around, just the two English girls standing side by side, nervously looking in all directions, waiting for their contact to arrive.

'He should be here any minute. Hold this,' Shell said, lighting a cigarette and handing the map over to Alison.

Alison couldn't talk. Her nerves were consuming her. She could barely make eye contact with Shell and silently scoured in all directions, partly looking out for the contact, but partly in fear of her safety should any unsavoury locals appear.

Then, unexpectedly out of the shadows, from a small patch

of wasteland to their sharp left, a dark silhouette started walking slowly towards them.

'This must be him,' Shell whispered.

Alison stood motionless.

'As-salam alaykum,' came a voice as he stopped in front of them. 'You are Shell?' he asked.

'Yes. You are, Tariq?' she replied, more confidently than anything Alison could muster at the moment.

'Yes. And you?' He turned towards Alison. 'You bring a friend?'

'This is Alison. A good friend. Trusted friend. She also knows Ali. She is okay,' Shell replied, trying to reassure him.

It was hard to determine any emotional response from his face as his thick black beard covered most of it, and his turban was pulled down, resting on top of his dark slug-like monobrow.

'Do you have something for me?' Shell asked.

'Yes. But not here,' he replied.

'We go somewhere else. Away from here.'

This was not what they were expecting. Meet Tariq and walk away with a sports bag. Job done in under two minutes. Back to the hotel in 15. Simple. That's what should be happening. Not this.

They had no choice now but to follow Tariq.

'Follow me. I have the goods in apartment. Just five minutes from here,' he said as he started to stride off in the direction where he'd come from.

The ground was rugged, strewn with shattered breeze blocks, loose gravel, bricks and clumps of knotted shrubbery. The only glimpses of light came from the faint orange glow of a few street-lights along the edges of the wasteland about 50m away.

They moved deeper into the centre of this desolate area, as

Tariq veered towards the left, appearing to pick up his pace. Now about 10 or so yards ahead, he glanced back and waved his arm forward.

Shell was struggling with her sandals. Not expecting to be going off-road, the sandals were slipping off and, at times, catching the edges of the rocks, making her stumble.

Alison looked back towards her and reached out to hold her hand, guiding her over and around the concrete debris.

She then swivelled back around to follow Tariq.

But he wasn't there.

She stopped and strained her eyes into the darkness, desperately hoping to spot him. Only silhouettes of trees and what looked like a discarded shipping container were all she could make out ahead. The glow of the streetlights was now just a pinprick in the darkness, far away from where they were standing.

They stood still in the eerie silence, surrounded by blackness.

Then 'as-salam alaykum' came a gruff voice.

They turned around and a stocky man was standing with his arms tucked behind his back, just a few yards behind them.

'As-salam alaykum,' came another voice. They turned round to where they'd been facing and another shadowy figure was now approaching just five or so yards away.

'You girls are lost?' the voice said threateningly from behind.

Alison and Shell looked back and forth at both men as they continued to edge towards them. Alison slipped her hand free of Shell's and dropped her arms to her side.

The man from behind stood in silence, then slowly brought his hands out from behind his back. His right hand was grasping what looked like a meat cleaver. Alison stared petrified at the cold sharpness of the metal blade pointing towards the ground.

The man in front was now grasping a wooden club and had taken another menacing step closer.

Alison quickly scoured the ground by her feet. She suddenly crouched down, grabbed a rock and threw it with all her might squarely at the face of the man with the club. He screamed, holding his face in his hands and dropped the weapon.

'GO! GO! GO!' Alison shouted at Shell, as she sprinted off to the right, heading towards the streetlights in the distance.

Shell darted to her right to follow. She was just a few yards behind Alison, running blindly in the darkness, trying to mirror every twist, turn and jump of Alison's across the wasteland, when suddenly, she fell crashing to the ground – her sandal had snagged on the rubble.

She tried to stand up, but her ankle had twisted and she dropped to her knees.

She grasped her ankle then looked up, in terror.

The club came hurtling down on her arm as she raised it to protect her head.

Alison bounded across the rugged terrain like a fleeing gazelle, not daring to look back or stop…

She kept running and running and running.

'HELP! HELP! HELP!'

Shell's desperate cries of help pierced the darkness like bolts of lightning. Alison could hear her harrowing screams repeating over and over and over. But her cries for help became fainter and were soon replaced by cries for mercy…

…then…

…silence.

Alison kept on running, tears streaming down her face as she feared the horrors of what was happening behind.

Finally breaking out onto the lit road, she stopped and dared to look back. Nobody was behind her. No attackers but… no Shell.

She didn't know where she was now, but headed towards the bustling streets ahead. Once she reached the crowded area, she stopped running, but her heart was still beating furiously as she struggled to breathe.

An hour later, she walked into the foyer of the hotel, exhausted and shaking. Keeping her head down, she quietly slipped past the lone receptionist and made her way to the lifts.

She threw herself onto her bed and sobbed uncontrollably.

Chapter 31

It was like the two of them were going on a hen weekend, when they realised they'd both be on the same flight for the first time ever. Granted, Lahore was not the most exciting, exotic or safest of places to party in, but it was clear as I watched them dance around their apartment these two wouldn't be holding back to make it a trip to remember.

I was fully expecting a tired (hungover) Alison to return to Dubai, and despite now being my bride-to-be, she probably didn't want to hook up for another 24 hours, giving her time to rest and recover.

My compact and bijou apartment had become even more compact since the arrival of the Technics, sound system and generator. Stacked up and still in their packaging boxes, they now partially blocked the way between the coffee table and the balcony.

Once Alison was back, I'd have to convince her that storing them at her place was a far more sensible idea, especially as I was about to give notice on this apartment and get the fuck away from Ali as well.

I couldn't wait to show her the flyers for *Paradise 49*. Laid out on the coffee table, I'd designed them at work as little A7 business cards. Easy enough to discreetly hand to someone in a bar or at the Marine Club. Printed on one side was an image of two female models in 70s roller-skating gear and sun visors, with both their eyes redacted in black ink. Above this was the title **PARADISE 49** and the tagline: *'A spiritual thing. A body thing. A soul thing.'*

On the reverse side was the date ***February 5th, from 10pm,*** and a phone number.

Anyone interested would have to ring that and leave a message, along with their fax number.

Once I'd screened the calls for anyone remotely sounding Arabic and potentially undercover UAE cops, I'd fax the coordinates over for the first *Paradise 49* rave.

There were three weeks left to promote it, but with Alison and Shell all over it as the marketing team, I was confident we'd drum up a decent gathering.

There was a KNOCK! KNOCK! at the door.

Shit. I didn't want Joe or Ali to see any of this, so I slid the boxes of DJing equipment out onto the balcony and closed the curtains. I pushed the pack of flyers under the bed, then whipped off my top and ruffled my hair as if I'd been sleeping.

I peeped through the spyhole. Oh. Hello!

I opened the door.

'Alison,' I said excitedly with a huge smile, reaching out to hug her.

She fell into my arms, bursting into tears as I carried her into the apartment.

I couldn't believe what I was hearing. Firstly, that Shell was doing a drugs deal in Lahore. Secondly, Alison had volunteered to go along with her, and now, what, that's she missing? Hurt? Dead? Murdered?

I hugged and stroked Alison's head, as she sobbed on my shoulder, and I tried to piece together the series of events she was explaining erratically.

'They think she's missing, Jimmy. AWA have reported her as missing to the police. But I know, Jimmy. I know what happened. She's dead. DEAD!! I was there. I heard it. Heard her screams! Her last screams!'

She pulled away from me, holding her head in her hands, and sat down on the side of the bed.

'I can't tell them, Jimmy. I can't tell them I was there.'

Alison was right. If she opened up to AWA or the police about what happened, there was a chance that she'd end up arrested herself. Even if she lied at first and omitted the 'drugs deal' part, I didn't feel convinced she would do well against intense questioning and risked collapsing under pressure to confess everything. Ali, Joe, Omar, Shell, me – she might talk about all of us!

No, the best plan was ignorance and silence.

It was another four days before Shell's body was found and two days later, her father had flown to Lahore to formally identify her. 48 stab wounds and her skull caved in – her body had been mutilated. It had been a brutally savage end to her life.

News of her murder unsettled not just those who knew her but cabin crews across the world. AWA issued internal staff memos, reminding personnel how they must take heed of health and safety advice when given, especially in politically or religiously volatile regions.

But they needn't have worried, for Alison and I strongly suspected Shell's murder was not a case of being in the wrong place at the wrong time. In fact, Alison was adamant it had been carefully planned – why else would two attackers be lurking in empty wasteland, tooled up, and why did Tariq suddenly disappear or fail to run back when he heard the screams?

'Someone was behind this, Jimmy,' Alison kept saying as the days passed. She was struggling to sleep, screaming herself awake in the night as she relived the attack over and over. Each time was more vivid and horrific, as her imagination played out the final few seconds of Shell's life.

'They're after me, after me, Jimmy, after me, Jimmy! No! No! Help! Help!' she would yell. It was only during these nightmares in the early hours of the morning when Alison would talk about Shell's death.

'Were they just after Shell or me or both of us, Jimmy?' she'd keep asking.

'Does someone want me dead? Is it me? Why would they want me dead or Shell dead? Or is it Ali? Is someone trying to fuck with his business? Jimmy, what's going on? I'm scared. Really scared.'

I didn't have an answer for Alison, not yet, but knew some of, if not all, the answers would lie with Joe and Ali.

'Shocking, man. I still can't fookin' believe it,' Joe said, as he poked his head around from his computer screen to get my attention.

'Such a nice lass as well,' he added as he continued typing up his story.

Then, a few minutes later, he said, 'Done,' sounding satisfied.

AWA AIR STEWARDESS MURDERED IN LAHORE

23-year-old mother of one killed in street mugging

By Joe Spencer

'Should be a front-pager that, Jimmy boy,' he said, as he logged off and shut down his computer.

'Will I see you at the fourth floor later?' he asked, standing up from his desk and lighting a cigarette.

'No, not tonight, Joe. Not tonight. Don't feel like partying, plus I need a quiet one. Got a busy day tomorrow,' I replied.

'That Alison got you running around with her wedding plans, has she?'

'Something like that,' I said, forcing a little smile.

Shift done, Joe strolled out of the newsroom and, as he did, I clicked the 'PRINT' button on screen.

I walked over to the printer and watched the four sheets of paper headed 'AL AWEER DUBAI CENTRAL JAIL – VISITOR'S PASS' slide out and into the printing tray.

Tomorrow, I had to make a long-overdue visit.

Chapter 32

It had been three months of boiled egg and bread for breakfast. The same serving every day. And always at 5am.

Six hours later, it was lunch. Always rice, vegetables and chicken. Dinner was slapped down at 5pm – more rice and more chicken.

Davey was ever-so-gradually coming to terms with the monotony of mindless repetition and routines, reluctantly accepting that this was as good as it'll ever get inside.

He'd seen the bad days, the days when there was no food. And yesterday was one of those bad days.

He'd only just sat down in the C Block canteen, scooping his hand into the lump of rice on the metal tray, when it all kicked off in front of him.

The Russians moved in on a fellow Brit. Davey wasn't acquainted with him yet, but he was a burly lad at over six feet, with a Leeds United tattoo down his right forearm.

The Eastern European gangs ran the protection racket inside, looking after the weak for some serious monies and favours in return. Anyone who fucked with one of their protected inmates would suffer the consequences.

Fuck knows what the Leeds boy had done, but as he sat there on the bench, settling down to eat his lunch, three of the Russian gang members encircled him. Seconds later it was a bloodbath, as the short and stocky unit with a completely tattooed face and neck brought a metal pipe crashing down onto his skull, then repeatedly on his back, as the poor bloke slumped forward.

Blood poured from his head wound, as the tables around erupted with inmates tearing lumps out of each other – fists, head-butts and kicks, as well as metal trays, tables, chairs and anything else they could grab tore through the canteen like a tornado.

But they weren't really fighting in anger. This was more to alleviate the daily boredom. This was their entertainment, their highlight of the week, their big game, their Match of The Bloody Day.

Davey watched his tray of food fly up into the air, as he seized a chair, holding it in front of him for protection. He tried to shuffle his way through the melee to the canteen's back wall and avoid any whacks on the way, but he wasn't lucky, as a right hook smashed into his ear with deafening force. He staggered towards the exit door, where the guards were now pouring in and tooled up. He took a few cracks of the baton to his back and arms as the prison wardens restored order, indiscriminately lashing out at any prisoner within reach before finally restraining, cuffing and dragging away two inmates, neither of whom were the Russians who started it.

The guards imposed a lockdown on their wing as punishment for the carnage and that was it, dinner was cancelled – no food for the rest of the day and no outdoor exercise. All 480 inmates in C Block were confined to their cells until 5pm the next day.

Three months ago, when Davey was first thrown into his prison cell, there were only six beds for the seven prisoners. A half-inch-thick rolled-up mattress and an unwashed coarse blanket were stuffed into the corner; this would be his bed, he was told.

At that point, Davey was still hopeful, though. He thought he could easily stick out a few nights of this, while the British Consulate and lawyers got to work on bailing him out. There was no need for him to be here. He was clearly innocent, and the authorities would soon realise this and do the right thing.

He was confident his British passport would guarantee him justice and the whole misunderstanding would be wrapped up in a few days.

He was wrong.

In those first four weeks, the British Consulate only visited him once and he hadn't even been in court for a hearing yet. Nobody from the Daily UAE had contacted him and he'd only had a couple of calls with his folks back home. Each time, he tried to reassure them everything was okay and they didn't need to fly out because, 'I'll be out by the end of the week.' But the end of the weeks came and went, and Davey was still curled up in his cell at night, flicking away the cockroaches.

He'd been appointed a lawyer, a UAE national, who coldly explained he was facing manslaughter charges for the deaths of the two children. All the documentation he was instructed to sign was in Arabic and he was totally dependent on the lawyer's summary explanation in English.

'Not guilty. I'm not guilty,' Davey insisted over and over to his lawyer. Yet his lawyer was trying to convince him that pleading guilty would lead to leniency and a lesser sentence versus pleading innocent and then being found guilty.

'Guilty! I'm not pleading guilty. It wasn't my bloody fault. Do you understand? It was not my fault. I'm innocent.' He felt he'd said these words a hundred times over to his lawyer, to other inmates, to the guards and to anyone who'd listen.

Inside this world of incarceration, everybody he spoke to had heard the innocence plea all before and the prison stats were not in Davey's favour: 94% of the inmates were foreign nationals and, in nearly 90% of the public prosecutions, the defendants were found guilty. Justice was corrupt and capricious out here.

Questioning by the police was brutal and not between your office hours of 9 to 5. Twice Davey had been woken up at 2am with a baton jabbed in the ribs and then dragged off to an interrogation room.

'I don't understand. I don't understand,' Davey pleaded, as he stared at the papers written in Arabic shoved in front of him by the officer.

The two guards standing behind hoisted him up off the cold plastic seat.

CRACK! CRACK! CRACK! The wooden batons smashed into his back dropping him to his knees. He slumped forward, with his hands cuffed behind, his right shoulder smacking into the concrete floor as he fell.

They forcefully hoiked him up. Davey lifted his head and caught a glimpse of the commanding officer giving another nod to the guards before CRACK! CRACK! CRACK! His back took the full onslaught of the batons again. The officer stood up from the desk and yelled in Arabic, smashing him across the face with the back of his gloved fist. He grabbed the papers and waved them in front of Davey, slamming them down on the desk, screaming in Arabic and forcing a pen into his hand.

Davey refused and let the pen drop to the ground.

Seconds later, a rope was flung around his neck and pulled tight. Davey fought for breath as every few seconds the guards twisted and tightened their stranglehold. His bound arms and legs battled for his life, desperately and instinctively trying to kick and thrash themselves free. But as the seconds went on, Davey felt his fight weaken and he slowly lost consciousness. Eventually, the rope loosened and he collapsed to the ground.

He didn't know how long that night's cycle of torture and interrogation continued, only that for the first time ever, he took comfort from feeling the roughness of his blanket against his face when he slowly regained consciousness. That meant he was back in his cell. The beatings were over, for now.

Five days later, his lawyer visited to give him some unwelcome news. An update which extinguished all immediate hope of release or even bail, which he still clung onto, thinking it was a possibility.

Sitting opposite Davey in his white Emirati robes, his stony-faced lawyer clasped his hands on the table.

'I have some difficult news,' he said. 'You are facing an extra charge. A charge which the public prosecutor says you have admitted to.'

Davey sat in disbelief. How could this hell hole be getting worse? What charge? What have I admitted to?

His lawyer continued.

'The police found hashish in your possession at the car crash. Three grams were contained inside your wallet.'

He paused to remove a two-page A4 document in Arabic from his file. He slid it across the table in front of Davey and pointed to his signature.

'This is your confession. You signed this when questioned five days ago? Correct? Is this your signature?'

The signature was indeed Davey's but only just. It wasn't his usual, confident, free-flowing scribble with the 's' and 't' Zorro stroke to finish off his 'Watts' surname. Rather it was a slow, prescribed spelling of his name with slightly wobbled lettering.

'I... I don't remember signing this,' he said, pushing his hands through his hair and rubbing his forehead.

'Those bastards, they beat me. Beat me! Fahkin' beat me,' he thumped the table with his fist staring down at the signature.

'Look! Look!' Davey tugged down the crew collar on his white prison overalls and pointed to the bruised rope marks around his neck. He then rolled up his sleeves to reveal the swollen blotches of blackened purple over his arms where the batons had relentlessly pounded.

The lawyer remained emotionless.

'Bad things can happen in prison. Prison... prison is a difficult place, Mr Watts,' he said, not engaging with the accusation of police brutality.

'This charge complicates matters,' the lawyer added. 'Possession of drugs is a serious crime in Dubai and more charges means more work. More time I have to spend on your case.'

Davey knew where this was going but had no choice. This greedy cunt wanted more money. The legal fees were already approaching 30,000 Dirhams and Davey had no idea how long his parents could continue funding legal support. His dad had made decent money in the City, and Davey was brought up in top-to-toe designer gear and holidays at their Marbella villa. They always seemed comfortable, but beyond the five-bedroom house and Range Rover, how much actual hard cash did they have nowadays?

Three weeks had passed since that meeting with the lawyer. Two and a half weeks since the extra fees were transferred into his account. But that cunt had not been back. There'd been zero communication from him. And zero contact with anyone else from the outside.

The loneliness was the hardest part of Davey's life inside. He was more alone than he'd ever been. He knew now the beatings would come and go, but the loneliness was a constant. A feeling that consumed him 24 hours a day. 'Nothing can harm a man as much as his own thoughts untamed,' he'd once read, when he briefly embraced Buddhism at uni (yes, a girl was involved in that flash of divine enthusiasm). He clung onto that philosophy and wrestled with it every day inside, trying to ignore the demons in his head intent on dragging him down to a world of hopelessness.

His dad had visited twice now. The second time was the hardest. By then, they had both realised this was a clusterfuck of a legal and cultural mess, and there was not going to be a quick fix. Seeing his dad's face boosted Davey's morale but only temporarily. The sight of him walking out of the visitor's room 30 minutes later, never sure when he'd return, hung heavily on his shoulders, along with the guilt, as he sensed the immense suffering his parents were going through.

He felt beyond his parents, beyond help, beyond hope.

Davey paced the outside yard for his daily exercises as he did every day: 182 feet long, 168 feet wide; 61 upright steel poles along the length of the fence to the north, 56 across to the east. He was just about to stroll over to the pull-up bars as usual when he was surprised to hear the call over the tannoy that 'David Watts' had a visitor.

Before I had headed to the jail, I'd planned to make a small detour on the way. The Disney-esque setting of the wadi-bashing and Alison's proposal had obviously remained vivid (or maybe scarred in my head) for lots of reasons, but now, fully kitted out with the mobile sound system and Technics, I wanted to revisit the area and explore for a very different occasion: *Paradise 49.*

The Audi was never going to handle the bashing from the rocky dry riverbeds, so I parked up as near to the gorge entrance as I could without fucking the suspension and tyres. Scanning around I could see there was easily enough steady ground on this patch for multiple cars to be parked.

Probably need to add some markings so folk don't drive too far and total their cars down one of the ravines in the dark. Don't want to deal with an emergency search and rescue operation at 2 in the morning, when we're trying to be inconspicuous from the Dubai cops.

I walked up and over the boulders, timing on my watch how far a stretch it was from where the cars would be parked. Five minutes so far – not an easy walk but not impossible, and, as far as I could see, no risk of death from a stumble. Twisted ankle, maybe, especially if anyone turns up in high heels, but nothing more serious than that.

I butt-inched my way down the face of the last boulder like a crab, then jumped down the final couple of feet to land in the centre of what was a naturally formed rock amphitheatre. A precipice overhung a shallow cave and opposite, the mountain walls leaned forward in rugged peaks, almost touching to provide a canopy over the area. There were plenty of alcoves embedded into the sides of the rock faces, providing natural areas to sit down, and a shallow rock pool led towards the opening of another ravine.

The acoustics around here would be cracking. This was it. This was the perfect location. And only a seven-minute walk from the entrance.

While perfect, I began to realise this was not going to be a one-man job. Clambering over the boulders carrying a crate of beer was one thing, but lugging speakers, a generator and records on my own was only going to lead to an expensive disaster. Then there was the whole marshalling and troubleshooting of people in and out of this place, and the whole setting up of a theme to create a bit of clubbing theatre.

My mind was racing with ideas, like that night at Vague when bare-chested and oiled-up 'Egyptian slaves' carried Vera Duckworth into the club at shoulder height in a golden sedan chair, or at Ku, when during the extended intro on 'Break 4 Love', acrobats dressed as devil-horned Satanic creatures slowly descended from the rafters and weaved their way into the crowd, freaking the hell out of us Aberdeen lads coming up on pills.

Okay, those production levels were maybe not achievable here, but clearly I needed a wingman or wingmen to pull this off.

There were only two people I trusted wholeheartedly who could do this: the Gaz Man and Archie. If Gaz wasn't offshore on a rig, I knew he had the money and would be over on the next flight if there was a party to be had. And Archie, while always short on cash, if the 'Bat Signal' was projected into the sky as a smiley yellow face, he'd find a way to get over… probably via Gaz's wallet.

I'd make the calls back home after visiting Davey.

Paranoid about any covert surveillance and police checks, I decided to take a taxi to the prison on the outskirts of Dubai, rather than drive the Audi. Guilty through association was a real fear among the expats, especially when someone you know is banged up on drugs charges, so I knew I had to be careful.

As the taxi pulled away to head back down the desolate road towards Dubai, I stood outside the prison gates and took in the harsh remoteness of where we were and the deliberate bleakness of the sandstone visitors building.

There were no other cars, no people; just me, the doors to the prison entrance and a barren desert, paralysed by the stifling heat.

The security guard inside buzzed the reception doors open and I stepped forward into the cool, air-conditioned space.

I was expecting something unpleasant like the Hanoi Hilton or Billy Hayes' Turkish sweat-pit of a jail at Sagmalcilar, but this was the opposite – modern and spotless, with clean, cool air flowing through. Two rows of curved white plastic seats were stretched in an L-shape along the walls, connected by a single steel rod running underneath. At either end were solid marble coffee tables with neat piles of magazines and today's copies of the Daily UAE, Khaleej Times, Gulf Today and Gulf News folded on the side. Portraits of Sheikh Maktoum hung behind the visitors' reception desk and on the wall above the visitors' seats.

After inspecting my documents, I was asked to take a seat. Two 20-something Filipinas sat opposite, both trying unsuccessfully to curtail the boisterousness of their three toddlers, who were wildly zigzagging baby buggies up and down the floor.

My visit was purely under the guise of journalism. This was not meant to look social. I was not letting on that Davey and I were friends, and I held the notepad and Dictaphone in one hand, looking primed to capture the awaiting story.

In truth, it was a bit of both. Yes, I wanted to check in on Davey and make sure he was alright, but I did want the scoop as well. Even if the Editor and Hamza didn't publish it, I knew the tabloids back in the UK would lap it up for a couple of hundred quid...

BANGED UP BRIT BREAKS SILENCE TO EXPOSE 'CORRUPT' DUBAI COURTS

Escorted along the white-walled corridors, I was led into a room of maybe 30 or so desks and chairs. Almost all were empty except two. In the centre sat a baby-faced Filipino with a shaved head, looking very relaxed, leaning back in his chair, waiting for his visitor. In the top-right corner of the room sat another man. His shoulders hunched and head bowed, he was resting his chin on his clasped hands. As he heard the guard direct me over to his seat, he gradually raised his head. It was Davey. But Davey without the flowing locks. He, too, had received the buzz cut.

'Alright, mite,' I said gently, trying to give him some familiarity in a Jockney accent, as I approached the table.

'Fahkin' hell, Jimmy. Jesus, it's good to see you, mite. Fahkin' good to see you,' he replied, forcing a smile, which momentarily lit his tired-looking eyes.

'I wish I could give you a hug, but these bastards won't allow it,' he said, looking over to the watching prison guard. 'How you doing?'

'How am I doing?' I replied, incredulous. 'How am I doing? Jesus, Davey, don't give a fuck about me. How are you doing? I haven't seen you since the night before the crash.'

I switched on the Dictaphone and held the pen to the notepad – journo training had drummed into me to always have shorthand notes as backup.

'Mate, I'm going to get all this down and help you. Get the story out there. What the fuck happened? Why are you still here?'

Five minutes into his story, my suspicion had been confirmed. Davey had not driven into anyone; it was the Dubai national who had smashed side-on into him.

'He ran a red. You know that crossroads by the Old Library and the ENOC petrol station? I'd barely got into first gear as the lights turned green and I headed across the junction, when bang! I didn't see him coming. Just like that, bang! I felt this almighty force smash into the side. I must have passed out, as next thing I know I was on a stretcher under an oxygen mask, being lifted into an ambulance, with everybody jabbering in Arabic around me.

'In hospital, nobody would tell me nowt about what had

happened. Nobody mentioned those kids had died or anything about charges.

'The doctors and nurses just kept talking about my health and getting better. Then, when I thought I was about to be discharged, they fahkin' cuffed me and brought me here.

'I've been surrounded by cahnts ever since, Jimmy. My lawyer is a cahnt, the prosecution are cahnts, the prison guards are cahnts and their fahkin' prison warden chief is the biggest fanny cahnt of all. Smacks me around at night like a coward, when his bitches are holding me up with my hands tied behind my back. And he pulls on black, leather gloves to protect his knuckles like a fahkin' perv. Probably got thigh-high boots and a gimp mask to match as well.'

I think Davey was having erotic flashbacks to his Berlin misadventure at this point, but now was not the time to mention it.

He continued...

'I've got to get out, Jimmy. That drugs charge is a fahkin' stitch-up. I don't even smoke pot for fahk's sake – you know that. I can't remember signing that bit of paper or any fahkin' paper. All I remember is they did a proper job on me, Jimmy.

'Rope around my neck. Strangling me. Punching me. Beating me. And it still goes on. Out of the blue, they come at night and drag me off.' He rolled up his sleeves to reveal the bruising along his arms. 'I think they just want me to plead guilty to everything.'

Davey paused. He was starting to wobble a bit as he rested his head in his hands again looking down at the table.

The Dictaphone tape slowly whirled around, capturing Davey's pain for the next 20 minutes, as I looked at my watch, realising we only had a few minutes left.

'Davey... I'll fix this. We'll get you out, fella,' I said. 'But before I go, mate, there's one thing I want to show you.'

I reached down into the brown, leather holdall by my feet, unzipped the bag and slowly, with a little smile on my face, placed the Gucci loafer on the table.

'My missing Gucci! No way! Ya beauty!' he shouted, attracting the guard's attention.

It was the biggest smile I'd seen on his face for the past 30 minutes.

'Oh, mite, that's fahkin' brilliant,' he said, reaching over to stroke the blue suede.

At that point, the prison guard blew his whistle and signalled our time was up.

'I'll look after it for you. Davey Tags will be back in his Guccis soon, pal. Don't you worry,' I said, leaving him with hope, as a guard behind Davey approached to escort him back to his cell.

I packed up the Dictaphone and notepad, knowing I had the right elements for the story and a couple of leads now to follow up on to prove his innocence.

Chapter 33

Gaz fell through his front door, tripping over his oversized Forbsmann Oil & Gas kit bag, but somehow miraculously managing to hold onto his 2am fish supper in one hand as he stacked it. Not a single chip had dropped.

'Saaaaave! Theeeeeo! Theeeo! Theeo! Theo!' he sang out loud, as if he was back on the South Stand terraces at Pittodrie.

He lay face down on the laminated floor, picking away at the fish and chips, trying but instantly failing to gain focus, as his living room swayed in front of him. It had been 14 hours since he stepped into the Nile Bar and ordered his first pint; eight hours since he'd started on the shots, just neat vodka at first for a wee livener; and four hours since he'd had his first Bolivian Landslide – champagne and tequila mix, topped off with a cheeky line.

It was his standard return to drinking duty after three dry weeks offshore on the rigs.

Blinking through his floor-level blurriness, a red dot kept flashing up ahead next to the sofa. Every so often it beeped. A beep way too loud for Gaz's head in this state.

He slowly rolled and pulled himself up onto all fours and crawled towards the sofa, nudging the vinegar-soaked chip wrapper ahead of him on the floor every few feet.

He reached up to the answering machine, pressed 'PLAY'

and rested against the foot of the sofa, tucking back into his cold chips, licking the ketchup off his fingers.

'Gaz Man. It's The Riddler. Fit like, min?!

'Ye know you wanted to come over to Dubai soon… well, how about in two weeks?

'Are ye free? Are ye back onshore?

'I'm doing a night, a desert rave and I need yer support to run it.

'Banging tunes and hoochin' wi' fanny. You'll love it.

'Give us a call back when ye hear this, pal. See ye.'

Gaz played back the message then grinned to himself, before leaning over and passing out on the rug. The gap between the coffee table and sofa was now his bed for the night.

'Too right. I'd love to, Jimmy,' said Archie. And then predictably…

'But, in two weeks? Dinnae think I can get the cash for a flight in just two weeks, Jimmy.'

'Archie, you're the operator, the planner, the general, Hannibal, Rommel, Charlie fuckin' Croker, Genghis fuckin' Khan, not Genghis fuckin' Khan't. I know you can make it happen. You just need 300 for the flights; the rest is covered by me – food, booze, bed. Trust me… It will be unbelievable,' I said.

'I've left a message with Gaz. You two have a chat and I'll call back in a couple of days.'

The gauntlet had been well and truly dropped and dipped in sugary-sweet honey, as I knew Archie couldn't resist a challenge, always wanting to prove to the lads he was undefeatable.

Archie was the one who'd dealt with the coach company, hiring the 60-seater to take us to his 'sister's wedding' 40 miles away in Marykirk, which then on the day of the 'wedding' was suddenly changed to a venue in Dundee, 70 miles away, because the original location 'had been flooded overnight'.

It was no surprise when the 'wedding' coach was pulled over by the rozzers 5 miles out of Aberdeen. 60 folk in dungarees, bucket hats, baseball caps, baggy sweatshirts and jeans did not look like a wedding party – there wasn't one buttonhole carnation to be seen.

Archie stepped up to smooth things over with the cops and the coach driver (after a whip-round for a healthy tip) to let us continue on our travels. 40 minutes and a Mitsubishi after arriving at the Dundee warehouse, the riot squad raided it and we were soon back on that bus heading up and *coming up* to Aberdeen.

Then it was Archie who within 30 minutes of us landing in Ibiza had made the call and jumped into a cab to the other side of the island to meet an Italian who was a contact of a contact to pick up 40 grams of powder, 50 pills and 12 tabs of acid.

I still remember him jumping out of the taxi two hours later, all victorious and proudly saluting up to us, as we looked down from the apartment's balcony.

This boy always delivered. He was a postman, after all.

After making the calls, I headed to the Marine Club to hook up with Alison. She was on two days' rest before her next flight to Hong Kong, which would be a three-dayer she said.

Maria on reception was looking fantastic, as always, flashing her brilliant smile and sparkling eyes... like she does for everyone, of course. Alison and 'the girls' were down by the jet skis, which had become their favourite spot on the beach, partly influenced, no doubt, by the presence of the two South African Adonises who managed the business.

Talk of Shell's murder was still never too far away in a conversation amongst the cabin crews, but as the weeks had gone on, the familiar cabin-crew themes of bitches, bastards, sex and parties were definitely rising to the top of the chat again.

It definitely sparkled. 'I'm convinced I saw a sparkle just bounce off her engagement ring,' I said to myself, as I approached Alison.

I pulled up a sunlounger to join her and the air hostesses staring at the ring on her finger. Joe (the fucker) had sown the seeds of doubt and been revelling in winding me up, ever since he'd casually said to her: 'Are there diamonds somewhere in there?'

From that moment on, I sensed there was an unsaid level of disappointment creeping into both our heads that the ring was not good enough – that I hadn't dug deep enough into my pockets to buy a ring that an 11-out-of-10 like Alison deserved.

But, I swear I just saw it sparkle. I'm sure it did, didn't it?

Jumping on the coat-tails of their spicy conversation about one of the cabin crew they knew who'd ended up in a threesome at a Jumeirah pool party, I pitched the *Paradise 49* night to them.

While all enjoying the likes of the Highland Lodge and Champions Bar, they all agreed they were missing and longing for a proper House night out here, like they'd been used to in their respective homes of England, Scotland, Holland and Italy.

The Dutch girl, Mila, sat quietly listening to the description of the location in the desert and the kind of vibe I was hoping to create, while Alison sung my praises of DJing at 'some private parties in Deira'.

'Ibiza, New York, Leeds, London, Rimini and now Dubai. We're going to put it all in the pot, stir it around and come out with Paradise 49 in the desert,' I said, handing out the flyers to all six of them.

'I know a few interesting guys, if you want to spice things up,' Mila said. 'Well, they're trannies, actually. Cabin crew but they keep it quiet for obvious reasons. There's about six of them.

Think they'd be up for putting on a bit of a show if you want them?'

'Trannies! Out here? Bloody brilliant,' I responded without hesitation. 'Look, if you're up for helping to promote this, take 30 flyers each. But we need to be careful. This has got to be invite-only. People you know and trust. There's plenty of undercover Dubai police mingling with the expats, looking to bust people for booze, drugs or sex.

'Get people to call the number on the flyer and leave a message. I'll vet the voicemails and if they don't sound Arabic then I'll fax the co-ordinates over to them on the night of the party.

'We only need a hundred for a good night. And we don't want to draw attention with bigger numbers.

'Don't... DO NOT whatever you do, leave the flyers lying around in bars or hotels or anywhere. They need to go into the palms of the right people.'

All six of them were on board.

The *Paradise 49* marketing team had just been recruited and briefed.

Chapter 34

ABUSIVE DRUNK SCOTS ARRESTED ON DUBAI FLIGHT

was the headline I really hoped I wouldn't be reading, as I waited at Arrivals for Gaz and Archie.

As the passengers from London Heathrow poured through the Arrivals doors, I struggled to keep up with the numbers passing in front of me and thought I might have missed them. But then, as five minutes became ten, and ten became fifteen, finally, like the last dregs out of a warm bottle of beer, the two of them came trudging along, the last of the passengers.

If The Krankies had been on a Middle East tour, there'd have been a good chance they'd have been mistaken for them. They couldn't have looked any more Scottish. Gaz, at 6ft 2" with cropped Lego black hair, was wearing an Aberdeen FC** 'Living Design' football top with the Daily Record poking out of his overstuffed RS McColl groceries bag, while Archie, at 5ft 8" with his 'strawberry blonde' curly curtains (it's ginger, Archie, admit it), was pulling along a battered tartan suitcase – the kind that even yer granny would be embarrassed to be seen with. Both had solid trainers on, though: Forest Hills and Sambas.

There was no denying the 'tourists were in toon', and we all cracked up laughing as we bear-hugged and the banter commenced.

'Fit the fuck's happened tae yer accent? Ye gan all soft on us?' was Archie's opening jibe after a couple of minutes chat, rightly picking up on how my Aberdeen dialect was starting to dilute out here.

It felt good to see them. No, better than that – it felt bloody amazing to have old friends out here and friends who had your back.

I'd explained to the boys that I could only take a couple of days off while they were out here for the week, but I'd make sure they were looked after and do all the intros at the right places like the Marine Club, The Radisson and, of course, Alison and the AWA girls.

They'd have free rein of my apartment, as I'd stay at Alison's for the week, comfortable now that her new flatmate was not the sort that would rat on us as an unmarried couple living in sin.

'Thank fuck,' a sweating Gaz said, as he gasped and stepped into my ice-cool, air-conditioned apartment. 'It's fuckin' hot, Jimmy! Baked-tatties hot. What is it out there? 28, 29, 30 degrees?'

'42, Gaz,' I replied, laughing. 'It's the fuckin' desert. What do you expect!'

We spent the next couple of hours cooling down and catching up over a dozen or so Heinekens, before heading back out into the searing heat to head over to Alison's apartment and make some introductions.

Thankfully, Archie and Gaz had made an effort with their sunshine beachwear. They'd both dropped into one of Aberdeen's designer men's stores before flying over, grabbing a couple of new shorts and T-shirts each in the sale. Gaz was sporting a white, crew-neck, Stone Island T-shirt and pastel-blue shorts, while Archie wore beige shorts and an Aquascutum checked T-shirt.

The Krankies-look had gone, thank God; the only giveaway to

them being tourists now was their peely-wally skin, which (apart from their heads and necks) looked like it had been deprived of daylight, let alone sunshine.

'Jesus, Archie, fit the fuck are they?' I said in the back of the taxi, pointing down at his clawed, blistered toes in his flip-flops.

'That's three years of being a postie. Pounding the streets, up and down stairs in the high-rises, walking in rain, sleet and snow for eight hours a day. These toes can tell ye a story, pal!' he said.

'Well, it won't be a *bedtime* story with those claws,' I said, laughing. 'The only bird that'll come into yer bed is the flapping kind.'

The banter and jibing continued without mercy, all the way to Alison's. I buzzed her apartment, which was answered by the new flatmate.

'Ello, Geemmy. She's at the pool on the roof,' she said in her French accent.

Alison sat on the side of her bed in her black Prada bikini, admiring the ring, wrestling with the emotions of guilt, desire, anger and love.

'*This* is what love really looks like,' she believed, entranced by the glistening diamonds radiating a spectrum of colours from the sun rays beaming through her bedroom window.

She held her hand out in front of her, spreading her fingers to admire the three-carat diamonds set in white gold in all its glory – a cut and clarity that would easily be valued at north of £10,000.

Hasan had been generous, very generous. He always was. The ring was just the latest in a series of flattering gifts he'd been showering her with over the past six months. But the jewellery, the jewellery always had to be kept hidden.

She wouldn't be able to explain away the bracelet, watch and this ring to Jimmy or her friends. They could only be worn when she was with Hasan. Designer bags and dresses were different, as that's a girl's prerogative, and you can never have too many bags and dresses.

'Love does have a price on it,' she was thinking. 'And it's not bloody cheap, Jimmy Irvine,' she said, frustrated at his lack of spending power.

Hasan had promised he would take care of her. She would never be left wanting. Not while she remained in Dubai.

There was one condition, though. She would never be *the* one. Instead, she would be one of many. Hasan's sexual appetite would never be satisfied by just a single woman. His wealth and social standing as an Emirati royal practically encouraged him to keep a merry-go-round of beautiful, materialistic girls from around the world.

She understood this and knew one day she might be replaced. But surely, until then, she had to keep making the most of the opportunity, she'd say, trying to justify her double life.

Alison carefully placed the ring back in its case and returned it to the bottom of her wardrobe, tucked behind the many shoeboxes and dresses. She knew Jimmy and his Scottish clan would be heading over soon, so it was time to relax by the pool for a couple of hours before the expected party shenanigans.

The high of flinging open the doors to the poolside and making a grand entrance of ourselves was swiftly deflated when I saw Joe sitting on a sunlounger among Alison, Mila and a couple of others from the *Paradise 49* 'promotions team'.

I was hoping to keep Archie and Gaz away from Joe for as long as possible during their stay, sensing it wouldn't take much to spark a flare-up between them, and I certainly wasn't wanting Joe to know about the *Paradise 49* plans, in case he, Ali and a load of unvetted, money-sucking, Russian hookers turned up. Plus, since the last feisty encounter with Ali when he accused me of syphoning off his gear and calling Alison a whore, I didn't want anything to do with the cunt and was making myself less conspicuous by spending more time at Alison's.

'Don't mention the rave,' I quickly whispered to the guys as we walked over.

Joe typically and loudly introduced himself first.

'Eh up, Cola Boy. This must be Begbie and Renton, is it?' he said, smiling, standing up to shake hands with Archie and Gaz.

'Alison told me the Scottish Mafia was in town,' he continued to jest.

It didn't take long before the Celtic charm took its effect, as Alison, Mila and the 'promotions team' hung on the jokey words of Archie and Gaz as they piled on story after story of abuse and embarrassment at my expense to keep everyone entertained. Even Geordie Joe, the self-proclaimed 'Talk of the Toon' found himself a spectator, drowned out by their constant barrage of japes and quips.

We all agreed that alcohol was needed to 'celebrate the joining of the clans Irvine and Wilson-Lewis' and the best bar in town was Alison's apartment downstairs. Thankfully, Joe had an evening press event to attend, so declined the offer and took the change of location as a cue for him to leave sober while he could.

'Good luck tomorrow, Jimmy son,' Joe said as he stood by the lifts.

'Tomorrow?' I replied, thinking, 'Shit. Did they tell him about *Paradise 49*? How the fuck does he know?' But I didn't want to assume and give everything away.

'What's happening tomorrow?' I asked, anxious to know where he was heading with this.

Joe walked up to me, glancing over at the rest of the gang who were now heading down the fire-escape stairs to Alison's apartment.

'Your AIDS test,' he whispered as he slapped me on the back. 'I had mine this morning. And I saw on Hamza's list you and a couple of the sub-editors are there tomorrow. Good luck, Cola Boy!'

The lift bell pinged and the doors opened, as Joe smugly grinned in my direction, before stepping into the elevator.

By law, all expat employees in the UAE had to take an annual HIV/AIDS test. It didn't matter if you were a construction worker from the Philippines or director of an American blue-chip corporation – if you were sponsored to live and work here, your employers had to ensure you were tested once a year.

The consequences of testing positive were unsurprisingly harsh and swift. You'd be denied all health benefits, then quarantined and eventually deported. Basically, you'd be nicked for being ill.

I'd been pushing the thought of the test to the back of my mind as the days counted down, not wanting to consider the consequences of a positive result. I kept trying to reassure myself that the chances of that must be slim. Back in Aberdeen, I hadn't been with anyone except Natalie for the year leading up to my departure, and when I arrived in Dubai, they sent me off for that first test and the result was negative.

Since then, I'd only got lucky twice before hooking up with Alison. Both were teachers, one from England, one from Wales, and they seemed 'decent' – also a euphemism for 'dull'. They just didn't seem the type that would be playing the field every weekend, I thought. And, since meeting Alison, there'd been nobody else in Dubai – there was no need to, as she was a banger in bed, when she wasn't tired and recovering from her three-day flights. The only seed of doubt was, of course, that at no point with any of these girls did we ever stop and say: 'Better put on a johnny.'

The morning trip to the clinic played on my mind, as the hours counted down. I'd been instructed to meet one of Hamza's assistants at the newspaper offices at 9.30am, who'd drive us to the clinic and handle all the medical paperwork and conversations in Arabic.

The party vibes in Alison's apartment were rocketing, as Archie and Gaz continued to charm Mila and the two other cabin crew, but despite the temptations and predictable abuse directed at me ('Ye big fanny'), I had to leave them to it as they all headed out to Champions Bar.

'I've got a meeting at 9.30 then working in the office all day, then we – that's WE – have to sort out *Paradise 49* and get the kit to the site,' I said, being all serious.

'Irvine is a fanny, Irvine is a fanny, nah, nah, nah, nah, OOH! Nah, nah, nah, nah, OOH!' was the compassionate response from Archie and Gaz, as they led their merry little conga out of the apartment.

'Don't get wasted,' I shouted after them. 'I need you boys on top form tomorrow.'

'Nae worries, Riddler,' said Archie, laughing back at me as they stepped into the lift.

Fuck, he better not tell them *that* story…

…Fucker, I know he will.

Chapter 35

I didn't tell Alison about the HIV test, thinking it's not really something you want to bring up in conversation, and – as I kept trying to reassure myself – it wasn't something to worry about. We'd both been together for a year now, so why bother mentioning it?

Alison, Mila and the promotions team had been briefed with a list of props to buy at the souks during the day, then we were to rendezvous in the car park of Alison's apartment building at 7pm. The AWA Cash & Carry of alcohol would be split among the girls' three cars in case anyone was pulled over for a spot check by the police; the Technics, sound system and rest of the kit would go in the Audi.

The HIV test in the morning had been daunting, as expected, as nervous paranoia overwhelmed any sense of composure or complacency. Being whisked past the winding queue of about 100 ASEAN men standing in the morning sun outside the Sharjah health clinic, I wondered how many of us were about to have our lives shattered with a positive result. We were all equal here – it was a life-game of percentages.

The nurse's wastebasket was overflowing with empty syringe packets and scraps of cotton wool, which lay discarded on the floor. While clean, I think, the area resembled a factory line, as five other nurses were positioned at tables around the room, with queues of men lined up, waiting for their turn to be called forward by the security guards.

Then, prick… dab… plaster and I was done. The nurse affixed a sticky label with my name and number onto the test tube containing the blood sample, and placed it into a tray with 50 or so others. I'd have to wait until next week for the results.

Back in the office, I filed the daily requisite of two stories. One was a tourist feature about Dubai's grand plans to build three 'Palm Islands' – man-made luxury islands constructed of three billion cubic feet of sand dredged from the bottom of the Persian Gulf that would ultimately house 80,000 people and boast more than 20 hotels. The 'Eighth Wonder of the World', it had been humbly proclaimed by Sheikh Maktoum. The other was a typically dry story about next month's Arabian Travel Market.

There was one other story I filed, though – the most important one I'd probably ever written: Davey's story. As predicted, the Editor said there was no chance it would get past Hamza and he just couldn't publish it in the Daily UAE, but he hooked me up with his contact back in London – the assistant editor at The Sun.

JOURNO BRIT JAILED AND TORTURED IN DUBAI HELLHOLE

He said it would be The Sun's front-page splash by the end of the week. On this occasion, I strongly insisted I didn't have a byline. Didn't want to attract any unwanted attention from the Dubai authorities, especially on the morning after the night before of *Paradise 49.*

At 7pm, we all convened in our cars at the back of Alison's apartment block and headed out of Dubai. Archie and Gaz had spent most of the day sleeping off their hangovers on the beach at the Marine Club.

Unbelievably, reports had been filtering in throughout the day that Gaz – yes, the Gaz Man – had actually pulled last night... and not just anyone, but the Dutch girl, Mila! The two of them, though, were in that slightly awkward-sheepish-hungover-barely-speaking state of post-drunken coital awakenings, as they sat in the back of Alison's car.

Everyone had a printed map to follow, along with the 42 other people who had left messages on the answering machine. Only one voice, I thought, was suspect, based on his Middle Eastern accent, and I didn't fax over any co-ordinates.

42 interested people was okay, I suppose. Maybe a third of them won't come, distracted by cocktails at the Highland Lodge as the night goes on, but those that do make the desert trek would probably bring at least one other person, so maybe we'll end up somewhere around 50 or 60. Just enough for a party.

'This is looking the nuts,' said Archie, as we surveyed our newly erected, twisting line of burning torches, which lit a path through the darkness from the cars to *Paradise 49's* natural amphitheatre.

'A torched procession for a disco inferno. A *Paradise 49* inferno!' he added, admiring his work.

Now was not the time to mention how the mainly gay Paradise Garage and New York disco clubs had blazed a trail for House music or the small matter of our guest trannies appearing later, having witnessed before Archie's irrational panic and meltdown at the slightest mention or introduction to anyone who's not straight. The last time was in Amnesia when, coming up on a double drop, he lost his way back from the toilets and was 'trapped' in a corner of the club with 100 bare-chested gay clubbers and trannies dripping in foam. I had to swoop in and 'rescue' him, as the charlie and ecstasy seemed to grip him with fear and he fell into a panic attack.

He'd soon see, anyway, that this night was not going to be your average banging House night. There was a show to be put on.

I wasn't expecting any trouble, but Gaz and Archie had been strictly briefed to act as spotters just in case. Spotters for police patrols heading our way, spotters for any undercover cops among the crowd and spotters for any blatant drug dealing and unwelcomed muscle.

At 11pm, the six of us were perched on the rocks in our sweatshirts and hoodies, looking out onto the vast blackness that stretched from just in front of us to the hazy city lights of Dubai in the distance. The darkness was only broken every so often as a truck's headlight passed on the main road a few hundred yards away. Behind and below us, the *Paradise 49* arena was lit and sound-checked, but there was nobody there.

'Hmm, what ye think? Nae looking so good, Riddler,' Gaz muttered, just before scoofing down his Stella. 'Ye'd expect some fucker tae be here by now, eh?'

I didn't answer him, thinking it surely can't stay like this. Surely, someone will get here. I mean of course we'd run some flops of nights in the past back home, but you'd always get a dozen or so folk in at least. We'd never flatlined and had a complete no-show.

'Maybe they cannae read the map,' Archie unhelpfully chipped in. 'Or just cannae be arsed. It's a bit of a fuckin' trek Jimmy.'

Alison and the girls looked over briefly and then glanced away to carry on chatting. I could sense the doubt creeping into their minds as well, as the desert coolness was setting in for the night and, so far, there was no people or energy to keep them warm.

I climbed back down the rock and stood behind the decks, swapping over from Roy Davis Junior's 'Gabrielle' to Danny Rampling's 11-minute remix of Love Corporation's 'Palatial' as I couldn't face listening to silence.

'Jimmy! JIMMY! JIMMY!!' Archie shouted.

Then…

'Jimmy! Jimmy! Jimmy!!' screamed Alison and the girls jumped up and down.

'Get up here,' they all yelled.

I scrambled back up the rock with a fresh can of Stella in one hand.

'LOOK! LOOK! LOOK!' They all pointed ahead at what was once this bleak horizon of complete emptiness. But now – *now* – I could see a convoy of headlights… one, two, three, four….ten, 11, more, all turning off the main road onto the desert track, heading this way. And a few minutes behind them, still on the road out of Dubai, there was a stream of more headlights, blurring into one long, winding, white stream.

'Fffffuuuckin' hell,' I shouted in disbelief. 'Look at them. Just look at them.' I stood frozen with shock, disbelief and relief, and then surges of adrenaline shot through my veins.

Archie and Gaz slapped me on the back.

'Fuckin' yes, min! Dubai's desert rave is on!' Archie and Gaz clinked their beer cans together, and danced around like they were already on it, raising their hands to the sky.

Hypnotised by the sparkling lights flowing towards us, I snapped out of the momentary trance as Archie booted me up the backside.

'Okay, okay. We're on. We're on! Let's fuckin' do this,' I shouted as we all raced back down the boulders. Archie, Gaz and Mila positioned themselves by the narrow passageway between the rocks leading into our area as the official welcome party.

Like scurrying ants transporting their spoils of the day, we could see the silhouettes of people now pouring over the rocks, as they made their way from the parked cars, loaded up with crates of alcohol, stopping every so often to carefully navigate down the face of the rocks.

I turned up the master control and the deep bass boomed out Rimbaud's 'Hard Times' around our little arena, instantly igniting the energy as the first few groups danced their way over to the decks and introduced themselves. I flicked on the projector and the *Paradise 49* flyer lit up the rock face opposite.

English, Scottish, English, English, English, Italian, Spanish, Scottish, Australian, South African, Italian, Dutch, English, English, Dutch: we soon had a global gathering of mad-for-it clubbers and, for the next hour or so, they just continued arriving, until there was no more space at ground level and they started scaling the rock walls to dance on top of the surrounding precipices.

'Shell would have loved this,' Alison said, standing next to me.

At 1am on the dot, I dropped the intro to Outrage's 'Tall 'N' Handsome', as Mila and Alison carried lit torches, leading their parade of glamorous trannies into the centre of the arena. With towering wigs to match their towering heels, they sashayed and vogued their way through the cheering crowd, radiating in their shimmering, sequined dresses.

Even Archie seemed impressed.

'This is mental,' he shouted into my headphones, admiring their performance 'safely' from behind the decks.

'Look at it. They're all loving them,' he gushed.

'I know. I know,' I replied, hurriedly trying to line up the next record.

Just as I was mixing it in, Gaz appeared to the right of the decks.

'Need to talk,' he mouthed.

'One minute,' I signalled back to him, ensuring the mixes were in time, before letting the next track fully drop.

'Some cunt is selling gear. Openly. An' he looks like an Arab to me. Aye, nae the Dundee kind but from out here,' he said.

'Shit. Where?' I asked, surveying the crowd in front.

'O'er there,' he motioned his head back towards the entrance between the rocks. Standing at the back of the crowd, nodding his head to the tunes, was Ali.

'Fuck, it's Ali. I know him. Okay, he's a pimp and a coke dealer and a bit of a nasty fucker at times. Get him to come over.'

'Oi! Oi! COLA BOY!!!' Geordie Joe suddenly popped up in front of the decks like a giant starfish. He held a bottle of Heineken in each outstretched arm, as his T-shirt inched up to reveal the bottom of the NUFC tattoo.

'Some fookin' party this, man. Let's fookin' ave it!' he shouted and, as quickly as he appeared, he spun away and wildly danced his way back into the smiling but startled and quickly parting crowd.

'Jimmy Irvine. So, here you are, my friend. I've been wondering what happened to you.' Ali smiled as he held out his arm and gave a strong hand clasp. Gaz stood a few feet behind, assessing the mood between us like a pit bull ready to strike on command.

'This is good. Very good,' he said, turning 180°, while motioning his hand to the crowd in front and those dancing above on the summit.

'Must be 200 or so here, Jimmy. More than the fourth floor, hey? The English DJ has done well – very well,' he laughed.

'*Scottish* DJ, Ali. Get it fuckin' right, you Moroccan cunt.'

'Ha ha!' Ali exclaimed, slightly taken aback by my bluntness. 'Very good, very good. Okay, yes, I get it. I know we had a small disagreement before.

'And okay, Jimmy, I'm sorry for what I said. But that's all in the past, Jimmy. This is the now.

'We should talk.

'Talk business.'

'Now's not the time, Ali. Look,' I said, punching my arm in the air as the crowd in front danced in time to the bassline. 'Tonight's a night to enjoy, not to talk business or do business. I don't want a night of arsey coke-heads and aggro here.'

'Don't worry Jimmy. No coke-heads here,' Ali patted me on the shoulder and nodded, acknowledging the tunes had to keep going. He wandered back to the outer edges of the crowd and stood not far from the passageway, observing.

Every so often, I could see Joe standing by Ali before he'd launch himself back into the centre of the crowd. Alison controlled the projector, flicking between images of the flyer to bondage guys kissing, girls kissing, a bare arse being spanked, a random shot of Dale Winton and, of course, one of our saviour – Her Royal Highness Jo Guest.

Four hours in, there was no sign of anyone going home. The energy levels kept rising and more people kept approaching the decks screaming, dancing and giving out hugs… lots of hugs… Even Gaz and Archie, I could see, were becoming magnets for a big bosie.

Their roles as spotters seemed to have evaporated, as I could see their focus was now split between talking to Ali and being entrenched in the centre of the clubbers, dancing and shouting out, 'Cummon, Cola Boy!' on the drops.

Eventually, Archie broke away and nodded his way up towards the decks.

'Fuckin' love it. Love it, Jimmy,' he shouted in my ear, before sweating a wet kiss on my neck.

I turned away from the records and looked at him.

He was off his chops. But pilled chops, not charlie chops.

'You're fucked, min. What you taken? You taken a fuckin' pill, Archie?'

He smiled, trying but failing to mask a gurn at the same time.

'Aye.' He hugged my right shoulder. Then, he raised his head, threw his hands in the air to the tune and turned around adding, 'We all have!'

He grabbed my hand and placed a little capsule in the palm before nodding his way back into the crowd to join Gaz, who unbelievably was now happily dancing with the trannies.

I cued up the next record then looked up at everyone dancing, smiling, gurning, some embracing, others happy in their own trance-like state. I opened up my hand, staring at the red-and-yellow capsule. Ali, still standing on the periphery, smiled and gave me a knowing thumbs up.

Maybe now was the time to talk business.

—END—

What Next?

In the follow-up book to Cola Boy, Jimmy is tempted by the trappings of a now burgeoning rave scene in Dubai fuelled by drugs. Building on the success of Paradise 49 he is faced with a decision of working with or against Ali. His desert 'Scottish Mafia' expands with the support of Archie, Gaz and some unexpected recruits.

Despite publicity from the media in the UK, Davey Tags is still languishing in jail, struggling mentally and being forced into increasingly desperate situations. But one encounter leads to hope for Davey and an opportunity for Jimmy to land his biggest scoop of all time.

Alison, who is now a 'face' by 'screwing a face' amongst the Dubai expats, revels in her parallel worlds until a return visit to the UK leads to some life changing consequences.

By Ryan Battles

Follow @cola.boy96 on Instagram | Cola Boy on Facebook

PERFORMERS

Irvine Welsh and Dean Cavanagh revisit the dying days of the 1960s to reimagine what happened during the making of the first true British cult film.

They Don't Think They're Gonna Let You Stay in the Film Business.

Performers deals with masculinity at the point when the sexual revolution was saturating culture. For many working-class men, it was confusing and threatening. As secularism started to replace traditional Judaeo-Christian attitudes, a lot of men found themselves torn between embracing the liberation and clinging to the simpler, more morally binary past.

In the swinging and hallucinogenic London of 1968, visionary Scottish filmmaker Donald Cammell joined forces with cinematographer Nicolas Roeg to make "Performance". The film would star James Fox, Mick Jagger, and Anita Pallenberg, but the casting process was frustrating for Cammell because he insisted on bringing "real villains" into the roles that supported the lead character of South London gangster Chas Devlin.

What Welsh and Cavanagh identify is that strange cultural moment in 1960's London when bohemian intelligentsia flirted with the world of organised crime

VARIETY

Book One of ZANI's Tales Trilogy

A CRAFTY CIGARETTE TALES OF A TEENAGE MOD

Foreword by John Cooper Clarke.
'I couldn't put it down because I couldn't put it down.'

'Crafty Cigarette, all things Mod and a dash of anarchy. Want to remember what it was like to be young and angry? Buy this book. A great read.'
Phil Davis (Actor Chalky in Quadrophenia)

'A Great Debut That Deals With The Joys and Pains of Growing Up.'
Irvine Welsh

'A coming of age story, 'A Crafty Cigarette' maybe Matteo Sedazzari's debut novel but it's an impressive story.'
Vive Le Rock

'It's a good book and an easy read. That's pretty much what most pulp fiction needs to be.'
Mod Culture

'A work of genius.'
Alan McGee (Creation Records)

'Like a good Paul Weller concert the novel leaves you wanting more. I'll be very interested in reading whatever Matteo Sedazzari writes next.'
Louder Than War

A mischievous youth prone to naughtiness, he takes to mod like a moth to a flame, which in turn gives him a voice, confidence and a fresh new outlook towards life, his family, his school friends, girls and the world in general. Growing up in Sunbury-on-Thames where he finds life rather dull and hard to make friends, he moves across the river with his family to Walton-on-Thames in 1979, the year of the Mod Revival, where to his delight he finds many other Mods his age and older, and slowly but surely he starts to become accepted...."

A Crafty Cigarette is the powerful story of a teenager coming of age in the 70s as seen through his eyes, who on the cusp of adulthood, discovers a band that is new to him, which leads him into becoming a Mod.

ISBN-13 : 978-1526203564

Book Two of ZANI's Tales Trilogy

THE MAGNIFICENT SIX IN TALES OF AGGRO

Foreword by Drummer Steve White (The Style Council, Paul Weller, Trio Valore,)

'A vivid and enjoyable slice of London life in the 80s, with a wealth of detail and characters,'

Meet Oscar De Paul, Eddie the Casual, Dino, Quicksilver, Jamie Joe and Honest Ron, collectively known around the streets of West London as The Magnificent Six. This gang of working-class lovable rogues have claimed Shepherds Bush and White City as their playground and are not going to let anyone spoil the fun.

Meet Stephanie, a wannabe pop star who is determined to knock spots off the Spice Girls, with her girl group. Above all though, meet West London and hear the stories of ordinary people getting up to extraordinary adventures.

Please note that Tales of Aggro is a work of fiction.

ISBN-13 : 978-1527235823

Book Three of ZANI's Tales Trilogy

TALES FROM THE FOXES OF FOXHAM

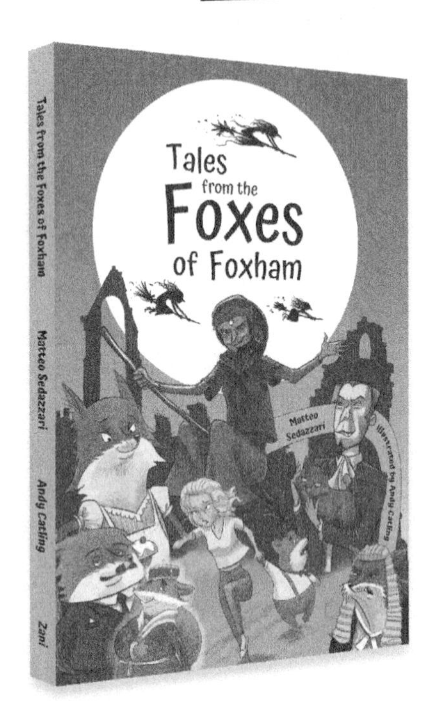

It is the late fifties and the Witches of Benevento are determined to plunge the world into darkness by kidnapping and sacrificing the jolly and young Neapolitan fox, Alberto Bandito, in a sinister ritual.

Yet, fortunately for Alberto, he is rescued, then guarded, by his loving mother Silvia and mob boss father Mario with his troops, a good witch Carlotta with an uncanny resemblance to Marilyn Monroe, the Bears of Campania, the boxing wolves' brothers Francesco and Leonardo, and other good folks of Naples and beyond.

However, their protection is not enough, for Alberto has been cursed. So, the young fox, along with his family, has to travel to the village of Foxham in Norfolk, the spiritual home of foxes across the world, to rid himself of this spell. The ritual has to be performed by a good fox witch, Trudi Milanese, but there is a problem, Trudi doesn't know she is a witch....

Tales from The Foxes of Foxham is a magical adventure story, packed with colourful characters and exciting situations, in a battle of good versus evil.

ISBN-13 : 978-1-8384624-0-6

Feltham Made Me – Paolo Sedazzari

Foreword by Mark Savage (Grange Hill)

The poet Richard F. Burton likened the truth to a large mirror, shattered into millions upon millions of pieces. Each of us owns a piece of that mirror, believing our one piece to be the whole truth. But you only get to see the whole truth when we put all the pieces together. This is the concept behind Feltham Made Me. It is the story of three lads growing up together in the suburbs of London, put together from the transcripts of many hours of interview.

ISBN-13 : 978-1527210608

The Secret Life Of The Novel: Faking Your Death is Illegal, Faking Your Life is Celebrated - Dean Cavanagh

"A unique metaphysical noir that reads like a map to the subconscious." **Irvine Welsh**

A militant atheist Scientist working at the CERN laboratory in Switzerland tries to make the flesh into Word whilst a Scotland Yard Detective is sent to Ibiza to investigate a ritual mass murder that never took place. Time is shown to be fragmenting before our very eyes as Unreliable Narrators, Homicidal Wannabe Authors, Metaphysical Tricksters & Lost Souls haunt the near life experiences of an Ampersand who is trying to collect memories to finish a novel nobody will ever read. Goat Killers, Apocalyptic Pirate Radio DJ's, Dead Pop Stars, Social Engineers and Cartoon Characters populate a twilight landscape that may or may not exist depending on who's narrating at the time.

ISBN-13 : 978-1527201538

7P'S Paperback – A.G.R

The 7 P's. An unusual title you may think, but its meaning will become as apparent to you as it did for four friends and comrades who, in a desperate move of self-preservation, escaped the troubles of 1980s Northern Ireland, and their hometown of Belfast, only to find themselves just as deep, if not deeper, in trouble of a different kind on the treacherous streets of London.

ISBN-13 : 978-1527258365

ZANI ON SOCIAL MEDIA

After enjoying *Tales from The Foxes of Foxham,* please follow ZANI on Social Media.

ZANI is a passionate and quirky entertaining online magazine covering contemporary, counter and popular culture.

Follow ZANI on Twitter
twitter.com/ZANIEzine

Follow ZANI on FaceBook
www.facebook.com/zanionline?fref=ts

Follow ZANI on Instagram
www.instagram.com/zanionline/

Printed in Great Britain
by Amazon